THE INCREDIBLE ADVENTURES OF VIC CHALLENGER
THE REINCARNATED CAVE GIRL

VIC
DOUBLE
TROUBLE

IF YOU RECALLED A PREVIOUS LIFE AND YOUR SOUL MATE – WOULD YOU HAVE THE GUTS TO SEARCH FOR THAT LOVE – NO MATTER WHERE IT LED YOU, NO MATTTER IF IT MIGHT TAKE A LIFETIME?

Double Trouble contains the full text exactly as printed and paged in originals of the first two novels in the series, The Incredible Adventures of Vic Challenger.

by Jerry Gill

Edited by
Keeley Monroy

Ann Darrow Co
Kaneohe, Hawaii

ISBN 13: 978-1-889823-66-9

THE INCREDIBLE ADVENTURES OF
VIC CHALLENGER #1
THE REINCARNATED CAVE GIRL

VIC
TIME
DOESN'T
MATTER

by Jerry Gill

Edited by

Keeley Monroy

Ann Darrow Co
Kaneohe, Hawaii

i

Paperback ISBN : 978-1-889823-38-6
Hardcover ISBN: 978-1-889823-55-3
Digital   ISBN: 978-1-889823-56-0

Library of Congress Control Number:
2017902285

Publisher's Cataloging-in-Publication Data
provided by Five Rainbows Cataloging Services

Names: Gill, Jerry.
Title: Vic : time doesn't matter / Jerry Gill.
Description: Kaneohe, HI: Ann Darrow, 2017. | Series:
    The incredible adventures of Vic Challenger, bk. 1. |
    Previously published in 2013. | Includes
    bibliographical references.
Identifiers: LCCN 2017902285 | ISBN 978-1-889823-55-3
    (hardcover) | ISBN 978-1-889823-38-6 (pbk) | ISBN
    978-1-889823-56-0 (ebook)
Subjects: LCSH: Women heroes--Fiction. | Cryptozoology–
    Fiction. | Adventure and adventurers--Fiction. |
    Reincarnation--Fiction. | Nineteen twenties--Fiction. |
    BISAC: FICTION / Action &   Adventure. | FICTION /
    Historical. | FICTION / Visionary &   Metaphysical. |
    GSAFD: Adventure fiction. | Historical fiction.
Classification: LCC PS3607.I4354 V53 2017 (print) |
    LCC PS3607.I4354 (ebook) | DDC 813/.6--dc23.

An Ann Darrow Co Book

Contents

This is a work of fiction. It is the first novel in the series, "The Incredible Adventures of Vic Challenger." These works are inspired by writers like Edgar Rice Burroughs, H. Rider Haggard, Jules Verne, Arthur Conan Doyle and H. G. Wells; and by characters like Nancy Drew, Lara Croft, Alan Quatermain, Doc Savage and his cousin Patricia Savage, and Dick Benson and his assistant Nellie Gray.

Historical and scientific facts are well researched and thought to be accurate. References are available at http://www.vicplanet.com

You will also find posters and other useful information on the site. Activities portrayed by or at any real person place or thing are purely fiction.

Dedicated to my inspiration(s) - the 4 best hanai nieces ever.

Erika, Elaina, Ocean, and Sky.

Biographer's Note

It is amazing what one can find at an estate sale. Recently, at one of these events, I purchased a massive old trunk from the first half of the 20th century. It was locked, contents unknown. I did not expect to find anything of great value, but the contents turned out to be priceless! The trunk held dozens of handwritten personal journals.

A young woman by the name of Victoria Custer penned those chronicles. She was a travel writer in the 1920's who wrote under the pen name of Vic Challenger. She traveled the far corners of the earth, and the stories of her trips made her very popular. The public stories, however, were never complete. Her journals tell the whole story of her treks, including things she felt *the public would not accept.*

I read her journals and researched her accounts. I have no doubt in the veracity or accuracy of her stories.

Victoria was an amazing woman who lived at an exciting time in modern history, and she dared many truly incredible adventures. It would be unpardonable if her exploits became lost. I decided to transcribe her handwritten journals and reconcile them with other references from her time. The work is now ready to be shared. I emphasize Vic's adventurous, brutal travels, but also share a bit of her home life. There was a sharp division between her amiable modern personality and the savage power which her primitive alter ego brought to her aid when needed.

Believe or disbelieve as you will. H e r e begins the uncensored saga of Vic's incredible and often strange adventures. They are tales of a re-incarnated cave girl, re-born in the final years of the 19th century - a cave girl who traveled the globe in search of her eternal love, her soul mate, whom she lost 100,000 years ago!

Part 1

Chapter 1

Savage Ending

Today Nu would change the history of his tribe. The caveman sought Gr, the long-toothed cat, apex predator of that time. In the collective memory of his tribe, no one ever stalked the beast. The cat could open the man with a single swipe of its razor-sharp claws. The fearful canines could pierce him through. Yet Nu had no fear. He intended to bring the head of the beast to his beloved Nat-ul, the warrior maiden. Nothing less could convey his love for the savage cave girl.

In that time, when the notion of love was in its infancy, millennia before the concept of eternity was first imagined, the two cave dwellers, in their way, swore fierce eternal love to one another.

Nu loved Nat-ul since the two were but children. Her father Tha taught the girl to wield an ax as soon as she could lift it. She loved the feel of the weapon and spent hours each day practicing. Then one night a low growl awakened Nat-ul and she fearlessly ventured out of her cave to investigate. As she came out, Ur, the giant cave bear, ambled over the beast fires and rent open the midsection of the warrior on watch. The valiant young Nat-ul grabbed her ax and called out for the tribe's warriors as she raced down to battle Ur! She met the bear without fear and inflicted many wounds, but as warriors charged down from the caves, Ur lashed out! A claw raked Nat-ul's left cheek and knocked her half-conscious to the ground. As Ur reached for the brave girl with open maw, a dozen spears pierced his hide, and he fell dead beside the young huntress!

That night Nu fell in love with Nat-ul. Each grew to be a consummate warrior and hunter, yet something beyond those traits strengthened their bond. They often concocted words for things without a name and pondered ideas which befuddled other members of the tribe.

On the previous evening, the two walked hand in hand beneath the great yellow-orange equatorial moon, along the shore of the Restless Sea. Nat-ul told Nu she would rather have him than the head of Gr, but the cave dweller could not be dissuaded. Nothing less than the head of Gr would suffice.

The Barren Hills were odd outcrops of giant boulders pushed up from deep inside the earth. Natural caves in the hills provided safe homes for the tribe, and the summit formed three domes, which the people could recognize from many miles away.

The tribe of Onu dwelt in one end of the small range. An especially large specimen of Gr lived on the distant end of the range, on the side away from the sea. Gr did not venture to

2

the sea side. The jungles and grasslands that lay away from the sea were a better hunting ground for the cat. An uneasy peace existed with the great predator, but today Nu would end it. He would confront the devourer of men and mammoths at his own doorstep and take his head.

The time of Nat-ul and Nu was incredibly brutal, so the killer cat was not the only danger which the caveman faced as he sought the trophy head. Yet those hearty souls did not think of danger, bravery or cowardice. It was all just living. If something needed done, it was done. If you needed to eat, you killed something. If something wanted to eat you, either you killed it first, escaped, or you died. Life was uncomplicated, but it was stupendously savage.

Earlier, a behemoth wooly rhinoceros charged the caveman and he took to the trees. Now his nostrils again warned of danger. The stink of the hairy ape folk was strong! Not a moment too soon, Nu dropped back to the ground to continue his journey. A dozen of the hairy ape folk showed themselves in the trees above and beat their breasts and taunted him. Nu understood what they said. His people shared a common language with the hairy ape folk and the lesser simians.

The hairy ape folk were less man than Nu but more man than the lesser apes, the gorillas, and monkeys. They were more vicious than any. They were as large as Nu and stronger than a bull. From their lower jaws rose a pair of four-inch tusks and canines nearly as long protruded from the top jaw. If they so decided, the hairy ape folk could attack Nu, easily tear him apart and eat him in short order, but the caveman didn't worry. Seldom would they attack a man unless he showed some sign of hostility. That is why Nu kept his spear on his shoulder and his ax and knife in his waistband.

An hour later, Nu came to the far side of the Barren Hills and was nearing the lair of Gr when the earth began to shake. This was not unknown to the caveman, but the fury of the tremors was unfamiliar. The ground rose and fell and shifted side to side. Nu went to one knee. There was a loud crack like a giant jungle tree snapped in two, but it was the fracture of strata miles below him.

When the convulsions subsided, Nu continued. A few days earlier, he was on this same path when the earth shook. On that occasion, he turned back to the caves, concerned for the safety of Nat-ul. Today though, Nu continued, for he was eager to take the head of Gr. Soon he could smell death in the air and knew he was near the lair of the killer.

Nu came out of the jungle a few hundred feet from the base of the Barren Hills. Between him and the lair of Gr lay an expanse of grass that stood taller than the man. Nu was grateful the wind came from before him so Gr would not be warned early. It would mean almost certain death to meet Gr in this grass. Just days earlier a mighty warrior from another tribe made Nu privy to the only tactic where he might slay the cat and live. Nu had a plan and wanted to meet the saber cat on open ground. He took the ax from his waistband and began to cross slowly through the high grass.

Shortly, Nu stood in a level clearing below several dark caverns. He did not worry that there were many of the great cats for Gr did not tolerate the nearness of another. The bones of many animals were strewn about the entrance to only one cave. Nu stationed himself before that grim portal, loosened the spear on his shoulder and gripped his ax with both hands. Within seconds, the flaming yellow orbs of the great long-toothed tiger glared out from the dark interior, and the devourer of men and mammoths issued an ominous, rumbling growl.

The majestic killer appeared slowly, mouth agape, and glared at the pitiful man-thing that dared to stand before his lair. Gr stretched his forepaws out and arched his back as might a kitten and seemed unhurried by the intruder. Nu was familiar with the ways of the predator, though, so gripped the haft of his ax and murmured, "For Nat-ul!"

Gr suddenly lunged at the man with a blood-curdling screech that made animals for miles around scurry for safety. The instant the cat came within reach, Nu slammed his ax against the head of the gigantic beast with all his might. That stunned Gr, and he stopped, his head hung low. Nu understood that the cat was only dazed so immediately pulled the stout spear from his shoulder and jumped forward. With his full strength, Nu drove the glass-sharp stone age weapon deep into the side of Gr. The spear tore nearly through the body of the cat but missed the mighty heart, the intended target. Now Gr, devourer of men and mammoths, was in pain and angry!

Much life remained in Gr, so Nu instantly jumped on the back of the colossal feline and held tight with his legs and arms. The hind and fore claws must both be avoided because a single slash from either could reduce him to Gr food!

The great cat jumped and turned and struck out with one paw then another. He tried to reach the rash creature on his back, but it was futile. Nu held firm. In time, Gr swatted the spear with a forepaw and snapped it. By so doing, the cat brought his own demise. The move drove the stone tip of the primitive weapon into his heart, and almost instantly his bestial rage ceased. Gr gave up a loud sigh and slumped, burying Nu beneath his great bulk.

With prolonged difficulty, the caveman removed himself from beneath his vanquished combatant and for a moment stood to admire the beast his weapons bested. Then as was the custom with his kind, Nu began to make shrill shrieks which mimicked Gr, then followed with a series of mighty, thunderous cries. It was the war cry of his tribe and to no less extent than the scream of Gr, it sent animals and birds alike to seek shelter!

With a few powerful strokes of the stone ax, Nu removed the head of Gr. The caveman's spear was broken in the last act of the great cat, and now Nu would repair that necessary implement. Before he began, however, an ominous hush came over the jungle, followed by an ear-shattering crack! The ground vibrated more violently than ever! The mountains shook, and massive boulders careened down the side of the Barren Hills! Nu grabbed up his weapons and the head of his kill and ran inside the lair of Gr to avoid the falling stones. Nu was aware other beasts might seek safety inside the lair of Gr, so he faced the entrance, ax in hand, prepared to defend the gift for his Nat-ul.

The caveman waited, but the wait was

short. More boulders tumbled down the side of the cliffs.   The quake knocked Nu to the ground, and a thousand tons of stone buried the entrance to Gr's lair.   There was only enough time for the caveman to cry out just once for what mattered most in his life. "Nat-ul!" Then the sanctuary of the mighty Gr, devourer of men and mammoths, became the tomb of Nu!

That was a hundred thousand years ago.

Chapter 2

Dangerous Encounters

Victoria Custer departed the compound early. The Waziri warrior Udur, and acclaimed big game hunter Lord Lawrence accompanied her.

Victoria first planned to hunt alone. Then, to allay the anxiety which beset her brother over her pursuit of dangerous encounters, she acquiesced to Udur's accompaniment as gun bearer. Her brother Barney, however, remained distraught over what he perceived as reckless behavior. Finally, the girl agreed to the escort of Lord Lawrence, a long time friend of Lord Grainger.

Days after their arrival Victoria caused a stir not to mention a great worry for her brother when she ventured out alone, without notice. Just before noon, those at the ranch heard a single shot from the weapon Victoria carried. It was a Wesley Richards .577, a powerful rifle that weighed fifteen pounds unloaded. Barney wanted to investigate but

Lord Grainger reassured him that of course he should hear a shot. After all, Victoria went hunting. She sauntered into the compound after lunch with a full grown male leopard slung across her shoulders!

Lord Lawrence accompanied Victoria and Udur on this hunt to ease Barney's concern. The three arose earlier than the rest of the household and were a mile from the ranch when the sun first peeked over distant hills.

A fourth member of the hunting party walked on all fours. Within an hour of their arrival at the ranch, a great wolfhound called Terkoz took a strong fancy to Victoria and was by her side whenever allowed. He evinced a desire to go on other hunts, but Victoria thought his presence might hinder her stalking. This day he was going and before they departed she whispered to the animal, "If three people tramping along don't frighten the game, you shouldn't be a problem, Terkoz!"

An hour from the ranch house, Lord Lawrence halted and pointed ahead. Victoria saw it. They were at the edge of the jungle, with hundreds of yards of open grassland ahead. Something was stirring up dust a quarter mile away beyond a small thicket. Lord Lawrence asked Victoria to wait with Udur while he investigated. "May be elephants or may be buffalo," he said. The great pachyderms were not hunted on Lord Grainger's property.

Victoria waited at the edge of the jungle behind an enormous fallen tree. Udur stood beside her as they watched Lord Lawrence stoop low and move in experienced silence across the open.

Again, Victoria carried a Wesley Richards

.577, an older single shot model. Barney argued for her to take a newer model with a dual barrel and single trigger. "It gives you two shots instead of one. It's safer. More sane," Barney told her. Victoria preferred the older single shot, not in arrogance or to gain an extra thrill, but simply because it was enough. So, in the way of big game hunters for decades, Udur, acting as gun bearer, carried the same. If a hunter missed a shot or if a shot did not bring an animal down, the second rifle was swiftly passed to the hunter. It was not unheard of for a hunter to have several bearers or to load up one unfortunate bearer with several rifles. If the hunter was a poor marksman, the life of both hunter and bearer often hinged on how fast the bearer could pass weapons to the hunter.

As Lord Lawrence moved across the open to the distant trees, he skirted a patch of small bushes. The brush camouflaged a hollow where water collected during rains. As he came even with the brush patch, a loud snort warned him of the danger lurking inside.

He swung his rifle around as a huge cape buffalo came from the brambles. The bull caught him between its horns and tossed him. By good fortune, the horns did not pierce the man, but the impact broke ribs and stunned him. The toss hurled him twenty feet distant and heaved his weapon ten feet farther.

Victoria knew well the buffalo might charge the helpless man again, so she didn't hesitate. Before Lord Lawrence hit the ground, she jumped the giant log to stand in the open and yelled to draw the buffalo's attention. The bull looked toward her and snorted and shook his head. He looked at the man again, so Victoria yelled more. The bull put his gaze back on her and lowered his head. "He's going to charge, Udur!" Victoria called to her companion.

The great wolfhound at that point looked like he might attack the bull. Victoria leaned and touched his head and said quietly, "Stay, Terkoz."

The Waziri moved to stand beside Victoria with the second weapon. Instead of jumping the log, he stood upon it to step over. The log appeared solid but was eaten out by termites. At his first step, Udur's foot broke through the shell, and he pitched forward over the log. The rifle slipped from his hand and discharged harmlessly into the jungle. Rather than scare the bull, the shot enraged it more!

The buffalo is a dangerous animal and each year accounts for a significant number of deaths. Every white hunter staying at the compound insisted the buffalo was at least as dangerous as a lion. The animal staring down Victoria weighed in at 1400 pounds and was five feet at the shoulder and over eight feet long.

As the bull lowered his head for the charge, a colossal rhino came from beyond the brambles and drove its fore-horn into the side of the bull. Its back was a foot higher than that of the bull, it was longer and much heavier. The effort of the rhino was all but invisible when it tossed the buffalo ten feet beyond Sir Lawrence. The bull hit with a crunchy thud and began to spurt blood and bawl in death throes!

When the rhino appeared, Lord Lawrence began to crawl toward his rifle to gain some means of defense. As it finished the brief dispatch of the bull, the rhino noticed the man's movement and turned toward him!

Barney was not able to sit still at the ranch house, so he and Lord Grainger followed the trail of the earlier hunters. They were near when Victoria and Udur began to yell but could not yet see what was happening, so they walked faster. When they heard the discharge of the dropped rifle, they broke into a dead run. As they came to the edge of the jungle at that stretch of grassland, they found Victoria waving her arms attempting to draw the rhino's attention. Udur whispered, "Lord Lawrence is a dead man!".

"No, he isn't!"Victoria growled. She began once again to shout and wave her arms, and Udur followed suit. Lord Lawrence froze. He understood the rhino had poor eyesight but excellent hearing.

Without warning, the rhino charged Vic at no less than twenty-five miles per hour, It kicked up dust, and snorted in rage as it came.

Victoria saw Udur reach for the discharged rifle and told him there was no time to reload. Udur did not retreat. He stood beside Victoria, for he was a proud Waziri warrior, the son of a chief.

Barney and Lord Grainger were both awed by that scene. The proud Waziri stood to the left of Victoria with arms folded across his chest and head high. On her right, Terkoz the wolfhound looked equally proud and calm.

Victoria threw the rifle to her shoulder.

The massive beast, head lowered, bore down on the three with the destructive fury of a runaway freight train. It was no more than fifty feet from the trio! Barney started to yell, but Lord Grainger put a hand on his shoulder and whispered, "Quiet, Barney. You mustn't distract her."

Relaxing most of her body, Victoria faced the rhino at an angle, bent slightly forward at the waist. The girl ignored the folding leaf sight - there wasn't time, the animal was too near. She focused with the forward open iron sight, pulled the .577 tight into her shoulder, exhaled, and with perfect composure squeezed the trigger.

The report of the rifle reverberated out across the plain and back into the jungle. The rifle's recoil pulled the barrel up a full foot, and Victoria took a step back from the force.

The .577 round exploded the heart of the rhino. Its forelegs folded and it went to its knees. Dust and pebbles peppered Victoria and Udur as the rhino slid to a stop just eight feet away.

"I don't know why Barney is always so worried. I'm a decent shot," she said as she handed the rifle to Udur. Victoria took a step in the direction of her injured companion when an awful roar halfway to Lord Lawrence announced the appearance of a huge male lion! It came from the jungle and moved for a swift attack toward the man and the buffalo. The blood-scent and bawls from the dying bull had its full attention.

Victoria never considered reloading. Before Udur could even suggest that action, Victoria was in a dead run at the back of the lion! As she ran, she pulled her knife and raised it above her head. It was a graduation gift from her father, a custom Bowie with a two-inch-wide, fourteen-inch-long spear-point blade. Victoria kept both sides of the tip razor keen for piercing.

Barney and Lord Grainger took two steps after the rhino went down. Both stopped and were stupefied when the lion appeared, and the girl charged. Udur was reloading a weapon, expecting to need it.

An arm's length before she reached the unsuspecting, confident lion, Victoria launched herself! The next few moves were so fluid they appeared to be one motion. She landed astraddle the cat just behind the head. She grabbed the mane above the lion's eyes and pulled back. She reached around and drove the entire fourteen-inch blade into the chest of the brute and pulled it sideways.

As she withdrew her knife, Victoria pushed off the back of the lion. She ran three quick steps back, her knife raised to meet any retaliation.

The girl's blade had slit the heart of the beast. It began a turn to get at the attacker, but the cut deprived the brain of oxygen and half-way through the turn the beast collapsed.

As the cat hit the dirt, Victoria raised both arms high and struck at the air with the knife. Those savage movements were accompanied by the most horrifying cry ever heard by anyone in attendance. Then, as suddenly, she re-sheathed her knife and went to Lord Lawrence who stood and used his rifle for a prop.

"Victoria!" Barney came running up with Lord Grainger. "Are you OK?"

The nobleman suffered broken ribs and bruises but was otherwise alright. He thanked Victoria, and Lord Grainger and Barney helped him toward the horses, past the dead lion where Terkoz circled, sniffed and growled.

As they walked away, Udur came to Vic, and she looked at him with a timid smile. "Sorry about that yell. I..."

"It is not a thing to cause shame or humility. Miss Victoria, you have the heart of a warrior."

As Udur walked away, Victoria wanted to tell him she was scared senseless and didn't know how or why she did what she did. She didn't say it, though, because she knew it wasn't true. She felt no fear at any time during the drama and now felt exhilarated and triumphant. As far as why, it was simply something that needed done.

Before they embarked for the compound, Udur assured her he would return quickly and collect trophies for Vic. Barney used Victoria's camera to take photos for her. She posed alone, then with Lord Lawrence and Udur and with the lion, rhino and buffalo. Of course, Terkoz was in all the photos.

Victoria's feat was phenomenal and amazed everyone at the compound. By noon, Udur brought the rhino and lion trophies and the meat of the buffalo and initiated a feast. The Waziri, the hunters, and Lord Grainger recounted stories of other great hunts, and all agreed they would not forget this day. Udur confided to Victoria that he attended many confabs with renowned hunters. Usually, each became his own jali and would use creative-license to recount his own exploits, This was the first where a woman was not only in attendance but was the center of conversation! That compliment kept her smiling for hours.

To look at her, you would never think Victoria Custer, of Beatrice, Nebraska, at all the sort of girl she really was. Her dreamy eyes and the graceful lines of her slender figure gave the impression of physical weakness which modern men often deem an inherent characteristic of true femininity.

The wavy, coal-black hair that topped her five-foot-nine-inch frame fell halfway down her back. She was quite particular about her hair and usually kept it in a tail or gathered with barrettes. She had an extensive collection of hair fixtures which she began to collect at age six. Her flawless alabaster skin and coal hair were striking, but without doubt, her eyes were her most notable feature. They were the color of light amber and possessed the translucence of that primitive sap stone.

In college, she began to collect cloches along with barrettes. All her life she adored pink and was enamored of frilly dresses. Victoria was the quintessential lady's lady – when she wanted to be. Yet an honest biography of the girl would never contain a hint of cowardice, sloth, nor mental or physical weakness. To her mother, she was a refined lady, to her father she was tough as nails. Both were correct.

Victoria Custer grew up a normal girl in most terms of description. Yet in a few odd ways, she was both precocious and possessed extraordinary curiosity. At age six she did usual farm chores. She fed animals, collected eggs, picked vegetables, and more. She also insisted on learning to cook from her mother and learned to keep accounts for the farm from her father. She was not good with numbers at first, but seemed fascinated by them and soon could do most common entries.

At age seven she began to hunt with her father and brother. Her aim was uncanny, and she proved herself to be a competent hunter on their first outing. She possessed extreme self-reliance. It took no time for her to learn to track

17

game. By her ninth year, she often went rabbit hunting alone. She hunted with only the most primitive of weapons - stones - and she never returned empty-handed. By the time she was twelve, she was an accomplished swimmer and equestrian.

Her elemental intelligence was remarkable. Yet formal learning was not easy. Her grades were always high but came with countless hours of study and difficulty. It surprised friends when she attended the University of Nebraska at Lincoln to earn a degree in mathematics. Victoria graduated cum laude and went straight to work on a second degree in astronomy. In spite of her difficulty, Victoria was an ardent advocate for education. She persuaded most of her friends to pursue degrees.

Victoria did have peculiarities. They began on the night of her thirteenth birthday. That night she dreamed vividly about the lives of two cave people. There was a cave girl, Nat-ul, daughter of Tha, and a caveman Nu, son of Onu. The two were warriors and hunters for the tribe of Onu who lived 100,000 years ago, beyond the Barren Hills, beside the Restless Sea. Their prowess was extraordinary, and Victoria always awoke from her dreams in a good mood. Those dreams continued for years, and the only person she ever told was her brother Barney.

Victoria awoke as a thirteen-year-old with an attitude as well. She was an attractive girl, so as she grew older, she had no shortage of suitors. However, everyone who tried to become more than a friend always brought to her mind the same words – pusillanimous weakling. None of them ever roused any interest whatsoever.

A more sinister affectation also surfaced on that birthday. Vic felt a morbid fear of earthquakes. Even reading about an upheaval of earth made her tremble and sweat and sometimes cry. The few times she felt even the most modest shaking, she froze with fear and lost consciousness. That morbid fear was all the more peculiar in that Victoria feared nothing else. Her childhood seemed a continuous series of reprimands from her parents. She often did things dangerous to the point of being deadly, but Victoria never felt concern, much less fear.

It was these peculiarities which Victoria took with her into 1919, shortly after she received her second degree. Soon after her birthday, Lord Grainger invited Barney to visit his African estate, and her brother suggested that Victoria accompany him.

Victoria accepted the invitation and immediately fell in love with Africa. From the day they arrived, she felt comfortable and secure. To the dismay of her brother she often wandered into the jungle alone.

More than once Vic ascended the heights of giant trees around the compound. She ran along the huge limbs with abandon, jumping from one to another, laughing as she went. On more than one such occasion, Lord and Lady Grainger disappeared into the house and came out in loincloths. They mounted the trees with Vic, and the three frolicked like children at a playground. Often they gathered fruits and enjoyed an exclusive picnic 80 feet above the ground. Later, Lord Grainger confided to Barney, "No need to worry about your sister.

She has a natural facility for climbing and seems to possess no native fear."

One place, however, did arouse dread for Victoria. On a group hunt, they rode south, and two miles from the compound, an odd outcrop of hills came into view. The hills towered in stark contrast to the plain and verdant jungle below. They were an almost vertical space occupied by only a few solitary cacti and tufts of brown grass. A series of three domes capped the small range and endowed it with a profound distinction. From a distance, Victoria stared at them and said to Barney, "Those barren hills are magnificent!" Yet, as they neared the hills, she began to drop back. Aware of her move, Barney slowed and fell in beside her to ask what was wrong.

"Those hills are so beautiful, Barney. I can't explain the feeling of welcome they rouse in me. Yet, they also fill me with enormous dread, and I find it hard to breathe. They overwhelm me with a feeling of unutterable personal loss as if a boundless love were taken from me!"

Barney rode with her silently for a bit then asked, "Have your avatars made the customary appearance?" He long before began to call the cave dwellers of Vic's dreams her avatars.

"Oh, Barney," she cried. "You are such a dear to never laugh at my eccentric dreams. I might become mad as a hatter did I not have you in whom to confide. They have been coming so often! Every night! Sometimes the girl Nat-ul is there, as is Nu the man. More often it has been me with Nu. I have walked hand in hand with him beside a restless sea, beneath a great equatorial moon. I have seen his form and features clearer than ever in the

20

past. He is tall and strong, and clean-limbed -- I wish to meet such a man in real life. I know it is a ridiculous thing to say, but I can never love any of the pusillanimous weaklings who are forever falling in love with me - not after having walked hand in hand with such as he and read the love in his clear eyes."

At this juncture, the hills came in full view. Their barren slopes and strange tri-domed crest loomed in austere contrast to the African plain. Victoria whispered, trembling, "It is so good to see them again!"

Barney looked questioningly and asked, "Again?"

Victoria was confounded, with no explanation for the comment. Then she claimed a headache and said she would return to the ranch. It was past noon, and the heat was scorching, so the entire troupe decided to return.

They reached the compound late afternoon and found a surprise. Two khaki-clad young men came walking out to meet them while they were yet a hundred yards from the gate.

One was a tall, athletic-appearing man. As Victoria Custer recognized his features, she did not know whether to be pleased or angry. Here was the one man she ever met who came nearest to the realization of her dream man. Still those words arose - pusillanimous weakling. His companion also came forward, and the set of his shoulders and his stride betokened his military vocation.

"Mr.   Curtiss!"Victoria   exclaimed,   and looked past him, "and Lieutenant Butzow! Where in the world did you come from?"

"The world left us," replied the officer, smiling, "and we have followed her to the wilds of Equatorial Africa."

"We found Nebraska a very tame place after you and Barney left," explained Curtiss. "When I discovered Butzow would accompany me, we lost no time in following you. Now here we are throwing ourselves on the mercy and hospitality of Lady Grainger."

That lady now joined the party at the foot of the veranda steps. "I tried to convince them that the obligation is on us. It taxes our ingenuity to keep the house even half full of congenial companions."

Throughout the day Curtiss made several attempts to draw Victoria out to the garden where he wished to speak with her privately. Victoria, however, avoided being alone with Curtiss.

The next morning, an hour before sunrise, the household was up as usual for a community breakfast. As everyone enjoyed the delicious fare prepared by the Waziri cook, Curtiss asked about Victoria. "Does she often sleep late?"

That brought brother Barney to his feet. "Never. She's likely gone out on her own again!" He rushed to find his sister but shortly returned alone. "She's not in her room," he announced and at the same time Udur came into the dining hall. "The rifle Miss Custer uses is gone. She must be hunting."

"I'm sure she will be alright. She can handle herself," reminded Lord Grainger. The episode with the rhino and lion curtailed Barney's apprehension some. Words from Lord Grainger helped. Yet he still held a sense of responsibility for his younger sister.

"Look here, Barney," Lord Lawrence spoke up. "In all my years of hunting all across the continent, I've never known anyone more capable in the jungle than your sister." That gentleman then reddened, and smiled at their host, "Except for Lord Grainger, of course!"

Grainger returned the smile and said, "I dare say her inherent skills are equal to mine, Lord Lawrence."

Lord Lawrence looked back at Barney. "There you have it! From someone who would know better than any man alive. Your sister is more than capable of dealing with any animal unfortunate enough to cross her path!" Muffled laughs and "Here, here!" were heard all around the table. Every hunter in attendance admired and respected the young woman from Nebraska. So Barney capitulated and sat down to finish breakfast and plan the day's hunt.

VIC: DOUBLE TROUBLE

Chapter 3

Kidnapped

Victoria Custer was an expert markswoman, physically strong, intelligent, and it seemed fear was something she never learned. Yet, there was one animal which did not enter the minds of Lords Grainger and Lawrence nor of any of those present at the breakfast table. It is an animal so cunning it can plan, deceive and be more vicious than any other. Man. Twice in as many days, hunting parties went out and both times returned empty-handed. Victoria reasoned that alone on foot, it would be easier to find another rhino. She took the .577 with six cartridges and set out two full hours before the sun rose. By the time Barney became aware of his sister's absence, she was miles away, skirting a grassland frequented by rhinos.

Soon after leaving the ranch, Victoria picked double handfuls of wildflowers. Their scent was less than pleasant, but it was strong, and she crushed them and rubbed their juices over her exposed skin and clothing. No animal would be completely fooled, but it would confuse and slow apprehension. Closer proximity by even a foot could mean the difference between a clear shot and an inhibited shot. That could be the difference between a successful hunt or a failed hunt.

There was a reason why usually that particular grassland was an excellent place to hunt. A cool stream flowed a hundred yards inside the jungle. Mid-morning, Victoria noticed her canteen was near empty, so went into the jungle for water.

A few feet into the dense vegetation Victoria heard the splattering stream, and presently it came into view. It was only six feet across and a foot or so deep. Straight ahead was a drop where the water cascaded three feet, and the splash created a fine mist.

Victoria knew it is a chore to keep rust from a weapon in the humid tropics, so she leaned her Wesley Richards against a tree a few feet from the mist. She also removed her cartridge belt and knife to keep the ammunition dry. Then she squatted at the stream to fill her canteen.

When Victoria entered the clearing, a trio of men spied her and ducked into dense brush to avoid discovery. They said nothing and the center man sent one companion to the left and one to the right. Those two went farther along the stream, then crossed over to get behind the unsuspecting girl. The soft rumble of the stream covered their movements, or they could not have surprised her. Victoria was unaware of their presence until the third man came from the jungle and smiled at her.

It was years since any ventured on the land, but Lord Grainger advised them of slavers. Based on descriptions and stories, there was no doubt this was a slaver. He wore the garb of an Arab. Two pistols and a machete hung from his belt, and he leveled his German Mauser Gewehr 98 at Victoria.

The girl scolded herself mentally for her carelessness. From somewhere in the recesses of her mind the thought came - In a place which appears safe, you should stay as alert as in a place of known danger. Wherever the idea originated, she was in complete, wholehearted agreement. She glanced back at the rifle to weigh her chances and saw that all hope was gone, for the moment at least. The other two men held her weapon and belt.

They did not treat her overly rude or rough but took her across the stream into the jungle. Two hundred yards from the stream they came to a trail where a great number of people lay resting. Eighty armed slavers watched over a line of captives twice their number. There were a few children and women, but most of the prisoners were men headed for a life of forced labor. Captives were attached at the waist to form a human chain of hopelessness.

Her captors spoke some English, enough for Victoria to understand an important point. They would beat or kill her if she tried to escape. Otherwise, they would treat her well for she would bring a higher price if she arrived at the block in good condition. Under the circumstances, Victoria decided that cooperation was her only rational choice and it would buy her time to study their habits and frame a method of escape. There was, of course, the hope also that Barney and the others could pick up the trail and come to her aid. For now,

Victoria Custer was just another set of knots in the unfortunate string of human misery weaving northward for the coast and the auction block.

For two days the march was endless marching from sunrise to sunset. At nightfall, they slept on the ground where they stopped. When they bivouacked for the night, they would eat, such as it was. A great pot of some thick unknown was carried down the line by slavers. Captives would cup their hands, and a slaver would fill them with the gruel. Meanwhile, the slavers feasted on sweet fruits and meat of boars or gazelles. In the morning before the march began, they watered the captives in the same way. Those were the only times and the only means by which anyone received any sustenance. It was a method intended to keep men too weak and disheartened to fight.

The huge iron pot used to make their stew weighed at least fifty pounds, and the captives toted it. The prisoner at the head of the column carried it when they set out in the morning. When he tired, he would pass it to the person behind him, excluding children. Thus it would make its way down the line and on a usual day Victoria bore the pot no less than twice.

On the third day, there was an incident which would become a part of Victoria Custer for the remainder of her life. A young native man, hitched but half a dozen bodies from her, stepped into a gopher hole and sprained his ankle. He rebounded immediately and tried to continue. From her vantage, Victoria could see that his ankle was blue and swollen to twice its normal size. The young man tried hard to walk normally but limped nonetheless. Though slight, the speed of the march slowed.

In minutes, one of the guards came along

inspecting each captive until he spied the injured man. He stopped the line and spoke to the man in his language. In seconds the man whom Victoria knew to be the leader came rushing back, yelling angrily. The guard said something and pointed to the man's ankle. The leader only glanced, then looked at the guard and drew a forefinger across his throat. With no evidence of reluctance, the guard raised his rifle and shot the native between his eyes.

Women and children screamed and cowered and men stared in silence. Victoria Custer looked in horror and disgust at the dead man. He seemed her age and was killed for a sprained ankle. The leader noticed Vic's look and stepped toward her. "If you cannot stomach a savage life, you should not have come to a savage land!" He laughed and turned toward the head of the column.

The guard removed the dead man from the line, and they continued, leaving the body where it fell. Victoria understood why her host swore a lifelong hatred for slavery and the upright animals who deal in human commerce. Under her breath, she swore that she, too, would be a lifelong enemy of the foul enterprise.

Two days after the young tribesman was murdered, the slavers sat the captives in a circle. Half a dozen guards remained with them, and the rest of their captors disappeared up the trail. Forty-five minutes later, gunfire erupted ahead, and the yells and screams of humans in distress could be faintly heard. The shooting continued for several minutes. All the time shots grew fewer and farther between. Then came the silence. Soon a slaver returned, and they herded captives in the direction of the gunfire.

Two miles up the trail they came to the

remains of a village and the sight dumbfounded Victoria. At the edge of the village, a group of three dozen new captives huddled. Men, women, and children were on their knees, already tied together for the march. Two slavers used whips to beat any remaining resistance from some of the stronger men. Every hut was burning, and Victoria recognized the acrid, oily stench. The slavers herded villagers into a hut and burned them alive! As horrible as all that, the worst was the six bloodied bodies of infants, none more than a year in age, lying in the dirt. "Why do you kill infants?" she asked the leader, stunned by the inhuman carnage before her. "I told you this is a savage land." Then he pointed to the center of the village. A slaver lay sprawled with a spear in his back. "They killed one of my men. The price was their children."

Three days later Victoria witnessed even greater offense to civilization and humanity. No slaver was injured, but the village was strewn with corpses from infant to grandmother. Slavers burned every hut and beheaded some of the men. In her mind, Victoria tried to put an adequate description to these men who deal in people. Barbarous, evil, subhuman all came to mind, but she found no series of words equal to the task. No mere display of vocabulary could convey the unholy horror of the reality. The bounty for that particular carnage was another fifty humans added to the line of misery. Victoria's hatred of slavers burgeoned.

The morning after Victoria went hunting, the household was searching. Except for the lady of the house and a few servants, everyone went out. They gave Terkoz a shirt Victoria wore the day before she disappeared. After sniffing it, the great hound bounded toward the north, and a troop of anxious, determined men followed him.

Within hours they discovered where Victoria entered the jungle. In short order, they found tracks of the slave caravan and raced northward. To be a slaver suddenly became a very unenviable occupation.

Two days later the rescue party came to the horror left behind by the slavers at the first village. Barney was beside himself when he saw firsthand the depravity of his sister's captors. The speed of the chase increased. In a little over a day, they came to the second village and realized they were gaining. At that point, Grainger consulted with Udur, and the two agreed. The slavers were working their way up an established route, and the next leg was an arc. They decided to split the troop. Grainger and the Waziri, armed with spears, knives and primitive archery gear, left the trail. They cut through the jungle and took the wolfhound with them. The remainder continued up the trail. Both groups now moved at a faster clip, sensing their quarry was near at hand.

Grainger and the Waziri reached the next village ahead of the slavers. Women and children and the old were rushed to safety in the jungle. Then, reinforced by a hundred warriors from the village, they took cover and waited as Barney, Lord Lawrence, and the other dozen well-armed, experienced and very angry men came up behind the slavers.

Vic's captors proceeded as before. They left the captives guarded by half a dozen men while the others went to raid the village. Grainger and the others were ready. A volley of arrows and spears dropped ten of the forward slavers a hundred yards from the village. The slavers attempted a charge against the ambush but failed. They could not see their attackers, so within seconds, another dozen lay dead or dying. The experienced leader realized then that the game was up. He and his two most experienced underlings made a hasty, covert retreat, leaving the others to fight the losing battle and die.

Back with the captives, the leader unhitched Victoria and a half dozen other prisoners. With four of his men, he took them and headed into the jungle to escape with what spoils he thought he could save. The leader ordered the other slavers to wait and continue to watch the remaining captives. Whether loyal or dimwitted, they did as bid.

Within half an hour, Barney and the white hunters came to the prisoners and their guards. In seconds the slavers went down, each with multiple fatal wounds. Questioning about Victoria was in progress when Grainger and the Waziri arrived. When Terkoz came on the scene questioning was unnecessary. He immediately began an ominous growl and charged into the jungle. Grainger, Barney, Curtiss, and the others followed.

The remnant slavers made less than a mile before they heard the howl of Terkoz closing. In moments the slavers, sans the leader, dodged behind trees and began to fire at their pursuers. The leader dragged Victoria on.

There was gunfire for a couple of minutes, then the silence told the leader his men were dead. He jerked to a stop and roughly slammed Victoria against a tree. He leveled his pistol at her face and spit the words, "Are you worth my life? Will they allow me to go for your life? I..." the man suddenly stopped speaking and stared at the girl. Twice before he got the impression that the girl's amber eyes changed to black. Each time he dismissed it as a play of light, thinking such a thing is impossible. Now, face to face with Victoria there was no doubt. Her eyes were like large, perfect black opals. Those dark eyes looked back at the man with no sign of fear. The girl spoke with undisguised threat, and the man's expression of menace was replaced by apprehension.

"You are weak. This was my land before it was yours. You should have never come to my savage land." Victoria's voice was even, and she looked beyond the man at his swiftly approaching fate. The man turned and saw the great hound Terkoz break from the jungle toward him. As he whipped his pistol in the direction of the dog, Victoria brought her tied hands up hard under his arm. The shot went high, and in the next instant, the hound grabbed the slaver's wrist in his mouth. The man dropped the pistol as the mighty jaws crushed the bones of his forearm and dragged him down. The man screamed only once before Terkoz released his arm, and closed on his throat. Terkoz held him off the ground and shook him until all signs of life departed.

Seconds later, Barney and the others charged into the clearing, and the ropes were off Victoria. She was in the company of friends and civilized men. Soon, they freed the other captives and the return march began. Throughout the trek, Victoria often found Billy Curtiss gazing at her with wide eyes. A few times he tried to position himself alone with her, but somehow she managed always to avoid that situation.

The longing gazes of Curtiss did encourage

a great deal of thought as they trekked. She was twenty-five with two degrees and no plans for the future. Most of the women she knew from college were married, many with children - some with many children. Even her two dearest friends, Emma Baker and Lin Li seemed to be settled. Emma was a third-grade teacher, her lifelong dream. Lin Li was a professional pharmacist. She worked part-time at Mortimer's Drug Store and with her parents in their Chinese herbal shop.

Still, the words "pusillanimous weakling" came automatically to mind. Vic would then envision the caveman of her dreams and find herself longing to meet someone like him.

Yet, perhaps now it was time finally to exchange dreams for a solid reality. Billy Curtiss was not unattractive. He was a former officer who served in the European trenches during the Great War. That he followed her to the wilds of Africa showed more than a passing interest and a certain daring. He was in the front line of those who came to her rescue. Perhaps she could finally make a decision based on reality, on something tangible. Maybe now she could leave her dreams behind.

Six days later they arrived back at the Grainger estate, and the other former captives continued to their villages. Immediately on arrival at the estate, the Waziri began to prepare a special meal. That night there was a great feast to celebrate Victoria's return and the defeat of the slavers. Udur himself prepared a rich hippopotamus stew. After one taste, Victoria declared it the best stew she ever tasted!

Late that evening, after dinner, Curtiss finally drew Victoria away from the others. At least he managed to pull her away from other humans. Terkoz accompanied them and lay with his head on the feet of Victoria, his eyes always on the man.

In the magnificent flower garden of Lady Grainger, the two sat on a bench. Curtiss began to speak, but not as the confident man of the world which was his usual demeanor. He stammered and hesitated like a bashful schoolboy.

Victoria attempted to listen but found it difficult. The great yellow-orange equatorial moon was full, and its beams worked magic on the landscape. Was it time to forsake her dreams? The moon seemed to draw something from the girls most profound memories. Something wondrous, and eternal struggled to free itself from the most obscure depths of Vic's mind.

With less than total coherence, Curtiss spoke of his love for Victoria. She would forever be the compass to direct his life. He would not sleep again until she promised to be his wife.

The same doubts assailed Victoria. Her thoughts spun like a tornado. The sincerity of the man was not in question. Victoria was flattered at his efforts to show his affections. Her two best friends were moving on in their professions. Other friends already had families. Perhaps it is time to abandon old dreams, she thought, and looked the young man in the eye and smiled.

"Billy," she began but spoke no further. At that moment, even as she prepared to speak words to put her dreams aside, the earth moved beneath their feet. It seemed to rise and then drop a bit and then slide from right to left. From deep underground came a terra borne thunder as strata shifted and fractured. From the south came a deafening roar of upheaval.

Victoria leapt up, filled with terror at the earthquake. An even greater horror gripped her at the thought of forsaking her dreams. She made a wild dash for the ranch house, and Curtiss followed, calling out to her. As he came out of the garden, he saw Victoria reach the veranda steps and meet her brother. Just then, the earth shook violently again, and Victoria swooned in her brother's arms!

Chapter 4

Back to the Stone Age

Nat-ul awoke to the cool, fresh welcome of a beautiful day, as always the first in her family to open her eyes. The girl was forever eager to dive into life. Life was the great wonder, and she cherished it and every experience it offered. The indirect light of the rising sun brightened the interior of the cave where she lay huddled in an enormous pile of furry pelts. Near her lay an older woman, and in front of them, nearer the mouth of the cave, two men slept. One was Tha, her father, and the other her brother, Aht. The woman was her mother, Lu-tan, who now opened her eyes.

"I am glad that it is light again," said the girl. "The shaking of the ground yesterday gave me terrible dreams in the darkness." The girl rose, stepped between the two men, and went to the ledge before the cave entrance. Behind her, the pile of animal skins shifted, and a ferocious head appeared. It was Zok, a canine, neither wolf nor dog, more massive and powerful than either. Shaggy hair covered Zok's frightening head and oversized teeth extended over its lips. The prodigious beast shook off a lion skin and followed Nat-ul out of the cave.

The sun just topped the horizon behind the Barren Hills. Brilliant rays reflected and rebounded over the continuous rise and fall of waves which gave the mysterious Restless Sea its name. The atmosphere was thick and hot, and countless creatures ranged through the jungle winged overhead and blackened the surface of the sea!

By this time, the others were up. Just inside the cave entrance, the older woman busied herself with flint and dry tinder. Tha and Aht stepped out upon the ledge to join Nat-ul. The three clambered down the steep outcrops and cavities which served as a trail to the beach. Nat-ul carried a bladder for water, Aht took a skin to hold fruits and Tha bore a stone-tipped spear.

Great Zok followed Tha and Aht into the lush, verdant jungle a hundred yards away at that terminus of the Barren Hills. Nat-ul's goal was a pleasant artesian spring at the foot of the cliff to collect fresh water. Here she joined other girls who were filling bladders with the cool, clear water. One was Una, daughter of Onu, the chief, and the sister of Nu. Beside her were half a dozen others, who laughed and talked as they collected water.

"Were you frightened when the earth shook, Nat-ul?" asked Una.

"It gave me terrible dreams," replied Nat-ul.

"Nu has gone to slay Gr," said Una.

Nat-ul looked surprised. "I told Nu he need

not slay Gr to prove himself."

Una told her, "Nu has a great desire to lay the head of the beast before the cave of Tha for Nat-ul. He has gone to slay the great Gr which dwells on the far end of the Barren Hills."

Soon their odd assortment of animal bladders were filled, and the girls returned to their respective caves. A minute after Nat-ul, Tha returned with an antelope and Aht brought the skin filled with fruits.

Nat-ul poured water into a hollow in the cave floor beside Lu-tan's fire where several stones were heating. Lutan slowly added heated stones to the water to bring it to a boil. Nat-ul cut flesh from the antelope and dropped the strips into the natural pot. Then Nat-ul gave Zok an antelope leg which he took to a corner and began to gnaw.

Breakfast conversation centered on the one thing which Nat-ul's people feared - nature. It was the one thing which none could stand against. Lately, the earth seemed angry. It shook more often and more violently than even the eldest members of the tribe could recall.

As the girls collected water that morning, Hud, a warrior of the tribe, passed them. He heard Una inform Nat-ul that Nu was gone to slay Gr. For many hunts past, Hud cast his eye on the daughter of Tha. He wished for the girl to be his mate, but she chose Nu, and in their tribe, a mate was the choice of the woman. Hud knew Nat-ul would not change her mind, so his one chance to have her as his mate was to abduct her. Away from the tribe, she might be persuaded to accept him as her mate. There was no other way, and with Nu gone, Hud decided to act.

Hud watched from his cave for an

opportunity to meet Nat-ul alone. At last, his patience was rewarded as she returned to the now deserted spring. Hud overtook her as she stooped to fill a bladder and came to the point in the most primitive fashion. "I want you to be my mate."

Nat-ul's instant response was laughter.

"Go fetch the head of Gr and lay it before my father's cave," she answered. "Then, maybe, Nat-ul will consider becoming the mate of Hud. But I forgot, Hud prefers to remain at home with the old women and children while the men - and I - go on the hunt."

Hud colored. Cowards were not bred until a later age, and the girl's remark was the ultimate insult. The discussion was over. Hud was twice the size of Nat-ul. He lifted her with one arm around her waist, his other hand clamped over her mouth. The girl struggled as Hud bore her down the shore of the Restless Sea, on the same path Nu ventured down earlier. They were at the point where Nu turned into the jungle when the earth vibrated and bucked and knocked Hud to a knee. He knew of the hairy ape folk, and that Nu took that route, so when the tremor subsided, Hud did not venture into the jungle. He dragged Nat-ul miles farther along the shore to a lesser version of the Barren Hills. He knew of a cave a few feet up where they could hide, and he might persuade Nat-ul to be his mate.

Bones which bore the teeth marks of Ur, the cave-bear, were strewn before the cave. Hud threw the sun-bleached thigh bone of a bull into the cave. There was no warning growl, so he pushed Nat-ul inside.

Hud rolled boulders, as large as he could

move, before the mouth of the cave, enough to bar the entrance to Ur. He left a small opening and squeezed through it. Nat-ul stood flattened against the farthest wall of the cave, and as Hud crossed toward her, the earth trembled again.

Nu traveled less than half the distance to the known lair of a gigantic male Gr when the earth began to shake. Ground trembling was not new to the caveman, but the power of that quake was beyond his experience. The ground rose and fell and rolled and threw Nu to the ground. That never happened before. Twice he rose, and twice more the vibrations knocked him down. When the shaking finally subsided the caveman rose and looked toward the lair of Gr.

Many sleeps ago there was an awful shaking. Boulders fell from the heights and crushed two members of his tribe. This crossed the mind of the hunter, and he wondered if Nat-ul was safe. Keen was his desire to bring the head of Gr to Nat-ul, but his heart was filled with what became known as love. Love has always, even in that time, co-existed with concern over the safety of the loved one. Finally, Nu turned back toward his home and loped as the antelopes of the grassland.

When Nu turned onto the beach, the earth shook again, but less violently and soon he reached the caves of his people. He was relieved to find no caves destroyed, but he could not find his precious Nat-ul. So he and Tha, sire of Nat-ul, called all the tribe together and asked if any knew where they might find Nat-ul.

For a moment there was silence, then a girl who collected water with Nat-ul at the spring spoke up. "I saw her leave with Hud. She has gone to mate Hud. I saw them leave together."

"No!" Nu bellowed and shook his head.

"I saw her with my own eyes," the girl continued. "Why should Nu be concerned? There are others who would choose you as her mate," and she smiled and stepped toward him.

"No!" Nu pushed the girl away.

A man in the crowd spoke up, "The choice of a mate is the right of the woman. Nat-ul has the right to change her mind."

"No," Nu repeated. "Have you forgotten? While yet a child Nat-ul defended against the great Ur. On her face, she wears the scar from the beast. She has hunted the mammoth. She has fought our enemies and always made a good accounting of herself. Nat-ul fears nothing. She would not cower and slither into the grasses like Nak, the snake. If Nat-ul desired another for her mate, she would stand before Nu and the whole of our people, and she would say it to my face. Hud must have abducted her! Which way did they go?" He looked sternly at the girl.

She could not hold his gaze so lowered her head and lifted an arm to point. "Hud took her in the direction from which Nu returned."

Nu inquired of Tha, "Where is great Zok? He can lead me to Nat-ul in short order."

Tha replied that Aht took Zok on a hunt and may be gone all day. That was an unacceptable delay to the caveman. So it was that Nu alone turned to retrace his steps toward the far end of the Barren Hills. He would slay treacherous Hud and return Nat-ul to their people.

Hud grabbed Nat-ul in his arms, as much for his protection as anything more. He looked fearfully at the entrance as the two swayed back and forth in the same quake which shook Nu on the beach. Nat-ul did not hesitate. She was a warrior and a hunter. As her abductor turned his eyes to the entrance, she pulled the broad stone knife from his waistband. Before Hud could react, she made a powerful upward thrust that drove the weapon's jagged edge through the man's liver.

The tremor knocked them both to the ground, and Hud reclined hard and sighed. Balancing against the sway of the earth, Nat-ul rose and bolted for the entrance. She slipped through the small opening to freedom and made her way toward the tribe of Onu until she came upon the hairy ape folk!

A group of hairy ape folk saw Nu enter the jungle which they staked as theirs, and after the first tremor watched him return the way he came. They followed him to the beach in curiosity about why the man came into the jungle then went out again.

The hairy ape folk found it difficult to hold any thought for very long. When Nu turned along the beach toward home, and the earth shook again, they stopped to stare at the sea. It was not the first time they beheld it, but it always filled them with awe. They gawked awhile and were set to return to the jungle when one spied something coming out of the surf.

A giant turtle pulled on shore, and whether to sun itself or lay eggs or for some other purpose would forever remain a mystery.   Some of the brutes tasted turtle flesh before. Were there such a word, they would deem it a delicacy, so they set out to confront the armored beast.

It was no giant tortoise as seen in modern zoos but a behemoth sea turtle. Only the tallest of the ape folk could see over the turtle's back, and its length was equal to the height of four of them. The head was as large as the head of Ur, and a single snap of the powerful beak could take an arm or leg! Yet with all its size and power and armor, on land, the creature was essentially defenseless. It was no match for a band of hairy ape folk who brought the cunning and calculation of near men.

The brutes circled the turtle. Two or three took hold of each flipper and the tail and lifted them. That eliminated the creature's ability to move. The other ape folk brought large stones and pelted the doomed creature's head until it lay still.

There was a score of the hairy ape folk, and it took them all to roll the turtle up on a side. They pulled, pushed and ripped at the carcass until the upper and lower shells separated and the internal contents of the turtle poured out. Then they squatted in the gore, argued amongst themselves, and proceeded to feed.

Nat-ul felt safe when she left the cave. Hud was dead, and her people were no more distant than what she considered a short walk. Yet in that stupendously savage time, there were witticisms as there are today. A favorite went, *do not begin to chew until the meat is in your mouth.*

As Nat-ul came over a dune, she beheld a scene of savage bestiality difficult for modern man to imagine. Gore covered the hairy ape folk as they feasted on gruesome chunks of mutilated turtle meat. The scene illustrated well their brutality which Nat-ul already understood. Thus, the split second she saw them, the cave girl dropped to her belly and back-crawled below the crest of the dune. She peered over the dune and saw that they were still in their revelry and yet unaware of her presence.

The hairy ape folk possessed a sense of smell many times keener than that sense in man even in Nat-ul's time, and she knew if she remained this near, even over the stench of the turtle's bowel contents they would eventually detect her presence. Staying low, she crawled safely back. Then she stood and rushed away from home and safety. Nat-ul ran full out for several minutes to quickly put distance between her and the brutes. Already she regretted leaving the knife in Hud's gut, for being unarmed in that savage world was something that never lasted long and seldom ended well.

After racing full out for some time, Nat-ul

slowed to a lope for a while, then began to walk. She was not tired, but she did not want to happen unaware onto some other predator. She no longer fled but moved as a huntress and constantly sniffed the air for the scent of danger. She listened, too. A crush of jungle foliage would forewarn of a dangerous plant eater like Ta, the rhinoceros. A stealthy footfall would warn of a predator like Gr, the long-toothed cat. Her eyes took in everything. Though most attentive to the 180 degrees ahead, she now and then glanced back. There was always the danger that an unfriendly fell in behind her.

Nat-ul wanted to put a great distance between her and the hairy ape folk. If they detected that a female human was recently near, it would be nothing unheard of for them to follow her. The most sensible action was to spend the night in unknown territory and return to her tribe in the morning. It was the most sensible plan but held a measure of dangers that would fill the skin of a bull mammoth.

The cave girl entered the jungle at a point less dense, where it would be more difficult for a predator to hide. She was well versed in the useful items of her world as were all her kind. It took no time at all for her to spot the tree she sought. The tree's wood was sturdy, and the limbs tended to grow straight. It was with this tree that her people made spears, and hafts for stone axes.

The strength of the tree hindered her. Having no ax, she hung from a limb and soon her weight and the force of bouncing provided a branch of acceptable size. She took another limb in the same fashion, then listened for a moment to determine if the noise roused some predator.

Next, she went out to the water line and dragged her feet through the sand. Within a few minutes, she gathered several sturdy scalloped shells. She returned into the jungle to collect stout lianas and used the shells to cut lengths of the natural rope. Not far from there, Nat-ul found a vine winding around a small tree. It was armed with thorns as thick as her first finger and longer. She cut a length of the vine and returned to the tree line with all her materials.

Nat-ul used the shells to saw, and after some effort, one end of a limb provided a serviceable point. Next, she wrapped a stretch of the thorny vine in a spiral below the point and secured it with lengths of the tough liana. Lastly, she attached a longer vine as a shoulder thong so her hands would be free when she traveled.

She repeated the process with the second staff and was thus then armed with two crude weapons. She could wield them as clubs, and the thorns made them formidable, or she could jab with the sharpened ends. The weapons would not slay a large beast but would serve her needs. Nat-ul would spend the night in a tree. A sharp staff in the eye could drive away any predator which tried to climb up.

When the job was done, the sun was poised just above the edge of the Restless Sea.

Quickly, Nat-ul gathered a portion of her skin garment, then placed the three best shells into the cupped material and secured it with a length of liana to form a makeshift pouch. The cave girl then returned to the jungle. Earlier she spied a giant fruit often eaten by her tribe. The brown and green striped, watermelon-sized fruit was soft enough to tear open with fingers. Nat-ul preferred animal flesh, but the fruit would satisfy both hunger and thirst for the night. After taking her fill, she smeared a handful of the pungent meat over her body to disguise her own scent and confuse predators.

Then she returned to the tree where she collected the lianas. She hung a war club over each shoulder and began to climb. Nat-ul pulled up the liana as well as any other upright.

The lowest limb was twenty feet above ground, large enough to walk on, with many lianas hanging from it. If she could use it to ascend, so could an enemy, so she used a shell to cut all lianas but the one she climbed. That one she pulled up and draped over the limb. Then she pulled herself up to a higher limb and then a higher limb to finally settle fifty feet above ground. It was twilight, and Nat-ul was preparing to sleep when she heard distant, booming.

More sure footed than you or I in daylight, the cave girl walked the narrow limb in near darkness. She didn't stop until it began to bend to her weight, and her feet told her they could not be accommodated farther. It was far enough, for she was at the tree line and below was the beach. The three-quarter moon gleamed on the relentless movements of the Restless Sea. The moonbeams made the wave caps sparkle like the tiny lights in the sky. For a moment, Nat-ul forgot why she ventured out on the limb. She appreciated the view and took in deep breaths of the fresh sea breeze. In all the world Nat-ul knew, only the full moon and her home in the Barren Hills were more beautiful than the Restless Sea at night.

Then she heard the booming again and looked up the beach away from her people. She saw fires in the distance and as she watched another fire ignited and then another. Someone was lighting beast fires for protection against predators overnight. One or a few people would not bother with that but would mount the trees as she did. It must be a tribe. Nat-ul experienced such booming before. She understood it was a signal made by beating sticks on fallen trees. With night falling, they likely warned anyone not within the beast fires to hurry inside or be lost.

They were no danger to her, so she gazed up at the moon for a few more minutes, and felt familiar yearnings. She longed to understand the moon. It looked like a round stone, but she knew if she threw a stone into the air it would fall. So if the moon was a stone, why didn't it fall? She knew a distant boulder would be much larger when she walked to it, so was the moon larger than it looked? And what were all those twinkling lights around the moon on a night without clouds? Nat-ul wanted to learn.

She could show 'many' stars or enemies by holding up all her fingers and waving her hand across in front of her, but she wanted more. Nat-ul wanted to give her people an exact account of mammoths or enemies or stars. She felt sure there must be a way. For some time her mind wandered in such fascination. Then, eyes fixed on the moon, Nat-ul whispered a promise to herself. *Someday I swear to learn of these wondrous things,* and she returned to the bole of the tree.

Leaving her weapons on her shoulders, Nat-ul straddled the limb with her back to the trunk. She leaned forward with her cheek on the smooth bark and let her arms dangle on either side. She fell quickly into a restful slumber and only twice in the night was she awakened.

At the first bother, she snapped awake, listening. From the ground fifty feet below, she heard great nostrils sniffing for prey. It was a long-toothed cat, confused by the smeared melon. Gr was not a tree climber like the modern house cat. Even if he stayed, it would serve no purpose, so he soon departed.

Later, an even larger nose awakened Nat-ul as it tested the air. At that episode, a rank musky odor came up to her. It was Ur, the cave bear. Ur possessed a habit which Gr did not, so the cave girl reached around the limb. She grabbed one wrist with the opposite hand and held tight. There was a grunt as the great beast stood upright and Nat-ul was glad she

50

climbed higher. That Ur could have reached her on the lowest limb.

She braced as Ur fell against the tree with forepaws backed by nearly a ton of force. Ur growled with anger that the giant tree hardly shook. He buffeted it again and again with such force that the fourth slam knocked Nat-ul over the side of the limb. She clung by her arms for three more attempts by Ur to shake something loose.

Only after she heard the bear drop to fours and amble off did she pull herself astride the limb again. She slid back against the trunk and lay forward, and in short order was once more in slumber.

Chapter 5

Beyond the Restless Sea

The sun was just above the trees, and the jungle was dusky when Nat-ul awoke. Birds made all manner of calls, a bee the size of her hand buzzed above her head and from the Restless Sea came shrill shrieks of battling saurians. Nat-ul stood and stretched this way and that, then descended to the jungle floor. She first revisited the giant melon plant and ate her fill. Then she went to the tree line and surveyed the beach before she ventured out.

Nat-ul began in the direction to her tribe but hesitated. What kind of people would live on the beach? Did they have caves on the beach? Never before did she see so many beast fires. It would be good for her tribe to know if they were many and whether they were warlike. She decided to investigate if they were not too distant. She planned to reconnoiter for her tribe, and slip away with the other tribe unaware she was ever there. She would go that direction until she must turn back to reach her home in the Barren Hills by next darkness.

Nat-ul moved with caution, near the tree line, always alert for signs of danger. Yet modern eyes would think her careless for she moved swiftly, alternating from a fast walk to full out run.

The cave girl traveled for what we would count two hours when she heard voices beyond the next dune. Immediately she dropped to her hands and knees and crawled. At the top of the dune, she inched on her belly to peer over.

In an area ringed by palm trees, well over one hundred men, women, and children went about their daily activities.   Many women and children scraped the hides of animals. Others chipped shards of stone to fashion spearheads. Across the clearing men were butchering a boar. These sights were familiar, but other things were mysterious to Nat-ul.

No caves were evident, but there were rows of square boxes side by side in straight lines. They seemed to be trees without limbs holding up leaves and animal skins. Nat-ul watched several people enter and leave the strange boxes and decided they must be caves made from trees. *No wonder these people needed many beast fires. Those sticks could not keep out a long-toothed cat or giant bear or an angry mammoth! My cave in the stone of the Barren Hills is the better home.*

Near the shore, there was more strange activity. Several men worked on large trees which lay on the ground, in various stages of whatever they were doing. Most were stripped of all limbs and men chopped to hollow out some. Fires burned within the hollows of others. Many were only a shell with the ends beveled to a point much like the weapons she carried.

Presently a group of men went down to hollowed logs at the water's edge. They were laden with an arsenal of spears, each with a long vine attached at one end. They placed the spears into three of the gutted logs, and pushed the logs into the Restless Sea and went with them! A few steps out, a hand count of men jumped into each of the hollowed logs.

Each man lifted a contraption which Nat-ul thought was a weapon until they used it. One half of a foot-long seashell, what we now call a bivalve, was lashed to a short, stout branch. Each man leaned forward and dipped the tool into the water at arm's length with the open side of the shell facing back. In unison, each pulled his shell back to him through the water, lifted it and repeated the procedure. As the men made the strange motions, the logs began to move toward the open sea!

Nat-ul never saw a boat before. The thought of riding a horse was millennia in the future. The wheel was not yet imagined, and even the concept of transportation was unknown to the cave girl. She would need to think about a seashell on a stick moving a log across the water. She had no idea how her tribe might use such things. Nor did she have a desire to venture into the Restless Sea filled with all manner of loathsome saurians. Yet, she was already eager to describe these things to Nu and her family.

Tur was one of the boatbuilders, the people Nat-ul was watching. While the people Nat-ul watched in the village were very much like her tribe, Tur was different. His well-muscled frame rose easily to six feet eight inches. While not a pelt like the hairy ape folk or gorillas, his skin was covered with hair. One thing especially made Tur look ill-natured. From birth, one of his eyes was blind, unblinking and the color of salt.

Tur left his village earlier to collect strong vines for cordage on the tribe's harpoon spears. With a huge bundle on each shoulder, he now came from the jungle a hundred yards behind where Nat-ul crouched. The moment he broke from the tree line, Tur spotted Nat-ul and froze.

Nat-ul's attention was so focused on Tur's people that she heard nothing when he came from the jungle. Tur gingerly laid the bundles on the sand and crept toward her. As he neared, Tur marveled at the sleek lines of her form and the luster of the crow-black hair.

Like all men and women who lived in that time, Tur was a stalker. He came closer to Nat-ul, but there was a dry twig. If the twig had been visible, Tur would have overstepped it. Sand covered the twig, though, so Tur did not see it. When his foot broke the twig, the sound was quiet and muffled, but Nat-ul was a warrior of that time, also. What we would miss was to her an unquestionable alarm to danger! She rose to her feet in a flash, slipped the war club from her left shoulder, then spun and slashed!

If the boatbuilder were a partial second slower, he would have his belly sliced open by the thorns on the club. He saw Nat-ul begin to rise though and instinctively stepped back. The girl held the club ready to swing again. From behind, her form entranced him. Now, seeing her from the front, he decided she must be the

most beautiful woman he could ever lay eyes on!
She seemed physically perfect but more
important, she looked him eye-to-eye. He could
feel the strength of a warrior and hunter, and the
scar on her left cheek verified her courage.
There was no cringing or cowering, no fear or
loathing at his visage as from the women of his
tribe. For the first time in his life, Tur thought,
this woman is my equal, not only beautiful but
powerful. There was an indescribable appeal in
her unflinching gaze and defiant posture.
Nowhere in all the vast wilderness of his world
could he hope to ever find another such as her!

Nat-ul did not fear, but she was angry at
herself that he was able to come so near. There
was no doubt the man claimed superior
strength, and she could imagine being lifted
with a single hand.

Before any part of the body goes into
action it makes minute preparatory moves.
The experienced hunter-warrior of a
thousand generations past learned such
things early or early left this life. Nat-ul saw,
or perhaps sensed, the man's muscles flex
and knew he was about to grab her. She
chose to move first.

Nat-ul would have made the war cry of her
tribe, but the other boatbuilders were yet
unaware of her presence. Instead, she hissed
at the man like the slithering death, Nak the
snake, and swung the war club at his face.

Tur stopped his forward movement, stepped
back, and leaned rearwards at the waist to avoid
the club. Nat-ul dropped the club so it would not
impede her next move, squatted, dived head first
between the legs of the huge man, and rolled up
to her feet already running! Tur, surprised but

smiling, turned to pursue her.

The two did not stand front to back with the long beach but were angled to it. As Nat-ul came up running, there was sand before her and no time for a question. A few yards from her start, she passed through a twenty-foot-wide portal flanked by palm trees. Right away she realized she did not pass palms to get there.

The dune that provided cover for Nat-ul was at the head of a promontory. It was on that narrow, three-hundred-yard finger of dry land where she now found herself. The Restless Sea lay on three sides, and the giant boatbuilder came behind!

Tur could not keep pace with the girl so was jubilant when she ran onto the promontory. She would be his! His mate would be the most beautiful woman in the tribe! Nat-ul could have given him good advice about not chewing before the meat is in your mouth.

Nat-ul slowed to a lope, to assess her options, and Tur matched her pace. He felt no need for haste. The prize would be his in moments.

Suddenly Tur called out in the universal language of uprights for her to drop. "Drop now!" he shouted. Nat-ul thought, *does he expect me to give up?* At that moment she was covered by a huge shadow and heard a tremendous swooshing sound. She glanced over a shoulder, and the sight which met her eyes brought an involuntary gasp.

Nat-ul often saw the terrible flying reptiles take animals and now one swooped down for her! She dropped, but it was too late. Like giant three-point pincers, a scaly talon closed on the girl and lifted her. The reptile's rise was swift - Nat-ul heard the man roar in anger once. Then there was only the sound of wind rushing past and a strange leathery creak of the reptilian wings.

It surprised the cave girl that the creature did not rip her in two and eat her on the spot. It gave her hope. No matter how dire the situation, she understood from experience that while there is yet breath in your body, there is a chance.

Nat-ul, of course, never flew before. She enjoyed the experience, but such thoughts were brief. More to the point of the moment, she sought a means to escape.

From her vantage, Nat-ul could see more of the world than she ever imagined existed! The pterodactyl soared at three thousand feet. The cave girl saw distant mountains for the first time, and the jungle stretched out of sight. A few islands were visible to her people. They were mystical lands protected by the Restless Sea and its horrible monsters.   Nat-ul could now see that there were many such lands of mystery, but one in particular interested her. Their path was a direct line to the largest and nearest island, and the reptile was declining toward it.

It was dusk when Nu, came near the far end of the Barren Hills and he happened on the same sight which Nat-ul saw earlier from her opposite vantage point. The hairy ape folk were still with the remains of the behemoth turtle. By then, less eating was being done than pelting one another with flesh and bones. Such jousting was often the case with the naturally irritable creatures. Nu keenly eyed the foul blood orgy and was finally satisfied that no human bones lay among the carnage. Nu saw no sign that anyone ascended the Barren Hills, and he knew Hud would not venture into the jungle toward the abode of hairy ape folk in the company of a female. Therefore, Hud took Nat-ul up the beach into unknown territory, and the hairy ape folk came afterward. This deduction relieved Nu. He knew a feeding was not a good time to be noticed by hairy ape folk, so he went back a few hundred yards. He found a crevice where Gr or Ur could not reach him. There, Nu fell into listless sleep and dreamed of perils which might threaten his Nat-ul at that very moment.

In the morning, Nu returned and found the hairy ape folk were just leaving. The brutish creatures would amble a few steps. One would slap another, and all would stop for a brief half-hearted fight. Then they continued a few steps and re-played the drama. Finally, the hairy ape folk were out of sight, and earshot and Nu continued his search.

Sometime later, Nu came to a small outcrop of stone, a miniature version of his beloved Barren Hills. On a ledge a few yards above, he spotted a cave with stones before it, obviously placed by man.

Ax held at the ready, Nu mounted the slope to the cave. He drew the ax high, poised to strike, and with his other hand pulled stones down to open the cave. When the entryway was adequate, Nu entered. The only sound that met him was the shrill squeals of rats, and several of the rodents scurried past him.

The instant he entered, Nu could see a body in the hindermost recess of the cave. In the gloom, he could not discern if it was his beloved Nat-ul or Hud. Glutted with apprehension, Nu made for the depths of the cave.

The relief was near overpowering when Nu determined the body was not Nat-ul. Rodents gnawed the face and other soft body parts, as well as the knife wound, but it was obviously Hud. So what became of Nat-ul?

Wind removed tracks in the sand, so Nu reasoned. If Nat-ul came upon the hairy ape folk, she would put distance between herself and their sensitive noses. That meant she traveled away from their tribe. Nat-ul was as capable a warrior and hunter as any in their tribe, but he also worried that she was likely unarmed. Further, if she went even a short distance in that direction, she would be in unknown territory.

Nu was eager to find his beloved cave girl, so he moved quickly up the beach. Miles later he came to the same village which Nat-ul watched with such interest earlier that very day. He immediately spied the war club which Nat-ul abandoned.

Nu held the club and lay in the very place Nat-ul lay earlier and watched the boatbuilders. He was as interested in their activities as Nat-ul, but curiosity was far less pressing than his concern for Nat-ul. For many minutes he watched but saw no sign of Nat-ul. Then a giant warrior roused his interest. The warrior was addressing a group of men in a very agitated manner, as he waved his arms and pointed to the sea. The men stood with arms crossed and shook their heads which brought an angry roar from the giant!

While that anonymous drama played out, Nu decided to look about for signs of his Nat-ul. Shortly, on the promontory where the damp sand held footprints better, he spied tracks

which he knew as well as his own. Nat-ul ran
here, out toward the Restless Sea!

Behind Nat-ul's tracks was a set of huge
footprints. Immediately they brought to mind
the giant arguing in the village. Nu followed
the tracks, and shortly those of the man
stopped. The giant returned the direction
whence he came. The tracks of Nat-ul
continued for another hundred yards, then
ended abruptly.

It confounded Nu. Nat-ul did not reach the
sea. She didn't turn to confront the man. She
simply vanished! Nu was neither of low
intelligence nor superstitious. He could not
imagine what happened, but he knew there was
an answer. If he could not see Nat-ul, then he
should watch the giant who seemed the one
who chased her along this finger of land. The
giant would know what happened.

So Nu returned to observe the strange
people, in hopes of an opportunity to draw
the giant out alone. The giant was a head
taller than Nu and broader. Yet it was no
matter for in that time it was the way to do
what needed done, and Nu would face anyone
for his Nat-ul.

The giant was not in sight when Nu returned
to observe. After a time, he came from one of
the strange tree caves with a war ax. He
stopped at a group of men and again spoke with
them, and again they shook their heads curtly.
The giant roared as before, stamped a foot and
loped toward the beach. He tossed his weapon
into a hollowed log, pushed it into the water and
after a few steps, jumped inside. Nu observed
the giant take a seashell on a branch and pull
it through the water and the log moved forward!

Nu didn't hesitate. He must follow the giant, and there was only one possible way - in one of the hollowed logs. A sizable dune hid the hollowed logs from direct view of the boatbuilders, so his rash plan had a chance. Haste was crucial, though, or the giant would be lost from sight.

Nu bent low and stayed behind reeds as he hurried to the canoes. There were six canoes in a row, each equipped with seashell oars, and it gave Nu an inspiration. Quickly he pushed all the canoes into the sea, and as he did, he threw the oars into the water. Then, he mounted one craft and used the shell-oar the way the giant used it. Nu made but a few strokes before a boatbuilder came over the dune and spied what was happening. The warrior's cry went up, and in seconds, dozens of the men were at the shore clamoring into the waves to fetch the canoes.

Nu was a fast learner. Within a few attempts, his awkward strikes at the water became serviceable strokes. He propelled his canoe forward faster than he expected. It made him smile until he looked back. Nu was doing a fine job for a relaxing afternoon on the lake, but the boatbuilders were experts. With the powerful pull of four men in each boat, the gap between Nu and his pursuers visibly narrowed. At the same time, the gap between Nu and the giant widened.

For a few seconds, the giant appeared to stop. Nu thought he saw the chase and was slowing for battle. That would put him between two enemies, but within seconds, the giant continued. Soon after, Nu saw wild thrashing in the water ahead and swerved the canoe to bypass a feeding frenzy. He passed within fifty feet of the fury. A dozen various sea creatures ripped at the body of a long-necked saurian. Nu spotted the head of the dead beast and recognized that it was cleaved by an ax. It was apparent the giant slowed to kill the creature.

Then a long-necked saurian rose up ahead of Nu! He turned the boat as well as his skill allowed, and as the snake-like neck reached for him, Nu swung his ax. The heavy, well-honed stone cut through the flesh and bone of one side of the jaw and knocked out several teeth. The wounded beast yanked its head high, and its shrill squeal sprayed blood across the water. It was an invitation for others of its kind to feed! Even before the wounded creature turned again on Nu, a dozen others sank their teeth into the doomed saurian.

An island soon loomed large ahead. Nu's pursuers passed too near a frenzy. Now they were engaged in their own death struggle with several reptiles. Nu bypassed another frenzy incited by the boatbuilder, then angled for shore. He could see the boat of the giant, though the man was not in sight.

A hundred yards from shore Nu heard a gush of water to his side as a colossal crocodile rose within feet of his canoe! The monster's mouth closed on the craft behind Nu and lifted it from the water. In a blinding instant, the caveman cudgeled the creature's head. Three times the caveman brought his ax down on the creature's skull, and on the third blow, the animal let go!

Nu grabbed up the oar and began to stroke. He glanced back and sighted the crocodile coming again, this time for the tail of the boat. Nu dropped the oar and moved to the rear of the canoe. When the colossal head came in striking distance, he swung his weapon into the beast's eye! With a blaring hiss, the thing brought its great bulk out of the water and twisted and thrashed in mid-air. The blow was painful, but it did more. Only a small amount of blood was drawn along with the raw fluid of the eye. That was enough in the deadly waters of the Restless Sea.

Concepts of belief and disbelief didn't yet exist, but something akin to disbelief now entered Nu's thoughts. That gargantuan crocodile was twice the length of his craft. Yet, as the beast hit the surface of the water, it was taken from below by a crocodile thrice its size!

It was then that Nu noticed his feet were in water. The bottom of the canoe bore two leaking punctures made by the crocodile. There would have been three, but a broken tooth acted as a stopper in one. Nu immediately broke Nat-ul's war club in two. He forced a half into each one of the punctures, then he grabbed the oar and pulled for all he was worth toward the shore!

Without further incident, the nose of the canoe met the beach. Nu jumped out and pulled the craft up from the water and glanced back to ensure no beast was following from the sea. Then he turned his attention to the interior of the island.

Chapter 6

Death-defying Descent

Dense jungle circled the island and ringed a rugged interior of mountain peaks and strange spires. The spires reminded Nat-ul of those she saw hanging from the ceiling or growing from the floor of caverns. These spires were mountainous, and the winged monster bore Nat-ul toward one of them. The top of the spire could accommodate three men lying head to foot and was concave, like a small volcano. Inside were tree limbs and grass, and bones and skins of past meals and three young pterodactyls! The three crowded to the side where their mother approached. Their long dagger beaks snapped in ravenous anticipation of fresh meat!

Nat-ul retained the second war club. It dangled from a shoulder, and the enormous scaly clawed foot of the reptile encircled her body, so her arms were free, but what good were four-inch thorns against the tough hide of the giant adult? Despite their inability to yet fly, the

reptile chicks in the nest stood nearly as tall as
Nat-ul. Their beaks were as long as her arm.
Even one of them might prove a deadly
adversary. Still, they would be easier to fight
than the adult.

Fortune often favors the brave. Fifty feet
above the nest it favored Nat-ul. Until then
she planned to fall into the nest fighting. Then
the pterodactyl urinated copious amounts on
the cave girl. The hot stinking filth of the
animal soaked Nat-ul, and she could only think
it was to mark her as food or to incite a frenzy.
Of greater usefulness, the unwholesome insult
to the condemned gave Nat-ul an idea. She
looked up behind her and could see where the
urine was excreted. A wound waiting to be
opened, she thought.

Twenty feet from the nest, Nat-ul sensed a
slight slackening of the talon that held her. She
knew the beast was preparing to drop her and
understood that she would have but one chance.
With her right hand, she grasped the club, took
it from her shoulder, and gripped it tight. She
could not lose her only weapon and expect to
survive.

The flying reptile came to a near stop at the
edge of the nest. Nat-ul twisted her body and
grasped the thing's leg tightly just above the foot,
not to inflict pain, but to keep from falling if the
reptile released her away from the nest. She
held the pointed end of the club wrapped with
the thorns against the pterodactyl.

The club was four feet long. Nat-ul thrust
hard, and a forearm length of the weapon
penetrated the reptile. In a fit of pain, the
pterodactyl screeched and lurched! Nat-ul now
hung over the nest away from the young, so she
let go the reptile's leg and grabbed the club with

both hands. Her weight tore the club from inside the pterodactyl. With the club came a chunk of flesh and gush of blood, most of which bypassed Nat-ul thanks to a friendly wind.

The pterodactyl continued to screech and back flapped up and flew away. Nat-ul dropped into the stone nest beside the only break in the cone wall. She teetered for a second, and caught a fight-inspiring look at the sharp rocks three hundred feet below!

It took but a second for the cave girl to regain balance and turn to face the three hungry young. As the nearest craned its neck to feed, Nat-ul slammed a bulging eyeball. Then immediately she raised the club and brought it down on the chick's skull. Blood ran from the head wound, and the eye dangled from the socket. The sibling on that side took advantage and plucked the eyeball like a berry. The wounded chick turned to peck and flap the other with unbelievable ferocity!

While two engaged one another, Nat-ul jumped toward the third and whacked the side of the head and it fell over. Before it could rise, the cave girl jumped with both feet on the long, spindly neck. She bounced her weight as she clubbed the head. For a moment the creature struggled, but finally, Nat-ul heard a crack and the beast gave a last gasp and lay still.

Now, Nat-ul turned her attention to the other two, but only one remained. The one-eye was hardy. It now picked out and devoured great chunks of meat and organs from a gash in the other.

Nat-ul saw the power of the wings when the wounded pterodactyl knocked its sibling down. As it now fed, a wing was outstretched, and she took advantage. She swung hard, and the thorns gouged a hole in the center of the membranous appendage. Nat-ul pulled back with her weight and made a huge rip in the wing. The creature shrieked and tried to strike with the wing but missed, so turned its beak to Nat-ul!

The sparring began. Nat-ul swung, and the thing dodged. The reptile pecked, and she parried. To Nat-ul, it was like practice with another warrior. The young pterodactyl never landed a blow. Nat-ul landed every second or third blow on its bony head. Yet the girl knew she would tire before the reptile so she must do better.

As she parried the deadly thrusts, she trusted her sense of balance and backed toward the break in the wall. Only when her heels teetered at the very edge did she stop. She began to thrust and swing as fast as she could. She intended to anger the reptile while preventing a counterattack. Then she stopped, and the brute took advantage of the feigned opening. It thrust its long neck forward and jumped toward her in a bold, angry move. Nat-ul side-stepped and swung into the back of the pointed head. The combined force of its jump and the clubbing almost took the pterodactyl over the edge as planned. At the last instant, it clutched the side of the cleft with the single sharp talon on the wing opposite Nat-ul.

Now behind the creature, the cave girl choked it and beat its head with the club, but she could not budge the thing. She kicked one foot from the edge, but it was back in place before she could kick the other. In a final effort, she dropped the club, and kicked one foot loose. While that foot yet dangled, she slammed herself against the body of the giant chick. The move broke the reptile's hold. It fell over the edge, and Nat-ul dropped forward behind it! She put a hand down to brace herself against the wall and watched as the creature attempted to fly. It was a bit young, and the torn wing hindered it. It screeched until it slammed onto the sharp rocks and lay quiet.

From the waist up her body was in the air! Nat-ul walked her hands back up and pulled into the nest. Now she must find a way down.

She worked her way around the nest to survey the walls of the spire from every vantage. There was no easy way down, but it was not impossible. Nor was there any choice. Nat-ul again circled the nest to choose the route with the best hand and foot holds for her descent. She was unable to verify footing to the bottom by any path. So she chose the location that appeared would take her the furthest. She was about to begin when a wondrous idea came to her. It was one of the greatest strides of humankind to imagine, and Nat-ul was experiencing it. The notion she envisioned excited her and filled her with daring!

Nat-ul gathered hides from previous chick meals and cut four strips of leather. She took a foot square from the wing of a dead reptile. She tied a leather cord to a corner of the square and tied the other ends to a stone. Finally, she stood on the nest's rim and first dropped a lone stone in the center of the nest. Then she tossed up the stone tied to the membrane. As expected, the stone plummeted, but the one bound to the membrane slowed and made a much softer landing. She felt no inclination to name her contraption, but Nat-ul conceived the first parachute, beating da Vinci by a very considerable span of time.

Nat-ul retrieved the stone and wing and climbed on the rim of the nest again. Holding the rock, she jumped to the center of the nest.

71

It did not slow her, and thus she understood an important concept - the larger the object under the wing, the larger the wing must be.

Nat-ul held no desire to spend the night in the nest to discover whether the mother might return. She worked at a feverish clip to upscale her invention. With a scalloped shell, Nat-ul removed the wing membranes from the chicks and tied them into one large patchwork. To each corner of that composite, she tied a stout tendon to tether the contraption under her shoulders. Nat-ul left the large single claw at the center of two pterodactyl wings. They would drape over her shoulders so the invention would hang loose until she was set to use it.

An hour before darkness, Nat-ul was ready. With her contraption attached, she stood at the break in the wall. She looked down and exhilaration filled her. Nat-ul felt no fear. The composite wing worked for the stone so she harbored no doubt it would work for her.

With a smile, Nat-ul hurled herself from the spire. The crude parachute was jerked from her shoulders by the uprush of air. By the time the cave girl fell twenty feet, the invention spread open and jolted her to a slower descent.

Nat-ul realized she was in the air at a height that would kill her if she fell! Instinct and reflex prodded her to grab for something. There was nothing to grasp but the tendons dangling her from the wing. After that initial moment of surprise, Nat-ul recognized she was not plummeting. Her movement was equally horizontal and vertical. The experience was electrifying, but she was moving backward and wanted to see where she was going. She had no idea how to turn, but again, human instinct served. Nat-ul began to twist her body to one side, over and over, as she kicked her feet and pulled on the cords.

It worked and just in time. At the moment she came to travel forward, the flattish crown of a small spire was feet away. Her descent was swift and slammed a grunt from her when she hit the spire. The impact knocked her on a side, and the contraption fell on her head.

Nat-ul lay motionless a second. The landing earned her a large bruise on the hip that slammed against the stone. She had a large scrape where her hip and thigh raked across the rough surface. She sprained an ankle but not severely. There were no broken bones or open wounds.

As she gazed around her, Nat-ul looked stunned for a moment. Then she broke into perhaps the largest smile ever experienced in that past age. In the universal language of uprights and lower primates, she yelled the equivalent of a modern "I did it!" Then she forgot it.

The sun was setting. Life was calling. Nat-ul studied her surroundings. On three sides were more spires. The jungle rose a hundred yards below by way of a forty-five-degree slope. To her right, a small stream flowed down from the mountains and into the jungle. She detached herself from the world's first parachute and dropped from the landing stone. She pulled the war club from her shoulder and began to limp her way through a maze of man-high spires.

Nat-ul's immediate plan was to get to the stream. She was thirsty and still sticky and carried the stink of the pterodactyl urine and blood.

She angled her way toward the stream when she heard deep, sonorous growls in the darkening jungle. The sun was out of sight behind the mountains. Even the open where she stood was in twilight, but she recognized the growls as the pack hunter, Wir. Wolves! Usually, they ran in small groups, and each was the size of a modern wolfhound! A single Wir would make a good fight. Against even a small pack, a lone hunter was doomed. Their fangs and brawn were deadly, but their cunning and cooperation were even more so.

Nat-ul dodged behind a spire and peered around it as four large black-gray Wir came from the jungle. They stopped and stared in Nat-ul's direction. They either saw or heard her. The cave girl remained quiet and watched. She held the club tight in her hand as her eyes searched for a place she might climb from their reach. There was no near safe haven, and she could neither outrun nor defeat them all. So she readied for battle and swore they would pay dearly if they came! Such was the determined way of man's early progenitors else we wouldn't be here.

Still several feet away, edging toward Nat-ul, the wolves unexpectedly stopped. They held their heads up high to sniff. Then the heads of all the pack hung low, and they looked around warily for a moment and made agitated growls. Then they turned and slinked back into the jungle.

Not understanding their behavior, Nat-ul looked about, alert and apprehensive. Was a deadlier threat nearby, something she missed? She turned and turned again looking for some greater beast, but there was nothing. Then the wind came just right, and she smelled herself. The stench of the reptile filth was strong. A modern human faced with that foul odor would likely drop to hands and knees and retch violently. In that time the putrid stench of both fresh and stale death came often. To Nat-ul, the rancid scent of reptile urine was a simple, un-noteworthy stink.

Nat-ul herself once witnessed a flying reptile lift a wolf and carry it away. It seemed even the scent of the creature was enough to send the always rapacious Wir to seek a meal elsewhere.

Nat-ul forgot the stream. Instead, she looked about and found a flat-topped spire to put her twenty safe feet above the ground. As the night covered the primitive world, Nat-ul lay on the bare stone and rested her head on her arm. She fell into needed sleep, undisturbed by the frequent cries of dying animals. They were the usual night sounds of the primeval jungle which the girl had always known.

Nu didn't know what manner of beasts or men might inhabit this mysterious island so pulled his canoe into the grass and covered it with branches. After caching his canoe, he ran up the beach and dragged the other boat away and hid it also. He used a branch to hide his tracks and those of the dragged canoes. If the giant returned first, he would have difficulty finding a craft. Then Nu searched for the trail of the boatbuilder.

Being on the island was mystical to the caveman. All his life, his tribe imagined what kinds of creatures might inhabit such a place. None of the imaginings mattered now. Nu must find the giant, and learn if somehow Nat-ul was on this island or dead.

Unaware that he was followed, Tur made no attempt to hide his tracks, so Nu found them immediately and set out to stalk the man toward the interior of the mysterious island.

The footprints of the giant were easy to follow. His weight made a deep impression, and his feet seemed twice the length of Nu's. Tur's size kept Nu on keen alert. It took no imagination to realize he would be a formidable foe, yet Nu held no doubt that they would fight.

Tur knew nothing of the island, either. The girl was taken hours earlier and by now might be resting in the belly of the flying lizard. Yet never in his life did he so desire anything as he now desired the stranger woman to be his mate! If she yet lived, nothing would stand in his way! That intent set, Tur keyed his senses for any sign of the woman or flying reptiles. Then he moved toward the center of the island.

Tur was inland over a mile when he heard hisses and screeches from miles away. He saw a flying reptile flapping erratically and wondered if the woman injured the thing.

Wounds and living did not coincide in those savage times. Without warning, another flying monster swooped down from a tall spire. It hit the weakened creature and sent it plummeting! Then from other spires, a half dozen more of the hideous things swooped down!

The flying lizard which became food for others may have been the one which took the woman. There were many in that area. There was no physical or other sign which way to go. Tur's instincts and experience urged him toward those beasts. He set his course along a natural stone trail beside a serpentine chain of small stone spires. The path twisted toward the center of the island and the loftiest pinnacles.

Nu also saw the mortal episode with the pterodactyls and wondered if one took Nat-ul. He once watched one lift a half grown Ta and fly away. What if one took Nat-ul? It would explain the strange end of her tracks, but wouldn't it devour her? Then why was the giant on this island? There was no doubt that it was his footprints following those of Nat-ul near his village. What did he know? The giant still seemed the best hope for finding Nat-ul, if she yet lived. Nu forgot the flying lizards and continued to track the boatbuilder.

Like Nat-ul, Nu was not unfamiliar with the spire shapes on the island. These were much larger than he ever saw in a cavern. Hundreds of stalagmites twisted out of sight up an incline toward the center of the island. Those curved lines created natural trails between them. Below them, to the right of Nu, lay the prehistoric jungle.

When darkness came, Tur found a crevice in rocks at his shoulder level and pulled himself in for the night. He was on the lowest of the spire trails, half a mile behind Nat-ul. Half a mile behind Tur, Nu found a suitable tree at the jungle's edge and climbed from the reach of predators to sleep.

Chapter 7

Prisoner of the Hive

The sun was still low when Nat-ul awoke. She stood atop the spire's planate summit and tested her ankle. The swelling and pain were both less, and she once hunted the mammoth with worse hurt than this, so she forgot it. Her plan for the day was simple. She would get to the Restless Sea and somehow make her way back across the monster-filled waters to her home.

As Nat-ul neared the bottom of the spire her survival instincts were aroused. The hair on her neck stood, and she got goose skin. She peered about and listened but neither saw nor heard anything out of place.

Then at the last step down, men jumped from around the spire and slammed Nat-ul back against the stone. Two men held her arms, and a third stepped up and held a knife to her throat. Another dozen men came from behind nearby stalagmites. The man wielding the knife spoke in the universal language of uprights and warned her not to resist or she would die immediately. Being a natural survivor, Nat-ul did not need to think of what to do. She was also fascinated, for she had never seen men such as these.

Nat-ul was equal in height to the men, so they were short compared to the men of her tribe. Clothing in her tribe consisted of an animal pelt loincloth or sometimes nothing. These men wore loincloths fashioned from animal hides, but the design was unfamiliar. They fell to the men's knees. Another square of animal hide sported a hole in the center through which the man's head protruded. A strip of leather closed this torso cover the same as the waistband Nat-ul wore. Each had a knife tucked under the leather strip.

The warriors carried other things which aroused Nat-ul's curiosity. A pouch fashioned from animal skin hung from a shoulder of each man and several small sticks poked out the top. A longer branch was bent, and the ends were connected by a length of braided leather, and this thing also hung over a shoulder.

The men of Nat-ul's tribe used sharp spear points to keep hair trimmed above their shoulders. Most pulled the hairs from their faces at an early age, and it never grew back. The head hair of these men fell below their shoulders. Hair also hung from their chins. What intrigued her most was the hair, skin, and eyes. Their hair colors ranged from yellow to white, and their eyes were pale blue, pink or colorless. Rather than bronze like her people and other tribes she knew, these men had skin as pale as their hair.

The cave girl asked questions, but the leader told her to stay quiet. He took the war club from her shoulder and threw it down. Then a man held her by each arm, and they began. The odd men were inattentive to their surroundings and talked loudly. Nat-ul considered it peculiar behavior for warriors or hunters. They only went a few yards when she learned the reason for their confidence.

From the dense jungle below came a sudden uproar. Half a dozen hairy ape folk dropped to the ground at the jungle's edge and yelled for the men to leave the female, and go in peace. The leader of the strange men laughed, and at that, the hairy ape folk moved upward toward the group.

Three of the blonde men stepped forward and took the peculiar stick with leather from their shoulders. Then each reached into his bag of sticks and pulled one out. Nat-ul suppressed a laugh but could not hold a smile, however. The sticks were little spears! On the end of each branch was a stone spearhead a fraction the size of what would be set on a spear by her tribe. What could spears for infants do against those beasts?

A slot was cut into the end of each tiny spear. Into that slot, each man fitted the leather cord on his bent branch.

The hairy ape folk were forty feet away.

Each of the forward men held his curved branch at arm's length and pulled back on the leather cord.

Nat-ul tried to break free and reach for a knife, yelling, "Give me a weapon! I will fight them!" Dying at the hands of hairy ape folk was horrible to imagine, but Nat-ul deemed it much worse to die in surrender. A warrior dies in battle! "Keep quiet," the leader said as he pushed her hand from the knife, and commanded his men, "Hold her tighter!"

The hairy ape folk were twenty feet away. Nat-ul knew when they came within ten feet they would leap in a mad attack!

The men each released the end of his small spear. Nat-ul heard a twang, and her jaw dropped! The small spears swooped through the air, and each drilled into the chest of one of the hairy ape folk! Almost before the spears hit their marks, the blonde men drew out more spears and fitted them to the cords. The leader said "Two," and two of the men let loose their small spears and two more of the hairy ape folk dropped. The sole remaining beast turned and ran for the jungle, screaming insults and threats.

What wonderful weapons were these tiny spears and the thing that made them fly! They impressed and amazed Nat-ul. She didn't understand, however, and asked why they didn't kill the last hairy ape folk.

"So he can tell the others," the man answered. "They are stupid and slow to learn, but in time it will sink into their dull minds not to approach us for fear of death."

Nat-ul judged it an amusing idea without merit. Having never developed the emotion of fear, she did not understand how this would discourage the hairy ape folk. Such an action toward her people would not make them afraid to attack. It would teach them to find a better way to attack.

The march resumed along the stone trail, and in late afternoon they came to a massive spire with a base fifty feet wide. It split the trail, and they went to the right.

When the hairy ape folk attacked Nat-ul and

her captors, Tur heard their angry jabbering. He could not make out what they screamed, but any activity might mean the presence of the girl if she yet lived. He headed straight for the sound of the beasts and soon came to the spire where the blonde men abducted Nat-ul.

Immediately Tur saw the club. It was the same as the club the beautiful stranger left on the sand near his village. The club filled Tur with hope!   Then he looked ahead and spotted the dead hairy ape folk and anxiety equaled his hope. Like Nat-ul, Tur had no experience with arrows, but weapons and death he understood. The war club told him the girl might yet live and the dead ape folk said she was in danger. The giant dropped Nat-ul's club, drew his ax over a shoulder and advanced.

A quarter of a mile behind Tur came Nu. The trail now moved over rock with no tracks, but from time to time a cache of windblown sand would yield a print. Also, he regularly ventured to the tree line to ensure no tracks led into the jungle. Of necessity, he moved slower than he liked. Anxiety over his speed increased ten-fold when he discovered Nat-ul's club and the dead hairy ape folk. Nu held no doubt that Nat-ul fashioned this club, but just as surely she must be in danger! The caveman took up the club of thorns, slung it over a shoulder and hurried on.

Hours later, the giant boatbuilder came to the large spire where the trail split, and he weighed which way to go. There was no sign to provide even a hint, so he went left. His pace was fast for the remaining hour of daylight. He never saw a sign of the beautiful stranger, but twice dodged dive attacks by flying reptiles. As darkness descended, Tur crawled into a crevice to sleep, now miles distant from either Nat-ul or Nu.

Not long after Tur, Nu came to the spire which split the trail and he was more perplexed. He was sure the boatbuilder was on this trail, but he judged it to be someone else who killed the apes and wondered if the two parties were aware of one another. With no physical sign which trail to take, Nu mulled it over and decided to go right. He was unaware that he no longer trailed the boatbuilder, but now followed the strange blonde men and his Nat-ul. He never saw any sign of human passage on the stone trail. As the sun began to set, a disheartened Nu found a high spire where he could sleep in relative safety.

Nat-ul asked many questions during the march, and at first, they ignored her. Finally, the leader of the party said, "You ask many questions. It is strange. Your kind cannot think like us." Nat-ul did not like the sound of that but bit her tongue against her true feelings. She replied, "It is a joy to hear about those who know more."

"A curious beast!" The man laughed and said, "Then I will tell you!" and he began a soliloquy of his wonderful people who, he assured her, were better than all other life forms. This was the land of Atla. Atla was their leader, and he owned everything and everyone. Even his own people were his chattel. For their obedience, his people were given slaves such as Nat-ul would be. They never needed to hunt or do anything dangerous unless they chose to be a warrior like him and his men. To be a warrior was a special honor which few sought as it sometimes meant a shortened life span.

Shortly before sunset, they arrived on the rim

of a colossal pit. It was a near perfect circle at least a mile across. From the base of the rim wall, the land sloped toward the center. There, a pile of boulders rose more than a hundred feet in a shape strange to Nat-ul.

The boulders were blocks - squares and rectangles. The structure was largest at the bottom and came to a point at the top. Spaces were between every second or third stone both vertically and horizontally. Nat-ul realized quickly they were entrances. Each higher line of stones was set back to create walkways all around the giant tower. Lianas hung from all levels, too, and she saw people climb up to higher levels or slide down. It was like a beehive for people, and Nat-ul thought it must house many more people than were in her tribe.

As they walked around, Nat-ul paid attention to the pit's walls. They were smooth, with no hand or footholds and from the pit floor to the rim was a height of four tall men. A modern human might succumb to despair. Yet for the primitive, hope was alive and well. On the rim where they first came to the pit, Nat-ul noted large boulders positioned near the brink.

The men walked her to the far side, and she found the genius of their home in a giant hole. A boulder higher than two men lay at the head of the only trail into the pit. It narrowed the path to only three feet. In that space, charred wood and ashes identified a fire site and behind the boulder was a large cache of logs. Nat-ul understood. This was the only way to enter or leave the pit, so they needed only one beast fire to stop predators.

There was no fanfare for her arrival. Few Atlans were outside, and they hardly noticed.

There were others like Nat-ul and it angered her when they looked upon her with obvious pity. Nat-ul never experienced the concept of slavery before that day, but already she didn't like it.

They came to the bottom of the pit near twilight, and they took Nat-ul inside the boulder hive at the lowest level. They left her with two women and ordered them to instruct Nat-ul in duties and behavior. The first instruction was a warning. Anyone who tried to escape at night would be thrown outside the beast fire at the pit entrance. Packs of Wir were always outside the fire at night. Nat-ul didn't expect to escape that night but did already have a plan.

The following day Nat-ul's first chore was to prepare and serve breakfast to Atlans. Later, the two overseers took her out and set her chipping stone to make points for the small spears. The day dragged, and Nat-ul worked steadily but also watched for an item she needed.

On that morning, Tur came out of his crevice and continued several more miles before he turned back. There was no sign of the girl, and he grew anxious. When Tur came to the split, he decided to return to where he found the war club and begin his search anew. If he found no further sign, he would return to the trail-split and go right.

At midmorning, Nu came to the great pit and the Atlan hive. With great care, Nu made his way around the pit to scrutinize the people and layout. If Nat-ul yet lived, this seemed a logical place to search, but people were too far away to recognize. Nu must enter the pit, and that must wait for darkness.

Nu took no food nor drink for more than a day now, so he decided to return to the jungle for both. As he walked, he pondered ways he might rescue Nat-ul if she were in the pit.

It was early afternoon when Nat-ul saw a group of the Atlan warriors return from outside the pit. They led several slaves laden with lianas used for climbing the hive. The workers stacked the bundles beside the wall of the hive, and Nat-ul asked the two women about them. They whispered that tomorrow it might well be their labor to replace older lianas on the hive.

Tur traveled to the site where he saw the club and the slain hairy ape folk. He reached the area at midday and immediately became confused. The club was gone! The giant walked down to the tree line where the hairy ape folk were slain, where now only gnawed bones remained. He coursed up and down the area alert for prints of the girl. He found only the old prints of hairy ape folk and fresher prints of Wir. Thinking the girl might be a tree dweller, Tur decided to search for a time within the jungle. If he found no signs, he would return as planned to the giant spire which split the trail.

Sometime after Tur entered the jungle, Nu arrived where the hairy ape folk were killed. He found the same chewed bones and also found tracks where the giant entered the jungle. Nu was as confused as Tur. These were fresh tracks, yet still no sign of Nat-ul. For a moment Nu considered whether to follow the giant's tracks, but in the end, decided against it. He reasoned there was no sign that Nat-ul was with the giant. The hairy ape folk were killed by someone else, likely the people in the pit. If Nat-ul yet lived, she was most likely a prisoner of the pit people. So, after drinking from the stream, Nu collected two fresh-water mussels for a moving meal and headed back to the pit.

Two hours later, Tur the giant boatbuilder came out of the jungle and found the tracks of Nu. It was clear that a single man came down from the stone trail and returned to it. Tur was unaware that Nu followed him so decided the tracks belonged to another enemy. The beautiful stranger was still his goal, and like Nu, he chose to assume the best.

With that in mind, Tur returned to the stone trail to retrace the path he recently traveled but made a slight change. He climbed to the second next higher trail. It paralleled the one he walked before, two hundred feet higher. As he went, Tur often climbed spires to get a distant view. It slowed his progress, so Tur was a mile from the split in the lower trail when the sun began to set. He chose a suitable spire to climb for the night.

There was a great commotion at the hive a couple of hours before sunset. A woman began screaming in the first level above ground. Her watchers told Nat-ul to continue working and ignore it until commanded otherwise. They would punish her for any other action.

Shortly, from a crevice 30 feet above ground, two warriors dragged out a screaming woman and threw her off! The screams stopped when the woman hit, but she yet lived and now moaned in pain. In seconds, two different warriors came and took the woman. They dragged her to a large flat stone, as long in both directions as the height of two men.

Then one soldier spoke. "Watch! This woman displeased her master. This is your punishment if you displease any Atlan. Do not avert your eyes or you will be on the stone!"

The woman writhed and pleaded after the men tied her hands to a pole that stood at one end of the stone. Well away from the wailing woman, the warriors took up large clubs and began to beat a great hollow log.

The booming echoed through the spires. Immediately, a half dozen of the flying reptiles swooped down toward the booming and screaming. The beasts provided a show of aerial combat for several minutes. Finally, the largest chased the others back to the heights.

The lone reptile moved as gracefully as a butterfly might. It alighted beside the woman who for all this time never stopped screaming. The beast sat with wings outstretched and for a few seconds turned its head this way and that. It was silent with its mouth half opened, perhaps watching to see if another reptile might return. Then with incredible speed and no forewarning, it made one pounding peck with the great beak. The screaming ceased. The entire middle of the woman, torso, with heart and other organs, was snapped up! The vicious reptile held the woman's parts in its beak and tilted its head back. With a little toss, the monster swallowed the chunks of bone and meat which were a human just seconds before. With two more pecks, the remainder of the woman was scooped up and devoured. Only a smear of blood and the bound hands remained. Then the hideous creature outstretched and raised the leathery wings to pull itself into the air and flapped away.

Chapter 8

Escape From The Pit

Everyone returned to work. Then one of the women said, "If they deem you unproductive you go to the stone." The other woman added, "Or if someone doesn't like you." As they worked, the three conversed freely as long as no Atlan was near. The two became slaves many years ago. They considered escape at first but lost that desire after they witnessed others tied to the stone or thrown to wolves. The Atlans were not native to that island. "They often brag of their travels. It may be that they do not know where they arose," one of the women told her. They did no work themselves. If slave numbers dwindled, they crossed the Restless Sea to capture more. Nat-ul described the crafts she spied at the boatbuilders' village. The women told her the Atlans had a much larger boat. They had one large enough to carry their entire population and twice more.

Nat-ul asked, "How can that be? I have never seen such a tree and how did they get it to the water?" The women told her it was not formed from one tree but many. Nat-ul did not doubt their word but had trouble imagining what they described.

The women had a friend who worked in the household of Atla. During one stretch of conversation, they said their friend recently heard disturbing news. Tis told Atla that soon the earth would shake with more fury than ever and the sea would wash over the island. Only if they left soon enough, could they be safe.

"Who is Tis?" Nat-ul asked. They told her he was a shaman who many believed held more power than Atla, for Atla always followed his advice. Nat-ul told them her tribe had a shaman when she was young. "He could make a wound heal faster and knew what plants make fever go away, but people thought him evil. He tried to take the power of Onu, and the people did not like it. I was but a child but remember. The people stoned him and drove him from the caves, and he fled down the beach, screaming like an old woman."

An hour before sundown, an hour after the Atlans fed the woman to the flying lizard, there was an earthquake. It was not powerful and lasted but a few seconds. The people paid it no mind, but within minutes, two slaves came onto a deck at the hive's pinnacle and blew into shells. The attention of all was immediately focused atop the hive where two men came into view. One was tall and blonde with many lines on his face. "Atla!" whispered one woman. Behind him came another, shorter, stouter and his hair and beard were black. "Tis!" the other woman whispered. Nat-ul found something familiar about Tis and it made her uneasy.

Atla addressed his people. Tis discerned that the sea would soon wash over the island. It would drown all life. So, on the next day, the Atlans would leave on their great boat. Slaves should give thanks for they would be taken, too.

During the short revelation, Tis looked over the crowd and espied Nat-ul. Their eyes met. Nat-ul sensed menace, so looked away and stepped aside behind a taller man. She could not place Tis, but he seemed uncomfortably familiar. When the address was over, the two men disappeared as they came. Atla strolled with a straight posture and stone age royal demeanor, a warrior on either side. Tis followed, with a forward lean, arms swinging, more the amble of the hairy ape folk than the walk of a man.

Nat-ul began, "This Atlan Tis doesn't..."

"Tis is no Atlan!" one of her fellow workers said with obvious contempt. "He is one of us and should be working as a slave. Rumor says Tis was abducted across the Restless Sea and brought as a slave. When Tis proved his value as a shaman, Atla elevated him to counselor and confidant, second only to himself."

Nat-ul didn't dwell on Tis. There was something more pressing. If the Atlans were evacuating tomorrow, then Nat-ul must escape tonight or die in the attempt.

When darkness came, slaves extinguished all torches and other fires in the hive. Only the small beast fire on the narrow trail burned, but night did not bring cover for the moon was near-full.

Nat-ul tried to persuade her trainers to

escape with her. The two women tried to persuade Nat-ul not to make the attempt. Neither side succeeded, but the women agreed to say nothing. So Nat-ul lay down to feign slumber until the other women in the room were asleep.

Two hours later, Tis summoned the guard to his chamber and commanded him, "Go fetch a slave. A new woman, one with a scar here," he tapped his left cheek. "I wish to question her so try to bring her alive, but my curiosity is not great, so if she resists you can kill her. It will save me the trouble." The guard nodded and withdrew to fetch Nat-ul.

All around Nat-ul were the sounds of slow sleep-breathing and in a few places a snore. She rose to leave the two trainers surprised her. In whispers, they again tried to deter the cave girl in fear for her life. They were unsuccessful, yet Nat-ul was glad they came to wish her good fortune, and she bid them well in return. Then the women retired to their sleep skins, and Nat-ul went out.

As Nat-ul entered the corridor, Nu stood on the far rim from the hive, fastened a stout liana to a boulder, and slipped into the pit. He kept against the wall as he moved toward the hive and saw no one save the distant sentry.

Nat-ul was just inside the door when a warrior came in, and they were both surprised. The man put a hand on his knife and asked, "What are you doing out here?"

"I am going out to relieve myself."

The guard spoke in a threatening tone. "You should know it is forbidden to leave quarters after dark! Are you new?" He stepped aside to let the moonlight fall on Nat-ul's face. With his hand, he turned her head and saw the scar. "Tis has

94

summoned you," he barked as he grabbed an arm and pushed her out the doorway.

Why Tis wanted her was a mystery, but she doubted it was for an amiable welcome. During Atla's speech, he looked at Nat-ul as intently as she gazed at him. "Can I go first?" Nat-ul asked the guard.

The guard told her no, and Nat-ul whispered, "If I soil the lair of Tis he will not be angry only with me!" The man looked at her a moment then pushed her and told her to hurry. The guard followed Nat-ul to boulders fifty feet away, where she saw what she needed. Even as she squatted, her hand closed on it. "Don't look at me," she said. "I am but a woman and a slave and I have no weapon. An Atlan warrior would not fear me, would he?"

Through clenched teeth, the man hissed, "Insolent animal! Tis gave permission to kill you, so take care!" He began to turn away.

Even before he made a half turn, Nat-ul sprang with lightning speed! She drove the sharp end of a large quartz crystal down on the crown of his head. The warrior made a hybrid sound, like a grunt and a sigh, as his knees hit the ground. Nat-ul slammed the top of his skull again, and he fell over on his face. Nat-ul dropped hard on his back, and again she pounded the crystal into the warriors head. Then she whispered to the dead guard, "Never trust a slave who prefers freedom, insolent animal!"

Nat-ul took the guard's knife and put it in her waistband. She dragged his body behind a boulder then clutched the crystal as she walked boldly to the fresh lianas delivered that day. She took one that felt stout and was of adequate

95

length, then started for the far rim of the pit.

Halfway to the hive, Nu ducked behind boulders when he heard footsteps. A lone figure walked toward him in the open. Thinking it must be a sentry, Nu tightened the grip on his ax. The sentry must die instantly to avoid immediate detection. When the steps told him the sentry was just the other side of this boulder, he would spring and swing the ax. If the sentry were his height, the blow would crush his breastbone and knock the breath out to repress a cry of alarm. If the sentry were shorter the face would be caved in, death instant! The sound was near, one second, one more step! Nu, drew back on his ax and tensed for the lunge!

Most of the pit floor away from the hive was loose rock and made it difficult to walk. There was one winding path where repeated walking had packed the stones. It made it easier and quieter to step. Most of that trail was near the center of the pit and in the open, but the speed it offered outweighed the risk.

Halfway to the back rim, the path veered toward the pit wall and a group of boulders. As she turned that direction, Nat-ul halted and stopped breathing. Did she see someone move behind that outcrop of rocks? Or was it a rodent scurrying across the top of a boulder? Or the shadow of a small cloud passing before the moon?

After a moment of apprehension, nothing more aroused suspicion, so she continued toward the boulders at the wall as far as the path took her. Two steps from a boulder, Nat-ul stopped to consider whether to go to the wall. She decided to continue on the trail as it was the most direct and sure-footed route.

Nu listened as the footsteps moved away. What if the guard found his liana? He took a step around the boulder to throw his ax and kill the sentry, but even as he drew back, he decided against it. Someone might expect the sentry to return soon. The dark liana might go unseen in the darkness against the dark stone. If discovered, the sentry would most likely think someone escaped. When the sound of footsteps faded, Nu continued.

The moonlight and smooth path did more than allow Nat-ul to walk faster. She was also able to tie the crystal into the center of the liana as she went. Her plan was simple. At the rim, she would hurl the crystal over the boulder up top. One tail of the liana would hang from either side of the boulder. She would then tie what her tribe called a pull knot. It could be tied with the two ends. Then she would pull one end to close the loop around the boulder and climb up. Children in my tribe could escape this evil place, she thought.

Nu came to the point where he was nearest the hive and hurried across the open ground to the building. He entered a wide, long corridor with door-less apertures on either side. Dabs of moonlight fell before each. Nu slipped predator-like into the first room. A portal ran the length of the room, so the moon lighted the interior well.

Nu's simple plan was to look at each sleeper until he found Nat-ul or someone raised the alarm. So he crept between the first two sleepers and bent down. Both were men, and he edged between the next two, and they were men, as were the next pair and the next. It occurred to Nu that men and women were quartered separately. With this insight, he made his way quickly to the next room. There he looked at only the first four sleepers and found them to be men. As he turned to leave, a man sat up and asked, "Who are you? What are you doing?"

For an instant, Nu tensed to swing the ax, then stopped and answered with the first thing that came to mind, the truth. "I look for Nat-ul, the new woman."

"Swamp toad!" the man grumbled, calling Nu the equal of a modern fool or idiot. He grunted, jabbed a finger toward the door, then rolled over to resume his sleep.

Nu hurried out and crossed the corridor. He entered the first door and began to move along to look at each sleeper. He was half-way through the room when a woman sat up and said, "What are you doing? They will kill us all if they find you here!"

Again, Nu told the truth, and the woman said, "She is not here! I do not know of her. Leave!" By now several women were awake, and all whispered for him to go.

"I know where she is," came a voice from the shadows and a woman crawled into the light and pointed a thumb behind her. "Two doors that way. She will be near the opening and light. Others have earned the dark corners for sleep. Now go!"

Nu turned and made his way to the room described. There he strode straight to the far side where the moonlight was brightest. He could see the women against the wall weren't Nat-ul, but there was an empty place as though someone was missing. For a moment, Nu stood wondering. He decided to wake someone and ask when he heard movement behind him and swung around, ax ready.

At the far wall of the pit, the boulder was easy to see in the moonlight, and Nat-ul walked straight to it. At the wall, she froze. A liana already hung into the pit, tied to the boulder as though waiting for her!

As she looked about, Nat-ul slid her hand an arm's length up the doubled cord of liana, away from the crystal. Held thus, she could swing it as a weapon if needed. She backed away and looked right and left and up at the rim. She listened a few seconds and became confident no one was near. It was a profound mystery. Did someone sneak into the pit, or did another slave escape by the same plan as her?

Using the guard's knife, Nat-ul cut the ends of the lianas holding the crystal to arms-length. Then she tied the ends together and slung the crude weapon over her head and shoulder and clambered out of the pit. She began to untie the liana to drop it into the pit but changed her mind. Whoever tied the vine was no friend of the Atlans, and might need it later, so she re-tied it and went her way.

When Nu turned, a woman stood there and said, "You must leave."

Nu told her he sought Nat-ul of his tribe and the woman told him slaves were nameless in the hive. He said Nat-ul came the day before, and another woman came beside the first and they looked at one another. Each took Nu by an arm, and one held a finger to her lips. "You must leave now!" said the other, and they led him out of the sleep chamber.

In the corridor, one woman whispered,

"There was a new woman, but she is gone." They didn't know Nat-ul's plan so couldn't answer Nu's next question but told him she left only a short time before he arrived.

In those days, the vacuous thank you that often seems obligatory even when nothing has been done to earn it, did not exist. Yet each tribe had an equal phrase only spoken with great sincerity. Though the words varied from tribe to tribe, any human would recognize such an expression.

Nu replaced the ax in his waistband and laid a hand on a shoulder of each woman. "May you always have meat for your bellies and may the long-toothed cat never know your scent.

The eyes of the women sparkled, and Nu's word gave them rare smiles. For years in the pit, neither heard a kind word except for secret whispers from the other. No one even knew they were sisters. On the first day of their captivity, they learned that only one member of a family could serve the Atlans. They slaughtered the rest of the family. Now in one night, they received a blessing twice. Nat-ul spoke to them the very words spoken by Nu, but the sisters didn't think to tell him.

After a time, Tis grew impatient and called for warriors to investigate. Why was his guard not yet returned with the girl?

Upon wishing the sisters well, Nu took one step toward the entrance when there came the footfall of many men outside. The two fearful women each seized an arm and whispered, "If they find you here they will kill us all!"

Nu glanced back into the sleep chamber, then dashed for the opening along the wall and dived through it. The other women in the room still slept, and the two sisters returned quickly to their skins and pretended.

A dozen warriors came into the sleep chamber with torches and began to yell and kick the sleeping women. They questioned the group en masse, but no one had anything to tell. They peered out the aperture in the wall, but by then Nu moved behind boulders, halfway back to the far rim.

Nat-ul headed for the spot where the Atlans captured her. She wished to put as much distance between her and the Atlans as possible. The crystal looped in the liana hung loosely from one hand. Her other hand rested on the stolen knife in her waistband. Her pace was rapid and as silent as any practiced predator. Thus, later that night, she passed unnoticed just 200 feet below the sleeping boatbuilder. A quarter mile past the giant, Nat-ul herself climbed to the top of a suitable spire and fell into instant sleep.

Nu returned to the wall. In the darkness, Nat-ul did not see the tracks of Nu, and now, Nu did not see the tracks of Nat-ul. Had he seen her tracks he would have a reason for hope. As it was, he only knew that a stranger woman was attempting to escape the hive that night. Yet he still hoped.

No sooner did Nu exit the pit than there came a great clamor. Torches were lighted around the hive, and Nu saw warriors discover a body. He decided it must be one of the blonde people for a great search followed the discovery. Warriors crisscrossed and circled the floor of the pit several times. Then a small group entered the hive. In moments an almost inhuman cry of bestial rage came from the upper levels of the hive. The cry made the hair stand up on the neck of Nu. The cry was very much like the war cry of his tribe. Yet it was eerily more like an animal, or if he knew such a word, he would think lunatic. Then guards began to snuff torches, and the pit grew silent.

Nu roamed around the pit for a time. He often heard cries of something dying, and a few times heard the angry roar of a predator thwarted. He sought a way someone might escape from the pit but found no way save his own liana.

Reluctantly, Nu withdrew to return in the morning. In the light, he might discover tracks to follow. He returned to the giant spire which split the original trail. It was not a short walk, but Nu decided he would sleep better if there were more distance between him and the pit. At the dividing spire, he turned down the original stone path for a time. Then he scaled a spire that put him out of most danger. He fell into a fitful sleep one-quarter of a mile before the location of Tur two levels higher, and half a mile from his beloved Nat-ul on that very trail.

Chapter 9

Hairy Ape Folk Attack!

At sunrise, Nat-ul dropped to the ground and went to the small stream to drink. Then, as she launched her journey for the coast, twelve pairs of small blood-shot eyes watched her. The cave girl moved along the stone trail, fifty feet from the jungle. The path was a repetitive rise and fall of diminutive hillocks populated by meager shrubs. She did not go far when she heard a series of thumps as twelve sets of bare, clawed feet hit the ground. A dozen hairy ape folk dropped from the trees.

Since a fight with twelve of the vicious beasts would not last long enough to qualify as a fight, Nat-ul bolted! She could not run noticeably faster, but she could run much longer, and that seemed her only chance. A s the hairy ape folk chased Nat-ul, they caused a horrible din of howls and brutish grunts. The large feet pounded the stone like twenty-four drums. Though they were extremely strong, hairy ape folk were neither built for nor accustomed to running, so already Nat-ul could hear the gasps of the horrible brutes. They jeered Nat-ul in the common language of all uprights, but their gasping and slavering made it sound like so much gibberish even to the others of their kind.

As he sat up from his sleep, Tur, the giant boatbuilder, heard the uproar of the hairy ape folk. He knew they were in pursuit of something and his first question was whether it was the beautiful stranger. Did she somehow escape the airborne reptile, and survive alone two days on this island? Was it her now chased by the abominable beasts making that racket?

It seemed improbable, yet in those brutal days, survivors beyond a certain age found it essential never to hesitate. A desired result and a meal were more often secured by action than by waiting, so Tur sprang up. A quarter-mile distant on the lower trail, he saw hairy ape folk pass from sight behind spires. Tur dropped from the spire and ran after them along the higher path.

Nu also heard the hairy ape folk and leaped from his spire to run in the direction of the howling. Was it Nat-ul who escaped the pit? Perhaps the howling hairy ape folk were chasing Nat-ul at this moment! His life and next action seemed predicated on a set of amorphous possibilities. Yet in that time even weak hope was more than adequate to send the caveman after deadly enemies.

The cave girl ran for her life, and twelve forms of hairy death were closing on her! Nat-ul dared not look back, not even a glance, for it would slow her and any hesitation might bring the chase to an end.

Tur topped a rise on the higher trail and saw the beautiful stranger running for her life from the creature most hated by man. The portion of a second it took Tur to take in the scene sent him at redoubled speed.

From the sound, Nu could tell the gap was closing between him and the hairy ape folk. As he ran, movement higher up caught his attention. It surprised Nu to see the giant ahead of him, higher up, angling down, running in the same direction.

Why was the boatbuilder running toward the sound of angry hairy ape folk? Nu trailed the man because he was the last known connection to his Nat-ul. He could only imagine now that Nat-ul might be up ahead and in danger!

The ape folk ran three abreast behind Nat-ul. She could feel the spittle of the nearest on her neck! Two small spires ahead created a passage with a gap of only two feet. Nat-ul felt a creature's paw touch her shoulder and sprinted for that gateway. At the narrow opening, the beasts did what the girl hoped. They were not especially intelligent but were greedy in the extreme. So the three in the lead, each desiring to be the first to feed, tried to pass through the span at the same time.

The screams of rage told Nat-ul what happened and she spun around, swinging the heavy quartz crystal. The pyramidal point of the crystal opened a jaw of the nearest beast from his ear to his mouth. He bellowed and jumped back, knocking down two more brutes. Their pile blocked the others for a moment.

105

Nat-ul paid a price for that maneuver. As the nearest ape fell back, he grabbed the crystal and yanked it from Nat-ul's grasp. In the same flamboyant move, the knife flew from her waistband! It would be deadly to continue without weapons, but instant death to try to retrieve either. Thus, Nat-ul did not slow, but finished the spin and raced away, and angled toward the jungle.

By then Tur was just above and saw the move Nat-ul made and grinned. Here was no woman to scrape skins and gather fruit. This woman was a warrior! He jumped from above the savage band and landed on the trail between them and Nat-ul. He faced the brutes, raised his giant ax high, and let out a roar that for all the world sounded like Zor, the lion.

Nu could not recall a man ever battling a pack of hairy ape folk by choice. He was topping a rise 100 feet behind them when he saw Tur roar the challenge and saw the near-human beasts attack. The man swung his huge ax, and it removed the head of the first creature from its body. In those times, respect by others, especially from another tribe, was seldom earned. Every day was so brutal and so deadly that everyone deserved daily what modern man calls respect. This man, however, won Nu's ungrudging higher regard. Even if he were not a link to Nat-ul, the man deserved help. If the warrior died, he would not die alone, not at the hands of these beasts, even if later Nu must kill the man himself!

Nat-ul heard the roar of Tur and thought that Zor was behind. Perhaps he would kill or chase away the ape folk and would follow Nat-ul and feast. Perhaps so many would slay Zor. Nat-ul would not wait for whichever death might come. She was determined to evade and fight, and if she lived, she would somehow find a way to return to her people and Nu.   Now in the jungle, those thoughts powered her as she sprinted. Tur and Nu were both behind her in battle, and cold-blooded death waited ahead!

By the time Nu came to the melee, another creature lay on the ground, gushing blood from where an arm was once attached. Two more lay still with their faces crushed in! Nevertheless, the giant was in trouble. Ragged, bleeding bites were on his legs and arms and back. Even as Nu came on the scene, an ape jumped on the back of the giant and began to bite his shoulder. Tur reached back and grabbed a tangle of the creatures matted hair. Then he slung the brute overhead into a spire ten feet distant. Nu ran up behind another creature and swung his ax with such force that it punctured the heart from behind!

Half a mile away, Nat-ul slowed to a lope as the jungle became less dense with fewer tall trees. There were few shrubs, and thick, knee-high grass carpeted the ground. Nat-ul was wary, tiny bumps covered her skin and the hairs on her neck were rising. Then she saw movement in the grass one step ahead and stopped!

Tur saw Nu run up and slay one of the apes then turn to face others. He had no idea who the stranger was nor where he came from, but welcomed him for his many wounds were painful.

An ape lunged at Nu, and his ax broke the things forearm then came down on the shoulder and broke the collarbone and left a blood pumping gash. The giant swung his ax beside Nu's head, and Nu heard the bone-crush and death grunt of an ape behind him! Tur and Nu looked at one another, and each gave a single nod of approval. Then they turned to bring more death to those hated creatures.

Nat-ul took a step, and the ground moved beneath her foot! Undulating, grass-colored skin moved with swiftness to match any rodent, and a great body encircled where she stood. Nak, the snake! The giant crushing death!

One who moved a partial second slower would have died then and there! Nat-ul vaulted over the behemoth and froze. There was no direction to run without stepping on the thing again. The grass moved on all sides as Nak sought her!

Nat-ul never saw nor even heard stories of such a Nak. A single creature surrounded her. The behemoth body was as thick as her own, and the length forewarned a mouth large enough to swallow her. Nat-ul stood within a giant coil which was closing as other coils formed beyond that one. The snake was lightning fast and so large it could surely bring down even a large mammoth! What could she do against such a monster? Any movement would give her away, and once Nak re-discovered her, she would die!

Nu and the giant Tur instinctively knew what to do. They stood back to back, and their great war axes cut down every hairy ape that came within reach. The warriors swung their weapons with power and ferocity unseen in modern times. Such was their calling, the thing they were trained to do from the time they could lift an ax.

Nak sensed vibrations, and his coils grew nearer the girl. *Is this how Nat-ul will end*, she asked herself. *Will I not see my Nu again?*

The two cavemen showed no mercy and shortly only two of the creatures remained. They apes must have understood the futility of further struggle and as if of one mind they turned to flee. One not versed in the ways of that primeval world might give a sigh of relief. Those warriors knew the hairy ape folk were vengeful and the two escaping beasts would return with tenfold the number slain! So when the apes bolted, a human followed each, and within a few paces, the last hairy ape folks were dispatched!

Nat-ul would fight to the end. Mankind has always preferred life to death and to the cave girl even another breath was worth the fight. There was also the chance some unexpected event might bring help. Her own father once lived through such a thing. That story sped its way through the girl's mind as she contemplated her next move.

A mammoth surprised her father and knocked him to the ground. The great bull would have trampled him, but its trumpeting attracted the long-toothed killer cat. Gr sprang to the mammoth's back and sank his fangs into the hairy neck. Tha, the father of Nat-ul, was forgotten and crawled to safety. Before the day ended, her tribe owned the skins of both creatures. From that day, whenever unexpected good fortune saved one, it was said that he had Tha's Gr. Perhaps Tha's Gr would find Nat-ul, but she would not depend on it, for such endings were rare. She would rely on herself.

Tur spoke first when the two cavemen retrieved their weapons and came together. "Do you come from this island?" he asked.

"I come from the same land as you," Nu answered. "I seek Nat-ul of the tribe of Onu. She is to be my mate. She will have my love until our lives end."

"I have never heard of this Nat-ul nor your tribe. How did this Nat-ul come to be here, and what is this other word you use - love?"

"She may not be on this island. She may be dead. I am here because I followed you. Tracks told me you were the last to see Nat-ul before her tracks ended in the sand near your tribe."

Tur understood. "The woman was taken by a flying lizard and brought to this island. I followed, for she is the most beautiful woman I have seen and Tur would make her his mate."

Nu's jaw and the grip on his ax both tightened.

"And she lives! By great Glu, I swear the woman is a mighty warrior! No less could escape the flying death, and here I watched her turn and knock down the entire host of brutes we have slain! As she passed from sight, Tur dropped before them to end the chase."

Nu's breast swelled with pride as the man boasted of Nat-ul's prowess! "Nu thanks you!" said the caveman as he ran past Tur to take up the trail of Nat-ul. She lived! She was near! The heart of Nu pounded in his chest, and nothing but his Nat-ul deserved his thoughts. As Nu dashed toward the jungle, Tur followed.

Nat-ul stood within a coil of the snake. She could touch the thing on any side. Nak was closing every body-loop in turn and in the end, would close on Nat-ul and crush the life from her! With cool composure, she searched for an answer. On one side there was a single height of the snake. Beyond that was a double height where the body crossed itself. Beyond that stood a gathering of four and five-inch saplings which reached up into a great tree. An idea was born!

Do not hesitate the cave girl thought to herself and she jumped on the single height of the snake. The great body closed lightning fast on the circle she abandoned. Without pause she bound up onto the double height and dived for the saplings, reaching high. Again the coils of Nak closed where she stood but a second before! She grasped a pair of the young trees and pulled herself upward, then again.

The coils of the monstrous snake encircled the saplings and rose. Then Nat-ul realized she could not make it to the larger tree! The saplings bowed with her weight, and she was still a body length from the lowest limb of the tree! Only one temporary refuge seemed available. Nat-ul slipped between two saplings and dropped to the ground. The young trees were strong and formed a protective cage, but as Nak's coils tightened, the saplings creaked. They would hold for a time, but eventually must fail!

Nat-ul possessed but one potential weapon, and it seemed so puny that a modern would likely dismiss it. To the cave girl, it was a weapon. Two, in fact. She quickly untied the bunched pouch of her loincloth and grasped the

111

two shells brought from the beach!

Tur ran behind Nu and called, "Tur would have the woman for his mate!"

"Nat-ul has chosen Nu to be her mate!" Nu called back without slowing. In seconds he spotted Nat-ul's tracks, and they encouraged a burst of speed.

"It is not for the woman to choose!" Tur yelled and continued to follow. "I choose the woman and Tur is the greater warrior!"

Without slowing, Nu replied, "In our tribe, a mate is the choice of the woman. Nat-ul has chosen, and it is not yet decided who is the greater warrior!"

Both men understood that a challenge had been issued and accepted. Yet neither slowed, for both put the safety of Nat-ul before all else, even a challenge. For Nu, it was without thought, the thing that meant more than all else since the night of Ur was his beloved Nat-ul. For Tur, the feeling was new and strange, but the vision of the defiant warrioress was a potent inducement.

A human of a later era might have dropped the shells in hopelessness and cried out for help or for swift death. Nat-ul lived her life with eternal optimism. To do otherwise would be to cower in a cave until thirst and hunger took your miserable life. She chose the sharpest shell and dropped the other. The seashell was thick and strong, as large as her hand and the serrated edge was keen. She grasped it along the raised edge and reached between two saplings. Nat-ul pressed hard and began to saw.

"You are a fine warrior Nu, but you cannot

beat Tur," the boatbuilder called as they ran on.

"That is not yet decided, but if it is so, then Nu will die for his Nat-ul!"

Both men were silent for a moment as they rushed to find the woman they would fight over. Then Tur asked, "What is this love? I have never heard it."

It aggravated Nu that the man continued to talk, yet he was eager to tell about his love. Alas, there was no exact way to explain it. Love is love, but he could proudly describe how it made him feel, and he did so at length. He also boasted that on returning to their tribe, Nu would slay Gr and lay the head before the cave entrance of Tha, father of Nat-ul.

After Nu explained how love made him feel, Tur roared. "This thing you say is good. It must be the thing that now makes the chest of Tur swell with hope! Tur must also love this woman, Nat-ul!"

In those days what modern man calls sadness did not yet exist. You liked or disliked a thing, or it made no difference. Tur was a great warrior, saved Nat-ul and seemed a good man. Yet Nu and Tur must do battle. One must die. It was inevitable, and Nu greatly disliked the idea of killing Tur.

\
\

Chapter 10

Eternal Vow

Within a few strokes, the shell prevailed against Nak's tough scales! Nat-ul etched a foot long gash into its side. Once she penetrated the outer scales, Nak felt the pain. As Nat-ul cut through its flesh, Nak twitched. He tightened the grip on the saplings, and two of the smaller ones snapped! Nat-ul ignored the failing protection and sliced deeper! Defense would not save her - she must attack!

The sight that met Nu and Tur when they entered the clearing stopped them cold. For a second they could only stare as the Nak reared its head and glared at them with lidless eyes.

"I have never seen such a Nak!" said Tur.

"Nat-ul! Nat-ul!" cried Nu. Nak hissed and the warriors separated. Nat-ul thought she must be dead or dying. That sounded like the voice of her beloved Nu, yet how could it be? How could Nu know where she was? How could he cross the Restless Sea with its swarm of monsters? "Nu!" she answered his cry.

"Are you also dead?"

"She lives!" cried Tur and his breast swelled with gladness, and he smiled one of the very few smiles of his harsh life.

"Nat-ul is not dead! She lives, and Nu has come for you!"

"Tur has come for Nat-ul!" the boatbuilder called. Then both warriors raised their axes and stepped toward the monster.

Nat-ul felt confused. Who is Tur? She knew of no one her tribe called Tur, but she could not dwell on it. Nu was there, and it would likely take their combined effort to slay this behemoth reptile. Nat-ul pushed down hard and continued to saw Nak's flesh.

The snake's tail twitched, the head weaved side to side. Bold Tur stepped toward the head, and brave Nu went to the tail. Nu struck the first blow, and his ax made a gaping hole in Nak. The beast hissed and withdrew its tail and looked in the direction of the attack. When the head turned, Tur swung his ax and opened a gash below the snake's jaw, and the head snapped back against the giant. The impact slammed him hard against a tree bole twenty feet away. With a roar, Tur once more charged as Nu continued to dodge the tail and slam his ax into the monster again and again.

The open mouth of Nak flashed at the giant, and he swung his ax and batted the head to one side. That volley repeated over and over.

Nu drove his ax into the body of the beast. Then without warning, the mighty tail came up from his feet and coiled about him! Nak's body pressed Nu's ax against him rendering it useless. Then the gargantuan muscles began to squeeze the life from him!

Nat-ul heard the groan of Nu and called to him, but he held no breath to reply. The clubbing continued as the snake and Tur sparred and instinct prompted Nat-ul to increase her efforts. She held the shell tight and drove both hands through the greasy meat of Nak to grasp his spine. The great snake vibrated, and Nat-ul knew he was going to move. She released the spine and shell and yanked her hands out as the snake slid forward. Nat-ul knew that had she not withdrawn, her arms would have been broken or torn from her body!

Tur continued to bat the snake's head, then saw Nu encircled by the snake and moved toward him. Nu flexed all the sinews of his muscular body to delay the looming death.

Except for crushing Nu, Nak ignored him and Tur. It sensed something deadlier was happening inside its body.

Nak's wound now lay on the opposite side of the failing cage and the trees were closer together there. Nat-ul could insert only one hand. The cave girl imagined that an effort to recover the shell, would spur another surge by Nak, and cost her arm. She also sensed Nu was in trouble since he did not answer her last call.

All this surmising occurred during the one step to the other side of the sapling enclosure. There wasn't time for more. As a single move, she raised a leg to brace a foot against the saplings and drove a hand hard and fast into the wound, palm up. Her hand hit the other side of Nak straight away, and she pushed up through the torn meat and grasped the spine.

At that same instant, Nak ripped the tops of the saplings away! Nat-ul looked up and saw the great head of Nak, the soulless eyes glaring upon her, its mouth agape!

Nat-ul gripped and fell back with her weight as she pushed with her leg. Nak poised to devour the rash creature within the saplings when his rear half became useless. When the spine separated Nat-ul's arm came out, and she fell to the ground.

The rear half of Nak slumped into the grass, now dead and useless. Nak threw back his head and made an eerie sound more like the mortal cry of a wounded man than that of a reptile.

Nak's sinewy tail fell away from Nu, who took a deep breath and ran to the head of the snake. Tur ran the other direction around to the head. Nu struck the snake behind its head. Before it could lash back at Nu, Tur made another wound on his side. Nak's head was now low. It swung back and forth, first in the direction of Tur, then at Nu and on each sway, a caveman made a new wound.

The snake with half its body dead could not maneuver or flee, so it became less and less a threat. Finally, it fell into the grass, too weak to continue. As the two men removed the massive head, Nat-ul pulled herself up the saplings and climbed out onto the dead tail.

Further mystery faced Nat-ul as she watched the two warriors work side by side. She recognized Tur as the man who tried to seize her before the winged lizard took her. How did they reach this island and come to work together?

When the head of Nak lay apart from the body, Nu and Tur both looked up and saw Nat-ul. The cave girl jumped from her perch and ran to Nu and threw her arms around him. "Nu! My

Nu! My beloved Nu!"

"Tur also came for you. You will be the mate of Tur!" said the other man calmly and Nat-ul turned toward him and took her club from the shoulder of Nu.

"How came you here with this man and how does he dare say that Nat-ul will be his mate?" she asked Nu. Then she looked up into the eyes of Tur and said, "Nat-ul will choose her mate.   It is the choice of a woman, and I have chosen. Nu will be the mate of Nat-ul."

Nu explained the story from what he knew, and Tur explained his story. Nat-ul marveled at the obstacles Nu overcame to find her. She marveled that Tur also came, but her love for Nu was not lessened and this she told Tur.

"If you do not consent to be Tur's mate, then Tur will slay Nu and take you anyway." The boatbuilder spoke in a sure, matter-of-fact tone.

"Nat-ul will not be the mate of Tur," the girl responded with equal certainty.   "I do not think you can slay my Nu, but if you do, then you must also slay Nat-ul or Nat-ul will feed your pieces to hairy ape folk!"

Without expression, Tur asked, "You would rather die than be the mate of Tur?"

"You are a mighty warrior. If there were never a Nu, Nat-ul would be proud to mate one such as Tur, but I know and love Nu. I will be the mate of Nu or the mate of no one. If it is the way of your people for the man to take the mate he wants, surely you can take any woman. No other in your tribe can be so mighty as Tur."

The breast of Tur swelled at Nat-ul's words. "There is none greater," he smiled but it was brief, and he said, "The women of my tribe will

119

not even look upon Tur. They fear my eye. You stare me in my eye, and there is no fear. I do not want a woman who fears me. I think the way of your tribe is better, that the woman may choose, but I cannot walk away. Nu has described to me the thing you call love. The same feelings he has, now fill the heart and mind of Tur. Nor would either Tur or Nu be worthy if they did not do battle for the love of Nat-ul."

Tur turned to face Nu and lifted his great ax to his shoulder. Nu nudged Nat-ul away, and drew himself up to his full height, tilted his head back to look up at Tur, and raised his ax. "Nu does not wish to kill the boatbuilder he has fought beside."

"You will not slay the boatbuilder, young Nu," Tur answered as he crouched and swung his ax at Nu's head!

Tur swung again and back swung. Nu dodged and, seeing the head of the man's ax up close, decided he must not try to block the weapon. The stone was twice the size of Nu's ax and twice as thick. It would likely shatter the head of his ax! As Nat-ul looked on, Nu dodged and weaved and fought with great ferocity.

Nu never before tired in battle but after an hour of dodging the giant's ax and swinging his own, Nu felt encroaching fatigue. Tur could see it. "Nu the rock climber grows weary. Soon I will give him a great rest!"

"Not on this day!" Nu replied and swung at the boatbuilder. Several more minutes passed. Twice the ax of the giant seemed it would take the head of Nu but somehow missed. Neither warrior made headway. The battle continued until by far it was the longest contest any ever

witnessed. Again the giant's ax almost took
Nu's head but somehow missed. Then in
mid-swing Tur stopped and spoke. "If Nu would
take the fangs of the long-toothed cat for his
woman he must remember this. You cannot kill
him with your ax. Tur has slain the cat. Twice I
slammed his head with my ax, and he shook it off.
To kill Gr, put the point of your knife or spear into
his heart. Anything less and he will feast on the
single bite that is Nu."

"Why do you tell me this?" Nu yelled.

"It is part of a gift before our fight is done.
It is a knowledge in return for your life."

"That makes no sense!" responded Nu.

"Does this make sense?" asked Tur and
swung the ax hard at Nu. Nu dived behind a
tree and Tur's ax lodged in the bole of the tree
and Tur pulled mightily to remove it. When his
ax popped free, the giant fell to a knee his arm
and ax stretched behind him. His body and head
were unguarded, and he looked at Nu with a
smile.

Nu felt an unfamiliar pang, a hesitation.
Instinct was strong though, and he swung his
ax at Tur. The giant reached out with his
empty hand. He failed to block the ax of Nu
but turned it, so the flat side of the ax struck
his head with much less than the intended
force. Tur let go of his ax and fell over on a
side. Again from instinct Nu raised his ax to
deliver another blow but Tur still smiled, and
Nu lowered his weapon.

Nat-ul came over, and Tur looked at her.
"Tur will die," he said, "but he will die for
something good. This thing you call love. It is
a much better reason to die than the carcass of
an animal or a hide full of flint shards or just

121

because someone is from another tribe."

Nat-ul disliked that Tur would die. She knelt down and took his hand, and Tur's good eye gleamed. "I wish you chose to live," Nat-ul told him.

The giant smiled and said, "Tur will rise from the dead anywhere Nat-ul declares if Nat-ul will be his mate!"

Nat-ul smiled back and told him "Nat-ul is to be the mate of Nu."

"So you will be happy with Nu?" the boatbuilder asked, and she nodded.

Tur kept his eyes on Nat-ul but spoke to Nu, "The thing you taught me, little warrior, this love. It is good. It is good that I die knowing it. Always be willing to fight as hard as today for Nat-ul. If you do not, Tur will rise, and you will not like it!" Tur released Nat-ul's hand, closed his good eye and eased his head down.

Nat-ul rose, put an arm around Nu's waist and looked up at the weary caveman. Nu looked down on Tur, and Nat-ul saw the eyes of Nu grow wide. Suddenly he took Nat-ul by the arm and turned her in the direction of the nearest shore. "The day is yet young," he said. "If we hurry we may be able to cross the Restless Sea before darkness."

Nat-ul held back a bit and said, "Should I take the ax of Tur? We may need it on the sea."

"No! The warrior earned the right to keep his ax in death. Let us hurry!"

After a few steps, Nat-ul said, "You act strange." Still pulling Nat-ul by an arm, Nu whispered, "Do not look back. Tur is not dead."

"What? I saw your blow and watched Tur fall, and he himself said he would die."

"He feigned his death that you and I might leave together while he yet could hold dignity in your eyes. It was necessary for him to fight for the woman he chose. He did not want you to think him a coward. It was the reason he fought strangely. More than once I thought I was dead, but his ax somehow missed me. Remember his words? *A knowledge in return for your life.* He gave me life, and it gave him the knowledge that I could slay Gr and that you would be happy."

"Why would he do such a thing?"

"I told him love is when the happiness and the life of the one you love are more important than your own. That is why he asked if you are happy."

"Are you sure he lives?"

"I saw an ant crawl under the skin of his good eye, and he blinked. A proud warrior as Tur would let ants devour his eye and make him blind before looking foolish to you."

As they walked, Nat-ul slipped her hand into the hand of Nu. "Tur is a great warrior and a good man. For Nat-ul he was Tha's Gr." She squeezed tight the hand of Nu, "My Nu is a great warrior and a good man, and he understands things which others do not. I will always love my Nu."

Tur brushed ants from his eye as the pair blended into the jungle, and a pleasant peace filled him. He understood what love is as well as anyone could and he was confident that Nu could slay the long-tooth. Nat-ul would be cherished and happy; at least as much as one could be in a world of constant death and savage peril.

Without further incident, Nat-ul and Nu

came to the beach. Nu pulled the crocodile tooth from the hull of the boat he paddled and gave it to Nat-ul. "Until I bring the fangs of long-tooth," he told her.

Because Tur was a boatbuilder it would be easy for him to repair the damaged boat, so they took the undamaged canoe.

As they pulled for the mainland, long-necked serpents reared up twice. Nat-ul killed both with her club.

From far out at sea, they spotted the village of Tur and veered toward the Barren Hills. Once ashore, they loped along the beach toward the caves of their tribe. As they went, they paid no notice to the cave which held Hud's bones, nor to the bits of the slain turtle which began the past days' adventures. In those days there was no time for reminiscence over things past. Life was too savage and short. You lived forward, breath by breath and only when that last breath was gone out of your cold body could you rest.

A wild welcome awaited them as the tribe gave them up for dead days before. Later, they walked hand in hand beside the Restless Sea, beneath the magnificent equatorial moon.

"Soon," said Nu, "Nat-ul shall become the mate of Nu. My father has deemed it, and so, too, has the father of Nat-ul. At the birth of the next moon, we are to mate, and tomorrow, Nu will slay long-tooth for Nat-ul as he promised."

"Nat-ul but teased," the cave girl said. "My man has proven himself greater than a mere hunter. I do not want the great toothed head, Nu. I only want you. For all my days I want Nu." She was silent a moment and looked up at the moon which stirred unnamed emotions, and inspired them to greater things. "No," she said and lay her hand on the face of the man. "Nat-ul does not want to be the mate of Nu for all her days, but for as long as the moon rises."

Nu smiled down at Nat-ul and could see her sincerity in the concept that boggled his mind - as long as the moon rises. He looked up at the full yellow moon which he was sure must hold magic, then back into the eyes of his beloved. "Then let it be, for any less time is too short."

Then Nu swore again that he would take the head of Gr for Nat-ul.

The next morning brave Nu set forth to confront the long-tooth. For   hours   Nat-ul awaited his return. She knew it might be days before his homecoming or that he might not return at all. Grave premonitions of impending danger haunted her. She wandered in and out of her cave, looking for the thousandth time along the way that Nu might come.

Long after Nu departed, a rumbling rose from far inland. The earth shook and trembled. Nat-ul's people fled upward toward their caves. The heavens became overcast, and the loud rumbling rose to an unnerving roar. From deep in the bowels of earth came loud cracking as days before, like giant trees snapped in two. The violence increased until the very cliffs rocked!

Nat-ul took a final look at the three domes of the beautiful Barren Hills she loved and proudly called home, then rushed up the stones to the innermost recess of her father's cave. Her family clustered about her, where for the first time ever, all were terror-stricken. Over her stood great Zok, who growled his readiness to defend loyally even against unconquerable nature. There she huddled upon the floor, her face buried in a pile of bear and lion skins. Amid the rampage of nature, Nat-ul thought her last thoughts and spoke her final words, "Where is my Nu? I swear I will love my Nu as long as the moon yet rises! I swear it!"

In seconds the end came. An awful convulsion shook the mighty cliffs. Behemoth boulders cracked and shattered and buried what once was the home of a proud people!

Chapter 11

Savage Recall

Victoria Custer jerked awake to a sitting position. The first face she saw was her brother, Barney. For a moment she stared in puzzled bewilderment.

"Who?" she began, then closed her eyes. Then Victoria looked up again and asked, "What has happened?"

"You're all right, Vickie," Barney told her. "You're safe and sound in our bungalow."

"Vickie?" It was a question. The girl knit her brows in perplexity, then shook her head. "Wasn't there an earthquake?"

"A little one, but there wasn't any damage done."

"How long have I been out?"

"You swooned three minutes ago," replied her brother.

"Three minutes?" murmured the girl. That night after the rest of the household retired, Barney Custer sat beside his sister's bed. Into the early morning, in simple words and without a sign of hysteria, she told him the story of Nat-ul and Nu. When she finished the strange tale, she told her brother, "I feel more complete now, Barney. Isn't that an odd word to use? Complete."

Barney smiled. "With the story of your avatars finished, perhaps you may be able to listen to what Curtiss has been trying to say." It was a half question.

Victoria Custer shook her head.

"No," she said, "I could never love him now. I cannot tell you why, but those three minutes revealed more about me than I ever realized. Besides, Terkoz doesn't like him, you know. He is a good man but," Victoria half laughed, "a pusillanimous weakling." Barney half laughed with her.

Victoria looked out the open window at the silhouetted jungle and distant mountains. As she stared at that early morning sky, she uttered a wistful whisper, "Must it be finished?"

Barney did not pursue the subject. As the east began to lighten to the coming dawn, he sought his own room for a few hours' sleep.

The last day of their stay, while the others hunted, Victoria and Barney stayed back to finish packing. When that was done, the girl asked Barney to go with her for a last ride in that beautiful land.

Before they covered even a mile, Barney saw that his sister had a particular objective in mind. She rode steadily as an arrow, with scarce a word, straight for the rugged mountains to the south. Her goal was what terrorized her before. Victoria didn't stop until they came to the foot of the lofty, triple-domed cliffs.

"What's the idea, Vic?" asked the man. "I thought you were through with all this."

"Barney," she replied, "I couldn't just leave. Something pulls me. If I didn't visit these hills, I would spend my entire life wondering."

She dismounted and scurried up the rugged escarpment. Vic amazed Barney with her agility and strength. She reminded him of a rock squirrel, and it kept him puffing to remain near in her rapid ascent.

At last, she stopped upon a narrow ledge, and when Barney reached her side, he paled. The earthquake dislodged a massive boulder that for ages formed a part of the cliff face. Now it resided outward a half dozen feet, revealing the mouth of a gloomy cavern.

"Come back to the horses," he said, "we've seen enough."

Victoria shook her head and answered defiantly, "Not until I search that cave!"

Together they entered the forbidding grotto, Barney in advance, striking matches.

Just a few feet inside, the feeble flame illumined something that brought Barney to a sudden halt. He tried to turn Victoria back as though there was nothing more to see, but she saw it, too, and pressed forward. She made her brother light another match, and there before them lay the crumbling skeleton of a large man. By its side rested stone-age weapons - a broken stone-tipped spear, a stone knife, and a stone ax.

"Look!" whispered Victoria, pointing to something that lay beyond the skeleton.

Barney raised the match until its flickering light carried to that other object. It was the grinning skull of a great cat, its upper jaw armed with two mighty, thirteen-inch, curved fangs.

"Gr, the long-tooth, devourer of men and mammoths," whispered Victoria Custer in awe. "And Nu, who killed him for his Nat-ul - for me!"

In an instant, Victoria Custer's mind filled with another life. It was complete with hopes and longings, recollections and instincts. All were intact, undiminished by time! Victoria realized the truth and looked up at her brother. "Those weren't dreams, Barney! They were memories!"

VIC: DOUBLE TROUBLE

Part 2

Chapter 12

A Perilous Profession

The boys were about to make a dangerous mistake. They pretended to read newspapers as they eyed a young woman stroll along that side street in downtown Omaha. Now and then the woman paused to view window displays, and the boys became more attentive to the paper while she stopped.

Victoria Custer was a lithesome girl, and her choice of clothing and her large dreamy eyes implied physical frailty. Pink flowers adorned her white cotton dress. Over her long, wavy raven hair and tilted a bit to the right she sported a pink Paris hat. It matched the flowers on the dress to a "T". In her right hand, she carried a folded pink parasol, and a pink wrist purse hung from her left hand. An average onlooker, like those boys, would characterize her as weak and vulnerable. Anyone who knew her growing up as a tough farm girl or who was privy to her exploits in Africa would recognize such a characterization to be absurd.

Two doors past the boys, Victoria stopped to admire a window display. The boys now approached her on the side where the purse hung loosely. As they came within a step of her, both dashed forward. One grasped the purse and wrenched it away while the other pushed her hard against the window! The boy who pushed her intended to continue the same direction, the one with her purse doubled back.

Victoria's response was instant. She righted, dropped the shopping bag and spun after the boy who pushed her. She kicked that boy in the back of a thigh and sent him stumbling. She continued the spin and swept the handle of her parasol hard at an ankle of the boy with her purse, and yanked!

The boy fell hard, and it was apparent he had the wind knocked out of him. Victoria glanced back and saw the other boy bulldoze a man who tried to stop him, then continue breakneck.

As the downed boy started to rise, Victoria dropped very un-ladylike with a knee on his back. With one hand she pulled his right arm behind him and bent it toward his head. With her other hand, she grabbed a fistful of his tangled hair and pulled his head back.

"If you try to get up, you will lose a very large clump of hair, and I may break your arm." To emphasize that second possibility, she pushed his arm up, and the boy yelped. "Ok, ok!" he said. "Go ahead, call the coppers!"

Victoria considered his profile then asked, "What is your name? How old are you?"

When he didn't reply immediately, she pushed his arm up, and he grunted, "Jason. Sixteen!"

She eased up on his arm and asked, "Is this to be your future, Jason? You are not very good at it. Your future is likely to include a lot of prison time. If the action of your accomplice is a sign, you probably can't count on anything from those you call friend."

"What's it to you?" he growled.

She prodded his arm until he yelped again then asked, "Why?"

Grudgingly the boy told her, "Got no schooling, can't get work, and I like to eat."

After a short silence, Victoria gave the boy some instructions. She told him to go to a shop and ask for any work. He was to take whatever a merchant offered if only an hour to clean a shop for a nickel or sweep the shop for dinner.

"When you finish, thank the shopkeeper and go to the next shop. Keep going until there are no more shops on that side of the street. Then cross and do the same thing on the other side. Always do your best. When you finish a job ask if you may return in a few days to see if there is more work. Do not refuse any work at any pay. Do that for three days. Then decide what to do next. Swear to do this, and I won't call the police."

The boy looked up at Victoria sideways and shrugged as best he could in his position. "Ok," was all he said. She let him up, and he handed her the purse and asked her name.

"Victoria," she answered and pointed

toward the shop next door. "That would be a good place to begin, Jason." The boy turned and walked away.

A small crowd gathered to watch the encounter. As the boy passed that next shop, the man knocked down by the other ruffian asked, "Are you letting him go?"

She looked after the boy. "What he did is inexcusable, but his reason is understandable and unfortunately too common. He's young so may turn his life around. If not, there will still be prisons when he does it again."

The window where she stopped held a display of cloches in many styles. A cloche for Victoria was like a licorice stick or a Mounds bar or a Double Zero to a kid. For that matter, Victoria definitely had a sweet tooth, too, so she entered the shop to pick out a new cloche.

For half an hour, Victoria tried on hats. She finally made a choice, paid the clerk and asked if there was a military surplus shop nearby. "I need clothing for an expedition."

The motherly clerk gave her directions to a shop on the next block. "For a brother, Miss?"

"For me," Victoria replied, then went out and turned toward the surplus shop. She made a few purchases there then rushed to catch the noon train for Beatrice.

It was a year since Victoria Custer returned from the African safari which transformed her life. The hunting was a patent success. Victoria brought lion and leopard skins with her on the return. Other things were too large to carry.

Three months later, an expected delivery came from a taxidermist in Africa.

Mr. Colter, the train depot manager, was kind enough to deliver three large crates. One was a cape buffalo head for Barney, the other was a rhinoceros head for Victoria. The surprise was a third crate, an animal carrier. When Vic opened it, out bounded the great wolfhound Terkoz. He was a frequent companion in Africa and saved Vic's life. The beast stood to place his forepaws on Vic's shoulders and licked her full in the face. Vic allowed it with laughs and a hug.   W i t h Terkoz came a letter from Vic and Barney's hosts in Africa. It related how the dog would sleep only in the room where Victoria stayed. Knowing that a mutual bond existed, they thought she might appreciate the odd gift. They also extended an open invitation for Vic and Barney to visit again, anytime, with or without notice.

Terkoz was most welcomed and took up residence at the family farm with Vic's parents.

The powerful experience in Africa transformed Vic and altered the course of her life. The vivid recollection of her previous life as a cave dweller could have dismayed her. Or it could have caused her to fear sleep or doubt her sanity. Or she could have pushed it aside and forgotten it. Instead, it invigorated and drove her.

On her return from Africa, Vic spent months in study. She read dozens of back issues of her favorite publications like *Adventure, Weird Tales, Vogue, Scientific Monthly, and National Geographic* magazines.

Victoria read extensively on the subjects of geology, geography, archaeology, zoology, and reincarnation. She made frequent trips to the library and returned with her bicycle basket filled.

She did not neglect her physical health. Her friend from high school, Lin Li, was teaching her a thing called gung-fu and she lifted stones. Vic also began a daily outing which was neither a run nor walk. She told Barney, "It's a lope. I always feel better when I'm done and think someday it will be a common practice."

For a short time, Victoria sported a fascination with the occult and the practice known as a séance. She participated on several occasions and discussed them at length with practitioners. Both her extraordinary experience and years of Sunday School left Vic confident there was more to existence than this life alone. She concluded that some séances may be genuine. Most practitioners, she decided, were charlatans.

It baffled acquaintances that Victoria Custer was not married. Most of her female friends were wed by the age of twenty-two. Friends often felt bad for her, but Vic herself gave it no thought. She was not interested, she told them. After the return from Africa she began to add, "But as Sherlock Holmes would say, the game is afoot." Of course, they had no idea what she meant, and Vic never explained.

A few weeks after their return from Africa, Barney asked Vic, "Have your avatars returned?"

"Yes, Barn," Vic answered, "most nights, but they are no longer a source of concern. They are reminiscences and visits. They exhilarate me and bring respite from the humdrum. I awake each morning no longer the pampered child of a weak civilization, and I'm filled with admiration for the cave girl I was. Those were stupendously savage days, brother, yet to her, it wasn't difficult. It was just living. No one fell on hard times because it was all hard. Every minute held the potential for your destruction. If you wanted tomorrow, you dealt with today, no whining, no shirking!"

Vic and Barney shared a small home in Beatrice, Nebraska, purchased from the Sears mail-order catalog with most of an inheritance from a distant uncle. That day, a year after their return from Africa, the day Vic finished her shopping trip to Omaha, was pleasant and sunny. Barney was in the third bedroom turned library, reading the Beatrice Daily Sun when he heard an automobile horn. It sent him outside, and he leaned over the porch rail.

The honking was from Emma's 1919 Ford Model T Coupe. All Model T's were black, except Emma's. Green was Emma's favorite color, and she was as headstrong as Vic. The day after she purchased it, Vic helped her paint it. With two gallons of green paint left from painting her house, Emma gave herself a green and black Lizzy.

Barney was not surprised to see his sister with Emma. The two were friends since they were five. Vic went to Omaha three days earlier for what she called a shopping trip. Emma drove Vic to the train station and evidently arranged to pick her up on her return.

"Don't just stand there, Barn," Emma called. "Come help your sister!"

Barney vaulted over the low railing beside the auto. Vic handed him two large cotton bags and took a third, smaller bag herself.

"These seem heavy for dresses, Vic. What kind of dresses did you get?"

"A lovely gown for fancy dinners and a wonderful barrette with a carved bison! And a stunning cloche which is the absolute bee's knees!"

Emma pulled away in her green and black Tin Lizzie and called to Vic, "Is the game afoot?"

"Seriously!" Vic yelled.

Barney noted, "Looks like the paint is wearing. I see a spot of rust on Emma's rear end."

"Don't talk like that about my friend!" Vic laughed and elbowed her brother on the shoulder.

"I've decided to get one too when we get back. Did you know Lin bought one last month?"

Vic started in and continued, "Yes, Emma knows about the rust. I promised I would help her repaint before we go."

"Go? Where? Who? Get one what?" Barney followed as Vic surged up the steps and into the house.

Without an answer, Vic went into the library. After they set the bags down, Barney asked again, "Ok, who is going where, and what are you getting?"

"I'm getting a Tin Lizzie," Vic pulled an envelope from a bag, "but I want to wait until next year. I hear they will have electric starters, so you don't need to crank like Emma's."

"It begins!" Vic advised her brother. "This is the start!" She pulled a letter from the envelope and waved it at Barney. "Of course you need not come. I will be fine, but if you have nothing else planned…..".

"What is that?" Barney asked. "What's happened?"

Vic informed her brother that she was to be published in The Beatrice Daily Sun, the very paper he was reading.

Her column would be syndicated and seen all around the world if she kept writing dramatic stories. The Sun already purchased a series of 3 stories about the trip to Africa and agreed to take more for a weekly column.

"A column?" Barney asked. "Stories of what?"

"Adventure dear brother! Adventure! I love adventure, and you do as well! You know you do! You've been listless since Africa. I have toiled, and it paid off!"

Vic would be a kind of globetrotting Nellie Bly from Nebraska. The paper would pay her to visit adventurous places and write about them. Barney pointed out that such a profession might prove perilous. Vic countered that there are occupational hazards in any profession.

"On the morrow," she informed her brother, "I book passage for the first adventure! Should I purchase a ticket for you? Victoria *Nellie Bly* Custer," Vic tested. "Or does Victoria Custer the female Burton or Shackleton sound better?" Her eyes gleamed.

"I do hope you are interested and want to go but, whether you go or not, I am doing this. I must, and it will be great fun!"

"Of course I want to go," Barney told Vic. "How could I sit home while you travel to exotic lands? No doubt, you will bring back exciting stories and bags of souvenirs!"

"Thank you, Barn," Vic said. "You are a terrific sibling!"

Then she opened another bag and showed her brother the three new cameras she picked up from the post office on her way from the train station. "I ordered them from the Sears Roebuck catalog," she told him.

Barney marveled at the new cameras. They were Kodak No3a autographic cameras which made postcard size photos.

Vic dumped a box taken from within the bag and rolls of film spilled onto the desk and onto the floor. "They use roll film, and I can make 10 photos from each roll. I bought 100 rolls! That's a thousand photos, Barn!"

"Holy moly!" Barney replied. "Do you think you can find that many things to photograph?"

"Absolutely," said Vic, "and these cameras have the autographic feature. Through this aperture in the rear, I can write a note on the back of each photo when I take it, so I will know where and when it was taken!"

Barney commented that he didn't think newspaper photographers used this kind of camera and he asked why three were needed.

"So we can each carry one and have a back up if one breaks. My esteemed editor expressly stated that photos must be part of the package. He loved the photos of me with the cats and rhino in Africa! What good is a travel article if the reader can't see a photo of the place traveled? Besides, I think I could make some nice picture books once I have enough photos. To me, these still seem bulky, but they are much easier to handle than those big boxes the professional photographers use, and less expensive, too."

"What do you plan that might damage cameras?" Barney asked. "Where are we going?"

Vic didn't answer but took a rolled world map from a bookshelf and spread it over the table.

"Do you have a coin?" Vic asked, and Barney gave her a new Buffalo nickel. She stepped away from the table, closed her eyes, made a silent wish, then flipped the coin.

The nickel bounced twice, and Vic went to look. With a smile, she finally answered Barney. "To the Yucatan Peninsula of Mexico!"

"That is how you decide where to go? Do you know what's there?"

"I've read articles about the area. Jungle and ancient ruins await! It will be a great adventure, a great place to begin!"

Barney really didn't expect his sister to change her mind but asked anyway. "Why can't you do a story about Paris or Rome or London?"

"Maybe another time, but the nickel has spoken! Besides, I miss the jungle."

Chapter 13

Passage to Mexico

The next day Vic used the train depot phone to book passage. The train station was a little over a mile away. It made a pleasant bike ride, and Vic was a long time friend of Mr. Colter, the station master. Many of their friends owned telephones, but Vic and Barney resisted. They felt their lives were already extravagant enough. They had running water in the kitchen and gas radiators in the bedrooms - things their parents didn't have. They even had a private room for the bathing tub with a radiator beside it! It was necessary to fill and empty it by hand, but they could use the kitchen pump for filling. Most of their country friends still had a tub beside the wood-burning cook stove in the kitchen. They needed to carry water from outside and hang sheets from nails in the ceiling if they wanted privacy.

After the nickel spoke, Vic had two bee busy weeks. She read about their destination, and almost daily she took a three-hour hike and dragged Barney along. Vic joked on the first day. "We might need to walk a great deal, brother and progress can't be slowed because you're out of shape!"

Barney replied, "Mexico is a modern country. They have roads and motor cars. They do have roads don't they?"

"Of course they have roads but from what I have learned, in the Yucatán rail travel is more likely. Even so, I doubt the animals will saunter up to the track and pose for a photo. I also want to photograph ruins which are off the roads and rails, ruins in the clutches of the jungle, unseen for centuries!"

Victoria shopped a bit more, also. At Mortimer's Drug, she purchased three journals to hold her notes. To ensure her capacity to write, Vic also picked up four Sheaffer lever-filled pens and four bottles of ink. For backup, she bought a handful of pencils. She was sure a knife or other cutting instrument would always be handy to sharpen them.

Barney teased her about going overboard on backups. "What if the ink all spills and the pencils fall in a river?"

"I'll put some charcoal from a campfire in a canteen cup, mix it with water and use a sharp stick to write. And if the journals get lost..."

Barney lost his smile and walked away.

Two weeks and a night after the coin toss, the adventure began early. They caught the six a.m. train in Beatrice and switched trains in Omaha for their ride to San Francisco. The trip was uneventful, but Vic did snap a photo or two at each stop for an article about train travel. She took a book about the flora and fauna of Mexico and also carried a copy of her favorite novel.

When Barney saw her pull that book out, he asked, "Are you reading that again?" It was *The Lost World* by Sir Arthur Conan Doyle. Over the years, Vic read it at least five times.

"It's a fabulous story!" she responded. "I wish I could find a story with a lady Professor Challenger, though.   Perhaps I'll write one someday." Vic took on a serious expression. "Wouldn't it be fabulous to find such a place as the lost world with primitive beasts and people?"

Barney nodded and said, "That would be fabulous." Then off-handedly he added, "Say, can't you use a pseudonym for your column? You could easily be as contrary and stubborn as the professor. How about Vic Challenger?"

Barney's flippant tease didn't have the intended impact. Vic stared at her brother a moment. "Oh, Barney! What a tag line! Hard-boiled Vic Challenger braves the sweaty, savage corners of the earth! You get the scoop, safe in your living room! I love it! Vic Challenger! Vic Challenger!   Thank you, Barney!   Vic Challenger it is!"

Vic took 200 photos in San Francisco. Reasoning she would likely take extra shots at sea, and through the Canal, she replaced those twenty rolls with thirty. She wanted to arrive in Mexico with film enough for 1000 photos. She sent the exposed film from the train ride and San Francisco to Emma, via the postal service. Vic enclosed a loaf of sourdough bread to thank her friend and mother-of-pearl barrettes for both Emma and Lin Li.

The stay in San Francisco was two full days, and on the second day Vic disappeared at noon and met Barney for dinner. When he saw his sister, his mouth fell open. "Sis, Vic," and for a few minutes, that's all he could say.

Vic smiled and spun around for her brother to see her new style. Her long waves were gone. Her hair now ended just below her ears with waves more pronounced than her natural hair. Her hair parted near the center with a thick curly set of bangs pushed over her right eye. "It's a finger wave," Vic said enthusiastically. "Isn't it spiffy?"

"Why?" Barney asked.

"It's fashionable and will enhance my look as a world traveler. The stylist said it is all the rage in New York and Europe. Besides that, it is utilitarian, easier to keep clean and remove ticks!"

The next day, Vic and Barney leaned over the rail of the Mexico Trader as it pulled away from the dock in San Francisco. Vic snapped photos of a ferry as it transported cars across the bay behind them. As they watched the city grow smaller, Vic wondered out loud, "Think they will ever build a bridge across the bay?" Another passenger heard her and shared his opinion, "Nah. Too many problems and the cost would be crazy. There will never be a bridge across San Francisco Bay."

Barney asked, "Why are we doing this, really, Vic?" Although he didn't yet frame a solid theory, Barney felt sure more than a little adventure or even a profession motivated Victoria.

"Adventure, Barney, and to learn new things, and I honestly miss the innate, captivating fury of the jungle."

Vic hoped for a reasonable amount of excitement but didn't expect the trip would actually be dangerous. If it was, no matter. Since birth, she always possessed perfect coolness in the face of danger. After her recollection in Africa, even the most ominous threat seemed trifling. It was just life.

Vic told Barney, "When I was in Omaha, I

visited the zoo. They have a tiger, you know, and people remarked how large and ferocious it looked. I wondered what they would think of Gr, the long-tooth." When Vic spoke of Gr, the devourer of men and mammoths, she envisioned his 13-inch fangs. In the table beside her bed she kept the two saber teeth brought from Africa, the fangs Nu won for Nat-ul.

Their trip would take nine days. The Mexico Trader cruised down the West Coast and crossed through the Panama Canal. Then it went northward, stopping in Cuba, and then on to New York. There, it would take on new passengers and return by the reverse route. There was no stop for passengers at Puerto Progreso where Vic and Barney would disembark. The ship did stop to unload cargo, so Vic arranged with the cruise line to go with the cargo.

From Puerto Progreso, they would travel inland to an archeological dig called Chichén Itzá. She expected it would make a keen first adventure and would supply material for many stories. She could write about the archeology, the cruise, plants and animals, history of the people, and of course the food! "The way my mind is racing, I will never be without something to write about!" Vic told Barney.

On the first night aboard ship, a woman came into the crowded dining hall alone. She spotted an empty seat at Vic and Barney's table and asked if she might join them. "My name is Ann Darrow," she introduced herself. There was an instant rapport between the two women, and it was immediately evident that much of their likes and dislikes were the proverbial peas from the shared pod. From that evening, Vic and Ann spent most of their waking hours together, and left Barney to his own devices. Every night they turned heads in the dining hall. They dressed elegantly, but it was their natural features which drew attention: Vic's raven waves in the stylish new hair-do and imposing amber eyes; Ann's strawberry curls draped over her shoulders and eyes like emeralds. On sight, no one imagined the adventurous disposition they shared.

On the second night, Vic wore the felt cloche she bought in Omaha. It was lime-green with an upturned chocolate brim and on the right side was a forest green, beaded palm frond. What a beautiful cloche!" Ann complimented. They discovered that each had a considerable collection and devoted the next hour to cloches.

On the third night, a portly gentleman from New York shared their table. When he heard some of their ideas, exploits, and plans, he seemed skeptical. "You two sound as though you believe yourselves female versions of Alan Quatermain!" His laugh seemed pretentious.

"Oh no!" Ann replied first, with an appearance of melodramatic shock as she sneaked a wink at Vic. "I consider myself more of an aspiring Mary Kingsley."

Vic also looked taken aback. "I am certainly more a version of Harriet Chalmers Adams than Alan Quatermain."

He never heard of those adventuresses, so the fellow became a student in the conversation.

First, they reminded him that Quatermain was a fictional hero created by H. Rider

Haggard, while Adams and Kingsley were real people.

Mary Kingsley was an adventuress with no formal education. She traveled with her father and aided him in studies of comparative religion. When her father died, she continued his work. She also brought many valuable biological specimens from Africa and wrote a book of her travels. "I love her story," Ann said. "Perhaps because I received no formal education, either. My parents schooled me. Some of my fondest memories are of learning with them!"

Harriet Chalmers Adams explored much of South America with her husband. She traveled the world and wrote for the National Geographic magazine. She also gave lectures about her adventures. "I've read some of Mrs. Adams articles," Vic said. "A friend had the honor to attend one of her lectures and described it as spellbinding. Mrs. Adams career confirmed my decision to travel and write."

Vic and Ann agreed their favorite adventuress was Nellie Bly. In 1887, she allowed herself to be committed to an insane asylum so she could report on conditions inside. Later, her newspaper sent a lawyer to rescue her. Her story improved treatment of the mentally ill in the United States. In late 1889, Nellie set out to beat the fictional record of going around the world in 80 days, penned by Jules Verne. The New York World newspaper sponsored her, and on the trip, she met Jules Verne. He held the opinion she wouldn't succeed. He was wrong. Nellie arrived back in New York, victorious, January 1890 - 72 days, 6 hours and 11 minutes after she began.

Vic and Ann found they were born just 2 months apart - Vic on a farm in Nebraska and Ann on a farm in East Texas. Both loved those early years, and they enjoyed sharing stories with one another.

Ann also shared stories of more recent adventures. "You've heard of Carl Denham?" Ann asked Vic.

"Yes! He makes movies and picture books of wild animals."

"I've been on three cruises with him. Not tourist cruises like this, though," Ann laughed. "My first cruise with him was particularly brutal and deadly. He wants to make a movie about it but may wait a few years to make it. That will make it more difficult for anyone to guess on which voyage it happened and to find the island. A frightening beast abducted me, but Carl plans to exaggerate a bit. You know, almost real. He wants to exaggerate the size of the beast, and the actress he wants to play my part is a blonde. He says the public loves blonde dames and unbelievably ferocious monsters. He expects they will buy more tickets to see those! I've met Faye, and she is perfect for the role, beautiful and a darling person. If she plays Ann Darrow, it would be a grand compliment!"

Ann continued with a more serious tone, "The beast handled me like a child's doll. I will tell you about it before you leave the ship, but you must promise to share with no one. It's to be a total secret until Carl makes the movie. He hopes the public will think the whole story is fiction."

On the fourth day, Vic confirmed details of debarking at Puerto Progresso with the ship's captain, Leonidus Walker. He invited Vic and Barney to dine at the Captain's table and said certainly Ann could join them. He found the trio so interesting that they dined with the captain for the remainder of their respective trips.

On the last night before Vic left the ship, Ann told her the adventure of Skull Island. It was a place of primitive men and monsters. She judged Vic would enjoy the story but didn't expect how much.

"It sounds marvelous, Ann!" Vic told her. "How I wish I could feel the steam rise from the ground, and see the beasts you discovered! It sounds so like Conan Doyle's imaginary land!"

"Except this was not fiction and many died."

Then Vic said, "Let me tell you my story." She recounted the trip to Africa and the 3-minute vision and what she found in the cavern. Ann immediately knew that Vic would love Skull Island. When Vic finished, Ann made her a promise. "Vic, I will do my best to persuade Carl Denham to supply you with the details of how to get to Skull Island. If anyone should ever visit there again, it's you. I have no doubt you would find it both thrilling and familiar, and we saw only about twenty percent of the island. Most of it is yet unexplored."

The trip to Puerto Progreso took nine days. The Mexico Trader took five days to reach New

York, including a twelve hour stop in Cuba. It would port at New York for twenty-four hours to take on new passengers and cargo. It would return to San Francisco by a reverse route, then repeat the circuit. Vic planned to finish her work and re-board when the ship next passed en route to New York. That allowed twenty-eight days for the adventure.

Vic took many photos of the captain and crew and sections of the ship. She promised a favorable story, and the Captain agreed to hold belongings they didn't need ashore as a favor to Vic and Barney.

The Yucatán Peninsula of Mexico lies between the Gulf of Mexico and the Caribbean Sea. It is always warm, and most of it boasts lush tropical jungles. The sea is too shallow at Puerto Progreso to accommodate a large ship. The Mexico Trader anchored three miles from shore. Rather than leave via gangway, Vic and Barney climbed into a motorized boat with a large number of crates. Ann was there to see them off, and the two friends vowed to write, to share adventures, and to meet again.

As the boat was lowered, Ann shouted to Vic, "Good luck Vic! May your quest be short and successful. I will talk to Carl Denham and let you know."

Vic called back, "Catch!" Then she reached inside her shirt and pulled out the cloche from Omaha and tossed it upward.

Ann reached over the rail to catch the cloche.

"You are a dear friend Ann, and that will look marvelous with your beautiful red hair and green eyes!"

The little boat hit the water, and the motor was started. "What does she mean? What quest?" Barney asked, but he didn't get an answer. Vic looked toward the shore and said, "Gee, Barney! This is so beautiful!"

It was a gorgeous day, but a stiff wind blew against them, and the boat bounced roughly. They sat at the front of the boat and Vic leaned over the side to enjoy the spray on her face.

The translucent turquoise water showed colorful fish darting along the white bottom. Magnificent beaches stretched out of sight to both right and left. Dead ahead, industrial buildings backed several wooden piers bustling with people.

Four piers jutted out into the sea from Puerto Progreso. Their boat tied up at the Porfirio Diaz pier and the skipper helped Vic out. His name was Sandoval, just Sandoval. He was a wiry gentleman of 70 if a day, who always stood erect like a soldier at attention and somehow always wore polished boots and creased trousers. Vic, Barney, and Ann all shared many great conversations with the charismatic old gentleman and he took a particular interest in Vic. "Buena suerte," he wished the two, and then to Vic, "Le ruego sea cuidadoso jovencita." *I beg you, be careful, young lady.*

"Si, Sandoval, lo seré" Vic answered.

Chapter 14

The Ancient City

They traveled light. Each carried a pack with a camera, film, journals, and pens. Vic and Barney both wore boots, and the Army surplus uniforms Vic picked up in Omaha. Each carried one extra set of everything. They met two boys at the docks who offered to guide them. They were friendly and spoke a bit of English, which Barney liked, and were hardy, so Vic hired them. Jaime and Diego brought Vic and Barney to Hotel del Mar in the center of Progreso. Vic gave them a list of provisions for the trip and asked if they could get everything by morning. They said it wasn't a problem. By the time the boys left, it was 6 p.m., so Vic and Barney went to the hotel dining room. Only a couple of other tables were in use when they arrived as it was early for dinner, but they weren't there to socialize. They last ate at breakfast aboard ship and were on the go since. Both went to the table hungry and amused the waiter when he heard their stomachs growl. The menu was only in Spanish, so Barney relied on Vic to order. It wouldn't have mattered though. Both Vic and Barney were adventurous diners and game to try about anything.

In Africa, they dined with the Waziri often. On the first occasion, they ate half the meal before they learned it was an ostrich egg omelette with corn and earthworms. They enjoyed hippopotamus stew another time. On every occasion, they enjoyed several helpings and praised the cook for the flavorful meals. Vic's favorite meal in Africa was without a doubt the bull buffalo from the encounter with Lord Lawrence. Udur boiled the meat to tenderize it. Then it was marinated in palm oil, onions, chili peppers, and garlic. Finally, Udur slow roasted it. Her mouth watered every time she remembered that meal!

Growing up on a farm, as a matter of course, Vic and Barney ate foods which many might consider with disgust. Some of their favorites were mountain oysters or beef testicles, scrambled eggs with calf brains, rabbit and antelope.

Neither worried about what might be served at a hotel restaurant. As it turned out both were very satisfied with their delicious dinner of poc chuc. It was salted pork cooked with orange juice and vinegar flavored with coriander and onions. Plenty of beans and corn tortillas accompanied it, so both left the restaurant agreeably full.

After dinner, they strolled the central plaza. By then, a sliver of a moon was bold in the clear sky, and a cool breeze from the sea replaced the heated air of the afternoon. Vic's intent was a short walk then "... get a good rest before we begin tomorrow." Then suddenly, "But first!" Vic spotted an elderly woman wearing a bright red shawl and holding a basket. She was a traditional tamale vendor, and Vic had to have one. Then after smelling them, she decided "Dos!". Though Barney insisted he was full, Vic bought him one, too, and after he tasted it, he was glad. Then Vic bought one more for while she wrote in her journal before retiring.

Before Barney went to his room, he went to Vic's, and they took a look at a map. "Looks rather wild, doesn't it," Barney commented.

"Yes," said Vic. "I hope Jaime and Diego know a fast way to get there. Then we can set up camp, and I will take day hikes for photos."

"I am so excited to be here! This trip is the onset of adventures that will last who knows how long or where they may take me! You know if you didn't come with me I would be here anyway, but I am happy that you are here. We have each become a great complement to the other over the years."

Barney agreed they were complementary. Both knew when their concomitance sprouted, and now and then, they would laugh about it. When Vic was in the third grade, an older boy pushed her on the playground. Barney promptly blacked the other boy's eye, and both were taken to the principal's office for licks. Barney said no one could push his sister around and refused to apologize. That bought more licks but Barney never regretted it, and Vic was ever after proud of her big brother for watching out for her.

Barney went to his room and was sound asleep in minutes, but Vic journaled for two hours.

In the morning, Barney thought he was up early, but came out to find Vic talking to Jaime and Diego. "We have time for breakfast," she greeted him. "Desayuno!" She waved for the boys to follow and led the way to the dining room. They all ate huevos con carne de chivo - eggs with goat meat - with corn tortillas.

Vic was especially pleased with the coffee they were served, a specialty of the hotel. She asked if she could get directions to make it, but they told her it was their secret recipe.

Vic loved pretty much all coffee. She developed the taste early. She and Barney rose each morning at 3:30 to do chores before breakfast and school. Her parents agreed if she could do work like an adult, she could drink coffee like an adult. In Africa, she learned to have coffee spiced with ginger and cardamom. She brought seeds home, and now, healthy young coffee trees grew in her hothouse.

Jaime and Diego each brought a "pack" of sorts. They were small wooden crates padded on one side with a blanket for comfort against their backs. Fishnets wrapped around the crates to serve as shoulder straps or handles. The crates held supplies for their trip. The boys bought them from a surplus store on the promise to bring payment that morning. Vic gave money to Jaime, and he ran to pay, and when he returned, the four walked two blocks and caught a tram.

It surprised Vic and Barney how easy it would be to reach their destination. They rode in a rail car similar to a trolley they saw in San Francisco, except this ran on gasoline. Like the trolleys, it often stopped to load and unload passengers. Barney was curious why there was such a great rail system, and the boys confirmed what Vic read. She told Barney, "Henequen is an agave plant which yields a fiber of the same name. You know what that is used for - to make rope and twine. It's a significant export for Mexico. They laid rails to provide a reliable way to transport henequen to the seaports."

The tram took them through the city of Mérida and on to Izamal in late afternoon where they decided to spend the night.

They ate at a home that operated a small cafe in the yard. Three tables sat under a thatched cover, and the woman cooked dinner in her kitchen.

They went into the jungle near the tram station after dinner and set up their pup tents for the night. In the morning they were up early and returned to the same home for coffee, then caught a tram. It wasn't a passenger car like before, but an empty flatcar meant to carry henequen. A bit after noon they arrived at the Hacienda Chichén, headquarters for a henequen plantation. From there they hiked to the ruins.

As they walked, Vic shared with Barney an abridged version of what she read. Chichén Itzá was a Mayan city built over the course of three or four centuries. The last major construction was around 1000 A.D. It was rediscovered in the early 1800s. In 1913, the Mayan scholar Sylvanus Morley devised a plan to excavate the ruins, but The Great War and ongoing Mexican Revolution prevented actual excavation.

The ancient city lay over several acres. Most of the site appeared to be grassy hillocks and mounds. On closer observation, they proved to be stone structures concealed beneath the profusion of plants. Mounds and trees prevented a view of the entire site, but one edifice rose above everything. It solidly affirmed they were in Chichén Itzá. The jungle encroached on the structure from every direction as grass and vines sprouted from cracks in its stone surface. A number of the giant blocks were broken loose and disarranged. Yet it was unmistakably a gigantic pyramid!

The first task was to select a place to set up for the night. They were surprised to discover four pup tents and three larger tents already set up amid the ruins.

First, they met the camp cook, Maria, who spoke some English. She shared that her husband Juan was somewhere inside the ruins with the professor. When Vic asked what professor, it dumbfounded her to hear, "Professor Morley."

Vic was speechless a second, then asked, "Sylvanus Morley? That Professor Morley?"

"Si, Senorita, and Professor Smith, and many assistants."

The prospect of a conversation with Morley elated Vic. They left their gear with Maria and went in search of the archeologist. "Do you realize what a feather this will be in my cap, Barney? First assignment and I land an interview with the pre-eminent Mayan scholar in the world! Of course, assuming he will grant an interview."

Morley didn't disappoint. He was a genial man, unperturbed by non-scientists at his work site. No actual excavation was underway. Morley and Smith were making sketches and notes, to update the old plan. "Seldom anyone from the states comes around here," Morley told them. "I look forward to a good chat this evening."

Vic and Barney kept busy the rest of the day as they wandered the over-grown city and took photographs. Her anticipation for the discussion over dinner made the time drag for Vic. It would delight her editor if she interviewed someone who was becoming a legend in his field, yet, Vic was even more excited to learn. She never tired of learning new things.

Vic read about Morley and some of his work. She considered it no overstatement to say he was the caliber of Stanley and Burton. H e n r y Stanley was a reporter. He became a hero in 1871 when he found David Livingstone who went missing in Africa for a year. Sir Richard Burton was a well-traveled soldier of the East India Company who spoke twenty-nine languages. Both men were internationally renowned. Morley appreciated the compliment but was modest and considered it a bit of a stretch.

161

At dinner that evening Vic kept the professors busy with questions. She noted every word in her journal. The plan for excavation was years old, and nature does not wait for man. Rumors ran that the Mexican Revolution might end soon. Morley wanted to update his excavation plan, so when he received a go-ahead, the actual dig could begin immediately. He told Vic it would take decades to recover the entire city.

Among other things gleaned that evening, Vic learned that an American owned Chichén Itzá. The Carnegie Institute in Washington, D.C. would fund the excavation.

The giant pyramid was El Castillo built to honor a Mayan deity, Kukulkan, the feathered serpent. Morley promised Vic a tour the next day to climb El Castillo and also see the sacred cenote. The terrain of Yucatán is largely limestone and cenotes are sinkholes in the limestone. Because there are few rivers or lakes, cenotes are the prominent source of water.

Of the three large tents, one served as quarters for Juan and Maria and to store supplies. The other end tent was quarters for the two professors. The middle tent served as the kitchen, dining hall, and office. They enjoyed dinner in the open by the light of campfires and torches and afterward, they moved to the middle tent for coffee and more conversation.

For a while, talk centered on the flu pandemic which at long last was abating. For three years it brought death to every corner of the globe. Millions died worldwide. The flu was responsible for more death than the Great

War. Vic and Barney both lost friends.

Then Professor Morley brought up cenotes again and described another role in Mayan life. The Maya used them in sacrifices to the rain god Chaac. One sacrificial method in particular interested Professor Morley. They gave the sacrifice a licorice flavored alcoholic drink made from miel y anís - honey and anise. They hoped it would induce a vision. Once the victim was sufficiently intoxicated, he or she was thrown into the cenote. They rescued victims who experienced a worthwhile vision and shared it. Otherwise, they allowed the victim to drown.

Of course, the professor happened to have some of the concoction for Vic and Barney to try. Vic took one sip. "It's actually tasty," she said. "I guess there could be more unpleasant ways to leave this world." She envisioned someone impaled on a horn of Ta, the wooly rhinoceros.

One sip was all Vic would have. She explained how she saw men return from the war and sink into addiction. Alcohol destroyed their health and families. Vic decided even if odds were slim that she might succumb, she wouldn't chance it. Potential results were so devastating that no odds were acceptable.

Amid their conversation, Vic glanced toward the rear of the tent. Suddenly, goose skin mottled her arms. Leaned against the back wall of the tent was a spear. Its head was a shaped and sharpened stone. It fitted into a split at one end of a stout limb, held in place with leather strips.

Vic pointed to it and asked, "Where did you get that spear?"

Morley told Vic of a graduate student helping them. "He is a genius at reconstructing ancient tools," Morley said and brought the spear to Vic. Goose skin rose again when she saw the fourteen notches below the stone head.

The professor noticed her reaction. "You know something of primitive weapons? This is an extraordinary replica, and Oliver made it using only tools a primitive man would have."

Vic glanced at Barney when she saw the weapon. He noticed too, but neither, of course, said anything. It could have been the mate of the broken spear in a certain cave in Africa.

Vic stood to admire the spear, and ran a finger over the fourteen notches below the stone head. Then she drew it back in a throw stance and hefted it twice before she returned it to the professor. "It is a fine weapon," she nodded her certainty. "The kind of weapon that could kill a saber-toothed cat."

"I don't know about that," Smith said. Without hesitation and with absolute confidence Vic replied, "I know. It is a magnificent weapon, the kind that only a great hunter would carry. It is heavy, and I have no doubt that the right man or woman could use it to pierce the cat's heart." Vic's authority and conviction left the professors speechless for a moment. Finally, Smith said, "I think women would never use a spear, but simply gathered fruits and cured hides."

Vic had what Barney dubbed her "attack" smile, and her reply was aggressive. "We speak of a time when creatures roamed which could rip you apart and devour you in seconds! The best food weighed ten tons and could crush a dozen strong and good men just turning around. If more spears were needed, women did not stay back to pick berries, and even older children would join the kill and learn! And when women didn't attend the hunt, they must be ready and capable of protecting the camp against enemies! It was a matter of survival. Women of the stone age claimed more pluck and resourcefulness than either women or men of this pampered age!" Vic's face flushed and her eyes for an instant looked like black opals.

For moments no one spoke. Then Professor Morley smiled and nodded. "I have never heard that argument nor the situation described with more conviction or eloquence! Victoria Custer, you should become an archeologist! Your insight makes you a natural."

Vic relaxed and chuckled. "Thank you, Professor Morley. I am honored that you would think such a thing, but for now, I'll stick to travel writing for the public. Primitive life and weapons are...just a hobby." Morley noticed Vic's keen attention to the notches on the spear haft, so asked if she had a theory. "The simplest answer is often the correct answer. They may be like notches on the gun of an Old West gunfighter, a simple testimonial for each major hunt."

Morley thought it was not implausible and shared that Oliver said it was simply the way he learned to do it. Vic wanted to meet Oliver.

"Unfortunately, Oliver is away right now," Morley told her. "Oliver and another graduate student went to investigate rumors of another pyramid between here and Tulum. I can't say when he might return."

Later, as they crawled into their tents, Barney asked, "Is that true about the notches?" V i c nodded. "Yes. Older warriors earned so many they no longer bothered. Younger men wanted to show their experience. Nu participated in fourteen successful mammoth hunts, and he was still a teenager by our count."

Chapter 15

Killer Swarm

Vic was up before the sun and joined the workers around a fire for coffee. They shared their breakfast of coati strips and armadillo meat kabobbed over the campfire with baked plantain.

All the workers were Americans, so there was no problem with communication. When questioned about their work, though, they offered little information. The archaeologists came out as the sun beamed its first streak of light over the trees. Vic stood and said, "Perfect timing! May I take a photo with the sunrise behind you?"

Vic snapped photos and took notes about the ball court where the Mayans played a game called pitz. Everyone played pitz for recreation, but there was also a grimmer purpose. Groups often settled arguments with a pitz match and the leader of the losing side was executed, or so some scholars thought. Morley believed they sacrificed the leader of the winning team as an honor. He got to go to heaven.

Vic made notes at the site for an hour then Morley led her to the top of El Castillo. The view from atop the pyramid was magnificent, so Vic took several photos. Then Morley showed her a stairway which disappeared into the core of the pyramid. "Strangest thing. It just dead ends. It's a stone wall at the bottom. Stairways are not made to go nowhere. There must be a hidden door, but discovery will need to wait until full excavation begins."

Vic wanted to go down and to take a photo. "I have flash sheets. It would be the first photo of the inside, wouldn't it?" she asked. Indeed it would be the first photo of the interior, and Morley agreed. Vic fetched a flash sheet, and the holder and Morley went to retrieve a surveyor's tripod and lantern.

Back atop El Castillo, they lighted the lantern and went down the stone stairs. A few steps in, the professor looked back at Vic and told her, "There could be snakes or rats down here you know." With a smile, Vic reassured him, "I tolerate rats, and I eat snakes."

"I can believe that," he replied. At the bottom, Morley pointed out a slim line on the wall. It formed a rectangle about five feet high and three feet wide. The line seemed deeper than the space between other stones, and he believed it might be a doorway. Vic wanted a photo of the professor against that end wall, so she prepared her equipment.

The professor took a position against the wall as Vic set the camera on her tripod. She set the f-stop at 11 and attached a sheet of flash paper in the holder. She stepped to the side and an arm's reach behind the camera. "Smile and stand perfectly still until I say," Vic told Morley, then opened the shutter and struck a match.   She faced the flash paper to Morley and pushed the burning match through the opening in the back of the holder.

An intense blaze flared and blinded them for a moment. Then Vic closed the shutter and said "Thank you, Professor Morley! This is far more than I dreamed for this trip."

Back atop El Castillo, Vic saw workers across the courtyard around the cenote sagral and snapped a photo. She then joined Morley making his way down the very steep steps. Loose stones and sprouted vines and grasses made it more hazardous than a simple walk down a stairway.   Vic was less than halfway down when a worker from the group at the cenote rushed past. He yelled to Morley as he passed. "¡Necesitamos escala de cuerda!"

The professor asked what was wrong and the man called back that one of the visitors fell into the sacred water.   Vic saw Barney and Jaime - Diego must have fallen into the cenote!

"There is no time for a ladder," Vic shouted, and her actions became a blur driven by pure instinct.

She bounded down surefooted, taking several steps at a leap. She more resembled a chamois negotiating a vertical rock face than a modern girl springing down a pyramid. By the time she hit the ground, her bag and camera were dropped, and she rushed full speed for the cenote.

169

"¡Quita! ¡Quita de ahí!" Vic yelled and put on more speed as she neared the men. She never slowed, and the men stepped aside. Their eyes were wide as the gringo senorita leaped over the edge of the cenote to the cold, dark water sixty feet below!

Vic kept vertical and hit the water with toes pointed. As she dropped, she noted Diego was to her right so as soon as she went under, Vic pulled in that direction.

Immediately, Vic rolled the limp Diego on his back. She towed him to the slippery wall of the cenote where a rock outcrop provided a handhold. She grasped the rock with one hand and used her legs and other arm to keep Diego's face above water. Then Vic pinched his nose and began to blow forcefully into his mouth.

Within minutes, a rope ladder was secured above and lowered to the pair. The ladder swayed from side to side as a worker hurried down. The man came down with a rope to put around Diego so they could raise his body. Everyone was sure Diego drowned.

Vic continued to blow into Diego's mouth even as the worker maneuvered the rope around the boy. The worker thought the senorita was loco. However, as he secured the rope, the boy coughed, and a gush of water came from his mouth and nose. He coughed again, and Vic stopped the procedure. She called out as men hauled Diego up, "Get him dry and warm quickly!" Vic slid both arms through the bottom rung to let her weight reduced the rope sway. As soon as Diego and the worker topped the edge, Vic clambered up the bobbing ladder.

They carried Diego to the central shelter and Maria was heating water for tea when Vic came in. He apologized for the trouble as Vic knelt on one knee beside the cot and joked that she needed a bath. Then one at a time she covered his eyes then moved her hand away to see if his pupils changed with the exposure to light. They reacted normally, so Vic stood and told him he should be OK, but ought to rest for a day.

The men were all quite impressed with Vic's actions. She shared that she was an excellent swimmer and grew up on a farm with a pond, a giant cottonwood, and a rope. A favorite entertainment as a girl was to swing over the pond and drop. Vic laughed as she related how her mother admitted the same activity growing up - so the jump was nothing.

Vic explained the breathing into Diego. It was a little known technique called expired air ventilation. It was first demonstrated by Dutch physicians over a century earlier. It only seemed to work when started quickly. If Vic hesitated, Diego likely would have died.

"Quite impressive, Miss Custer," said Morley. "Writer, astronomer, mathematician, primitive weapons expert, photographer. Crackerjack diver and trained in emergency medical care to boot." Vic laughed and replied, "All farm girls grow up to be a Jill-of-All-Trades!"

Vic postponed the trip to Tulum for twenty-four hours. Vic didn't want to break up their group but wanted Diego to rest a day. Since she wanted to do some day hikes anyway, she could hike and take photographs for a day then go as planned.

Vic hiked alone so she could write about it accurately and honestly say she did it. After Vic's performance the day before, no one tried to dissuade her from a solo hike, but they did give advice. Don't go farther than you can return from before dark. Don't corner a jaguar and if you see one don't run because it may instinctively consider you prey. Watch for snakes. Avoid contact with anyone except a family. A lone man or small group of men could be banditos, mal hombres. Morley put particular emphasis on this last advice.

Vic assured everyone she would be OK and took a recently sharpened machete with her. She carried it to cut through the jungle. Without saying so to the others, for Vic, it would also be an adequate weapon. Vic took a journal, pen and ink, camera and two rolls of film, smoked squirrel strips and a canteen of water.

There were no trails to the northwest, so Vic went that direction toward no specific target. She wanted to take photographs and write first-hand about chopping through the dense jungle under a tortuous sun. It excited Vic to imagine how much more difficult and adventurous it was for early explorers. They traveled with less equipment, no map, and no knowledge of the plants, animals, and natives.

The jungle was sparse for a few seconds. Vic could push aside most lianas and brush, or step over or stoop under. A hundred yards into the jungle she ran into a solid green wall. She pulled her machete from its sheath and began whacking. It was already hot at eight in the morning. Vic knew swinging a machete can wear a person down in short order. Thus, she chopped a path just wide enough to slip through. Vic navigated by compass and aimed directly northwest. She peered through the brush to select a notable feature which fell on the desired azimuth. After she reached that object, she chose another target along the same azimuth and hiked to it.

Her bearing wouldn't be exact but would keep her from veering too much. Without some method, she knew that in a dense jungle she could actually start to wander in circles. It is human nature to take the path of least resistance, unconsciously and if that makes a circle, that's where we go.

After an hour of cutting through extreme jungle, Vic got a break. She cut through to a small, but obvious trail. Only about two feet wide and four feet high, it had branches forming an arc above. Vic knew it was an animal track used by larger animals like peccaries, tapirs, and jaguars, and probably it led to a watering hole.

Vic cut a large X on a tall tree at the spot. To return she would retrace the game trail to her mark, then follow her own cut path back to Chichén Itzá.

In hopes to snap a photo of some animal, Vic pulled her camera out and moved as alert and as quietly as the tangle allowed.

She heard howler monkeys often, but they kept out of sight. She did manage to snap a photo of a woodpecker.

Half an hour after she began to follow the game trail, Vic heard something in the jungle ahead. She could tell it wasn't small, and it was coming toward her at a respectable pace, so she was ready with her camera. Vic knew a jaguar wouldn't be making that much noise and they often sleep in the day. So whatever it was, she suspected it would stop when it saw her and go back the way it came.

Within seconds two tapirs broke through the jungle no more than twenty feet ahead. The larger one stood a good four feet high, and Vic guessed it would weigh around four hundred pounds. The other was almost as large. They looked straight at Vic, and their ears stood up and one snorted. Yet they never slowed but lumbered toward Vic at a slow trot.

Vic didn't fear they would attack, but they obviously wanted to pass. Getting hit by a pair of four hundred pound animals at a run couldn't be healthy, so she snapped one photo and stepped aside. The duo rushed past with more snorts and disappeared into the jungle.

Vic got goose skin, and all her senses heightened. Then the thought came. Tapirs are nocturnal and don't like people. Yet they were in a hurry in the heat of the day and passed   undeterred   by   her   presence.

Something they disliked or feared more than a human must be behind them. Vic rolled the camera film for another shot, then pulled the machete from its sheath and listened.

For a full two minutes, Vic stood stone silent. Something didn't seem right, but at first, she couldn't identify what. Then she realized she could hear howlers and birds behind, but not ahead. Straight ahead, from where the tapirs came, the silence seemed threatening.

Vic sniffed for a predator scent, but there was none, so she advanced to discover the mystery.

After a few yards, Vic came to a fork. Freshly broken limbs told her the tapirs came from the left. She went left and in minutes heard movement in the underbrush. At the same time, she encountered a parade of small creatures crossing the trail from her left to right. Scorpions, centipedes, grasshoppers, beetles, mice, and lizards were all in a mass exodus from exactly where she was headed.

Vic glimpsed something strange about twenty feet into the jungle on her left and stopped. The brown-black weaving motion seemed like a snake, but it was more than a foot wide!

Vic could not resist the intrigue. She pushed some branches aside and took five steps and stopped cold! The moving black-brown mass was a column of ants. A colony of millions of flesh-eating army ants was on the march!

At her feet, ants swarmed over a lifeless snake, and all along the column workers carried whole insects. Others carted chunks of flesh torn from larger animals.

Vic slid the machete back into its sheath. She snapped one photo of ants dissecting the snake and another of the central ant column.

Then she noticed dozens of ants on her trouser legs. None were in her clothing yet, but they were climbing. Vic brushed ants from her as she backed away from the ominous mass. The ants didn't move fast enough to run a person down, and the central column was several feet away, but scouts were everywhere. She knew from reading that ants at the front of a column spread into a fan shape to detect prey over a wider area.

As fast as Vic brushed ants off, more came. She read the bites were extremely painful and held no desire to verify the fact. She also knew that if she was bitten, somehow scouts communicated to the main column they found more food.

Walking sideways to keep an eye on the column, Vic moved faster. She first walked parallel to the ant column so she now should be moving perpendicular and away from it. She was at least 20 yards from where she encountered the column. Still, there were so many scouts, and she wondered why.

Vic decided she might need to run a bit, so while still moving, she re-sheathed the machete and pulled off her pack. She wrapped the camera in her rubberized poncho and slipped it inside then slung the pack on again. Vic tightened the pack straps to cut bounce, and pulled the machete to clear a path.

Vic knew the distance a swarm would move on a raid was no more than 500 - 600 feet in a day. By now, she should be at least 200 feet from her nearest contact, yet the population of scouts was increased. Suddenly, Vic heard a howl. It was a howler monkey in trouble and in pain, and it was dead ahead!

Most of her attention was forward, but on a glance to her left, she glimpsed a brown ribbon in motion. Right away she knew it was the horde of ants! She was parallel to the central column again, and that horde was now only ten feet away! Vic quickly realized the path of the swarm made a right angle turn, and she turned with it. She still walked with the deadly column, but now was nearer!

Three things happened simultaneously. A snake covered with ants slithered non-stop over her boot. Another scream brought her attention to the young howler. He was less than ten feet ahead and rolled and slapped at hundreds of ants!

Vic understood that confusion was the danger to an able-bodied person or monkey. Multiple bites could cause incredible pain and encourage an attempt to remove ants. That distracted from what the victim most needed to do - get away to avoid attack by more ants!

The third occurrence at that moment of decision was a sharp, fiery pain on the back of her neck. An ant made its way up! Something must happen immediately!

Vic stood under a monkey pod tree and above the howler was a horizontal limb with a six-inch diameter. The limb was just low enough for Vic to reach so she again slipped

177

the machete back into the sheath. Vic felt another bite under her collar and crushed the ant in place. Without hesitation, she took two bounds, jumped for the limb, and caught it with both hands.

She pulled herself onto the limb in time to crush another ant beneath her shirt after it bit her. Vic took two steps, and the howler was directly below her and fought hopelessly against an increasing number of ants.

Vic sat on the limb and leaned back and over until she was hanging by her knees. She was about to reach down for the howler when she saw another snake crawling along the limb toward her. In two seconds, she released the safe tie and drew out the machete.

The snake was about a foot from Vic and assumed an S-shaped strike stance. V i c swung the machete and buried it in the limb. The snake's head came off and fell to the ground and reflexes wrapped the body around a smaller branch.

Vic looked down at the howler. It was young, and she guessed its weight at about fifteen pounds. She thought it would be safer to grab the monkey by the neck, but on her first attempt, she couldn't quite reach it.

Then the howler's tail flailed in the air, so Vic grabbed it and sat up as strange sounds came from her throat. The sounds were a language as old as man and once shared by the apes and people of another time. The words flowed from the mouth of the twentieth century Victoria Custer with ease, and she understood.

The young howler understood as well.

She pulled the monkey up, and it leaped onto the limb where Vic helped brush ants off. Then it told Vic it never saw an ape like her before and thanked her in a sound you and I would think was a growl. Vic nodded, and the howler ran down the limb and disappeared into the thick canopy.

Vic was well balanced and relaxed on the narrow limb but collected more bites under the cuff of each sleeve. She crushed those intruders and brushed more ants off then recovered the machete from the limb and sheathed it. Ants were already harvesting the snake's flesh. Vic brushed them off and stuffed the snake into her pack.

More ants were climbing the tree, so Vic ran to the trunk and pulled up to a higher limb. After a quick survey of the surrounding trees, Vic went along that limb to where it ran side by side a similarly sized limb from another monkey pod. She leapt without slowing, and the limb bounced from her weight, but her balance was steady. Not once did fear arise.

From that tree, she moved nimbly to another and then another, as surely-footed as a jungle squirrel. Vic traveled at heights greater than fifty feet above the earth. Never did Vic feel concern as she leaped spans of six or seven feet.

Dozens of trees later, Vic knew she must be at least 300 yards from the swarm and was no longer in danger. She descended to a low hanging limb and without hesitation dropped ten feet to the jungle floor.

Chapter 16

The Beast!

The ants were no longer a threat, but Vic had several bites. One in particular, above her left thumb, was very painful, so Vic examined it. This bite was from a true soldier. It was huge beside the other ants. It also sported larger mandibles that curve and lock inside the victim like a fish hook. When Vic brushed at the bite through her shirt, it pulled the ant apart, but its head was still embedded. Using one tool she would always carry, Vic pulled out her tweezers to pry the mandibles free one at a time. She found a whole ant inside her shirt which she swatted as it crawled up her side.

Vic wrapped the small trophies in a page from her journal and stowed them in her pack. She hoped the photographers at the paper could make close-up photographs.

Next, Vic pulled out the dead snake. The upper skin was brownish-green with dark triangles, and the belly was cream. She skinned the reptile and in a few minutes rolled the skin like a narrow scroll and placed it into her pack. It would make a gorgeous hatband or belt.

Vic stared at the skinned body of the snake. Finally, she shrugged and took one bite of the flesh. She ate that bite then another. Then she made a face and tossed the carcass aside. She thought, *Not bad, but I would prefer it fried, with onions, and salt and pepper.*

Vic took a drink from her canteen, and that was the last mouthful. It was mid-afternoon, so she needed to begin her way back to the ruins. She decided not to search for water but to drink from vines and watch for a cenote as she traveled.

An hour later, as Vic found a mango tree and knocked a fruit down, she heard a loud slosh. Vic pulled the mango open with her fingers and ate the juicy pulp as she went toward the splash.

She came to a clearing on a steep incline that ended at a pool of water at least thirty feet across. It was a cenote with walls collapsed on two sides. That allowed her to walk to the water's edge where she squatted and held the mouth of her canteen underwater to fill.

The canteen was half full.

Vic's eyes were on the canteen, so her peripheral vision may have warned her. Maybe it was the primitive survival instincts she reacquired in Africa. Whatever it was, anyone with lesser reflexes would have died the next second. Vic let go the canteen and pushed herself up and back from the squat as the water exploded where she knelt. In the space she occupied but an instant earlier, the savage jaws of a crocodile clamped shut!

When Vic thrust herself back, the crocodile followed. She leapt back twice more before the reptile stopped, hissed, and retreated into the water. As it did, Vic heard a swoosh, and a huge shadow fell over her. She tried to turn, but was suddenly grabbed by both shoulders and jerked roughly into the air!

Although the impulse did arise, Vic didn't scream. She realized it would do no good. As she experienced a sense of déjà vu, she looked up to see what creature controlled her - for now.

The thing was repulsive! She tried to compare it to a known bird simply because it flew, but no accurate comparison came to mind. The body equaled the bulk of two adult ostriches, with a wingspan of fifteen feet or more. Its beak was broad and curved like a parrot, and a fleshy mass fell over it like the wattle of a turkey. The design seemed perfect to crack nuts and seeds, but the only seed that large, which Vic knew, was a coconut.

As it flew, the great beak opened and closed. A muscular, serpent-like split tongue slipped out and receded in rhythm with the breathing. Its great bloodshot eyes bulged and withdrew within the square skull at the same cadence. One feature of the thing was more reminiscent of a bat than a bird. It had external ears like cupped hands on the sides of its head.

It held Vic tightly by the limbs sprouted from the lower body, positioned as legs. They ended in three-clawed feet and wrapped forward over her shoulders. The opposable rear facing claws pressed into her back but were blunt, so they didn't break the skin. The upper claws on the arm-hand-like limbs were raptor-like. With one swipe they could easily eviscerate any animal or Vic.

The basic shape of the thing was human, but besides the limbs placed like arms and legs, a pair rose from the back. The wings were flaps of skin attached along the flanks. They were supported by that third set of limbs and thin, rib-like extensions which folded accordion-style.

The beast's beautiful variegation amazed Vic. The primary color was pecan, with striations of white, and two tones of gray. The patterns gave the appearance of feathers. From her proximity, Vic could see the thing possessed a leathery skin.

Vic noted those characteristics within a few seconds. Then she turned her attention to the jungle below and escape. The thing flapped its way toward the declining sun and was never more than 100 feet above the tallest trees. The flight exhilarated Vic but she didn't doubt the intended conclusion would be unpleasant. A stinking, slimy drool dripped from the beak and made the flight more disagreeable. For ten minutes, the creature flapped steadily westward, ever farther from help.

The situation appeared dire, and might fill the heart of another with helplessness. Yet Vic had no inkling of defeat, even as the monster bore her toward some unknown terror. The awareness of her stupendously savage life a thousand generations before did not allow fear to exist. Defeat only came when the last breath went out. She thought, *Life is precious. I will not leave it peacefully.*

During the flight, Vic saw nothing which might help determine her position. They passed over only the densest jungle for the full flight. Finally, she saw a clearing in the trees ahead. It was a hundred yards across, and therein was an opening into the earth which half filled the clearing. Experience told Vic it must be the beast's lair and to enter would be to accept death. She subscribed to the axiom, you always lose if you don't fight back.

The beast's grip put her upper arms to a disadvantage but left her forearms and hands free. Vic drew her legs up to bring the machete handle within reach and pulled it out. Timing was important. She couldn't be over the hole, nor did she fancy a 100 foot fall into the trees. Either death or freedom was seconds away.

Vic could just reach the thing's leg. When they came to the edge of the clearing, she placed the blade of the machete against a thigh and pulled it across, as her other hand pressed. The blade sliced through the muscle with ease, and the beast released that hold. In a flash, Vic switched hands to repeat her action. The instant the beast felt pressure on the other thigh, though, it dropped her!

Vic fell from twenty feet. She tossed her weapon before she hit, slammed down hard on her side, and momentum rolled her into the hole! Inches below the surface were exposed roots from nearby monkey pods. Vic caught one with a hand, then her other hand. She swung her legs up and gripped the abyss's rim with a foot.

In seconds Vic was out and dove for the machete as the beast nose-dived for her. As she lay on her back, it hovered above her and reached with a hind talon. Vic swung and just nicked the sole. The creature jerked into the air and tilted forward. It reached with a fore talon, gripped Vic's ankle and began to rise. Her body was off the ground by a foot when Vic sat up mid-air and swung her weapon.

The thing's screech was whispery but horrible as it jerked back minus a fore claw. Blood sprayed Vic as she thudded to the ground. The creature fell to earth on its hind legs, and before it could rise again, Vic sprang up and sliced down. The machete broke a wing bone and ripped the membrane from the center through the bottom edge. Vic took the initiative. She swung at the thing again and again. It backed to avoid the machete, until it teetered at the edge of the hole for a second, then fell silently inside.

Vic went to a knee at the rim and looked down. One hundred foot trees shaded the hole, making the interior murky. Vic did not see the beast but could tell the hole opened to a gigantic cavern. Below the opening was a bone yard of skulls from humans and many animals. She laid down to see further inside, and for only a second she saw two lights in the distant recesses. They resembled carried lanterns. Then she heard what sounded like a human voice and the lights were gone. Vic rolled away from the hole before standing. The idea that people might be in that cavern was as strange as the beast.

There was no time to ponder. The creature carried Vic miles. She could not return to Chichén Itzá before nightfall, but she could put distance between her and the cavern. The appendage Vic hacked off still gripped her ankle, so she pried it free and stuffed it into her pack. She set an azimuth the reverse of what she traveled that morning. She would not try to be exact but would bear left since she veered left coming. If she missed the game trail, that should eventually take her to Chichén Itzá. If she missed the ruins she would hit the north-south tram rail which lay beyond. Until an hour after sunset, she alternated a lope and rapid walk. Then she mounted the heights of a monkey pod and slept.

By evening on the day Vic set out on the hike, everyone became worried as night settled. By then, it was too dark to send out a search, so instead, they built a fire atop El Castillo. The flames were visible for a considerable distance and would guide Vic if she traveled after dark. Barney nursed the blaze until midnight and scrutinized the jungle for movement or light from a fire or torch.

The next day, two search parties went out. Each ventured as far as they supposed Vic could travel then returned by a different route. Barney accompanied the group which came upon the collapsed cenote. They spotted Vic's canteen in the water, and when a man tried to retrieve it, the croc surfaced. Everyone but Barney felt sure that Vic fell victim to the croc.

In Africa, both Barney and Vic learned a great deal about tracking. He pointed out that there was no blood nor any of Vic's gear or clothing. Tracks showed she went to the water, knelt, then stood and backed up. There were croc tracks in the mud, but they did not go as far as Vic's tracks. To settle the matter, they performed an impromptu autopsy. Though already sure it didn't get Vic, it relieved Barney to find no human remains inside the animal.

The following day was the same for Vic. Chop and walk; chop and walk. She often stopped to pick fruit or to cut a liana for water. She did not forget her vocation and stopped twice for photos - once for a brood of peccaries and then a squirrel. A bit before darkness, she again found a safe, suitable tree and slept.

Others gave up hope the afternoon of day three, but Barney planned to take Diego and Jaime out one more day.

On day three, Vic again began her journey at first light.

An hour before darkness, Vic stumbled upon the open game trail she followed the first day. As the sun sank below the horizon, she found the "X" she marked and decided to forge ahead in the darkness. Two hours after night settled on the moonless night, Vic spotted a fire, high, two hundred yards or so ahead. Barney decided to light the beacon fire one more night, and that guided Vic into the ruins of Chichén Itzá.

Vic thanked them for the signal fire and apologized for the worry. She assured them she was fine, so they wanted to hear about her ordeal. No one had eaten, and Vic was hungry, so she suggested she tell her story over dinner.

Vic washed up, and they all convened in the dining tent. Maria served squash, beans, tortillas, and shredded meat and Vic piled her plate high.

"This isn't howler is it?" Vic asked Maria.

"No, senorita, esta carne de venado."

"Yummy! I love deer."

Then Vic had a little fun with the tale.

"Well, first, I was nearly trampled by a pair of 400-pound tapirs. A swarm of army ants stampeded them and I inadvertently walked into it. I was bitten several times and collected these souvenirs," and she pulled out the ant trophies. "A snake intended to bite me while I hung from a tree," she related, and pulled out the skin. "By the shape of the head, I believe it was a fer-de-lance. Isn't this skin beautiful! I helped a young howler escape the ants and then followed it through the trees to safety. Then I nearly lost my head to a crocodile."

Her companions all stared in silence. Finally, Barney asked, "Are you serious?"

Vic laughed and said, "Oh yes!" Then she reached into her pack which was on the ground beside her chair and pulled out the talon of the beast. She tossed it onto the table and said, "Then things got really curious. A bit unpleasant, also." There was a uniform gasp and then more silence as they waited for Vic to continue.

She detailed her experience but offered no explanation of what the thing was. Maria listened, and when she heard the description, held her hands to the sides of her face and shook her head. "It was a thunderbird, senorita! No one has ever before escaped a thunderbird! Only those who see it from a distance live to tell!"

Vic gave the talon to professor Morley to do with as he chose. "I don't think my readers are ready for this. I have no photos, and a big bird foot would undoubtedly bring cries of hoax. I will protect my reputation for now, and let science do with this as it will. Science can make better use of it than I can."

Professor Morley seemed more interested in the lights, and possible voices, and in directions to the cavern.

After dinner, Vic asked Maria to make chillatolli, corn gruel with chili peppers, for breakfast. "Ciertamente!" Maria loved that such a pale woman from so far away enjoyed her Mayan food so much.

When the others retired, Vic first lighted a candle and wrote in her journal for 2 hours. Then she slept and dreamed of a time when days such as those just lived wouldn't be worthy of mention.

Chapter 17

Evil Slavers!

The next morning Vic was up early and eager to get moving. Already a week was lost from the planned schedule.

Vic and Barney packed their gear and with Jaime and Diego made the walk to the same tram line that brought them. It was hours until a scheduled tram, but luck was with them. A family living beside the track owned an old flatcar large enough for their group. By hand, they lifted the car onto the rails, a boy from the family hitched a burro to it, and they were off.

They rode for about twenty miles when the boy needed to return. As he moved the burro to the other end of the car, he told them about a small settlement a mile from the track. They thanked him and began to walk.

It was early afternoon when they came to the collection of small houses. As they approached, a young American met them. He was bespectacled, and wore a dirty, sweat-stained ten-gallon hat and was outfitted with twin six-guns. He appeared tense with his hands positioned at the revolvers.

Vic broke into a big smile and said, "My God, William S. Hart! Return of Draw Egan!" Vic referred to a famous cowboy actor and one of his popular movies.

The man smiled and relaxed, and said, "You're Americans."

"Yes." Barney introduced himself and the others and shook his hand. Then Vic shook hands with the man and said, "You must be a big fan of Hart."

"Absolutely! I've seen all his movies."

"Me, too!" said Vic enthusiastically.

The young man introduced himself as Jimmy Jones. It turned out he was the other archeology graduate student.

"Where y'all from?"

"Nebraska," answered Barney. "Beatrice."

"We're almost neighbors! Just a couple of states between us. I'm from Indiana," said Jones. He apologized for being so dramatic and explained.

Jimmy and Oliver with four assistants arrived early that morning. The previous morning slavers took two young girls ages twelve and ten. Nearby a woman sat on a stump, with her arms wrapped around a young girl. "That's Lupe, their mother," Jimmy said. "The little sister, Carmelita, was with them. Men surprised them in the jungle, and the older girls fought the men and told her to run."

It surprised Vic that slavers were in Mexico

as in Africa. The Civil War ended legal slavery in America, and like most people, Vic assumed it was gone elsewhere. Her own captivity in Africa fostered in her a keen hatred of the practice. It far exceeded her prior academic dislike shared by most people without personal experience. It appalled Vic when Jimmy shared some statistics. He told her slavery was pervasive worldwide under various names and for various purposes. Jimmy thought the species of vermin in this situation wanted physical laborers. They didn't try to catch the youngest, so probably she was too small to do the work.

Oliver and their four assistants set out trailing the slavers. Oliver was in charge and left Jimmy so if things didn't go well he could get their notes and maps to Morley. Aware that slavers in Africa sometimes ran in bands of a hundred or more, Vic asked Jimmy how many men Oliver was tracking. The little girl said there were about a dozen, but from tracks, Jimmy believed there were more.

"Those are not good odds," Vic said. "Five men are up against a dozen or more, all presumably armed and no doubt vicious." Vic recalled Africa when the young native was murdered for a sprained ankle. She needed to do something. She asked if Jimmy had weapons they could borrow and offered to try to catch up with Oliver and help even the odds.

It was quickly clear that Jimmy didn't like waiting in the village marking time. After a little back and forth, he agreed to loan them weapons and go along. Jimmy gave the papers for Morley to a man in the settlement to take to Chichén Itzá. "Oliver won't like giving those papers to an unknown foreign national," Jimmy told them, "but if two civ... tourists are going after those guys I should go, too." Vic considered it odd for one graduate student to care what another might think.

Jimmy armed Barney with a pump shotgun and told him, "It's a Winchester 12, a military trench gun." It leaned against a hut, and when Jimmy went for it, Vic saw a primitive stone ax leaned against the hut with the shotgun.

Vic strode to the ax and took it up and held it before her easily with one hand. Jimmy was surprised as the ax was heavy. "It's a hobby of Oliver's. He makes primitive weapons. He has a spear with him."

"I want to take this," Vic stated flatly.

"OK," Jimmy agreed, "but take this, too." He removed a belt and gave a revolver to Vic. "Do you know how to use it?" he asked.

"Sort of," Vic answered. She strapped the weapon on, slipped the handle of the ax through the belt and said, "Let's go get the bad guys, Draw."

Barney spoke up, "I've seen Vic pull a revolver and without taking clear aim, put a bullet behind the ear of a moving coyote from fifty paces or more. Every time and I'm talking more times than I can count."

Jimmy looked at Vic and said, "Wow! I guess she can use it fine. Miss William S Hart, huh?"

Vic grinned with a guess-so-shrug.

At that point, a man standing near the mother of the abducted girls came over and spoke excellent English. "I want to help," he said. "I have lived here all my life and know the jungle well." His name was Pablo, and he was eager to assist them. He returned from visiting a nearby settlement following Oliver's departure. Otherwise, he would have gone then. So Vic, Barney, Jimmy, Pablo, Jaime and Diego, started off to help rescue the abducted girls. Two were armed with firearms, three with machetes, and Vic was armed with a firearm and a primitive war ax as hunters used 100,000 years earlier.

They began where the men grabbed the girls. Their pace alternated from a fast walk to lope. During a walk period, Vic asked Jimmy about Oliver and the weapons. He told her he watched Oliver make some of them and it amazed him at how fast he could create a lethal weapon. He agreed with Vic, the weapons appeared as authentic as anything he ever saw in a museum.

The march continued all day without a stop.

Next morning, they were awake before sunrise. The group rolled up their hammocks, and Pablo started a fire within 3 minutes. Jimmy packed a good supply of venison jerky which they shared along with a cup of coffee each. By first light, they continued after the slavers. A mile later they came to a fork. It was clear the slavers and Oliver both took the trail headed right. Pablo hesitated, and Vic asked about it.

Pablo explained. The path taken by the slavers led to a small settlement about five miles away. It was likely the slavers went that way to kidnap more children. Pablo figured they would then go south to other small settlements of a dozen or fewer families.

They could follow the trail on the right and attempt to catch Oliver, or they could take the path to the left, and try to get ahead of the slavers.

"If I am wrong, we may lose them, but I think very much this is how they will go," Pablo said. Vic trusted Pablo's instincts, and it made sense. As though rehearsed, Vic, Barney, and Jimmy all said, "Let's go left." They knew it was time for a plan, too.

"I know Oliver," Jimmy told them. He was sure Oliver wouldn't take rash action. He would follow within striking distance and look for an opportunity with a good chance of success. "He will likely be near the slavers to their rear. If we can get ahead and spring an ambush, Oliver can rush in like the cavalry. Of course, our plan should assume Oliver is nowhere near and be capable of success whether he shows up or not.

Jimmy asked Pablo if he knew of a place where they might set a good ambush. He wanted an area they could reach before the slavers, and terrain that limited where the slavers could run.

After a few minutes of deliberation, Pablo had an answer. He described a stretch where the slavers path made a ninety-degree turn. A wall of jungle blocked movement to the left for twenty-five meters. To their right was a six-foot vertical drop, an intermittent stream, dry this time of year.

Jimmy summed it up. "If I picture it right, one armed person in the creek bed, one in the jungle up ahead, and one behind at the right angle turn. We'll have them in a 25-meter kill zone with fire from 3 sides. The dense jungle will make it difficult to run on side four. Like shooting fish in a barrel if it wasn't for them shooting back. Jaime, Diego, and Pablo, one each with the others to be a second set of eyes and ears and close quarters if it comes to that. You have machetes, do you have any problem using them?"

The three said the cause was just, and they would use the machetes without hesitation.

"Good," said Jimmy. "These guys are bad. They will not walk away, surrender or negotiate. Once we engage, it will be to the death."

They continued. Pablo led, followed by Jimmy then Vic. Vic said to Jimmy as they walked, "You seem to know a lot about ambushes, and you're an archeologist? You sound military and sure look the part."

Without looking back or losing stride, Jimmy answered, "Just a hobby."

That amused Vic - that was the line she gave Morley when he asked about something she didn't want to explain.

Barney heard and moved up and tapped Vic on the shoulder. She looked at him, and he held a finger to his lips then pointed to the butt of the trench gun. There was a stamp, *USN.*

Barney whispered, *Navy*, and dropped back.

A mile later, they left the trail and plunged into dense jungle. After a few minutes, the jungle opened up, with less undergrowth. They followed what almost seemed a trail. It was a wide channel where rain flowed when it came down too fast to be absorbed.

It was about noon when Vic's group reached the ambush site. When Jimmy saw the location, he said, "Excellent! This is right out of a field manual!"

"You really get into your hobby, don't you Jimmy," Vic said, and Jimmy ignored her.

After some discussion, the plan unfolded. Barney was positioned with the trench gun at the right angle in the trail, centered behind the slavers. Jimmy with a revolver would post a little off center to their front. Vic would wait in the stream bed with a revolver and rocks. Vic suggested a twist which Jimmy finally agreed to. She would begin the assault with rocks. She was a dead aim with a baseball-sized stone and Vic's reasoning: "A stone is silent until it hits some guy's noggin. I can take out a couple of guys before they know what's happening." When attention turned to Vic, the others would open up. Barney and JJ would fire one at a time, in succession, to confuse and rattle the slavers. Hopefully, that would let them cut the odds way down before a give and take gunfight ensued.

After they settled the physical preparation, Jimmy spoke to Vic. "You're obviously fit and smart, and you may be a good shot, but I have never known a woman who..."

Vic tightened her fist. Barney feared she might punch the guy, so he stepped forward and said, "Don't worry about Vic. She has nerves of steel. In Africa, I saw her stand her ground without a flinch and drop a charging rhino just ten paces before he reached her." He didn't mention the cave or the lion or leopards. Barney also thought about a few days earlier out of Chichén Itzá, but he didn't need to say any more.

Vic said, "I guarantee I will do what needs done. However this day ends, if I don't try to help those children, I doubt I could ever sleep again. You do bring up a good point. Jaime, Diego, Pablo. You only have machetes. If you want to go into the jungle and wait, there is no shame in that. You are nearly unarmed against men with pistols or rifles."

Jaime and Diego answered together, "I'll stay." Pablo said, "As you senorita, I would never again rest if I do not act. The children are not animals or things for men to buy and sell. I will do what is needed."

So Jaime went with Vic, Diego with Barney, and Pablo with Jimmy and they all waited in silence.

An hour and a half after the three pairs were settled into their positions, they could hear voices from up the trail. The slavers were coming!

Chapter 18

Deadly Gunfight!

In his apology for ruining the nest of a field mouse, in the eighteenth century, Robert Burns wrote, The best-laid schemes of mice and men often go awry. Approaching the status of a universal law, that force was at work that day on the Yucatán Peninsula of Mexico. Small bushes grew along the edge of the creek bed in several places. Vic took position behind one of those. It would put her about center of the slavers when they entered the ambush zone.

Six men came into view and behind them were two young girls and four boys all tethered together at the waist. Beside the children, evenly spaced, were three more men. Vic's determination elevated and her focus sharpened when nine more men came behind the children. There were eighteen well-armed slavers, without a conscience among them! She tightened her hold on the stone in her right hand and loosely held the stone in her left. Another was lying in an indentation of the earth where she could grab it quickly.

As the lead men passed Vic's location, the smaller girl stumbled and fell. One of the men jerked her up roughly and slapped her. "Stop holding back!" he shouted and drew back to slap her again. Before he could strike, the older girl jumped on him and scratched his face as she yelled, "Leave my sister alone!" The man punched the girl off. As she hit the ground, he pulled the rifle from his shoulder and shrieked, "I will kill you for that!"

Pablo screamed "No!" and jumped up. Jimmy tried to grab him, but he was out of reach. Vic heard Pablo running.

Oh God! was the only thought with time to fly through Vic's mind. She stood, and with no hesitation, she sent the first stone at the head of the man who threatened the girl.

Pablo charged the front men with upraised machete. The second stone was on its way when Vic heard the first man's skull crack.

A slaver fired, and the bullet ripped through Pablo's right lung!

Vic sent the third stone at another slaver as she heard the second skull crack.

The children all dropped to the ground and huddled.

Pablo's machete flew with deadly accuracy. It split the breastbone and sliced the heart of the man who shot him, and the slaver fell dead without a sound.

The remaining slavers saw where the stones

came from and Vic ducked as they all fired on her position.

Pablo dropped on all fours and spit blood.

Jimmy opened up with his revolver and was a deadly shot. Three more slavers lay dead by the time the others wheeled to return his fire.

Barney stood and fired as quickly as he could aim. He got off three shots and as many of the slavers fell before return fire forced him down.

When she ducked the hail of bullets, Vic dashed twenty-five feet to a new position. She now peeked over the top and saw all attention was elsewhere.

Pablo took the rifle of the man he killed. Another slaver was walking toward the trench. Pablo tripped him and put a round through his chest as he hit the ground. Then Pablo slumped on his side.

Vic stood on tiptoes and fired. The shot struck a slaver in the head, and he dropped.

The girls cried out, "Tio! Tio!"

A slaver turned to target Vic and took her next bullet in the throat.

From the ground, Pablo pointed the rifle upward at another slaver and fired. The bullet struck the man in the armpit, passed through his shoulder and his head.

As that slaver pitched backward dead, Pablo dropped the rifle and rolled on his back. Vic sent hot lead through the heart of another slaver before ducking a hail of bullets.

Vic heard Barney fire the trench gun twice in rapid succession. She hunted with her brother often, so figured there were two more dead slavers. Most of the remaining slavers turned their fire again on Barney.

Then Vic heard Jimmy's revolver, and another body hit the ground. She looked down the trench to see Jaime peer over the edge and throw his machete. She heard a scream and glanced over the side. Jaime's machete protruded from a slaver's leg, and he was on a limping rampage toward the boy's position!

Vic raised and fired twice at the man. The first bullet hit the man in front of his ear. On her second trigger pull, there was a click. Vic dropped behind cover just in time to avoid a bullet in front of her ear.

More shots rang out, and more bodies hit the ground.

Three slavers remained. One was the leader, and he was the proverbial trapped rat. He jerked up the older girl and held her around the waist and jammed his pistol under her chin. "Come out of hiding immediately, or I will blow her brains out!" Vic thought it curious that he spoke in English with a European accent. He hesitated for only a second then struck the girl on the crown of her head with the pistol barrel. Blood ran down the girl's face.

Barney and Jimmy were reloading.

Vic pulled the ax from her belt and grasped it so tightly her knuckles were white while rage reddened her face! She yelled don't as she jumped from the safety of the ravine.

The slaver turned his attention toward Vic, and as he did, the girl twisted away from him and fell to the ground.

The man saw a lone young woman with an ax and laughed at her. He turned his attention again to the girl and leveled his pistol at her head and smiled. "Watch her face!" He spoke the words without emotion.

With a yell so savage it once cowered the primitive long-toothed cats, Vic hurled the stone ax. That barbarous war cry of her ancient tribe reverberated through the jungle, as the ax flew unswervingly!

The leader only began to look back at Vic when her ax stuck. The heavy stone crushed his skull like an eggshell and dropped his carcass three feet back. He left this world without a sound, without pulling the trigger and without knowing he died by the weapon of choice of warriors 100,000 years ago.

Barney couldn't see what happened but sensed that attention was off him for the moment. He began to rise, the trench gun reloaded.

The final two slavers turned her direction when Vic yelled her war cry. They leveled their rifles at Vic and their trigger fingers squeezed.

 Barney saw what was about to happen, but before he could fire, two shots rang out from his left. The last two slavers fired! Their shots went wild as both pitched forward dead, each with a hole in the center of his back.

Barney looked in the direction of the shots. Vic looked in the direction of the shots.

Four young boys huddled in the clearing.

The two girls were beside Pablo, crying. The oldest was trying to stop the bleeding from his chest with a scrap of cloth torn from her dress.

Jimmy immediately began to search the pockets and packs of the dead men.

Standing in the trail at the edge of the clearing was a large man, at least 6 feet 6. His arm muscles were pronounced, he was dark from time in the sun, and his hair was shoulder length, thick and black. A stone-tipped spear hung by its rawhide thong down his back. He lowered his .45.

Behind the giant were four other men.

Jaime and Diego came into the clearing.

Vic hurried to Pablo. The older girl made a heroic effort to stay the bleeding, but it was no good. Blood flowed from the chest wound, out the exit in his back and from his mouth. His eyes fluttered. He looked at Vic and whispered, "Gracias senorita, Vic. Get them home safe, please."

"I swear it," Vic said, hiding how numb she felt. "Te lo juro por dios."

Pablo coughed blood then said, "We wondered how the day might end. For me, it ends happy. My precious nieces are safe."

Then Pablo looked at the two girls and smiled through his pain. "As a child, I played Indians and Spaniards in this very place. I love you girls. Tell my sister and your sister that I love them. Take care of each other. I do not want to see you in heaven for a very long time." Pablo looked back at Vic, stiffened and fought to speak. "I tell you, my nieces will be great women!" Then he closed his eyes and stopped breathing.

Vic stood with the girls and held them. Pablo never mentioned that the girls were his nieces. Perhaps if she knew she would have insisted on a different plan, but she didn't dwell on it. She couldn't change any of it.

"He loved you so much," Vic told them, knowing nothing she said could ease their pain. She learned that when their father died, uncle Pablo helped raise them, and taught them to read and write both Spanish and English.

Vic's only regret over the gunfight was that she didn't shoot sooner or kill faster and save Pablo.

For twenty minutes Vic listened to the girls cry and tell stories about their uncle. As they talked, Vic took out a handkerchief and wet it to wipe the blood from Juana's head wound. When she did, Rosa held out her hand and said, "Can I do it? She's my sister."

After the head wound was clean, the girls asked, "Is Carmelita safe?"

"Oh yes! Your little sister is safe with your mother. You two girls were so brave. Carmelita slipped away and was able to tell what happened. Tres niñas estás heroínas! The three of you saved one another. What wonderful sisters each of you has!"

Then the girls sat beside their uncle and Vic finally turned to the large man who saved her. He now waited with Barney and Jimmy.

"You must be Oliver!"

"That I am," he answered. Barney watched Vic closely.

Vic shook the big man's hand and thanked him. "I guess we need to get the children home now," she said. Barney sensed disappointment for Vic; in her eyes and the way her shoulders dropped when she shook hands with Oliver.

"I need a bathroom break before we begin," Vic said. She went into the jungle farther than she needed, out of earshot, and sat on a rock. She cried quietly for one minute. She swore Vic Challenger would never fail to help someone in danger. Nor would she ever hesitate, because even one second is long enough for a good person to die. Then she wiped her eyes and rejoined the group.

There was still an hour of daylight, and all agreed they wanted to leave that place. Before leaving, the girls expressed their wish to bury Uncle Pablo at home. Generations of their family rested in the small cemetery at their village. When he heard this, Oliver said, "Your wish is granted muchachas." Oliver wrapped the body of Pablo in a blanket and announced he would carry him back to their village.

They began immediately. As they set out, Vic saw Jimmy show Oliver papers taken from some of the bodies and heard him tell Oliver "No doubt. It was them, but definitely not all."

The group pitched camp just minutes before dark. Everyone collected sticks and logs to contribute to a heap of firewood. The panorama of stars beyond the jungle canopy was unbroken so promised a dry night.

They kindled a fire and everyone had a strip of jerky and a share of a coconut someone brought. Then Vic, Barney, Jimmy, and Oliver talked around the fire. The children and others fell asleep.

"You're an excellent shot, Oliver," Vic told him. "Thank you again for today. Do you practice much?"

"You're welcome," the big man answered. "No, I got plenty of practice in Argonne."

"You were in the Grand Offensive? In the Argonne Forest?" Barney referred to the massive assault by the Allies that ended the Great War in 1918.

Oliver nodded. "For sixty days there was hardly an hour I didn't get practice with either a rifle or my .45."

"Now I understand why you were calm today and able to shoot straight in the circumstances," said Vic.

Oliver did not seem inclined to dwell on the war. After a bit of general small talk, Oliver said to Vic, "Jimmy says you asked about me."

"The weapons you make," Vic answered. "They are remarkable, authentic, and built to the task," Vic tapped the ax which was back in her belt. "Where did you learn to make them so well?"

Oliver explained that a street artist taught him. "He sold his paintings leaned against a tree near my office. They were beautiful. Making these weapons was just a kind of hobby. Most of his paintings were of primitive people and animals and landscapes. His work was so realistic I thought he must be a trained paleontologist. He told me he was a self-taught artist and the ideas and images he created came from dreams." That gave Vic goose skin.

"One of his most vivid works was a Neolithic man armed with an ax like you used today. He stood over the body of a saber cat and held up its severed head in triumph. He called it *For Love.*" It seemed to Barney that his sister was in a near hypnotic state as she listened with the keenest attention.

"My favorite," Oliver told them, "was a painting of a Neolithic woman, a cave girl. It was another exquisite work of art, and the subject seemed alive. Her thick black hair fell almost to her waist, and her eyes were like black opals. Her skin was paler than I expected for a primitive human. When I mentioned it to the artist, the artist told me everything was accurate, and there was no model. She was from a dream."

Oliver paused and looked at Vic intently. Vic noticed his stare and asked about it.

"We came to the battle, you came into view, just when you threw the ax. For a moment it seemed the painting had come to life. You could be her sister. Her hair was long and her eyes were black, but for those two points and one other, you are identical to the girl in the painting." He said the third point was a scar on the cave girl's left cheek and by then Vic scarcely breathed. Through her mind raced the declaration, *My supposition seems to be correct - Nu lives again, too!*

"Every painting was for sale except the painting of the girl. He said that painting was to keep him company when he painted or hawked his work on the street."

"I told him I would pay well if he would paint another for me, " Oliver continued. "But he said no, there could only be one."

Vic questioned Oliver at length. The artist's name was Stewart James, but he liked to be called Stu. "Stu was happy to teach me to fashion primitive weapons and was reluctant to take payment for the lessons." Vic asked if Stu said where he learned the skill and Oliver admitted he never asked.

"So Stu lives in Washington?" Vic probed.

Unfortunately, Stu was a nomad. He was in the capitol for the summer but was headed for a warmer climate for winter. He didn't know himself where he would end up. He did agree that if he returned to Washington, he would look up Oliver.

Vic got information for how to get in touch with Oliver if she found herself in Washington. She also gave Oliver details to contact her and asked that he please let her know if he did see Stu again.

As conversation wound down, Vic asked if she could carry the spear and ax back to Chichén Itzá and Oliver agreed.

"May I give you this?" Oliver pulled a stone knife from his belt and handed it to Vic. "You have such a striking resemblance to the cave girl in the painting that I feel it belongs with you." Then he hastened to add, "I mean nothing unfavorable when I compare you to a cave girl."

Vic said, "I take such a comparison as a compliment, and with the greatest pride."

Barney hid his smile. He was sure Vic didn't notice. She sat more erect, pulled her shoulders back, and was grinning from ear to ear. For just a second, as she took the stone knife, her amber eyes looked like black opals.

Then the four left the dying fire and turned in.

Chapter 19

Savage Challenge!

After the others were into a well-deserved sleep, Vic lay awake marveling at that clear night sky. She both imagined and recalled, admiring such a sky long ago. The sky and its mysteries will always be beautiful. Those same stars were up there 100,000 years ago and will be there still, 100,000 years from now. It gave her strength to realize she met two lofty challenges set by herself a hundred millennia ago. She learned about numbers and the stars. Now she told herself with unwavering conviction, *I will find Nu!* Vic finally managed to fall asleep - for a short time.

Suddenly, her eyes opened, and she came to full wakefulness in the time of a blink. Instinct kept her quiet and motionless.

The jaguar is a fearless and powerful cat. It roams the jungles from the southern-most tip of South America up to the border area of Mexico with the United States. A grown cat can weigh from 100 to 250 pounds and may grow to 6 feet long. They will prey on animals which weigh as much as 600 pounds. They can kill prey with a single blow, and their bite is more powerful than either the lion or tiger. They climb trees and swim so seldom does prey escape. Derived from a Native American word yaguar, jaguar means he who kills with one leap.

Jaguars prefer to hunt at dawn and dusk but will hunt anytime if hungry. Jaguars were not uncommon in the 1920 jungles of the Yucatán Peninsula. That night, Vic's party camped within the marked territory of a large male. The cat was on the prowl for its evening meal and passed a mere 100 feet from the camp as the fire reduced itself to embers.

Twentieth-century Victoria Custer was not trained to detect the near-silent footpad of a predator. Her primitive survival instinct drafted her ancestral senses into service. Ever so slowly, nearer came soft sounds of some stealthy creature like a saber cat! Vic knew there was no more long-tooth, she knew she wasn't dreaming, and she knew about the jaguar.

Cautiously, Vic moved her hand to feel the stone dagger in her belt. When her fingers clutched the cold stone, part of Victoria thought, so what - it's a sharp rock. Yet another, deeper part of her, felt reassured and undaunted.

Vic heard sniffing and discreetly turned her head toward the sound. Her eyes narrowed. The wrapped body of Pablo lay eight feet from Vic, between the hammocks of Barney and herself. From the tree shadows beyond Pablo, the large jaguar crept and nosed the body.

Slowly, Vic slipped the stone knife from her belt and fit it between her teeth for quick access. The great cat raked the razor-like claws across the body and shredded the blanket.

To Vic, it was a desecration. Faster than deliberate reckoning could put it together, she rolled out of the hammock! As she hit the ground, she growled through her clenched teeth, her eyes ever on the jaguar. She hoped the sudden movement and growl would cause the cat to bolt for the jungle, but it chose differently.

The jaguar was only eight feet away and could easily reach her in one spring. The spear and stone ax lay beneath her hammock. When Vic rolled from the hammock, she grabbed the spear and planted the butt of the weapon on the ground. She held it firm as the great cat pounced with a blood-curdling snarl!

Vic met the savage challenge without doubt for long ago a friend shared how to kill a great cat. Your blade must find its heart. That was Vic's intention, but the stone point missed its mark. The sharp stone ripped into the abdomen, and the cat's 200 pounds drove the weapon deep. Vic felt it scrape the spine of the jaguar.

The cat twisted in mid-air to escape the impalement. The spear snapped as the cat flipped and landed on its feet astride Pablo's body. On raw instinct alone, Vic hurled herself onto the back of the cat. In a single move, she held it tight around the throat with one arm, and a tight grasp of the cat's neck hide. She wrapped her legs around its middle and locked her ankles. With her free hand, Vic took the stone knife from between her teeth.

By now everyone was awake and standing. Barney and Oliver shouldered rifles, and Jimmy was poised with both his revolvers. None saw a clear shot. A round from any of their weapons would pass through the cat and hit Vic.

Fortune favored Victoria Custer as it is ever credited with favoring the brave. Desperation, perhaps, played a part, also. Vic knew if she let go, and let the cat face her, even for seconds, she would die. The mighty jaws could rip out her throat or crush her skull with ease. A single swipe of a powerful paw could break her neck or open her belly. So even when she felt at her limit, and the muscles of her arms and legs began to cramp, Vic gave more and held tight. She called on reserves of strength she never realized she possessed. She pushed her body to the utter limits of its potential. As all the party watched first in horror, then in awe, Vic thrust the stone knife into the chest of the cat again, and again!

The salt of sweat stung her eyes and made her vision blurry as the cat whirled around and rolled to dislodge the death it sensed. It went onto its back and twisted side to side in an attempt to depose the tormentor. As it did, excruciating pain surged across Vic's abdomen that made her want to scream and let go, but she did neither.

The mortal battle lasted two full minutes, and the jaguar and Vic growled with equal ferocity. Vic finally found the heart and felt the pounding organ burst as the tip of her stone dagger pierced it. With a final screech and spasm, the jaguar laid still.

For another minute, Vic held tight. The reflexes of the cat could yet rend her flesh with those claws.   Indeed, after a moment, the cat stiffened for the last time and raked the air with lethal force. When Vic let go, she pushed the cat to one side and rolled away to the other.

Vic leapt to her feet and raised both hands high. She stabbed at the air with the bloody knife and began the primal war cry of her ancient tribe, and that brutal, unnerving howl gave a chill to the men around her. When Vic noticed their odd looks, she cut it short. "Sorry," she said. "That's a little something I picked up while in Africa." She saw Barney purse his lips and roll his eyes.

Oliver prodded the cat with the rifle barrel. "That was unbelievable," he told Vic.   "I wouldn't want you mad at me."

Vic shook with exhaustion, and her heart pounded. Her breath was labored, and her muscles ached from the effort of the battle. Yet, she managed a jest. "As long as you don't bare your fangs and pounce, you're safe!"

Jimmy just said "Wow!"

"Are you OK?" asked Barney. "Am I in a dream? I don't believe what I saw my little sister do." Then he pointed to Vic's abdomen. "The cat bled all over you." Rips crisscrossed the lower front of her shirt, and it was soaked with blood.

"No," said Vic. "I think that is mine," and she pulled up her shirt a couple of inches. Everyone gasped at the battery of gashes across her midsection.

"It's OK," Vic said. "They're not serious. Just skin deep."

Concerned about rabies, Oliver asked her, "Did he claw you or bite?"

It was neither. With a boot toe, Vic pointed at the cat's back. The tip of the spear penetrated maybe a quarter of an inch out of the back of the cat beside its spine.

Then, ever the professional, Vic said to Barney, "Snap some photographs of me and the cat, Barn. My editor should love this."

After the photos, Vic washed the wounds with canteen water. Then she gritted her teeth as Juana and Rosa applied iodine tincture from Oliver's first aid kit. As they dressed her wound, Vic couldn't help thinking how she would like to have a daughter someday. When they finished, Vic went into the jungle and changed to her one spare set of clothing.

Oliver was re-wrapping Pablo as Vic left. When she returned the fire was ablaze again, and Jaime and Diego had the jaguar hung from a tree and were skinning it. They thought she would want a trophy.

Vic didn't consider that before but decided yes she would. Vic took four claws and the incisors and most of the skin. She already had plans for the claws - one as a pendant, two for earrings and the fourth would adorn a barrette.

Each of the children got a claw. Vic also gave the girls enough white belly hide to make sashes and hair ties for them and their sister. "Pablo must have sent this cat and helped me subdue it," she told the girls. They nodded agreement and smiled proudly.

The men roasted meat from the hind legs, and Vic ate with them as they talked about past jungle adventures.

They all considered it a wondrous thing Vic did. Vic stayed silent but considered it more wondrous than anyone. Indeed, she found that the farther in time the event drifted, the more she marveled at her actions.

Everyone settled for about 2 hours sleep that night, and for the first time in her life, Vic was the last one up. Everyone else already circled a fire when she crawled out on all fours, moaning, and stood very slowly. "I have never been so sore in all my life!" she declared as she joined the others for coffee.

That day went almost as planned. They returned the abducted boys home by noon. The group needed to keep moving, but accepted a quick meal of menudo before they continued.

The next leg to the girls' home took longer than expected, and they didn't arrive until after dark. After a general heartfelt round of greetings, the older girls hugged Carmelita and told her she was a hero for telling everyone what happened. "If you didn't, they could not find us. Thank you, little sister!" Carmelita looked so proud!

All the neighbors came, and everyone was elated over the girls' return but grieved about Pablo. Thanks and blessings were bestowed on everyone, especially Oliver for returning Pablo's body. The villagers fed the troop, and once more the girls retold of the rescue and Vic's jaguar battle.

It was late before everyone went to sleep, but at sunrise, the little community gathered to bury Pablo. Afterward, Lupe came to Vic with a gift. It was a huipil, a traditional garment in the shape of a rectangle with a hole in the center to place over the head. It can be worn loose, a bit like a blouse or poncho, or tucked into a skirt. It reminded her of the Atlans' garb. Vic thought she recognized the fabric and asked to confirm. "Cieba?" It was indeed made of kapok fiber.

The troop split. Oliver asked Vic and Barney to take a locked satchel to Morley. He and Jimmy led their group to map more pyramids - *supposedly*, thought Vic.

Vic's group hiked a wagon trail which ran parallel to the rail for part of the route back to Chichén Itzá. After walking the trail for a couple of hours, a wagon came up behind them. The white-haired driver offered a ride which they gladly accepted. The man said he would drop them where they could catch a tram.

The wagon moved slowly enough that Vic

jumped off from time to time to snap a photo. Among goods the vendor carried, were papayas and cuyche or sapote fruit. Vic bought some of each for them. The ride was like a moving picnic and reminded Barney and Vic of a hayride in Nebraska. The vendor dropped them off in the late afternoon.

As the wagon pulled away, the four travelers went a few yards into the jungle to pitch camp. Diego started a small fire, Jaime collected firewood, and Barney opened a coconut. By dark, the four sat around the fire eating fresh coconut and recounted their adventures. Before retiring, they all needed to answer the call of nature. The men entered the jungle one direction, and Vic took an opposite course.

The men were soon back at the fire and shortly, Jaime and Diego crawled into their tents. It wasn't until then that Barney realized Vic was still in the jungle. He waited a couple of minutes but heard no sounds of Vic returning, so called to her. When there was no answer he became apprehensive and stepped into the jungle on the same path as Vic. Barney called out a second time and then a third and fourth. Alarm became fear, and he walked quickly into the jungle for several yards. He called again and again, but the only replies were insects and leaves rustled by the slight breeze.

Jaime and Diego heard Barney's repeated calls to Vic and joined him.   The three searched the area for an hour, but they neither found a sign nor heard a reply to their calls.

At length, Barney called the boys to join him at the fire. He felt they did all they could until morning, so Jaime and Diego crawled into their tents to get some sleep. Barney dozed but maintained a vigil. He kept fuel on the fire in hopes that if Vic were somewhere near, she could see the light.

The next day, the three searched 400 yards in every direction. Jaime walked to the rail, and when the tram came by, he asked if they saw an American woman. They didn't.

There was no moon the night Vic disappeared and she didn't carry a light with her. It didn't make sense that she would wander off into the darkness, Barney reasoned. If something attacked her, surely she would have called out. There were no footprints or broken branches to show someone passing. Vic somehow vanished without a trace within a few feet of the camp. That night, Barney again kept a fire burning.

By morning, Barney decided they should go on to Chichén Itzá. If Vic weren't injured, she could find her way back there. In the meantime, he could get help from Morley and locals who knew the area. The three caught a tram and rode atop a load of henequen back to Chichén Itzá.

Chapter 20

Dark River!

Burns and his field mice were back that night Vic vanished. Otherwise, how could picking flowers go awry?

When Vic entered the jungle, she intended to go no more than a few feet. Even in the moonless night, she spotted the tiny night jasmine blossoms ahead. Their sweet fragrance drifted to her on the night air and was like a magnet. She walked straight for the stand of the sweet fragrance to gather a small bouquet. On her third step into the carpet of vines and grass, she reached for a large sprig of the star-shaped flowers.

So suddenly did it happen Vic didn't think to call out. When her foot came down that third time, the carpet of greenery gave way and Vic plunged into utter darkness! Instinctively, she reached out, but jerked her hands back when the sinkhole wall sliced one! Vic fell for about two seconds. She called on high school physics and figured at thirty-two feet per second she likely fell about sixty-five feet.

Her hand was bleeding, and she thought of the crocodile. While she trod water, she tore the collar from her shirt and wrapped her hand. It was then she realized she was moving. She wasn't in a pool; she was in an underground river! It was slow moving, but by now she must be several yards from where she plunged inside!

The seriousness of the situation hit Vic. No one knew where she was, and she was being swept away by an underground river! Cenotes were so common that the underground of the Yucatán was often compared to Swiss cheese. That was probably how the croc made it inland. There was no way to tell where this river might take her. There could be a way out one mile ahead. Or, the next entrance might be 100 miles away! She could see nothing, and if there were crocodiles in the river her cut hand would be like a dinner bell!

Vic closed her eyes. In the dark grotto, visibility was no less with her eyes closed than open. Yet, the act produced a psychological effect as might sleep or meditation. Nat-ul was there and was pointed with Vic. "This is not the time for nerves or despair." For just a moment, Vic felt the heat of shame on her face, but for only a moment. "I do not give up!" Vic said. "I know," replied Nat-ul. Vic opened her eyes to the darkness and reassessed her situation.

I can tread water for hours. I can float for an indefinite time. Just two years ago, I swam seven miles down the Republican River. This river current is not strong, so if needed I can swim against it for a while. I was lucky to fall in water and not onto rocks. My hand has stopped bleeding. I have no other injury, and I have my knife. I will get out of here.

Vic swam from wall to wall and found the river was about thirty feet wide. She dove for a couple of seconds and didn't hit bottom, then decided to float on her back, and leave her eyes open. Perhaps she would pass below another sinkhole and see light.

To pass the time, Vic imagined all the shops she could visit in New York and all the cloches and barrettes! "Jeepers!" Vic said aloud at one point. "I would love to have a thick juicy steak right now! When we get to New York...."

Vic was unsure how long she floated but time didn't matter. A change in circumstances mattered. She knew she was in the river for a significant time, though. She dozed often and didn't know if it was for seconds or minutes or longer. She was cold and tired and hungry. She wondered more than once what it would be like for a croc to grab her in the darkness and begin a death roll. Then things changed.

Vic bumped into the wall to her right. She pushed away and found the opposite wall was only ten feet distant. Within seconds, her feet dragged bottom, so she stood in water to her waist. Vic waded across from wall to wall, then continued to move with the river. She walked for a considerable time in waist-deep water with a hand on the wall and eventually came to a ledge at shoulder level.

Moments later she found what she feared half-consciously. The river came to a rock wall and continued below the rock! She was exhausted from a very long time in the water and knew she was in no condition to make a proper decision nor to carry out whatever action she decided, so she made her way back to the ledge. She pulled herself up and found the shelf was several feet long and about two feet wide.

As she settled on the ledge, Vic realized that she was very thirsty. In spite of being in the water, she never drank, so now she reached down and brought a cupped hand of water to her mouth. It was cold and tasted good. It might carry disease, but that represented a potential future problem. Right now she needed to avoid dehydration, so for several minutes, Vic drank.

Her thirst quenched, Vic removed her boots and socks and set them away from the edge where she might kick them into the water while she slept. The prolonged immersion wrinkled her feet and hands, so she massaged them a few minutes. Finally, she secured her knife, laid against the wall, and fell into a deep sleep of exhaustion.

There was no way to know precisely, but Vic was sure she slept a lengthy time. With no sound but the movement of the river, and no light, her sleep was deep and restful. When she awoke, her stomach was grumbling, and her skin was no longer wrinkled. She drank again and recalled fragments of her dreams. In her sleep, she walked with Nu, fought saber cats, and wandered grasslands under a bright Nebraska sun where she played as a child. She stared into the darkness and asked herself what one of her heroes would do. Then she laughed aloud in the language of uprights, "More to the point, what will I do?"

Vic saw three options. She could lie there and wait for death. Second, she could fight her way back upstream and hope for circumstances to change in her favor. Third, she could dare to dive under the rock. If she dove, the river might come up into a cavern again in a matter of feet. Or it might be 100 miles before there was a place to rise again to breathe.

Vic chose to dive. She pulled on her still damp boots and socks and again checked that the knife was secure in her belt. She held her hand in the water to test the strength of the flow. Vic could hold her breath for four minutes. She could swim with the river safely for a minute and forty-five seconds. If she found no opening, she would have two minutes to return against the river.

There was nothing to gained by more deliberation. Vic dropped into the flow, took a deep breath, and lay on her back. She pulled herself beneath the water, and in the utter darkness and wet cold, she moved under the rock wall with the subterranean river. She didn't swim, but stayed on her back and pulled herself along the top. It used less energy, and if there was a cavity that could provide an air pocket, no matter how small, she might feel it. She counted as she went and pulled herself as fast as she could.

At a count of one hundred and five, she felt strong so decided to go farther. She moved blindly through the cold water for a full minute more and realized she must turn back or die. *One more second*, she thought, and reached ahead to pull herself a final time. Then she thought *just once more*, and reached again, but her hand found nothing! Vic kicked and reached upward, and seconds later her head broke from the water. She made it at least to another cavern!

The water was still waist deep, so Vic walked with the river for a couple of minutes where she came to a right angle turn.   She sloshed zigzag through the cold water and darkness. Finally, she satisfied herself that the river continued as before, but there was another way, too. The water's movement in that new direction was almost imperceptible. That might mean a dead end, so she decided to investigate.

After half an hour Vic discovered a large tree limb caught in a crevice. Farther along, there were other large limbs. No doubt they fell in through some sinkhole and washed into this side tunnel. Vic continued with an arm in front of her face to avoid jamming a limb into an eye. Before long she noticed the slippery feel of the water. There was also a rank odor. Both verified the river did not run here. It was a stagnant tributary with an end.

Vic noticed something else. The floor of the river was smooth before, worn by ages of flowing water. Now she began to kick things on the riverbed and tread over rounded objects which she was certain were not rocks. She also stepped on many stick-like materials.

Then the wall gave way to a ledge, and Vic pulled herself out of the water and crawled along the cold stone. She found the ledge to be at least several feet wide. Hope soared when she discovered an accumulation of dry tree branches back from the water.

Vic worked meticulously by touch alone to break branches into a pile of short lengths. She sat beside them in the darkness and broke many even smaller. Then she shaved some sticks with her knife until she had a double-handful-sized pile of tinder. Then she unsnapped her watch pocket and pulled out the small waterproof tin. It was the only thing she carried besides her tweezers and watch.   Hoping the tin was indeed waterproof, Vic opened it. Into her hand poured twelve precious Diamond matches - all dry!

Vic returned all but one match to the tin and sealed it. She scratched the head of the one against the strike strip on the tin. A tiny flame burst to life, but after untold hours of darkness, it was like staring into the sun! Reflex closed her eyes, but she immediately re-opened them in spite of the discomfort. The precious light of a single match could not be wasted! She held the match to the pile of tinder, and it ignited. Vic added finger-sized sticks to the young fire and once it safely blazed she jumped up and broke larger limbs to feed the flames. Soon, there was a sizable fire with a healthy pile of fuel beside it.

The next order of action was to satisfy her curiosity about the objects in the water. Vic re-entered the river and pulled up what she expected - a human skull! In the knowledge of past death, Vic found hope. There were dozens if not hundreds of skulls. Vic felt sure that many people didn't fall into sinkholes and end up here. More likely they were Mayan sacrificial victims. That made it reasonable to think there was another way into this underground cove!

Suddenly, Vic heard explosions followed by gunfire! The sounds came from the direction of the dark river and were far off. In a few short minutes, the sounds lessened and ceased. She knew now without a doubt she would get out of the cavern. Gunfire meant people, and they got in here somehow, but did she want to go toward gunfire? Mexico was having a revolution after all. She decided to make a thorough investigation of her present location first.

Right away she noted a similar stony beach across the tributary. It was much smaller than her side, and she could see both ends decline into the water.

Vic then prepared to explore her side. She feathered the end of a four-foot limb and held it in the fire until it burned steady. It could serve as a feeble but acceptable torch. She walked around and found the rock beach angled up from the water about fifty feet to a rock wall. Shortly, she discovered a breach in the wall.   It was five feet high and three feet wide, and steps led upward. Vic hurried up the stone passageway for more than a hundred feet to where it dead-ended!

For a moment she stared at the wall.   She could imagine what Nat-ul would say. Never give up until all the life has left your cold body! Vic nodded agreement with that sentiment.   The savage ways death might take her could not be counted, but this was not the day for any of that.

Vic scrutinized the wall carefully and recalled what Morley said a few days ago: *A stairway isn't made to go nowhere.* There must be a way beyond the wall. Within a few minutes, she brushed enough dirt away to expose an outline the size and shape of a door. She scraped the seam, and before long it was two inches deep along four sides. Vic pushed, but it didn't budge. By then, the torch was quite short, so she began back down the stone steps for a replacement.

Chapter 21

Return of the Beast!

As she came out of the stairwell, Vic felt a sudden sharp pain at the back of her head and fell to the ground. Her head hurt, but she didn't lose consciousness, and Vic realized she was slugged. She looked up and started to rise.

"Slow!" The European accent echoed through the cavern. A tall, bony man stood over her and pointed a pistol at her head. Caked blood covered one side of his face and blotched his hair. His clothing seemed soggy and was discolored, and he reeked strongly of gasoline and oil. His small eyes narrowed into a squint.

"You!" His voice was low but shrill and violent, and frenzied hatred contorted his face. "I'm going to kill you! Slow and painful death!"

"Who are you? Why do you want to kill me? I just want out of here," Vic said.

"You were at the cavern. You injured the beast. You almost killed it! You're the reason they found us!"

Vic remembered the light and voices as she escaped the beast. It wasn't her imagination. "If you're going to kill me, please tell me something first. What was that incredible creature?" Vic made a bid for time to think.

Luckily, the man enjoyed boasting. He was one in a band of scientists and army officers who fled Europe. They discovered the cavern and found it the perfect place to begin plans to *return in glory.*

The creature dwelt in the cavern, feeding mostly on small animals and fish. They taught it to prefer human flesh as a means to keep meddlesome locals away. His group planned to create an army of the creatures. "Finding the thing was a stroke of luck! It is a female and reproduces by parthenogenesis! Asexual reproduction! She gives birth to perfect clones, but you injured her, and the soldiers you sent, killed her brood!" Vic's wounds prevented it from flying, but he said it was otherwise well.

Vic considered what the man said, and a few facts - the only people she told were Morley and Smith. There was a definite military feel to the way Oliver and Jimmy talked and worked together. There was the 'USN' Barney pointed out on the trench gun. Her earlier, vague suspicion began to jell.

She hoped the man would look away or move closer, but he did neither, so she tried to keep him talking. For several minutes the man bragged how they would get even. Eventually, though, he seemed to tire of listening to himself. Vic knew time was running out.

"How did you train the beast? Is it like a pet now?"

"A pet?" The man's laugh sounded insane. "The thing is wild and ferocious, a natural killer. It could never be a pet, but it understands power and pain. A whip and a club - that's how I made it do as I bid!"

He looked at the dying fire and smiled. "I am tired of talk." He looked straight at her, and then an ugly form of good fortune cast its gracious shadow on Vic.

Something rose into the gloom of the cavern from the cold, dark river. It was the hideous flesh-eating beast the man boasted of beating. It came up behind the man, and its movements were smooth and quiet like a predator.

"Is that your plan? To feed me to that?"

"What?"

"Your beast, there," Vic said and looked beyond the man with a nod.

"Fool! Do you think I would fall for..." As the thing opened its beak, there was a sigh, and the man tilted his head back to look up. Like a giant piston, the opened beak slammed down!

The man tried to twist away and made a half scream before the parrot-like beak snapped shut on his skull!

Vic jumped aside just as the man's dead finger pulled the trigger.

Part of the man's brains became a messy projectile squeezed from one side of the beast's mouth while the rest of his head was mangled and gulped. A round hit the rock wall behind where Vic stood a second before. At the same time, the pistol fell from the dead hand, and she caught it in mid-air. Vic started for the stairs, but the beast stepped between her and the doorway!

Vic raised the pistol, but the creature snapped out a wing, and the bony edge smacked the weapon from her hand!

Against the weak firelight, the beast was little more than a silhouette. That was enough for Vic to read the movements when it raised a lower leg and struck at her like an ostrich!

Vic dodged and stepped back, and the creature stepped forward and clawed again.

She jumped back and tripped over a rock and fell. Lightning fast the creature leapt at her. Vic rolled just as the beast slammed a ponderous foot down!

Vic came up but stopped half standing as the creature again clawed at her with a foot. She twisted and stepped to avoid the attack, but the claw hit her shoulder and shredded her shirt and raked a bloody furrow in her back!

The blow knocked Vic down, and she rolled again and again until her hand splashed the water. There she stopped and looked back. The beast stepped toward her, so Vic went up to a squat and dove into the river. The rock beach was only thirty feet away and in three seconds Vic pulled herself up, and at that same instant, she heard the massive beast hit the water!

On hands and knees, Vic waited and listened. In seconds, the form of the creature showed against the faint glow of her dying fire.

The creature had to be surprised. As it rose from the water, Vic pulled the only weapon she had, the stone knife Oliver gave her. The cavern reverberated with the war cry of her ancient tribe. Vic hurled the knife at the center of the shadow as she charged it!

The creature's wings had a reach of three arms' lengths. Just short of its grasp, Vic angled, took two leaps, dove into the river again and stroked with all her might!

Vic came out on the other side and began to search for the pistol. Little more than embers remained of the fire, so the light was nearly gone! She heard the creature hit the water again! Her eyes desperately combed the dark beach for the pistol. At the same time, she dragged a foot to feel for it!

The creature came up from the water, and she heard it approaching when she tripped on the body. Vic remembered how she reacted when she struck the first match. She went down on a knee beside the dead man and dug in her pocket.

Vic couldn't see the thing, but the footfalls told her it was almost within striking distance!

She opened the tin of matches and poured them in her hand then let them all drop but one. If it didn't work, there would not be time for another! She raked the match over the strike strip and when the tiny flame lighted she held it against the gasoline impregnated clothing. The shirt flared and burned her fingers before she pulled away. In an instant, the entire length of the body was ablaze.

The creature reacted as Vic did earlier. It closed its eyes and turned its head for a moment but a moment was all Vic needed. In the bright light of the blaze, she spotted the pistol and jumped for it!

The animal opened its eyes and looked for Vic just as she lifted the pistol and fired. The first bullet hit the creature in the chest, as did the second and third!

The thing opened the beak and made its horrible sigh sound. It sprayed Vic with putrescent drool as it folded at the knees. Vic wiped a glob of the disgusting slime from her face and from a safe distance put one more round between the eyes. She figured it should be dead, but she didn't know how hardy it was, or about its nervous system so she watched for movement for two full minutes. To be sure, she then stepped closer and put one more round in the top of the head.

After she had the fire blazing again, Vic chose two limbs for torches. Once one was lit, she returned up the stairs to the wall. With her stone knife, she scraped at the indentations which might outline a door. After only a few minutes, she heard someone call faintly, "Hello." At first, she thought her imagination was playing with her, but she heard it again, and it was unmistakable. It was Barney!

Digging at both sides, it took more than an hour to loosen the stone door and move it

238

enough for Vic to squeeze out. Vic was at Chichén Itzá in the pyramid at the wall she visited with Morley. Barney heard the shots. If Vic didn't put the extra slugs into the beast, he could not have traced their origin.

It was morning when Vic came out and learned she was underground for four days. Barney, Jaime, Diego, Maria, and Juan were the only people there.   Two days earlier, a dozen armed Americans arrived with a dozen armed Mexicans. Morley, Smith and the four "workers" went with them into the jungle, and headed in the direction of Vic's   earlier adventure.

First, Maria dressed Vic's back wound. Then the day was spent sharing the events above and below ground over the past four days. Vic rested, and did a lot of eating and just lying in the sunshine.

Late the next morning, Morley and the others returned. Morley explained their short foray was to investigate rumors of a large pyramid - but it was a false alarm.   After hearing of Vic's adventure, he and Smith spent an hour in the underground cove. Then he directed the other men to put the door back in place. Morley told Vic they would leave the next morning for Puerto Progreso.   The Mexico Trader would be back in two days, so the timing was perfect.   Jaime and Diego decided to remain with Maria and Juan at Chichén Itzá. Morley promised them work when he returned for proper excavation.   Vic and Barney didn't need the camping gear so left it with the boys.

That last morning, Maria made breakfast by request for Vic. She cooked scrambled eggs, black beans, chay, and fried plantains served with queso blanco and local coffee.

After two servings of everything, Vic showered Maria with compliments. "I will miss your terrific Mayan and Mexican cooking, but I will use the recipes you've shared!"

Maria wrote several recipes for Vic. One was how to make the special cinnamon-vanilla coffee she tasted in Puerto Progreso. She also gave Vic three small bags of seeds. One bag was epazote seeds, and one bag was Hoja Santa seeds. Both were for Mayan cuisine, and Vic loved the flavors. The third bag was coffee cherries to grow her own trees. Soon she would have a miniature hothouse coffee orchard in Nebraska!

Chapter 22

Going Home

When the tram arrived at Puerto Progreso, Morley's band met up with Oliver and Jimmy and their men. Together they disappeared down the street without a word. Vic and Barney took a room at the Hotel del Mar as before. In the morning, Vic insured that everything was watertight and they headed for the dock. The Mexico Trader sat anchored three miles out, and another ship lay anchored beyond. The motorboat was already unloading as Sandoval greeted them.

Unloading was fast. Barney was aboard, and Vic was climbing in when they heard the first rumble. People at the pier teetered, and their boat rocked side to side.

"¡Terremoto!" Earthquake! "¡Debemos hacerlo rápidamente!" Sandoval shouted as he pushed the boat from the dock and jumped in. He powered the motor to full throttle and aimed for the cruiser. A hundred yards out they heard another, louder rumble.

It lasted ten seconds, and onshore it knocked people down.

They did half of the ten minutes to reach the cruiser when the regular gentle waves ebbed. The sea became flat, and a barrel-thick wave surged from beyond the ship! It stopped their movement, raised the launch and dropped it sideways to their course. The engine died, and Sandoval worked to restart it immediately. It shook the three passengers without harm. Not expecting an earthquake, the gear was not lashed down. Vic saw the pack full of film tumble over the side but couldn't catch it. She thought the trip would be a near disaster if she lost the photos.

The box was 10 feet from the boat and without hesitation Vic dove and came up beside it. She grasped the rope handle and pulled for the launch.

Sandoval got the motor started and waited for Vic. At the boat, she yelled for Barney to take the box and for Sandoval to go.

Barney yanked the box aboard and held Vic by an arm. Sandoval knew Vic was an expert swimmer and could see that she held tight, so the launch shot forward.

Barney pulled Vic aboard quickly. As she came into the boat, Vic saw the cruiser turn to face the open ocean and saw a cargo net dropped down one side.

"We need to climb the cargo net, don't we?" Vic asked Sandoval. The old sailor nodded.

"Why climb the net?" Barney asked.

"There won't be time to hoist the boat. We heard two rumbles. That wave was from the first and the second rumble was much larger."

"Holy moly!" Barney remembered the much louder second rumble.

It seemed prudent and safe to climb the net with only one pack. Vic donned the wooden box full of film and left her personal gear. Barney slipped on a pack, and they waited.

Before they reached the Mexico Trader, a larger launch pulled alongside and paced them. It was Morley and company. "Everyone OK?" Morley called to them. They nodded and yelled back yes. "Board your ship quickly!"

Vic smiled, nodded and saluted. Oliver and Jimmy started to return the salute, but stopped halfway and looked at Morley sheepishly. Morley grinned and shook his head then saluted Vic. Their launch shot away with ease, heading for the ship beyond the Mexico Trader.

Sandoval brought their launch hard against the Mexico Trader and killed the engine. The old man then held the net as Vic and Barney climbed.

Just after Sandoval left the boat, a nine-foot wave rolled under and lifted it high. It banged against the side of the cruiser and Sandoval pulled his legs up just in time to avoid being crushed. Crew members hauled Vic and Barney over the rail to safety as the ship rose and swayed. They looked back over the side to see the cracked boat begin to sink. Sandoval pulled himself up, and in a moment other crew members helped him over the rail.

The cruiser rose and rolled, but the wave

was not large enough in the deep water to cause damage to a ship the size of the Mexico Trader. Vic looked out toward the other ship and could see the men all boarded safely.

Vic and Barney went to their cabins. The wooden pack endured a lot, but to Vic's relief inside was dry. She finished inspecting the contents when Barney knocked and entered.

"Come in Barn," she said almost laughing. "All is well. The cameras and film are safe!" Then she sat on the bed with a sigh. "I do wish I could have saved my notebooks, though, so I wouldn't need to write from my poor memory. And the mementos!"

Barney dropped a pack beside his sister. "Poor memory? You remember things from 100,000 years ago," Barney laughed. "You won't need to rely on your memory, Sis. Your notes are all safe. As well as your mementos."

Vic looked at the pack. "This is mine? But I took what mattered most to me - the film. It was my choice. Why didn't you save your pack?"

Barney replied, "The only thing in my pack was clothing, dried monkey meat, and one empty camera. Sis, we stored clothing on board, the camera is replaceable, and Captain Walker will see that we eat. And to tell the truth, I'm not overly fond of monkey meat. You could not replace the mementos." The logic was undeniable, so Vic thanked him.

They dined that evening with Captain Walker and others and shared the adventures - mostly. They did not divulge they were forced to kill eighteen people who may have been enemy agents or war criminals. Nor did they share they likely did so alongside U.S. Naval Intelligence and other special military troops. Vic and Barney felt comfortable with that episode of the trip. Anything less, and Juana, Rosa and the boys might now be laboring for war criminals in an underground cavern. Outside the group who experienced it, the story was watered down. They fired shots into the air, and the bad guys ran away.

After dinner, Vic went on deck to enjoy the salt air and moon. Barney joined her and was silent a few moments, then said, "It's none of my business, but I must ask."

"Out with it, Barney."

"Ann Darrow wished you a short, successful quest. Was it successful?"

Vic sighed and said, "Not yet, Barn. It may be just beginning. What happened in Africa was extraordinary. I have in my possession the physical evidence of its reality.   If Nat-ul has returned as Victoria Custer, it is reasonable to assume Nu is also returned."

"That would seem logical," Barney said. "So, if he is, you want to find him."

"Yes. And yes, I understand the odds are against it. It was the dual coincidence of visiting the site of that past life and the earthquakes that fully awakened my memory. Without such a combination of circumstances when I find Nu, he might have no recollection. He may think I'm a fruitcake." " Vic shrugged.

Barney said, "Or he may be ten years old,

and you will need to settle for being his auntie. Then again, it may be destiny that you are back together as you were then."

"There is no destiny, Barney. God gives life and free will. Then it's up to us. Our futures are neither pre-ordained nor haphazard. We create and re-create our lives daily with our decisions and actions. Nu will not walk into my life by some grand plan. I must find him."

Vic looked Barney in the eye and spoke with passionate sincerity. "I was given a miraculous opportunity to remember. I have re-experienced that time and an unspoiled love so powerful that a thousand centuries have not dulled it. Against all odds I cannot, I will not ignore it!"

"Why adventure writing?" Barney waited.

"Nu may be predisposed to love the jungle or any wild place, as I do, and my job will let me travel to such places. Of course, after what Oliver told me, a wilderness may not be the correct place to look. Nu may be on a street in Paris painting saber cats. Or as you say he may be a ten-year-old boy in China. So, I will continue as planned, with a visit now and then to an art exhibit. I've already waited for a thousand generations. Time doesn't matter."

"If you never find Nu?" Barney asked.

"Then I shall live following my dearest desire. I will listen to my heart, and enjoy many extraordinary adventures." Vic looked at her brother. "And I will go to my grave without a visit by that dreadful question, *What if I had tried?* Do you think I'm bonkers, Barn?"

"No, Vic. I was there. I heard your vision. I have held the teeth of the saber-toothed cat. The task you have set for yourself seems enormous, but your desire and plan make logical sense. If I were in your place, I hope I would have the conviction and courage to take on the task as you have."

"Thank you, Barney."

"By the way, I noticed you didn't seem frightened by the earthquake today."

"They don't bother me anymore, Barn, at least no more than they should concern any sane person."

Vic gazed up at the moon. It was the same magnificent moon she walked beneath on her last night with Nu, 100,000 years earlier. She seemed like she might be lost in the long twisting tunnel of time, so Barney left her to revel in her thoughts.

Vic borrowed a typewriter from the captain and for two hours each day punched out stories. In Havana, they went ashore for a few hours, and they stayed three nights in New York where Vic kept a self-promise made in the underground river. She ate a lot of steaks. Vic tried to get in touch with Ann Darrow but found she left the morning Vic and Barney arrived. She went on a private ship with Carl Denham, destination unknown. "I hope Ann and I can share an adventure someday. I think that would be the cat's meow!" Vic confided.

Barney laughed. "I think that Misses Ann Darrow and Victoria Custer are equally nuts...I mean adventurous. You two became so naturally chummy that such a duo will indubitably occur!"

Before they left New York, Vic purchased several children's books in English and Spanish and mailed them to Juana, Rosa, and Carmelita.

Back home, Vic approached Mrs. Simpson, her ninth grade teacher about a project for her class. Vic would provide funds every month for her class to buy books from the Little Leather Library. In return, Mrs. Simpson's class would choose three books to send to the sisters in Mexico.

Mexico was Vic's first opportunity to help someone in trouble, and it set a precedent for her life. She would always help if she could.

That trip had a result that Vic didn't learn until years later. She became a mythical being. A young howler returned to his clan and told a wild tale of a hairless white ape. She spoke his language, slew the poisonous viper, saved him from ants, and ran through the trees as he did. Of course, as often happens with legends, Vic, in the howler's stories, could soon breathe fire, and fly, and lift mountains.

Two weeks after Vic returned from the Yucatán, her editor gave her a surprise. He was so pleased with her stories and future plans, he renovated a spare room and turned it into an office for Vic. It was complete with a brand spanking new Underwood No 5 typewriter. It also included a glass candy jar which her editor knew was necessary. Vic needed a place to hold the licorice sticks, and Mounds and Double Zero bars, and homemade peanut cookies he knew were inevitable.

On the door was painted *Vic Challenger, Adventuress & Writer.*

Of course, the Mayan trip was just the beginning. Vic understood and accepted she might need to brave several extraordinary and dangerous adventures in her search for Nu, who slew Gr, devourer of men and mammoths, for his one and only eternal beloved, Nat-ul, daughter of Tha, of the tribe of Onu, that once upon a time dwelt beyond the Barren Hills beside the Restless Sea.

The best-laid schemes of mice and men go often astray - Robert Burns, "To a Mouse", 1785. Something of a universal law (Mouse Law?), because they do.

If the first plan doesn't work, try something else. Vic Challenger's corollary to the Mouse Law.

Follow your dearest desire, give it your all, and even if you don't achieve your ends, you will likely have a rich and meaningful life. You won't go to your grave under the shadow of that suffocating question, "What if I had…?" You may enjoy a measure of real adventure to boot! – Vic Challenger to her brother Barney in 1920

You don't need to be brave, just do what needs done. Vic Challenger's motto.

The Adventures Continue...

Join the further adventures of Vic Challenger.
Visit http://www.vicplanet.com
Or Amazon, Barnes & Noble or ask your
bookstore.

#1 *Vic: Time Doesn't Matter* 978-1-889823-38-6
#2 *Vic: Mongol* 978-1-889823-60-7
#3 *Vic: Never Give Up* 978-1-889823-61-4
#4 *Vic: Terror Incognita* 978-1-889823-63-8
#5 *Vic: Fast* 978-1-889823-62-1
#6 *Vic: Event* 978-1-889823-65-2
ISBN's are for paperback editions.
More to Come!

Howlers Illustrated story 978-1-889823-37-9

Love bacon? Get
*Vic Challenger's Incredibly Delicious Recipes
for Bacon Lovers.* ISBN 13: 978-1-889823-10-2

Several Vic Challenger journals are available.

Authors appreciate and need reviews. If you
have a couple of minutes, some places you can
leave a review are Amazon, Barnes and Noble,
Goodreads or your own web site / blog.

If you enjoy Vic Challenger adventures,
share the fun and tell others about Vic!

*Want to be first to know when another Vic
novel is out? Sign up at*
http://www.vicplanet.com/joinvic

Get free posters at http://www.vicplanet.com

Curious?

1. Victoria Custer has a favorite modern weapon - the Westley Richards single shot .577. It was a favorite of big game hunter in the 1920's and is still used. The company began in 1812 and continues to manufacture sought after hunting rifles. One famous owner of the .577 was Ernest Hemingway. Learn more about the history here: https://westleyrichards.com/

Here is a good description of a 1923 double barrel at Cabela's:

Westley Richards .577 NE Double Rifle
Description:
Westley Richards, exceptionally fine vintage boxlock ejector double rifle in .577 NE, ca. 1923. Weight: 15 Lbs. Stock Dimensions: 14 ¼"x 1 3/8"x 2 ¼"x 3/8" cast-off. Superb 28" chopper-lump steel barrels with pristine bores, 100gr. Cordite and 750gr. bullet proofs, have a quarter rib with a single fixed 100 yd. rear sight and four folding leaves out to 500 yds.

http://www.cabelas.com/product/Being-Kicked-By-A-Mule-The-Nitro-Express/532275.uts

2. Can you kill a lion with a sharp weapon? Yes. For generations Masai boys become a warrior and adult by single handedly killing a lion with a spear. A 14 inch Bowie would be adequate - it would just require the person to be faster and closer! I suspect our ancestors in the dim past were called on to kill even larger felines with a spear, knife, pointed stick or whatever was handy.
   Recently, the Masai have tried to replace the lion kill with the Masai Olympics. Read about it

https://www.washingtonpost.com/news/morni
ng-mix/wp/2014/12/15/african-tribe-ditches-
lion-killing-as-proof-of-manhood-embraces-
running/

3.   Sylvanus Morley was the pre-eminent
Mayan scholar of the early 20th Century well
known for excavations at Chichen Itza. He
was also a graduate of Pennsylvania Military
College and served with the Office of Naval
Intelligence during WWI as Agent 53.
http://pennsylvaniamilitarycollege.org/agent-
53-sylvanus-morley-class-1904/
http://www.yucatanliving.com/history/sylvanu
s-morley

4. Cryptids The most basic definition is a plant
or animal whose existence is questionable.
Well known examples include the yeti and
Loch Ness monster.   There is so much
interesting information available on the subject
but no room here to list them all, so here are
three you will enjoy:
http://www.newanimal.org/
http://cryptidz.wikia.com/wiki/List_of_Crypt
ids
https://en.wikipedia.org/wiki/List_of_cryptids
      Sightings of the Thunderbird have been
recorded for centuries and are generally related
to Native American traditions. This is Vic's
first cryptid.
      Vic meets bad guys and at least one cryptid
on every trip.

5.   The Little Leather Library mentioned
became the Book of the Month Club in 1926.
https://en.wikipedia.org/wiki/Little_Leather_L
ibrary_Corporation

Reference materials for all Vic Challenger novels are available through the Resource Hub at
http://www.vicplanet.com

BOOK 2 OF
THE INCREDIBLE
ADVENTURES OF
VIC CHALLENGER

VIC MONGOL

by Jerry Gill

Edited by
Keeley Monroy

Ann Darrow Co
Kaneohe, Hawaii

257

©Copyright 2013, 2015 2017, 2019 Jerry Gill
ISNI 0000 0004 5345 9704
Paperback ISBN: 978-1-889823-60-7
Paperback ISBN: 978-1-889823-73-7
Hardback   ISBN: 978-1-889823-58-4
Digital   ISBN: 978-1-889823-40-9
LCCN: 2017904501

This is a work of fiction. Activities portrayed by or at any real person place or thing is purely fiction. Historical and scientific facts are thought to be accurate.

Publisher's Cataloging-in-Publication data

Names: Gill, Jerry Wayne, author. | Monroy,
    Keeley, editor.
Title: Vic : Mongol / Jerry Gill ; edited by Keeley
    Monroy.
Series: The Incredible Adventures of Vic Challenger.
Description: "The Reincarnated Cave Girl" | Kaneohe,
    HI: Ann Darrow Co., 2017
Identifiers: ISBN 978-1-889823-60-7 (pbk.) | 978-1-
    889823-58-4 (Hardcover) | 978-1-889823-40-9
    (ebook)
Subjects: LCSH Mongolia--History--20th century–
    Fiction. | Reincarnation--Fiction. | Travel writers–
    Fiction. | Women--Travel--Fiction. | Adventure
    and adventurers--Mongolia--Fiction. | Action and
    adventure fiction. | Historical fiction. | BISAC
    FICTION / Action & Adventure | FICTION /
    Historical
Classification: LCC PS3607.I4355 V53 2017 | DDC
    813.6--dc23

The beautiful symbol on the title page is the word "Mongol" written in Mongolian script.

Then came the big one. In an instant, Vic was in total silence, and her other senses were anesthetized. The ground billowed the way a sheet on the clothesline ripples in a breeze. The earth lifted beneath her and tilted. Just as suddenly it reversed, and Vic had the sickening sensation of a sudden fall. Hot air and dust engulfed Vic and her knees buckled from a sound so violent it made her bones vibrate! Like a flare of lightning, the broiling memory of her final breath in a cave a thousand generations before seared Vic's brain! Then her world went black!

From Chapter 10

Special appreciation to these super professionals with the Hawaii State Public Library System for helping make Vic: Mongol accurate. You will not find Dulan Bulag on a present day map or earlier maps for that matter. It is now called Dalanzadgad. I searched for days. Finally, I gave in and asked for help from librarians at Hawaii State Library. They could find no reference. They contacted colleagues in Mongolia. They could find no written source so consulted with senior professors who remembered that time and had the answer! Never underestimate a librarian!

Jessica Hogan/Language Literature and History
Marie Claire Hutchinson/E-Reference Librarian
http://hawaii.sdp.sirsi.net/client/default/

Dedicated to
Ashley.
"How's the writing coming?"
&
Hosea
"Hurry and finish the next one so I can read it."

It helped!

Contents

About the pagination: The number before the dash is original novel page.   The number after the dash is page in this book.

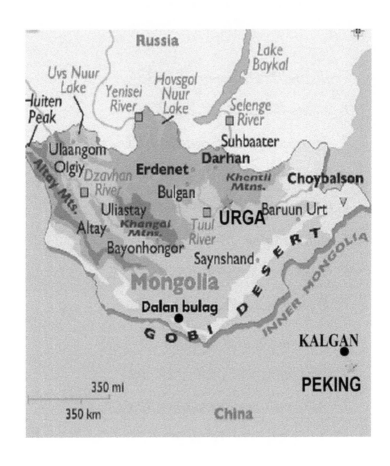

Prologue:

100,000 years ago when life was stupendously savage and every day was a test of your will to live, an epic love was born. Two cave dwellers, Nat-ul, daughter of Tha, and Nu, son of Onu, each a stupendously mighty hunter and warrior to match that time, vowed to love each other as long as the moon would rise in the night sky, which, in their primitive fashion, meant forever. They both died in geologic cataclysms on the very day following their sacred oath. Buried by mountains, one would think their story ended. Yet, since that time the wise of every generation and every culture have proclaimed that true love never dies. There is a reason they say this. In 1896 the moon still rose in the night sky when Nat-ul was reborn as Victoria Custer and as a young woman, the educated Nebraska farm girl vividly recalled her former primeval life and eternal vow. One thousand generations did not cool her love and the recall restored her savage, stone-age instincts and defiant boldness. Now, under the pen name Vic Challenger, she writes adventure travel articles and her work allows her to comb the globe in search of present-day Nu. She realizes her quest may take a lifetime and mortal peril may become her incessant companion, but she is determined to do whatever it takes to reunite with her eternal love and time doesn't matter!

In 1919 Vic remembered her primitive past, and swore to find Nu. In early 1920, she began her search in Mexico and learned of Stu, a nomadic artist who painted primitive people and fashioned stone-age weapons so might be present-day Nu. By September of that year she was ready to venture out again. Vic and high school friend Lin Li visit Outer Mongolia, an exotic locale with wonderful people, breathtaking scenery, a fabulous array of wildlife and a plethora of ways to die a violent death!

VIC: DOUBLE TROUBLE

Chapter 1

Beats Being Dead!

The wind picked up mid-afternoon. Now it blew a steady forty miles per hour, and it bore a cold, pummeling rain.

One bedroom in Vic's house was re-purposed into a library and office. Vic sat in her favorite reading chair beside her map-and-planning-table, absorbed in the latest issue of National Geographic. She enjoyed the occasional crashes of lightning and rumbles of thunder and otherwise didn't pay much attention to the rising storm until she heard a loud crash out back. She was up in a flash and ran to the back door to see what happened, but the sheets of rain limited visibility to about twenty feet. Vic decided to return to her reading when there was another crash, and even above the din of the howling wind and pounding rain, she heard the unmistakable sound of breaking glass.

Without hesitation, Vic plunged out into the storm and dashed for her hothouse. It took only seconds, but by the time she was inside, her cotton day dress was soaked. Halfway down the length of the 100-foot hothouse she immediately saw the broken pane and the tree limb which poked through. Wind and rain blasted through the breach in the window-glass and whipped her young African coffee trees and hot peppers.

Instantly Vic was back in the tempest and strained against the wind to make her way to the shed at the far end of the hothouse. She seized the handle and pulled, and the wind ripped it from her grip and slammed the door against the wall.

A coffee can hung on the wall beside the door, and Vic reached into it and pulled out a handful of two-penny nails. She dropped the nails into the large pouch-like pocket of her dress, then took a hammer from the wall and slipped it in with the nails.

Two panels of corrugated sheet tin were on the floor against a wall. One would do the job if there   was no more damage. Vic lifted one and carefully stepped out with the thin edge faced into the wind. When she turned the corner to go back down the side of the hothouse, the wind was at her back, and it was good for a second. Then a blast jerked the tin sheet broad side to the wind.

Vic didn't lose hold but tightened her grip, and the storm dragged her forward faster than she could step!

The bottom of the tin sheet suddenly whipped upward, and Vic found herself two feet off the ground, flying at forty miles an hour! Within a pair of seconds, she would either smash against the old elm tree or the pointed uprights of her wrought iron fence would fillet her!

Vic released the tin, and one end hit the tree. It spun 360 degrees, and the wind plastered it against the fence. Vic sat up from the three-inch puddle of water she was lying in and checked that the nails and hammer were still with her, then dashed to retrieve the tin.

It was no easier, but Vic learned or perhaps relearned the lesson - a massive result can sometimes derive from meager change or effort. Accordingly, she moved slowly, careful to keep the thin edge into the wind, and backed the tin against the wall beside the damage. She leaned against the tin and reached to pull the intrusive limb from the window. It wasn't an easy task but the branch finally came out. Vic let it drop and the wind tumbled it toward the house and promptly lodged it firmly against the fence.

Then Vic carefully maneuvered the tin over the broken pane and held it in place with a shoulder. It was difficult, she dropped a nail a couple of times and it took longer than expected, but she managed to secure the tin to the frame.

When that task was complete, she headed inside to check her plants but stopped short outside the front entrance. The hothouse was on level ground but it rested at the bottom of a slight down-slope and water seeped under the door in sheets. Water wouldn't harm the dirt floor but would make it a muddy-mess-of-a-work-area.

Vic fought her way again to the shed, retrieved a spade, and returned to the front of the hothouse. The wind and rain were unrelenting, so it required concentration to stand in place. Her vision was impaired by the rain in her eyes, but within a few minutes, water no longer flowed against the building. A trench diverted the runoff to either side. Vic went inside the hothouse to examine the plants and found they lost only a few leaves. Just enough jalapeños were shaken loose for a breakfast scramble. She collected those and headed for the house.

Vic was on the front porch scraping her shoes over the edge to remove the thick mud when a coupe pulled up. Barney visited friends in Lincoln, and this was another friend bringing him from the train station.

Barney shut the automobile door and held his Newsboy cap in place as he dashed from the car. When he was on the porch, Barney pulled off his headgear and shook the water from it.

"Got a nice new wool cap and it is thoroughly soaked! Rain won't shrink it, will it Vic?"

"Well, actually, …," Vic hesitated to deliver the bad news and Barney looked up, froze and stared.

Not a square inch of Vic was free of mud. He noted the mud-coated Mary Jane's and the pouch pocket now ripped by the hammer and nails, and said, "Vic, why didn't you change into work clothes to muck about in the rain?"

Vic's friend from high school, Lin Li, worked part time at Mortimer's Drug and the next day after work she came to visit. The sun was bright, there was no wind, and the mud was well on its way to drying out.

Lin greeted Vic, "Wow! Yesterday was wild, wasn't it? Mortimer's closed, and I went home and had a swell time with the family. We all sat in the living room and watched things blow down the street and told stories and drank hot tea and hot chocolate! Bet you were curled up and comfy with a hot cup of fresh coffee and a book, weren't you?"

Vic stared at Lin and answered, "Eventually."

The two went into the library where Vic already had a large map laid out on the over-sized map-and-planning table.

They talked about their trip scheduled to begin in four days and Vic pointed to a spot on the map labeled *Kalgan* and said, "Here is where I expect we will commence to rough it."

"From what your editor told you," said Lin, "let's hope it really is desolate and we don't meet anyone we don't want to meet. After watching limbs as big as me blow down the street yesterday, I'd like to miss out on those legendary sandstorms we read about, also."

"We'll keep our fingers crossed. I'd like to avoid storms, too," Vic laughed, "but even the best preparation and intentions can be turned topsy-turvy by the unexpected. Remember

Burns and the field mouse, from Mr. Gavin's literature class?"

Lin nodded, "Oh, yeah. You mean the best-laid plans thing. Well, my guess is, we will get on just fine even when it gets cold as an icicle."

"I'm so glad you are coming, Lin! It will be such fun to travel together again. Remember how we thought the trip to Chicago was such a big thing?"

"It did seem monumental at the time," replied Lin. Vic walked Lin out and watched her crank her Tin Lizzy and drive away.

Their friend Emma painted her Lizzy half green, but Lin's Lizzy was all original black. She did individualize it, however. On the left side of her windshield, she painted a red, upside down bat. Red is the color of joy and prosperity and general good luck and an upside down bat symbolizes happiness has arrived. Lin wanted to paint two identical bats to double all that it meant, but her mother insisted and helped paint a carp. Lin told everyone it was because she liked to go fishing, but confided the reality to Vic. A carp may symbolize strength or persistence, or *abundance of children*. That last was her mother's intent. "Since mom had six of us and I'm the only one who turned out right, I'm not sure I want an abundance," Lin joked.

The next morning, Vic went to her office at the Beatrice Sun to type an article about Mayan poc chuc, a recipe she collected while in Mexico. It was the last of twenty articles written for publication in her column while she was gone on her next trip. It was almost noon and Vic was about to wind up the day and the week when her assistant Jenny delivered some letters.

"Lots of fan mail, Vic," Jenny said as she dumped a couple dozen letters into Vic's in-box. "Most from here in Nebraska but one from New York."

"Wow!" said Vic, "I love it when someone from way off reads my work, but I hope it's not someone just impressed by the jaguar photo!" Jenny handed her the letter and said, "Open it and see!"

Vic took the letter and slit the top with the opener she embellished herself - the handle was wrapped with genuine jaguar skin from the Yucatán. She scanned the letter quickly then told Jenny, "It's from a seamstress in New York. She passed through Nebraska by train returning to New York and picked up a paper. She read my piece about how to make a huipil, has already made a couple for customers, and just wanted to say thank you. That's so nice!"

"That's exciting," said Jenny. "Someone all the way in New York used something you wrote in Nebraska about what you learned in Mexico! No wonder you are always glad when mail comes. Well, back to work."

Vic sorted through the other letters quickly, with the intention to read them when she returned, but one caught her eye. It was from Jason Saxby of Omaha. Although she couldn't quite place it, the name rang a bell, so Vic decided to open it.

To Miss Vic Challenger,

I found your address upon recognizing your photo in the newspaper with your article about jaguars and your personal encounter with one. You indeed looked different from the young lady in pink I first met, but I could tell it was you.

I am the boy who tried to take your purse in Omaha and whom you soundly throttled. It was a point of humiliation for a time, to have been bested by a girl, but after I saw the photo and read the story of you and the beast, it became a point of pride.

Thank you for not turning me over to the police and for trusting me to follow your advice. I avoided my promise for two days, but on the third my conscience would no longer allow it. Most of those I approached shooed me away but one and then another gave me a project and I always did my best. Without belaboring the details, I now have my own business doing maintenance and cleaning for shops. I have hired five former street acquaintances and we have much brighter futures than was evident a few months ago, all thanks to the throttling and advice you gave me that day.

Unfortunately, my long time friend Matt, who was your other attacker, thought it was useless and we parted ways. I thank you for that, as well. Two weeks later he was shot dead in an attempted bank robbery. If not for your direction, I almost certainly would have ended in similar fashion.

If you ever have an office in Omaha, I would be glad to clean it free of charge."

Vic was sad that his friend came to such an unhappy end, but was thrilled that Jason took her advice and it helped him. When the boy tried to rob Vic in Omaha several months earlier, she didn't realize her advice would be that helpful, but it sounded like Jason had a bright future.

Vic went out to Jenny's desk and asked to use the phone. She telephoned a friend in Omaha who owned a millinery, the source for many of the cloches in Vic's considerable collection. Vic asked her friend to spread the word among other proprietors and suggest Jason Saxby for custodial and maintenance services and vouched for his hard work and honesty. Vic insisted that her name not be used. Then she headed home.

A chum from college drove Barney around that day to visit friends in Beatrice and returned him just before dark. When he came in, Vic told him, "Tonight we are going to be kids!"

"What do you mean?"

"I fried some chicken and roasted us each an ear of corn. I made 3 dozen molasses cookies, large ones. What we don't eat you can take on the train. On the way from the paper, I bought us 2 bottles of sarsaparilla each and a box of Crackerjack and fresh butter for the corn."

Vic walked over to a hutch and opened it. She pulled out a box and held it toward Barney. "And tonight you go down in abject defeat,

273

brother!"

Barney laughed and took the box. "At least your imagination is healthy. You know that I am the master!"

Inside the box was the game of Prosperity. It was a Christmas gift to Barney when he was fourteen and Vic was nine. They played more games than they could count, sometimes with their parents and sometimes with friends. Barney won probably 95 percent of all games, everyone else won the other five percent. Vic never won a game. She asked Barney once, while he never helped their dad keep books and she did, and now she had a degree in math, why couldn't she win a game about money? Nevertheless, she always enjoyed games!

That night Vic and Barney, as kids, ate an unnatural dinner and played three long games of Prosperity, all won by Barney. It was near midnight when they headed toward their rooms and Vic told Barney sternly, "This means you owe me another match, you know. So you can't be gone forever. It wouldn't be right to fail to offer me a rematch."

"I can't promise when or where, but I promise you will get a rematch."

"Fair enough, brother." Then they went to their beds and slept well, which is a benefit of kid-ness at any age.

The weekend was a blur. Saturday, Vic prepared for Barney's going away party, then hosted it that night. At the party, everyone ate too much. A friend of Barney's brought his banjo and there was singing for a while. They played charades and friends relived good times from school days. Everyone had a blast!

On Sunday the brother and sister attended church with their parents and Vic cooked a big meal for the family - with unsolicited help from her mother. Then the four went to the pond where their parents watched Vic and Barney compete as who could swing highest before dropping and who could do the fanciest dive. It was an activity they enjoyed since they were children and that is where Vic always shined over anyone and why she didn't mind, too awfully much, losing board games.

At seven Monday morning, Lin pulled up and honked her horn. She drove them to the train station where they had only a few minutes wait before Barney's train departed. When it was time to board Barney hugged Lin and Vic and said, "Off to separate adventures sis. We should have some great stories to share later." Then, where Lin couldn't hear, he wished Vic success on her search. Barney boarded the train just before it began to move and in moments it was lost to sight.

Vic and Lin were quiet during the ride back to Vic's. When they arrived, Lin grabbed her overnight bag from the back seat and went in with Vic. She was staying the day and night with Vic and Emma would pick them up in the morning to drive them to their train.

When they were inside, Lin dropped her bag and stood in front of Vic. "Ok Vic, do something. Say something. You're going to miss Barn and you haven't said a thing about it, not even how glad you are. You know my all-time favorite funny story is your mom telling how Barney helped watch you and when you wouldn't stop crying he stuffed the bottle farther in your mouth to shut you up and choked you. And when he hit you in the head with a baseball. And the time he dropped on you in the pond and nearly drowned you. Say, you're gonna be safer!" Lin laughed.

Vic laughed with her. "I will miss Barney but I'm ok. The part I find unpleasant is uncertainty about when or if he will return. That is annoying!"

A little before lunch time Lin drove them out to Vic's family farm where they were greeted by Terkoz, Vic's gifted wolfhound from her African adventure. Over past weeks, he came to like Lin and especially enjoyed when she scratched his back.

Vic and Lin wore dresses to the farm. Both dresses were lightweight and rippled in the gentle Nebraska breeze. Vic's was pastel pink with a white sash and she wore a cloche with pink butterflies on a white background. Lin's tastes leaned to darker colors. She wore a black Paris hat trimmed in red and a small jade turtle was pinned on the front center. Her dress was simple black with dime sized white and red polka dots. Both wore black and white saddle oxfords. Vic sported pink ribbon through her eyelets, tied in a bow and Lin used black and white stripe laces. They both looked decidedly chic.

After a chat with Vic's parents and a good back scratch for Terkoz the two went to Vic's old bedroom where they changed into khaki trousers, shirts and boots, and retrieved several weapons with ammunition. Terkoz lumbered along behind them as they proceeded, now appearing somewhat less than fashionable, to the backyard target range.

The range wasn't elaborate but sufficed. With her dad's help, Vic built a simple waist high bench. Twenty five feet out from the bench was a row of four fence posts. To the right end of those posts were two holes, just about a foot apart.

They laid the weapons on the bench and Vic asked, "Which routine do you want to do?" "Toss," replied Lin. "I think just basic," chose Vic. The two developed several practice routines and whenever they came out, each would choose one routine they didn't use on the previous visit. Vic began to load the modern weapons. Lin went to a pile of tin cans and lumber on the side and gathered cans for the top of each post. She retrieved two planks, each five feet long and six inches wide, and placed them upright in the perfectly sized holes so they stood vertical from the ground. Then Lin used chalk to mark two X's on one board, one a foot above the other. They didn't talk as they set up for they did this often.

Vic was kidnapped by slavers in Africa and took part in a lethal gunfight in Mexico, so decided it prudent to keep survival skills sharp for her travels. The question crossed her mind as whether she might encourage the brutal encounters. Perhaps the resurgence of her primitive and savage instincts attracted similar. She had no sense of how that might happen, but after her recollection in Africa, she was open-minded to any possibility.

The weapons on the bench were a 12 gauge shotgun known as a trench gun, like the one Jimmy Jones from Indiana introduced to Vic in Mexico, an old Winchester 73, lever action which belonged to Vic's dad, a .44 revolver and a surplus 9 mm Mauser picked up at the local hardware store. There was also a large modern dagger, plus a stone war ax and stone-tipped spear which Vic fabricated. The weapons were laid out in a row.

When the targets were rigged, Vic asked, "Want to go first or shall I?"

"Go ahead," Lin said.

Vic went to the end of the bench to her left. Lin quietly stood a moment then shouted what had become their shorthand for *make a move.* "Next!"

Vic jerked up the trench gun quickly, smoothly, and fired once. A can spun on its post. As she set the shotgun down with one hand, she lifted the Winchester, cocked it and fired. Another can clanked. Vic moved so fast and smooth that the sound of the rifle yet reverberated when she fired the .44 which made a hole in the next can. The revolver just settled on the table when the Mauser sounded and another can spun.

Without slowing, Vic took up and threw the dagger and then the stone-tipped spear and buried them in one of the upright boards. Both were within six inches of an X which they agreed was acceptable. A split second later, the war ax splintered board number two.

"Excellent!" said Lin. "Just about fifteen seconds."

"Not bad," Vic said, "but I should be better by now." She went to replace the board she halved with the ax and to retrieve the ax, knife, and spear.

Then it was Lin's turn. She repeated Vic's performance in about the same time. Perhaps the only noticeable difference was that she didn't power the ax as much and it hit the board a foot lower than Vic's.

"Wonderful!" Vic told Lin.

Then they prepared again. This time, though, the weapons were all gathered at the right end of the table and Vic stood at the left end. Lin took position with the weapons and talked about her family in China a moment, then mid-sentence, without warning, shouted, "Next!" As fast as she could, Lin threw the ax, the knife, and spear in turn and Vic caught and threw each in turn. Next, Lin tossed the rifle then the trench gun and a blast from each battered a can. Last of all, Lin tossed the handguns to Vic who fired the pistols twice each, one shot at a time and every one hit home. As she laid the pistols on the bench, Lin told her, "Perfect."

The targets were all reset and Vic tossed weapons to Lin whose execution was equally perfect.

They then replaced the cans and boards on the

pile and gathered the shell casings. "I really don't think we will need weapons," Vic told Lin. "However, my editor's contacts in China tell stories that make it sound like our American West a hundred years ago and after Mexico, I will never discount any possibility."

Weapons practice was not their only preparation. Several times a week they did what Vic called loping. They would run slow, run fast, then walk. They would go several miles at the three speeds in a mix of sequences and for various distances. Twice every week they practiced their equestrian skills. They took the horses loping and practiced short turns at full gallop and obstacle jumps.

Vic would always give full effort to her job as a travel writer, but the core motivation for her travels was the search for Nu. She would question people about artists, and observe and sense for a sign of Nu, but she tempered hopes for she was well aware the odds did not favor her.

Beyond the search for Nu, Vic looked forward to photographing beautiful, unspoiled landscape, wildlife and rugged people. Everything she read about Mongolia or heard through her editor promised all of that in spades. Except for a wolf and wapiti, Vic expected to do all of her shooting with her camera but considered it prudent for her and Lin to prepare for unforeseen possibilities.

The two changed back into their dresses and lunched with Vic's parents. During the meal, Vic's mother, Victoria, said, "While you're on the trip I hope you girls don't need to do any of the things you practice. Hope the practice isn't an omen of things to come." After a moment she added, "But then I guess to be over-prepared beats being dead."

Vic and Lin agreed wholeheartedly!

Back at Vic's home, they lifted stones for an hour, then practiced with their gear one more time. "It might sound silly," Vic told Lin. "but there may be times when it is beneficial to set up or break down camp quickly or in the dark with no more thought than to tie shoe laces."

Lin replied, "After your mom's observation, I'm willing to practice all you want!"

They carried identical gear. Each had a two compartment pack with buckle straps on the upper compartment and snaps on the lower. On the bottom were straps to secure their custom pup tents. They re-engineered standard pup tents for this trip. With a standard pup tent, two halves are carried by two soldiers and joined to make one tent for two. Vic and Lin would each have her own tent.

They joined and modified canvases to be one eight-foot by six-foot piece which required only two poles instead of three. It made for a smaller interior but to Vic, the tents had only two purposes - a place to sleep or to get warm, and protection from a sand storm or blizzard.

Vic ordered sheets of MacIntosh material, to serve as water resistant blankets they could either wrap up in or use for ground cover and they folded very neatly to take up no more than a third of the upper compartment. The only other item stowed in the top section was an over-sized homemade haversack, taken to be used as extra luggage if needed.

The lower compartment held camera, film, a flashlight and for Vic, a journal also. They carried one extra set of clothing identical to what they would wear - socks, military surplus trousers, and a flannel shirt. Each also carried a down-filled jacket which could be tightly rolled and tied under the lower straps with the tent when not needed. There were no spare boots, just those they would wear, kangaroo leather boots ordered from Sears Roebuck. So plenty of room remained. Each would carry two items which served Vic well in the Yucatán; tweezers and a waterproof tin of matches, plus a small magnifier and a compass, and Vic carried a pocket watch to keep them on time for rides.

After one practice taking their gear apart and putting it back together, they ate a small supper of Vic's locally famous fried chicken with biscuits and gravy, as they recalled good old days in high school. Lin took a quick bath before heading for bed, then Vic laid in a tub of hot bubbles for an hour before she turned in.

By six the next morning they thanked Emma for the ride, boarded, and waved her bye as the train departed Beatrice. It would deliver them to Omaha where they had an hour wait before boarding the train for San Francisco.

Originally, they intended to visit Mongolia in the Spring. Lin's cousin Lao in Peking said he knew the perfect guide for the trip. Later he contacted Lin to say the guide preferred they come in September. At first, they weren't sure they wanted to wait until autumn, but then Barney announced he was returning to Europe at that time so things came together perfectly.

The trip to San Francisco was uneventful but not dull to Vic and Lin. They brought a Sears and Roebuck big book and the pages with women's fashions became ragged by the time they reached the coast. Each made a score of mental notes about what she wanted when they returned. They also looked at homes. Lin wanted to buy a house from Sears like Vic and Barney. Each also brought a book to read and they got off at every stop. They took Oreo Biscuits to snack on and in Denver, they managed to wolf down two I-Scream bars each – after having lunch. The train trip was a fun, pocket vacation.

In San Francisco, things changed.

Chapter 2

Murder in San Francisco

Their train arrived in San Francisco on Saturday a bit before noon and their ship was scheduled to embark early Monday morning, so they had a day and a half to be tourists and relax. They left their books and the Sears catalog in the train station for someone else to enjoy and after they registered at their hotel the first order of business was lunch.

After forty minutes of up one street and down another, they settled on an Italian restaurant on the second floor of a building on a short street behind the Embarcadero. There was no view of the bay, but the aromas which emanated from inside were enough to make them forget the view.

After their meal, they went out and stood in front of the restaurant deciding which way to go. They only took half a dozen steps when they heard a woman scream and turned to see a young Chinese woman come from around the side of the building at a dead run. She saw Vic and Lin and dashed to position herself between them. As she did, three scruffy, rough-looking men sprang from around the building. When they saw the other woman, one yelled, "There she is! Get her!"

"Stop! What's going on?" Vic asked, but the men didn't slow or appear to hear. They rushed up to the three women. Lin stepped in front of the girl and the lead man reached out to push her aside. Mistake.

Lin was trained in gung-fu by her uncle Longwei – for over three years now, minimum of an hour each day, seven days a week. The man reached with his right hand and Lin parried, grabbed his wrist, twisted his arm back over his shoulder and took him to the ground and held his arm outstretched with her left hand. She used the palm of her other hand to slam the back of his elbow and it bent unnaturally in the wrong direction. The man screamed in pain and rolled away, then managed to rise and run unsteadily back the way he came.

The second man swung hard at Lin. Lin dodged the fist and the swing went over and beyond her. She stepped into the man, back to him, swung down hard and hit him in the crotch, drove that same elbow into his breast bone and swung up under his chin so hard she could hear his teeth chip. As his head snapped back from that, she used her elbow once more to slam his throat. He stepped back choking and Lin gave a side kick to his chest. He just sprawled on his back as two more thugs came from around the building.

Vic was learning gung-fu from Lin. True, for only one or two hours, once or twice a week for almost three months, but she was inspired when she saw what Lin did to the two men in less than 10 seconds. She stepped to block the way of the third man and he swung at her. Vic dodged and swung at the man who dodged and swung. Again, Vic dodged and swung at the man who dodged and swung. Then Vic kicked at the man's crotch but he crossed his wrists to block it and kicked at Vic. Vic crossed her wrists and blocked the kick, then stepped sideways and shot a side kick at the man's chest. He turned sideways and let the kick pass. Vic went with the momentum and spun around as the man stepped toward her with a punch that missed.

Vic was irritated. When the man punched at her again, she stepped to the side just enough so he missed, grabbed his arm and used his momentum and her weight to whirl him around and slam him into the side of the building. Immediately she locked her arm around his neck and spun around again to ram his head into the wall. He didn't fall so she gripped a shoulder, grasped his hair for leverage, and drove his forehead into the wall and then did it again. She let go and the man crumpled to the ground unconscious.

When the last two men came on the scene, one grabbed the stranger. The other began a match with Lin which was pretty much a stand off. Vic stepped toward them to help. As she did the man got lucky and Lin moved a bit too slow. A kick intended for her chest clipped her shoulder, but still with enough power to knock Lin down. It surprised Vic when he suddenly spun, backhanded the side of her head and sent her sprawling!

Without hesitation he turned back to Lin who was about to rise. He reached behind and from under his jacket he pulled a Bowie knife and drew back to throw!

Vic saw the knife before it was fully out. A small flower bed beside the building was lined with red bricks. As Vic rose, she grabbed a brick and hurled it into the back of the man's head. He bellowed, spun, and snapped the knife! Vic turned sideways just in time and the knife was buried in the plank wall!

That gave Lin time enough to stand, kick the man's groin from behind, and slam her elbow rapid fire three times into his lower spine. The man howled and spun with his arm out to strike Lin but she expected it and dropped. Then the man jammed his hand into a pants pocket and pulled out a Derringer. Vic saw the small pistol coming out and so fast it was a blur she yelled as she pulled the knife from the wall and hurled it underhanded! The man turned toward Vic when she yelled and raised the Derringer but he never fired. His knife went into him just under his ribs, and pierced the lower lobe of his right lung. The man gasped and dropped the Derringer as he looked down at the knife. His knees locked and he toppled forward like a hewn tree. His own weight drove the knife guard through the grisly wound until most of the handle was lodged inside the now dead body.

Instantly, Vic and Lin's attention were drawn to the other woman who struggled against the one remaining man. With two of their band unconscious on the ground, one on the run with a mangled arm and another dead, the one with the girl let her go and ran as soon as he saw Vic and Lin coming. The woman was knocked to the ground but was up in a flash.

"I've got to follow him!" she said in a loud whisper and waved for them to follow. "I deputize you both!" Then she ran after the last man.

Vic and Lin looked at each other for a second, and noticed the crowd gathered around the men on the ground. "Our adventure may be officially begun," said Vic. "Want to follow?"

"Why not?"Lin said and they ran full steam after the woman, for she was already out of sight. When they came out at the end of the alley, Vic spotted her half a block down the street and they turned after her.

They followed the woman into another alley and found her moving slowly along the brick wall. The alley was a dead end with several doors along both sides. The woman stopped to listen at each door. Lin joined the woman and Vic went to the opposite side of the street to listen at doors. She didn't know what she was listening for, but figured if she heard anything unusual, she would let the stranger know.

When they met at the end, the woman asked Vic, "Did you hear anything?"

Vic shook her head then said, "Why don't

you tell us what this is all about."

"Yeah," said Lin. "We killed a guy back there. We could go to prison. Are we really deputies? You're not a crook are you? Those weren't policemen?"

"Police? No. Definitely not! I'm Evelyn Chan. I'm a detective." She shook their hands enthusiastically and thanked them for the help. "I guess you aren't legally deputies but I know people at police headquarters so you are OK."

"Your gung-fu is swell! I wish I could do what you did," she told Lin with a big smile, then looked at Vic and said, "You're gung-fu isn't so good but you seem to be a tough nut." Vic and Lin both laughed and thanked her for the compliments.

Then Lin pressed Evelyn to explain. Evelyn asked where they lived and they told her they were visitors. They began to walk toward the hotel as Evelyn recounted her story.

First she assured them not to worry about prison. "I was in danger and you helped. He died by his own weapon. If he hadn't pulled those weapons he wouldn't be dead.

"So you are with the police?" Vic asked.

"No. I'm a private detective."

"But you work with the police?" Vic repeated.

"You look kind of young for a private detective," Lin said.

Evelyn looked a little sheepish as they walked on. "Well I don't work with the police," she emphasized WITH. "But when I solve this case I could contact them. Several inspectors know my uncle and that would make everything OK."

"Is your uncle on the police force?" Vic asked.

"Not here. He's a detective in the Honolulu Police Department in Hawaii, but he has helped the police here on cases and they know him well." Evelyn's pride and enthusiasm were both evident.

By then they were back at the hotel so they went out on the coffee shop veranda. Lin and Evelyn ordered tea and Vic drank coffee as Evelyn continued the story.

A local dowager, Miss Ernestine Gage, arranged a house party for the weekend at her estate just outside the city. In attendance were a great nephew and his wife, a third cousin and her husband, and a niece Cora with her fiancé, plus three servants, an attorney and Evelyn. Evelyn was invited by Cora and her fiancé, Seth.

Miss Gage was a blunt, to the point person. She let it be known that she was unhappy with some of her potential heirs and called them together so she could give new instructions to her attorney in their presence and explain why. Evelyn knew Cora on a casual basis. They met each other at another party and a couple of times for lunch. Cora knew Evelyn was a detective and knew her uncle's reputation so she confided in Evelyn that she heard two of the other heirs make threats toward her aunt and when she told Seth, he insisted they invite Evelyn to attend the weekend get-together. He convinced Cora that with an attorney and detective both in attendance, tempers might be managed better.

Evelyn gladly accepted the invitation even though at the time she felt there was probably no reason for Cora to worry. After all, wills are changed every day, and people threaten people every day but there is no epidemic of murders. She thought it would be valuable experience, though, and it might serve as a preventive measure. It didn't.

Evelyn arrived at the estate late afternoon Friday with Cora and Seth. The others were already there. Cora informed Miss Gage earlier that Evelyn would attend and why, so as soon as they arrived, Miss Gage took Evelyn into the library and spoke with her privately. She told Evelyn that she felt she was in no danger because she thought the whole bunch except for Cora wouldn't have the backbone to carry out the threats, and Cora was the only one she trusted. Even so, Miss Gage said Evelyn was welcome to stay the weekend. She also hinted she might hire Evelyn for further work after the weekend, but didn't elaborate.

On condition of secrecy, she confided in Evelyn that only one change would be made to her will, but she wished all involved to know why. She especially wanted those who would benefit to know that it was not because of any goodness on their part.

Then Miss Gage leaned to Evelyn and whispered that her physician said her heart was weak and predicted she would not see Christmas, only 100 days away, so there was no time to lose. She wished for a friendly dinner, and in the morning, she would share her plan with the group, then she and her attorney would go into her study, draw up the will and she would sign it right there and then. As they left the room, Miss Gage whispered, "I hope I'll be forgiven."

"It made me sad to hear she had so little time," Evelyn told Vic and Lin. "She reminded me of my grandmother except not Chinese, of course. She was a sweet lady."

"So what happened?" Lin asked.

The maid served the first course of thick beef stew and cowboy toast and shortly afterward, it happened. Miss Gage looked startled and put her hand on her upper chest and in a raspy voice told the butler to call her physician. She wheezed and scratched at her throat, then began to thrash and fell out of her chair. Seth lifted Miss Gage onto the settee in the room. The maid brought smelling salts, but it was no good. She was gone. Cora and the maid cried. "The others seemed upset but not overly so, and they all eyed one another accusingly.

"Why were you following those men? Why did they grab you? Was their attack related to this?" Vic asked.

"It must be," Evelyn told them. "I'm not working on any other case, but I wasn't following them."

"What were you doing when they grabbed you?" asked Lin.

"I was following the suspects. All of them!

I couldn't believe it when both couples came down here together!"

"Four suspects?" asked Vic. "Aren't there six, even if you don't count the servants?"

"And didn't she have a heart attack?" asked Lin. "Wasn't it just someone's good luck that she died?"

Evelyn didn't think so. "I had a cousin die from a heart attack a couple of years back. I didn't see it, but I've heard the story at least a dozen times. He grabbed at his heart. He got pale. He grabbed his left arm. He sighed, and his eyes rolled back in his head, and he fell down, deader than a doornail. That doesn't sound anything like Miss Gage. She scratched at her upper chest, and her voice was raspy, and she couldn't breathe. Her physician was surprised, too. He just saw her and confirmed the bad news last week. He really believed she might have three months or more. Those circumstances plus the social situation smells like sour mackerel in my book. I'm working alone so I decided to just tail one couple to see if I could learn something or at least rule out someone. It was a surprise when four of them came together down on the Embarcadero. I was a block from them when they went into a building, and that was when those guys tried to grab me!"

Then Evelyn nodded at Vic, "You're right, Vic, there are six suspects. I can't let my personal thoughts interfere. Uncle Charlie has told me that often. Except he says, *Even most gentle puppy will bite most kind master if have rabies. Chance at easy money like rabies to greedy person."*

Evelyn looked over at Lin and said, "You look so young and sweet, Lin, but your gung-fu is brutal! I heard that guy's arm rip!"

"Uncle Longwei says you should only fight to defend yourself and your family, but be brutal and finish each enemy quickly in case more come."

Evelyn said, "That lesson came in handy today! There was another and then another! Thanks again for coming to my rescue! I'm pretty sure they planned to kill me."

It took little persuasion for Evelyn to enlist Vic and Lin on the case as both were intrigued and all three felt like friends from the first. So they agreed to help her through Sunday night.

The first move was to find out why the two couples came down to the waterfront. The couples entered a building around the corner from where Evelyn met Vic and Lin, so that is where the three began.

They found the building to be a ticket office run by a lone woman who eyed them suspiciously when Evelyn questioned her. The woman was Chinese and at first spoke English but then lapsed into Cantonese and Pidgin, and shook her head a lot. It was only after considerable persuasion from both Lin and Evelyn that she told them what they wanted to know.

The reason for the visit surprised them all. Both couples booked passage for Monday morning on the Red Dragon, a steamer on its way to China via Hawaii.

Holy cow was Lin's response when she

heard it in Chinese and Vic exclaimed the same when Lin told her.

"What's up about the Red Dragon?" Evelyn asked. Vic and Lin were booked to board the Red Dragon on Monday morning.

Things moved even faster after that. Evelyn talked to inspector Blake, an old friend of her Uncle Charlie who knew Evelyn, but he said he could do nothing unless the physician confirmed there was a homicide. So Evelyn bought a ticket to share the room with Vic and Lin on the Red Dragon. She contacted Cora and told her what she planned. Then she grabbed a suitcase of things from home and joined Vic and Lin at their hotel. That all happened Saturday.

Sunday morning Cora and Seth came to the hotel and told Evelyn they booked passage on the Red Dragon to Honolulu. "Aunt Ernie was so dear and always so good to me," said Cora. "Seth thinks we should go along to see what happens. Maybe we can help you in some way."

"Besides, we think we might be married in Hawaii," said Seth. "Isn't that right, dear?"

Afternoon Sunday, Evelyn visited Inspector Blake and was gone until sunset. She also visited the Gage estate and talked to the butler and maid. She didn't elaborate further.

The three ate dinner that night in the restaurant of the hotel and talked of many things and eventually the case came up. "I wish that I knew more about poisons," Evelyn told the others, as she leaned back and sipped hot tea. "In my gut I know it was murder. I just know it, and poison is the only method which fits."

"You're probably right," agreed Vic. "Did she eat anything different from everyone else?"

"No. We only got to the first course, the stew, and the maid served everyone from the same serving dish. I thought maybe poison was painted on her plate or the rim of her glass, or her fork or spoon was dipped in poison, but I slipped them each away. Inspector Blake did me a favor and checked them and there was no poison. Besides, even though they are technically suspects I've basically ruled out the butler and maid and they were the ones with best opportunity to do something to the dinnerware. The food could have been poisoned by anyone. Everyone, including me, wandered into the kitchen at some point while dinner was prepared and you could dump poison in a bowl in one second while the cook looked away, but like I said, we were all served from the same dish so it can't be that simple."

"Wow!" said Lin. "Fork dipped poison, rim of the glass painted with poison! You really are some detective! What normal person would think of things like that?"

Evelyn smiled and thanked Lin. "But I'm running out of ideas. I hope I can come up with something before we get to Honolulu."

The three sipped tea in silence for a few moments. Then Lin spoke, "You know, I've thought about how you described the way Miss Gage died. Most poisons would take a little longer or cause abdominal pain, or she may have puked or defecated right there even."

"Holy cow!" Evelyn almost shouted. "I didn't know that. Are you a doctor?"

Vic and Lin laughed and Lin said, "Hardly!" Vic answered the question. "Lin is a pharmacist."

"No kidding!" Evelyn said with a touch of awe in her voice.

Lin explained. Growing up she worked with her parents who practiced Chinese medicine and owned a small shop. She wanted to learn about the herbs and other Chinese remedies from a Western perspective, too, so attended university to become a pharmacist.

"You're really a pharmacist!" Evelyn exclaimed.

"Yes, " smiled Lin. She was very proud of her degree and profession. "I sometimes help at Mortimer's Drug when Mr. Mortimer wants to take time off or things just get really busy. I still help mom and dad, too."

Evelyn frowned and her shoulders drooped. "So maybe I just have a great imagination. Maybe it wasn't murder if you think it wasn't poison."

"Maybe it was murder," offered Lin. "There is something else."

Evelyn got wide-eyed, set her tea down, scooted her chair up to the table, and said to Lin, "Tell me everything you can, please."

"Of course," Lin answered and moved her chair closer to the table. "There is a condition called anaphylaxis. It's a very serious allergic reaction which causes throat and lung tissue to swell to the point the person can't breathe and that could make their voice raspy. It can also cause heart failure. Just a few years ago a Frenchman was given the Nobel prize for his work on anaphylaxis. He was researching immunity and injected toxin in dogs. When he repeated the injections a few weeks later, the dogs all died immediately! Turned out, the toxins didn't give immunity, but induced a very severe allergy."

After a moment of silence, Evelyn asked, "How do you trigger such a reaction? Does it require an injection?

Lin answered, "No. Just touch the allergic substance like poison ivy, or breathe it, but a really common way is to drink or eat it."

"Can clams cause it?"

"Absolutely. Shellfish are a very common cause."

Evelyn leaned back and slapped herself on the forehead. "Geez Louise! Would it take much, would it take an actual shellfish? Would juice do it?"

"Juice would do the trick. Doesn't take much. Squeeze a clam, got enough for sure," Lin replied.

Evelyn explained what she was thinking. On the way to the estate with Cora and Seth, she casually asked if they might expect a course of yummy chowder and sourdough for dinner. Cora told her certainly not. Years earlier Miss Gage suffered a reaction to clams that nearly killed her and she was advised to never eat them again. As a result of that incident, she

299

never again allowed sea food of any kind in the house.

"You have a possible method," said Vic.

"Still no fewer suspects. The servants would certainly know the problem and all the family members would likely know about it also. But yes, it is a step closer. The game is afoot!"

Vic and Lin looked at each other and laughed.

"Not another one! You must read Sherlock Holmes. Vic loves Sherlock and is forever saying *the game is afoot*," Lin told Evelyn.

"Really?" Evelyn grinned at Vic. "Well, Sherlock Holmes may be fictional but the plots are brilliant. Every detective should be required to read them." Evelyn paused, then said, "Now I just need to discover who did it. Or maybe who didn't do it. You know, eliminate the impossible and see what's left. I don't yet have a satisfactory answer to why both the other couples are skipping town and now Cora and Seth decided to go, too. Is everyone involved? Wouldn't only a guilty party want to disappear?"

"That does seem to confuse an explanation, doesn't it?" said Lin.

For a moment no one spoke, then Evelyn snapped her fingers, "Or maybe it begins to make things more clear. A guilty party would certainly want to leave, but someone with just a guilty conscience might want to skip out to avoid embarrassing and compromising questions. If you planned to kill someone and someone else beat you to it, wouldn't you be nervous about police interrogation? If police discovered a weapon or incriminating note, you might get pegged for the murder even if you didn't do it! Excuse me for a minute, I need to make some phone calls," Evelyn was obviously excited as she headed for the lobby.

Chapter 3

Mayhem at Sea

All the players were at the dock at sunrise Monday morning, ready to board along with three dozen other passengers, including a Danish priest and his wife headed for Urga.

All the suspects were smiling and cordial, but an undercurrent of tension was evident. Except for Cora and Seth, they were surprised to see Evelyn. They knew by now she was a detective, but Evelyn asked Cora and Seth not to mention she still was on the case. She was just traveling to visit her Uncle and his family in Honolulu in the company of her friends Vic and Lin. Evelyn judged that if her other suspects sensed they were in the clear, they might be more candid in conversation. That first day, she avoided them all until dinner.

The Red Dragon was built to serve as a cargo vessel, but the passenger trade became so lucrative that it was refitted to accommodate up to 125 passengers, while it also still carried about two thirds the cargo load as before.

The dining tables seated eight persons each. With her six suspects, Evelyn made a table of seven. Vic and Lin sat at another table for all meals. They discussed whether one of them should sit with Evelyn for moral support but decided she didn't need it. Their twenty-five years of life experience offered scarce advantage over a lifetime desire to become a detective. She was alone on the case before they met her and she might feel insulted if offered moral support. If she got in trouble or wanted help, fine. Otherwise, it was her show.

They would only be aboard ship four nights before they docked in Honolulu. After that first night at dinner, Evelyn paced the cabin and talked to herself as much as to Vic and Lin. She was more confident than ever that four of the suspects disliked Miss Gage substantially, but that didn't help her case.

The next day they were all tourists on a cruise, except maybe Evelyn. She paced the deck, looked deep in thought and seemed eager for dinner.

During the meal, Vic and Lin attempted to overhear if Evelyn brought up the case. Early on they heard her do some fishing. She related a famous case which her uncle solved and introduced it with a question. "Did you know that if a person has a dangerous medical

304

condition and someone deliberately induces that condition, it is considered murder?"

Later, Evelyn casually asked her table mates how long they would be in Hawaii and two couples were unsure and didn't make advanced plans for return. Cora and Seth happily said they would be there long enough to be married and enjoy a proper honeymoon. After that, the conversation centered on wedding ceremonies.

Following dinner when they all stood to leave, Evelyn positioned herself so she could observe the entire group and offhandedly said she read the medical records of Miss Gage and discovered she was severely allergic to shellfish. Cora remembered telling Evelyn about the allergy on the drive to dinner and fought a smile, but winked at Evelyn.

Evelyn innocently exclaimed what a sad affliction for a resident of San Francisco and asked if her table-mates knew of the allergy or was it kept a secret. Everyone nodded and said yes they all knew. Evelyn said goodnight and turned to join Vic and Lin, but as the others moved to leave, she did a quick about face and said, "Oh, in Miss Gage's record her doctor said her allergy was so severe that she could die from something called anaphylaxis. I'm curious. The doctor wasn't there to ask, and I haven't had a chance at a medical reference. Do any of you know what anaphylaxis is?"

They shook their heads and murmured as they glanced curiously at one another. "That's OK," said Evelyn. "Just curious. I can ask Uncle Charlie when we get to Honolulu. Good night." Evelyn turned away and smiled as she approached Vic and Lin. The answers about anaphylaxis were fruitless, but the question caused a posture change for one party. The head and shoulders went back almost imperceptibly, and only a trained eye would catch the change in the jaw line as the muscles tightened. To Evelyn, it was a silent proclamation of mental discomfort.

As soon as they were alone on deck, Vic and Lin questioned Evelyn. "That is a Eureka smile if I ever saw one," Lin told her. "Did you get a clue?"

"Nothing for a court but it was sure a clue. Not one I'm happy with, but when murder is done, justice must follow where the clues lead."

When asked what it was, Evelyn said she didn't want to say yet. "When you tell what you know before you know surely, it's just chin music, and gossip from a police officer can cause great harm. I sound more and more like my uncle, but it's true." Evelyn suddenly stopped, snapped her fingers and told her friends to go on. She wanted to see the captain who was still eating when they left, so she turned back toward the dining hall.

Vic and Lin decided to walk the deck for a time as it was a lovely night. A host of stars sparkled brightly across the perfectly clear sky, and the damp salt air was comfortably tangible. For a time they watched the lights from a distant ship, no doubt headed for San Francisco.

The three left the dining hall which was forward and starboard and casually strolled the long way back to their cabin which was port and aft. When Evelyn left her friends, she went through a passageway amidships because it was quicker. There was an intersection with a perpendicular passageway at the midpoint, and because Evelyn was hurried and immersed in her thoughts, she didn't notice a masked figure step out behind her as she passed that juncture. She did, however, feel the solid thump against the back of her head which knocked her to her knees.

Evelyn began to rise, but her attacker pulled a burlap bag down over her head and arms and lifted her. She twisted and kicked to break free, which made it difficult for the assailant, but he held on. Then Evelyn heard the door open and the sound of the ship cutting through the water and realized her attacker's intention. He was going to throw her overboard!

She was suddenly icy with fear but not frozen. With the terror came an adrenalin induced surge of strength. Immediately Evelyn began to scream and fight harder. She kicked relentlessly into her captor's shins, but although he growled in pain at each blow, he didn't let go, and with the sound of the sea against the ship and the wind, her cries drifted away in the night.

Evelyn felt her captor lean back and raise her higher and she knew he was about to heave her over the rail! She stopped kicking and held her feet together, and in a make-this-work-or-die move, Evelyn waited a second until she felt another slightly backward bend of her assailant.

Then she drove her feet out in front of her, and they caught the rail!

Evelyn pushed with all her might, and it worked. The captor was forced back against the bulkhead and the jolt combined with Evelyn's dead weight was too much. She hit the deck hard and instantly rolled away and pulled at the burlap bag as she screamed at the top of her lungs. It only took two seconds to get out of the bag, but the deck was deserted. Evelyn jumped up and looked into the walkway, but no one was there. She pondered the incident for a moment then continued, more cautiously than before, to see the captain.

Vic and Lin just started to worry when Evelyn finally returned. She told them about the attack but assured them she was OK. They were curious of course about her mission with the captain, but she was yet mum and said she needed to gather more evidence.

"Sorry, but Uncle Charlie would really frown if I shared suppositions without evidence."

There was a moment of silence, then Vic said, "I need to talk to you about that. Please don't take this wrong. You are not your uncle, Evelyn. You can never be him. I have experience entrusting my efforts to what someone else might presumably do in a situation. We can learn a lot from those who have come before and done before, but we cannot be and are not meant to be them. We learn and build on what we learn from others so some day someone can learn from us. Don't try to be your uncle. Be Evelyn and be the best you can be. I have no doubt whatsoever that someday the name Evelyn Chan will command as much respect as does Charlie Chan, and will cause criminals to quake in their boots."

Evelyn just stared a moment, then said "Thank you," and gave Vic a hug. "No one has ever told me to be me. It's always *why don't you be more like*, or, *why don't you do what so and so did* or *you can't* or the worst of all, *you're a girl.*" From now on, I'm Evelyn Chan, detective, and I will use what I've learned, but I'll get the job done my way. There is something I can share, too, although you likely surmised this already. I am no longer working on a hunch. The attack leaves no doubt. Miss Gage was murdered, and the killer is on board!"

When Evelyn returned, she carried a small box, and Vic now asked what it was or was it a secret to do with the case. Lin answered for Evelyn, "It's a mahjong set isn't it?"

It was a mahjong set which Evelyn borrowed from the captain. "Let's play!" she said.

"No," said Vic. "I'm no good at games. I lose too often."

"C'mon, " said Evelyn.

"She's not kidding, Evelyn. She stinks. She always loses."

"Not always!"

"Yes, always, Vic."

"But we need four people," Vic stalled.

"No, we can play with three. I'll show you," said Evelyn. "Do you know how to play with three people, Lin?"

Lin looked at Evelyn with wide eyes and said, "What? Did you really ask me that? Did Beethoven play the piano?"

"I'll be a gracious winner, Vic," said Evelyn.

"You? You forget me," said Lin.

"No, I just know how good I am," answered Evelyn with an exaggerated smile and shrug.

"We cannot let that misconception continue," said Lin and pushed Vic toward the table in the center of the cabin. "Sit down Vic. We're playing mahjong!"

"You two are just going to have a shoot out in Dodge with me in the middle! Don't I get a say in this?" Vic asked.

Evelyn and Lin both said with unequivocal sincerity, "Absolutely not. Sit down."

Then Lin said, with a wicked smile, "You don't even need to learn three handed well, Vic, since you will lose anyway."

"What? That's not nice!" Vic grinned, too.

Evelyn said, "You two can joke, but mahjong is serious. I apologize up front for my brutality. I plan to maul both of you. Take no prisoners! Or to put it so you understand, Lin, your vicious gung-fu is like patting a kitty cat on the head compared to my savage tiger mahjong."

Lin made an exaggerated gasp and began to tap the table hard with an index finger, "OK! OK! Get that box open. Get the salt and pepper. When you eat your brag, it will taste better if you season it!"

So the three were up until one-thirty in the morning and played eight hands of mahjong. Evelyn and Lin won an equal number of hands and Vic scored a perfect record of losses, and all three had fun and never once thought of murder and murderers.

The next day they napped, talked, read, napped, and napped. Twice Evelyn excused herself for a few minutes but came back mum.

The third night nothing fruitful happened at dinner. Afterward, with the help of Vic and Lin, Evelyn tried to lay a trap. She strolled the promenade and passageways with Vic and Lin always near.

It was a dangerous ploy which almost ended badly. Vic and Lin waited around a corner up ahead. Evelyn strolled the deck, looking out to sea. She passed a door to a service closet and didn't notice that it was not quite closed.

Just as Evelyn passed, a man who wore a bandana over his face below his eyes opened the door and slipped out quietly behind her. There were no elaborate flourishes. Evelyn wasn't aware of his presence until he grabbed her. In a single movement an arm swept her above and behind the knees, a hand grabbed her collar, he lifted her, and tossed her over the rail!

Evelyn made one continuous scream until she hit the water!

"Did you hear that?" Vic moved quickly toward the corner.

"What?" Lin asked.

"A scream!"

They came around the corner and could see all the way to the other end of the ship. The walkway was empty!

"Where's Evelyn?" Apprehension was strong in Lin's question and an answer came immediately as Evelyn managed to scream again, this time the word, "Help!"

Vic shouted, "It's Evelyn. She's overboard! Tell the captain to stop the ship!" She took a life preserver from the wall, kicked off her shoes, climbed over the rail and jumped!

En route to the water, Vic yelled for Evelyn and she yelled back "Here!"
Vic heard Evelyn but the sound was faint. She knew if she hesitated one minute longer she could not hear Evelyn and odds of saving her would be cut by at least half.

Vic swam toward the voice and every few strokes called out to reposition Evelyn. In minutes she found Evelyn and they clung to the preserver together for nearly two hours before the ship found them and they were onboard.

The captain and Lin had towels and blankets waiting. Evelyn asked the captain not to say anything about the incident and after they were less than dripping, they wrapped in the blankets and headed for their cabin.

The full moon was just a few days away and Vic wanted to stay outside awhile. Alone, leaned over the rail, Vic's thoughts were soon lost to another time and another sea beneath the same moon. Vic closed her eyes and in an instant, she walked hand in hand with Nu along a trail on the side of the Barren Hills and was filled with perfect contentment.

"Vic," came a familiar voice from another time. "Vic," it came again and her hand slipped from Nu's hand and she opened her eyes.

Lin laid a hand on Vic's arm and shook her gently. "Vic. I'm sorry I fell asleep and didn't know you weren't back. You've been out here for over two hours! Are you OK?"

Vic turned to Lin, and Evelyn who stood behind her, and they both did a double take and looked startled for just a second.

Vic noticed and asked, "What is it?"

"Your eyes. Just for a second they looked as black as mine," Evelyn said.

"They did, Vic," said Lin. "I swear your eyes looked black."

"A trick of the light no doubt," said Vic.

"Had to be a trick of light," said Evelyn. "People's eyes don't change color like that."

The next day was the last full day at sea before they docked at Honolulu. For a considerable portion of it, the three were on a lower deck where other passengers wouldn't see them. They fished with the cook and other crew who lent them fishing gear. They caught a few small fish, but nothing they could expect to see at the table. One of the crew pulled in a four-foot shark, and when Evelyn saw the teeth, her eyes popped! "Were things like that in the water last night?"

The crewman laughed and Vic replied, "Likely."

Before dinner, Evelyn dressed quickly and told Vic and Lin she would see them in the dining hall. "I need to check the radio room for a telegram. Wish me luck!"

Vic shook her head and said, "No. You don't need luck." Then she touched her forehead and then put her hand over her heart and said, "You have all you need here and here, Evelyn."

"Anyone who can tie me in mahjong can out think any criminal. You'll get the killer," said Lin.

Evelyn pulled her shoulders back and said, "You're right. Thanks, girls! See you later."

The dining hall was full and Vic and Lin were eating when Evelyn arrived. They looked up and she gave them a big wink and went to her table.

Evelyn brought two folded papers with her, which she slid under her plate as she exclaimed, "I'm starved!" Cora asked what the papers were and Evelyn just said, very pleasantly, that she received two interesting telegrams and they would make great after dinner conversation. Vic and Lin were both highly intrigued and listened intently as on previous nights, yet not once during the meal did they overhear any mention of the case. Once Vic leaned over and whispered to Lin, "Something is afoot, without a doubt."

When everyone at Evelyn's table finished with their meal and her plate was taken, Evelyn lifted the telegrams just before a dessert plate was set down. "Oh! That smells great! Is that apple pie?" The server told her it was indeed apple pie, and Evelyn licked her lips and took a full minute to explain how much she loved apple pie. Then one of the wives asked Evelyn about the telegrams.

"Oh yes!" She shared that one telegram was from Miss Gage's attorney and one from her colleague, Inspector Blake with the San Francisco police department. On hearing that, Lin tapped Vic on the hand and whispered, "Hear that! Colleague, not uncle's friend!"

Evelyn stood and began to pace slowly. She asserted there was no doubt whatsoever that Miss Gage was murdered, that the heart attack was not due to natural circumstances. "Her physician was so surprised. He felt she had at least two months or more if she took it easy and the maid and butler both confirmed that she was extremely careful not to exert or excite herself. She was determined to live to change her will and talk to all of you. It meant a lot to her. I am very angry that she was denied that final wish. Miss Gage was murdered and I WILL send the murderer to prison. Folsom has a length of rope just for you!"

Evelyn began to circle the table slowly. She stood behind each person for a time, then moved on. She conspicuously spoke with volume enough that everyone in the dining hall could hear what she said, and by now she held the undivided attention of one and all.

"Then, there was the social situation. From what I have found four of you didn't especially like Miss Gage." One of the men started to protest but Evelyn stopped him. "Nothing is especially incriminating or strange about disliking or having differences with a relative."

Evelyn continued, "Then there was the planned changes to the will. Someone was obviously about to inherit less and someone more. Her attorney could not tell me the particulars of the will, but he did confide that the estate was extensive. In addition to the property which must be worth a tidy sum, Miss Gage's bank accounts totaled nearly three-quarters of a million dollars. Many people have been murdered for a great deal less."

"I must admit I was confused for a while. Why is every heir on this ship? However, as the facts were gathered, it became clear that most of you are here from guilty conscience. Whether you made physical preparations for murder or not, you harbored deep-seated ill-will and malicious intent and preferred to avoid any questioning."

Evelyn was back to her chair and leaned forward and smiled "I am probably boring you, so let me get to the crux of the affair."

"Miss Gage died of heart failure and failed blood pressure due to extreme shock brought on by a terribly severe allergy to shellfish. I have consulted with a professional pharmacist and am assured that the condition known as anaphylaxis can kill an allergic person in exactly the manner which we all witnessed Miss Gage die. I further learned shellfish products are known to be a common inducer of this anaphylaxis, and that it would take but a very small amount. It would be undetectable to the tongue in a bowl of beef stew."

At that, Lin tapped Vic's hand, pointed to herself and whispered, "Professional pharmacist!"

Evelyn was on a final assault. She told how

the police lab, at her suggestion, examined the food and utensils a second time, to look for signs of shellfish, not poison, and indeed found remnants of clam juice in the serving dish which held the stew.

Evelyn talked with the attorney about the possibility that someone knew the contents of the will. He assured her that was impossible but he did happen to mention that three weeks earlier his office was burglarized. Locks on several file cabinets were broken but the only thing taken was a few dollars from a cash box. Yet, someone could have easily looked at any will in the files and then taken the money to hide the true purpose of the burglary.

The second telegram confirmed that just two days following the burglary at her attorney's office, both the butler and maid observed Miss Gage in a heated discussion with a man in the garden. They couldn't see his face, but voices were raised and the man vaulted the fence to leave rather than take the gate past them.

The first telegram, from Inspector Blake, provided more evidence. "It is about a gang who tried to murder me in San Francisco, but was foiled by my friends and associates, Vic and Lin." By now the entire dining room was so quiet that the proverbial dropped pin would sound like clashed cymbals. "The visitor in the garden was a member of that gang. Miss Gage learned of his connection and was going to expose him if he didn't go away on his own." Evelyn gripped the chair back, rocked back on her heels and looked

317

grimly at the heirs.

"What brought it together for me is something Miss Gage told me the night of her death. She wanted those who would benefit from the change in her will to understand it was not due to some goodness on their part. It was cryptic on its own but makes perfect sense with this other information."

"If I didn't already have enough evidence, on the past two nights, right here on the Red Dragon, two attempts were made to murder me!" A united gasp buzzed throughout the dining hall and Evelyn paused a moment for effect. With raised voice, Evelyn snapped, "He actually threw me overboard last night. He obviously failed both times, and during the first attack I kicked the stink out of his shins. No doubt it left incriminating bruises." A single gasp came from Cora as she pressed the back of a hand to her lips and her eyes began to tear.

"I'm truly sorry, Cora," Evelyn said solemnly and directed a harsh gaze to Seth.

Everyone looked at Seth who frowned at first but suddenly smirked and stood. He glared at Evelyn and growled, "You meddling dame! You won't pinch me for this!" His acerbic and vicious tone and countenance caused many diners to recoil in their seats!

Suddenly Seth bolted and was through the door before anyone could react. Every occupant of the dining hall rushed the door after him. Vic, Lin, and Evelyn were first out and behind them, the Captain. Seth, however, was nowhere in sight. "Which way did he go?" Evelyn asked with a bit of frustration in her voice. The captain suggested Seth didn't like the sound of the rope Evelyn mentioned, so took the easy way out and jumped overboard.

Cora was beside Evelyn and spoke up, "Seth didn't jump. He's a physical coward and he doesn't know how to swim."

"Then he must be hiding somewhere on board. When we dock in Honolulu, I'll get a small army of policemen to search every nook and cranny. We'll find him," Evelyn vowed.

At the mention of an army of police, Vic noticed that the captain stiffened and paled a bit.

Evelyn said, "Nothing to do right now. I want my pie," and she went back into the dining hall.

"Geez, Evelyn, you like to eat as much as Vic!" said Lin.

"I like apple pie," replied Evelyn.

Vic said, "Food is good for you, Lin." Then she invited the captain to join them, and with stern, unblinking eye contact added, "Please."

The other passengers had retired to their cabins. Vic, Lin, Evelyn, Cora and the Captain sat at a table and the cook brought them slices of fresh apple pie. "What is it, Captain?" asked Vic. "You didn't seem too happy at the suggestion of police searching your vessel."

Evelyn looked at Vic, then the Captain, swallowed some pie and asked, "Is there a problem, captain?"

He replied that he simply preferred not to have police on board and that it might keep them in port over schedule. Evelyn assured him that all she wanted was the murderer.

Vic made fists, leaned forward and spoke again. She made no attempt to disguise the menace in her voice. "Do you deal in people, Captain? Is this a slave ship? I despise slavers! They are less than human, and don't deserve their next breath and given the opportunity, I would personally take the last breath from every one of them!"

The captain could not forge his resentment and shock. Vic judged them to be real. "My God, no!" The captain was not a man given to fear but Vic's tone and posture sent a chill down his spine for they were not empty words. He was a man of great and varied experience and could tell that Vic's statement was not an idle threat but spoken on authority of her own experience.

"Do you take opium to my country," asked Vic and watched the captain closely. "No!" The captain snapped and again Vic sensed his sincerity.

"Then I agree with Evelyn, our only concern in this matter is that a murderer is brought to justice."

Then Cora spoke, "Seth murdered my dear aunt and attempted to kill Detective Chan and he must pay for his crimes."

For several moments there was silence then the captain crossed his forearms and leaned forward on the table. "I'm not Chinese," he began.

"You're Mongolian," said Lin and Evelyn

together and looked at each other with a nod.

"I've seen photos of my parents' Mongolian friends from before they came to the United States. You just look Mongolian to me," said Lin.

"When I was in your cabin to borrow the mahjong I saw your name in the log on your desk," said Evelyn. "I have a Mongol friend with the same name, Chuluun.

The captain nodded. "This is a time of turmoil in my country. Even in a country where life is naturally rugged, these days it is doubly so. Simple, daily survival can be very challenging for my people...."

Vic held up a hand and said "Stop. If you are helping your people, without harming others, we don't need to know more. We can never reveal something we don't know. Leave it there."

"Couldn't your men search the ship now?" Evelyn asked.

"They could do a better job and faster than the police who don't know the ship," said Lin. "They'll miss some sleep but for a good cause. Or for two good causes."

"They could. They will," agreed the Captain and he rose. Vic, Lin, and Evelyn would wait in the dining hall, and the Captain would walk Cora to her cabin then muster the crew to begin the search. Before he could get out the door, Evelyn held up her plate and asked, "Captain, would you mind if...." Before Evelyn finished, Captain Chuluun called to the cook to bring out a whole pie, then left with

Cora.

At one in the morning, Evelyn finished the last of the pie and pushed her plate away. Lin bent over and looked under the table and said, "I don't understand."

"What?" Evelyn asked and she and Vic both looked under the table.

"Where did that big pie go?" Lin asked.

Vic laughed and Evelyn answered simply, "Apple is my favorite."

A few minutes later they heard someone running on the deck and expected Captain Chuluun, but when the door burst open it was Seth with a .45 in his hand and murder in his eye!

Seth didn't pause and as he came, he raised the pistol at Evelyn.

Vic's hand was on the plate in front of her and she grasped it the instant she recognized Seth.

Vic saw there could be no talk, no time to stall. She knew that if Seth made it all the way to the table, it would be too late. Someone would die.   "You and your bimbo friends..." Seth muttered as he neared the table.

"Next!" Vic rapped as she drew the plate across her body with her right hand. At the same time, she slammed Evelyn on a shoulder with her open hand and knocked her off her chair.

Lin understood their *magic word*, saw what was happening, and grabbed her plate.

Seth's gun fired!

Vic slung the plate toward Seth and it hit his gun arm at the biceps, and he dropped his weapon.

No sooner did Seth drop the gun when Lin's plate hit him hard in the forehead, snapped his head back, and he crumpled to the floor.

Vic and Lin were both up and moving immediately. Vic kicked the .45 away from the unconscious Seth. Lin took a lace from one of his shoes, rolled him on his stomach and tied his hands behind him. Seth began to rouse as she finished and Lin slapped the back of his head. "I don't like to be called bimbo! The way you won't like being called fish when you start to flop at the end of that rope."

Evelyn watched them and rubbed her shoulder. "I will definitely have a bruise, but it's better than being shot." She half turned toward her chair and stuck a finger in the bullet hole in the chair back. "Right about where my heart would've been. You guys are good!"

Just then the door burst open and the Captain and two of his men came in. He stopped when he saw Seth on the floor and slipped the revolver he carried back into his belt. "I see you got your man, detective. My men will lock him up and watch him until we dock."

Evelyn went to the radio room and sent a wire to Honolulu police. Vic and Lin woke Cora and told her. Then the three friends met up at their cabin, with the intention of resting a couple of hours, but the evening had been far too dramatic to let them sleep, so they talked.

Evelyn told Vic and Lin the second telegram included information which would please them.

She asked Inspector Blake if a body was found down near the bay. She wanted to confirm a reason for the attack and questioned the inspector without admitting she was there. It turned out the man was a member of a group called the Ragland Gang and Inspector Blake found that one of the members was a Seth Malone.

The young detective pieced it all together. Originally, Seth wanted her around for cover. After all, a murderer wouldn't want a detective around, and if a detective witnessed Miss Gage apparently die of a heart attack, that would be the end of it. He evidently considered Evelyn incompetent, but became concerned when he saw she was suspicious and followed the other heirs. So he sent the gang to get rid of her. That didn't work, thanks to Vic and Lin. When Seth learned Evelyn was joining the cruise, he worried she might rule out the others which would narrow the field a bit too much, so he needed to stop her.

As far as the incident near the docks, Inspector Blake told Evelyn that a waitress at an Italian restaurant saw three girls "beat the tar" out of five men and one of the men got killed when he pulled a gun. Evelyn asked if, theoretically, someone was about to be killed and someone else came to help and things happened like the waitress said, would the people in the theoretical situation be in much trouble. In a rather indirect manner, the inspector told Evelyn that particular death was designated as gang related and the theoretical people acted in self-defense and there would be a lot, emphasis on a lot, of theoretical paper work if the incident needed to be rewritten to include others who might be theoretically involved.

"I think that means," Evelyn told them, "none of us should worry about going to jail," which was a relief to both Vic and Lin.

"I'm glad we got Seth but I wish I could have prevented murder in the first place as intended."

"You did," Vic said. "There is no doubt that Miss Gage would have died anyway, and very shortly after their wedding, Cora would have been victim to an unfortunate accident. You prevented Cora's murder and Miss Gage would be pleased. She planned to disinherit Cora so Seth would have no reason to marry her and kill her later. Now Cora will get her inheritance and Seth will get his proper reward, too!"

Within minutes of docking, the Red Dragon was boarded by five policemen. The ranking man was Inspector Hu and he knew Evelyn. Young Detective Chan took full charge and told Inspector Hu she would come to the station and write a full report later. Vic and Lin were proud of how their new friend metamorphosed into a confident, self-assured professional.

The Red Dragon had a one night stay only. Vic, Lin, and Cora stayed over at the Chan residence and they had a swell time. Cora was invited to stay and see the island with Evelyn while she was there, and those two drove Vic and Lin down to the Red Dragon the next morning. When Vic and Lin boarded, the Captain welcomed them and thanked them for how they handled the situation with Seth. Soon, the Red Dragon began to ease away and Vic and Lin leaned over the rail to wave 'bye to Evelyn and Cora.

Chapter 4

Beyond the Great Wall!

Four days after the Red Dragon left Honolulu it made a 24 hour stop in Yokohama, Japan. Vic and Lin went ashore and tried some curry rice, fish (raw, steamed and battered), fried tako, buckwheat noodles in broth with green onions and udon, miso soup, pickled vegetables, grilled unagi, yakitori, and plenty of other goodies. To finish off the excursion they purchased a bag of red bean paste anpan to take with them.

Two days later there was a 24 hour stop in Kirun, Formosa which the captain called Kelang, the old name before Formosa came under Japanese control. Then the Red Dragon doubled back North into the East China Sea and docked at Dairen where Vic and Lin entered China.

The pier was busy, but not with tourists. It was mostly dock workers unloading ships.

Friends came for the missionaries, and after they were gone, Vic and Lin were the only passengers who remained from the Red Dragon. Impatient, they were already questioning how long they should wait when a young man about their age approached and spoke to Lin in Chinese. The man and Lin shook hands, and bowed, then laughed and launched into a conversation. After a couple of minutes, Lin said, "Excuse my impoliteness. This is my friend, Vic. Vic, this is cousin Lao."

Vic shook hands with Lao and bowed from the shoulders as Lin taught her. "Ni hao," she said.

"Ni hao," Lao answered. "I am pleased to meet you Vic Challenger! I have read the story of you and the jaguar. I was most impressed," he told her.

Vic blushed a bit and said, "Thank you, Lao. I am honored. I am also relieved that you speak such fluent English. I have exhausted my knowledge of Chinese."

"It is not for you to worry," Lao told her. "I will be entirely at the service of you and my cousin while you are in China, and I have arranged for my close friend Chu to guide you in Mongolia. You are in good hands with my cousin, also. Although she has been raised in an English speaking country, her Chinese is flawless." At this Lin thanked Lao in English and then the two reverted to Chinese and began walking. Vic followed and took mental notes to write about later and just enjoyed the new sights.

They only walked one block before the

smell of food triggered the usual response. "Mm mm! That smells good!" Vic said and walked over to a street vendor cooking meat on a portable grill. "Oh, those look like squirrel legs. I love squirrel," Vic said. Lao laughed. Lin said, "I don't know for sure but from what my parents told me that isn't squirrel, Vic."

Vic looked at it a moment, then said. "Oh. They're a big rat's hind legs, huh?"

Lao nodded.

"Well," said Vic, "We can call it street squirrel. It looks good and smells really good. I think I'll have some. Do either of you want some?" Lao told her he wasn't hungry and Lin said, with just a little hesitation, "OK. I told my parents I would eat and do as many things as I could to experience their homeland. I guess rat drumsticks would be a good place to begin."

"These may not be fresh," said Lao. "Sometimes, meat on the street may be what didn't sell on the day before. Let's go to a restaurant where you can get a whole, fresh rat." Lao was from Peking but knew Dairen, and in a few minutes, they stopped at an outdoor restaurant. An overhead plank door was propped open in the side of a building. There was a counter and behind it was a grill with pots boiling something, a worktable and one man and two women.

In front of the restaurant there was a long narrow table with bench seats. Two bamboo cages were stacked at one end of the counter and each held about a dozen live rats. "Here we can get fresh meat," said Lao. He greeted the man behind the counter then turned to Vic and Lin. "Pick the one you want."

"Pick one? How?" Lin asked. "What's the difference? They all just look like rats."

"If you are really hungry you pick a large one, otherwise a small one. Look for good coat. If its hair is falling out it may be sick and taste bad. If he is lively the meat will be more lean. A large rat that doesn't move much will have more fat."

Lin seemed a bit hesitant so Vic said, "I've eaten armadillo, opossum and squirrel. They are all rodents and good. And you ate squirrel at my house before and liked it."

The two chose their rats and the man behind the counter reached into a cage. "I know. I'm sure I'll like it," said Lin. Then she began, "How do they k…" Her question was answered before she got it out. The man pulled a rat from the cage by its tail, flipped his wrist and sent the rat into a high arc. It fell behind the counter head first and made a soft thud when its head hit the brick floor. The man bent over and grabbed the rat and tossed it onto the table in front of a woman who immediately began to gut and skin it. Vic chose a plump rat and in seconds the other woman had it on the prep table. In just a few minutes, two well done rats were set in front of them and Lin admitted, "It does smell pretty good." They ate tentatively at first, but in the end only picked skeletons and rat heads remained.

Shortly, they were at the train station to begin an hour wait for the train to Peking. They were surprised when the Danish missionaries and their friends arrived and boarded the same train. Lao and Lin shared a seat and spoke in Chinese most of the trip. Vic chatted with the missionaries and their friends to learn about Mongolia directly from Westerners who lived there.

"We don't have permits to enter Mongolia, and our ship Captain said it may be difficult. Do you have any suggestions?" Vic asked the missionaries from Urga. They told her don't draw attention to yourself, act like you know what you're doing even if you don't, and don't even apply for permits. "You won't like this, but they don't pay much attention to women."

Lao heard this and nodded his agreement. "I have a friend who is a head guard at the gate in Kalgan where you will enter Inner Mongolia and from there it is no problem. They are correct, it is likely you could not get permits. On the other hand, the government will not care if you go without them. They do not like to give permits to foreigners because you might get killed and your country would blame them. However, if you go without a permit, it doesn't matter. The blame will be yours."

"Holy cow, Lao," said Lin, "is it really that dangerous?"

"It could be. Depends on where you go and how lucky you are."

"Oh. I like that. We won't get killed if we

331

are lucky," said Lin, sarcastically.

Vic said, "Mexico was having a revolution and I saw nothing of it. Lao is probably right that it depends on where we go."

"Yes, but I think beyond the Great Wall will yet be more dangerous than Mexico. They were near a conclusion to their revolution. The same is not true in Mongolia. There are too many hands in the pot. The Chinese took control of Mongolia last year. The Russians want to push them out. Mongols want their own country. There are rogue Russians who would have Mongolia for themselves. There are Mongol bandits, often led by rogue Russians, and Chinese bandits, the Red Beards, who kill anyone they like and take whatever they want. They are the biggest danger. Both Russia and China want to seem friendly to the Mongol people to gain favor. The rogues don't care about favor. Chu told me there are rumors that a renegade Russian, Baron von Ungren has raised an invasion force. He plans to rule as the new Genghis Khan, and he condones and encourages his forces to every known atrocity. Chu will know how best to avoid danger. If you want to see rugged country and wild animals, Vic, Chu will do a first-rate job for you, and hopefully bypass the conflict."

"Who is Chu?" Lin asked. " Chinese?"

"He is," said Lao. "He married a Mongol woman and has lived there about six years now. He used to lead trading caravans with his father into the most remote places, on the old

332

trails where the trains don't go. That is how he met his wife. We grew up together. His parents still live in the house next to my family."

"Sounds like a perfect guide," Vic said.

"He is. Besides Chinese and Mongolian, he also speaks English and Russian well and he has friends throughout Mongolia from his days on the caravans. At the gate you will meet Chin, another friend. The three of us were always together when we were kids."

They reached Peking an hour before sunset, and after farewells to the missionaries, hired rickshaws for a one hour ride to Lao's home. When they arrived, the household immediately became a hive of activity. They were served tea and cakes and Lin answered questions for two hours. Lin's aunt Jing-Wei, Lao's mother and the sister of Lin's mother, spoke a bit in English, as when she welcomed Vic, but mostly they spoke Chinese. At one point the aunt laughed and clapped her hands and Vic asked what that was about.

"She told me she was so glad her sister raised a big family and she gets to meet her eldest," Lin couldn't stop smiling. "She is really neat and she misses my mom. Mom is her little sister. They haven't seen each other for almost thirty years! They were really close as little girls, though, and have written each other twice every year, without fail. Every Lunar New Year and every autumn. My mom keeps every letter and I've seen them. They almost fill a hat box!"

The next evening there was a dinner

attended by what seemed to be every one of Lin's distant relatives. The family was fairly well to do and several large tables were set up outside within a fenced area and Vic counted 63 adults seated. Many children who ranged in ages from what looked like maybe four up to ten or so played near the tables.

During dinner, whenever Vic's plate seemed to have an empty area, someone would rush to fill it. At one point Lin came over to tell Vic a secret. "I know you love to eat, Vic, but your plate may never empty no matter how much you eat. And you might actually find something you don't like that much."

"Why are you whispering?" Vic whispered.

"I'm not sure. It may be rude to tell you this with the host and hostess here, but mom told me that everyone does this. When you are full, leave just a bite of each food on the plate. If you don't like something or there is too much, call one of the children over and give it to her, or him, and smile. You will be seen as generous and compassionate. If you take a bite first and smile as though you enjoy it, then give the rest to a child, you will be seen as even more generous and compassionate. The children learn fast and will begin to gather near you in hopes you will feel generous again. They like everything so will take anything you don't like – if there is such a thing!"

Two days later, they were up and on the move early. They left their dresses and Oxfords with Lin's aunt and caught a train to Kalgan. Even though the Great Wall at that point was in disrepair, Vic and Lin were thoroughly impressed. Armed soldiers were at the gate and eyed everyone. They waved some travelers through without a second glance, while others were stopped and questioned and a few were searched.

All the soldiers but one were armed with rifles. It was the one with a .45 that Lao went to. "Chin!" called Lao and the man turned to him. They bowed and talked good-naturedly for several minutes. Then Lao introduced Lin and Vic and told his friend Chin they were visiting Mongolia to take photographs and maybe hunt wolf and wapiti. Chin laughed his envy to Lin - he wished he had time to hunt and enjoy wapiti steaks!

Beyond the gate the area seemed no different for a distance, then the crude structures became fewer and fewer. Finally, when buildings were about to run out, they came to a low block structure with a large open barn surrounded by pens which housed horses and camels. Several automobiles were parked inside the barn, all open coupes in dire need of paint. A man of about thirty was seated on the back of one and jumped up when he saw them. It was Chu.

After Vic and Lin were introduced, Lao and Chu talked for almost an hour. "I hope you both can ride a horse well. If not, you will learn," Chu laughed. "Lao thinks you can ride."

They assured Chu they could ride, but perhaps not as well as a Mongol, since they are renowned for horsemanship. On the steppes and in the deserts, distances can be great between habitations or water, and a horse can be the difference between life and death. Just as horse theft earned you a hanging in the Old West of America, a horse thief in Mongolia would be killed immediately when found by the owner.

"But," said Chu when he saw Vic and Lin eyeballing the corral, "we won't go horseback from here. This is our ride for now," and he patted the boot of a large convertible.

Vic's first question was, "Do we need to change our dollars into Mongolian money? Will it make things easier?"

Chu answered, "Mongolia does not have its own currency. You probably won't need money but if you do, you can use your dollars or British pounds or Russian rubles or Yanchan, the Chinese-Mexican dollar. You can also use salt or tsai bricks, tea bricks in English. Trading posts as this one will always take most any of those."

Chu suggested Vic obtain some rubles, some salt and tsai and keep some dollars.

"How do you want to be paid?" Vic asked.

Chu got a strange look and said, "You don't pay me. You are Lao's friends."

"Yes I pay you. My boss provided money for a guide and Lao said you are a guide. We will be here two months or more. You can't guide us around for free. You must earn a living." Lin and Lao also assured Chu it wasn't wrong to charge them. "It's two things.

We will be friends and our tour will be business," Lin finally convinced Chu.

Once Chu agreed they went into the trading post and came out with some rubles, bags of salt blocks and tsai bricks, extra batteries for their electric lights, and American military surplus canteens. After short goodbyes to Lao, Vic and Lin threw their packs into the back seat and Vic jumped in with them. Lin rode up front with Chu. Vic took the watch out of her pocket and noted, "3 p.m. I'm not likely to need this for awhile," and she stowed the watch in the bottom of her pack.

As they rode, Chu told them about his days with caravans and about how he met his wife. It was obvious he missed her and he admitted as much, and also said he worried because there was so much lawlessness in Mongolia at that time. "Often, there can be even more trouble for my family. Most Mongols think a Mongol woman should never marry a Chinese and many Chinese think no worthy Chinese should wed a Mongol. Then the twins! My daughters are orles, half breeds, and looked down on by both races." Chu drove in silence for a minute then said, "My baby girls are the most beautiful in the world. Just wait. You'll see!"

Then Chu explained about dangers, warning them first that if they see a group of men, avoid them. It didn't matter who they were. "If they don't like you or don't trust you, or if you have something they want, you will be in danger."

"Ugh! I've heard that advice before, in Mexico.

Why is it that so often, whenever people get in a group, they want to hurt and kill other people? It disgusts me." Chu didn't understand the word disgust so Vic explained and Lin told him in Chinese.

"It is disgusting, isn't it!" Chu agreed .

The greater dangers, Chu told them, were the rogue Russians and the Hung-hu-tzes, or Chinese Red Beards. "White Russians are those who supported the tsar in the 1917 Revolution. They are not faring well in the ongoing civil war. The Hung-hu-tzes are bandits that have existed for centuries. Both are dangerous and kill anyone they wish and take whatever they want."

"Most feared by everyone is the Mad Baron. He is a White Russian with vast experience at war but said by some to be insane. He has amassed a large force to invade Mongolia, but I hear that his recruitment efforts have slowed."

"If less men join him that's good," said Lin.

"Yes, but the reason is what Vic would call disgusting. He held a large recruitment day and, because of his reputation, thousands came to join him. He inspected every man personally and if a man possessed any physical defect or any Jewish blood, the Baron killed him on the spot. So now, one who doubts his perfection is hesitant to enlist with the Baron. Most battles occur farther North, especially around Urga, but it can spread anywhere, overnight, so we must stay wary and hope the Mad Baron stays in Russia."

By then they were away from Kalgan. "Did

Lao give you weapons? He told me you can both shoot," said Chu as he stopped the auto. Vic and Lin both raised their shirt a couple of inches to reveal Colt .45 double action revolvers Lao loaned them. "He gave us fifty rounds each," Vic said. Chu got out and walked back to the boot. He pulled out a wool blanket and unwrapped three semi-auto carbines. "Winchester carbines, 20-inch barrel so they're easy to use on a horse, .351 caliber and the magazine holds 20 rounds. We each have three magazines."

Chu gave Vic and Lin each a carbine and a box of cartridges. "These are fine weapons," said Vic. "Looks like French writing on the stock. How did you get your hands on these?"

Chu told them about eighteen months earlier three men appeared one day from nowhere and hired him as a guide. They spoke English and Russian and just made maps and didn't want Russians or Chinese to know. A very quiet and mannered giant man was in charge. The others called him O. "When they left, I took them to the steppes where an aeroplane landed for them. I asked O earlier if I could just have a rifle and some ammunition for my pay instead of money since they would be more useful, and I might need them to protect my family. Before they climbed aboard the plane, O told his two men to throw their weapons on the ground along with his and all their ammunition, and then he pulled 2 full cases of ammunition from the plane and dropped them. Before he climbed in he said,

Chu, I've lost my weapons somewhere, doggonit. It means a godawful lot of paperwork, but if they ever show up it'll mean even more paperwork and I don't like paperwork. Thank you for your help and take care of your family."

Vic thought O sounded very familiar. "Were they French?" Vic asked.

"No. I'm sure they were American."

"Did this O have arms bigger than your legs, stand about two meters and have a soft voice?" Chu said yes.

"Did you hear the names of the other men?" Vic asked.

"They also only used letters. One was GQ and the other was JJ," answered Chu.

Vic half smiled and shook her head,"Oh, my... Did the one called JJ wear six guns like a cowboy?"

Chu said, "Yes! And a big cowboy hat and he had sand colored hair and always looked ready to jump. Do you know these men Vic?"

Lin looked back at Vic and said, "Yeah, Vic, do you know them? They sound kind of cloak and dagger or maybe Uncle Sammish. How would you know them?"

"I'm pretty sure I've met them. Oliver, I never learned his last name, and Jimmie Jones. I don't know about GQ. I met the others briefly in Mexico. My but they do get around."

"How did you meet them? I never heard them in the story of your Yucatan trip. What did you leave out?" asked Lin.

Vic didn't answer and by now Chu had the

auto rolling again. They were on a trail turned road, used by wagons and horses and camels for centuries, and they followed it for several miles through a deep gorge. Chu told them that for centuries the gorge was a route frequently used by Mongols to invade China. Chu probably never got the automobile over about 25 miles per hour on the better parts, but it was a guess because the speedometer didn't work. Vic noticed Lin looked a bit sullen so leaned up and whispered, "I'm sorry Lin. It's just something no one needed to hear, but now that we are traveling together I will tell you later and...tell about something else that began in Africa."

While in the gorge, they stopped a few times for Vic to snap photos. Then later when they climbed to the Mongolian plateau and were on the steppes, they stopped for Vic to take a photo of *nothingness*. "And I thought the grasslands of Nebraska could look desolate," said Vic. Lin added, "Grass and wheat look like a forest compared to this."

"Much of Mongolia is beautiful," said Chu. "There are mountains and forests and lakes and rivers. Though Westerners think of desert with the name Gobi, much of it is what you call prairie.

"I know, Chu," Vic said. "Personally, I think this is beautiful. Wide open, uncluttered, free, unlike anything many of my readers have ever experienced." They were all silent for several minutes, then Vic said, "Hear that?"

Lin asked, " What? All I hear is my own

heartbeat."

Vic nodded, "Exactly. Isn't it marvelous?"

Chu told them, "If you are unfortunate enough to be in a sand storm you may hear the opposite of silence, the banshees of hell as they wander the sands in search of souls. I don't think you will like that sound."

Just before dark, Chu drove off the road for a distance he called one li, and parked behind a small thicket of scraggly trees. Vic told Lin a li was half a kilometer or about one third mile. Lin smiled and replied, "It is also the name of a very prominent family in Nebraska."

The temperature was in the mid-fifties in the daytime but as the sun disappeared, it dropped quickly so they all pulled jackets out of their packs. They built a small fire on the opposite side of the car from the road and Chu brought out a can of corned beef and a can of hardtack for each of them. They were from the trading post in Kalgan.   "These are American military rations. Rations are given to soldiers in packages, but merchants tear them apart and sell the separate items to make more profit," Chu told them.

"Ok," said Chu as they ate, "Lao told me you two want to take photos and do some hunting. Is there anything you especially want to see or shoot?"

Vic and Lin told him they each wanted to bag a wapiti and wolf. Vic wanted photos of scenery, animals and plants and Mongols in native dress, a ger, and generally anything uncommon or exotic to her readers.

Chu didn't understand wapiti but when they described it, he said, "Oh, you want to shoot a maral. Easy enough! First stop is Dalan bulag, 70 Springs. It is what you might call a frontier town. It is the first place we come to and it will take all day tomorrow and a little more the next day to arrive."

Chu was silent a moment as he reached into one of their "money" bags to pull out a dark brown block, tsai leaves pressed together to make a brick. "Would you both like tsai?" They both answered yes so Chu set out three tin cups beside the fire. Then he scraped the tsai brick with a knife and let the shavings fall into the cups. "It's that easy and you cannot drink money in your country." He poured hot water over the shavings and handed cups to Vic and Lin.

"From Dalan bulag we go to the mountains and my family. There we take horses and make runs for maral and wolf if we don't see one before we get there. Then we will cross some dunes for photos, and I will show you a canyon where there is art from very long ago."

"Like cave art? Like ancient men would have made?" Vic asked. "I would really like to see that."

Chapter 5

Dalan Bulag

Hardtack and coffee served as the sunrise breakfast for Vic and Lin, and they asked Chu if he would like a cup of George. The instant coffee's trade name was Red E Coffee, but it was the product child of George C. L. Washington, and during the Great War, soldiers nicknamed it *cup of George.* Chu stuck with his tsai.

That day was mostly driving. They stopped a few times for photos and once for lunch. For the most part, the scenery altered little, dirt and brown grass out of sight, and even to someone seeing it for the first time, it soon became monotonous. The road changed now and then, from bad to worse, and forced Chu to slow to a crawl because of potholes or large rocks and small boulders in the road.

Two hours into the drive that day, Lin asked, "When will the scenery change?"

Chu laughed and said, "Not this day. Didn't you look at a map before coming here?"

"Of course," said Lin, "we looked at lots of

maps, but a flat paper on a table isn't the same."

"We have numbers in our head," said Vic, "but until you are here, and look ahead and behind, and see nothing to the horizon, it isn't easy to imagine the distances."

"Well, now you are down on that map. Let me try to describe where you are on the paper and where we will go," said Chu.

"Kalgan is where we met at the Great Wall, or Lao may have called it Dongkou, the Eastern gate, and it is a Chinese city. We have been traveling northwest. The distance from Kalgan to Dalan bulag is about 200 kilometers.

"That's about 125 miles," said Vic to Lin.

Chu glanced back and said, "That was fast."

"She's a numbers nut," said Lin. "Mathematician."

"Numbers are interesting, not to mention useful," defended Vic. "How else could you warn your.... friends how many bandits are coming or tell how many maral are in the herd?"

Chu nodded and continued. "From Kalgan, we traveled across Inner Mongolia which is an autonomous region of China. Now we are in Mongolia, a separate nation. From Dalan bulag, we continue northwest. We will avoid crossing the els or empty sands. We could visit beautiful canyons to the west of Dalan bulag, but I think you will find it more interesting to explore other canyons which few people have seen, even Mongols. We will travel another two and a half days beyond Dalan bulag to reach my home. There we will park this automobile, and use horses to hunt wolf and maral. Then we will ride across the els, where they are narrow, to the canyon with the ancient art."

When Chu pulled off the road as the night

before, the sun was just down. Although its light was no longer on the ground, it made the western sky white-yellow which turned to blue then black. Dinner was a repeat of the night before. As they sipped coffee and tsai, Chu told more stories of the days leading caravans with his father, and Vic followed with stories of big game hunting in Africa.

As they crawled into their pup tents, Lin told Vic, "Thanks for inviting me to come with you, Vic. You and Chu have such neat adventures to tell. The best adventure I can talk about is our trip to Chicago."

"I would have asked you to go to Mexico, but the only trips we ever made together were to Lincoln and Chicago, so for some stupid reason I just assumed you would prefer more civilized travel. I won't make that mistake again. I'm sure we will have a little adventure here. Wolf hunting ought to be exciting. And adventure is measured by experience of the adventuress. At the time, shopping in Chicago was a fantastic adventure to both of us!"

Most of the next day and evening were the same. The one difference happened in the afternoon when they scared up a flock of prairie chickens and managed to shoot two for dinner.

On the third day, early light heralded the coming sunrise when they were up, and the sun itself just topped the horizon when they pulled away. They sighted Dalan bulag one hour out of camp and reached it an hour later.

There wasn't much to Dalan bulag. A dozen stone buildings and five times that number of gers. Chu knew where to go and stopped at a single level block structure. Men loitered outside, and horses and camels milled around in small corrals beside the building. Just before they came to a stop, Chu said, "Put your revolvers where they can be seen, nod but do not smile if you pass someone. Some of the men may be bandits, and many have never imagined let alone seen a woman from the west nor eyes like yours, Vic. Try to look mean or, as they would say in Mexico, like a bad hombre."

Vic and Lin looked at each other. "I'll see what I can do," said Vic. Lin said to Chu, "So I already look like a bad hombre?"

Chu held his laugh and answered, "Chinese women are not as rare here."

Vic and Lin carried their revolvers inside their pants with their flannel shirts draped over them, so before they climbed out of the auto, they tucked in their shirts, to place the revolvers in plain view.

As they walked toward the entrance, a group of five men eyed them, and just before they reached the door, one stepped in front of Chu. The man nodded toward Vic and Lin and spoke in Mongolian in an obviously unfriendly tone. He looked at the other men, spoke quietly, then laughed unpleasantly. Then he abruptly stopped smiling and laid his hand on the pistol which hung from his neck by a leather cord.

Chu kept his eye on the men and said to Vic and Lin, "He doesn't think a Chinese should have a gun, especially a woman, and he thinks you are Russian Vic, and he likes Russians even less; but whatever you are you shouldn't have a gun."

"Whatever...." Vic started and looked straight at the man, with the most offensive 'bad hombre' look she could muster. "Would it help if he knew we can find the trigger? And won't shoot anyone. Accidentally."

Chu said, "Huh? What do...."

Before he could spit his question out, Vic said to Lin, "There are a lot of rocks around here. Let's do our rock routine." Lin nodded, and they bent down. Both kept their eyes on the men, and each took up a rock roughly the size of a softball. "Next!" said Vic and underhanded her rock straight up. Lin drew and fired and hit it twice before it dropped to head level.

Immediately Lin underhanded her rock. Vic drew and fired. Her target wasn't as solid, and the first slug cracked it in two, so Vic fired twice more and hit both halves before they were down to head level. The whole episode didn't take more than six seconds. Vic turned and held her revolver at her hip, pointed toward the man who did the talking.

Suddenly a man burst from the building. He spewed Mongolian loud and fast and waved a long shotgun! When he saw Chu, he smiled and lowered the gun, but kept talking loud and fast. Chu nodded toward the men and said something and the man from the building looked toward them, and they turned and walked away. Vic watched them and noticed that Lin also kept her revolver out and pointed meaningfully. "Lin, it's

scary how much we sometimes think alike."
They holstered their .45's, but kept them in sight.

Chu introduced the man as Bat, and they
followed him inside.   Bat   only spoke
Mongolian, so Chu explained that Bat was a
good friend of his father's for many years. This
business was half his and half his sisters'. It
was the local store, surplus, garage, stable,
restaurant, and bar. Bat took them to a table
and got them seated and called to someone. He
sat with them and talked with Chu, loud and
fast and patted Chu on the shoulder every few
words.

After a few minutes, a woman came out
with several dishes. She placed a bowl in front
of each of them gave herself one and centered
a tray on the table. Then she went around and
hugged Chu. The woman was fifty or better,
and her skin was toughened and dark from the
harsh weather and sun on the steppes.
Nonetheless, Vic and Lin were still taken by
her good looks, her perfect oval face framed by
thick, still black hair, high cheek bones, a
radiant smile and almond eyes which sparkled
like those of a ten-year-old.

Chu introduced her, "This is Bayarmaa,
my...my lawless mother I think."

Vic and Lin looked at each other puzzled,
then Lin asked Chu, "Do you mean mother-in-
law? The mother of your wife?"

"Yes!" said Chu. "My wife's mother! And
Bat is her brother."

While conversation continued among Chu
and Bayarmaa and Bat, Vic and Lin ate.

The bowls in front of them held a thick stew of hearty chunks of meat, most still attached to bone, with carrots and cabbage and it gave off a delicious smell. "Khorkhog," Chu told them. "This is goat, but any meat can be used." From the platter they took dumplings which Chu called khuushuur, meat filled and deep fried in sheep fat. "Bat says the meat is zeer he shot yesterday." After Chu described it, Vic and Lin realized that a zeer was a local antelope.

Vic and Lin both ate all the stew, and two dumplings then suddenly found their bowls filled again by an old man who appeared quietly from the kitchen. Then he reached into the large pocket of his apron and pulled out two more dumplings and placed them in front of Vic and Lin.

"If you get your fill, leave a little. Otherwise, he will continue to bring more," Chu told them.

However, that didn't seem like an imminent problem. Both thoroughly enjoyed the food, although Vic was slowed a tad as she made notes in her journal.

Chu enjoyed a very lengthy conversation with his in-laws while Vic and Lin ate a lot. They also roamed around the store and then went outside. Vic got her camera and took photos of the stables, gers, and buildings, and pretty much the whole settlement in a dozen shots.

Around noon Chu was ready to leave. Bat brought out gas cans and refilled the cans in the boot of the car and then he filled the tank. They

351

refilled their canteens, and Vic gave Chu about half the rubles and dollars and asked him to pay for the gas and get anything else they needed or which he wanted. Vic and Lin then said goodbye and through Chu's translation profusely thanked his in-laws. Chu came out, after Vic and Lin, with two bags. One was a large burlap bag he carried on a shoulder and dropped in the back floor beside Vic.

Lin reached back and opened the bag to find it full of flat round chunks of what looked like dried grass held together with something. "Is this more tsai?" She took one out, turned it over to examine, and sniffed it.

Chu laughed, "No. That's argol. For fires."

"Is it grass, or what?" asked Lin.

"It's dried camel dung."

Lin replaced the argol brick, closed the bag, wiped her finger on it, and used the sleeve of her shirt to wipe her nose where the brick had lightly touched. "Camel patties, huh?"

The other cloth bag was the size of a football and Lin asked "What's in that bag? Or would I rather not know?"

"Bortz," Chu answered and pulled one out of the bag. It was dark brown, the size of a finger.

"It looks like a stick," said Vic. Her journal was out again and she made notes.

"It's dried meat," said Chu. "Grind it up, put the powder in water and use it to make stew or just drink it if you don't have anything else. It is for Narakaa, my wife."

Vic and Lin looked at each other and said,

"Mongolian bouillon cubes!"

As they left the trading post, Vic asked, "What were your mother-in-law and her brother wearing?"

Chu's in-laws both wore clothing very similar, except for a bit of styling. It resembled a robe with a single button on one side, with a sash, and the billowing sleeves extended beyond the wearer's fingertips. The garment ended just below the knees and both Bayarmaa and Bat wore trousers beneath.

"It is called a deel," Chu told them. "It is the traditional dress. If you like I will have Narakaa make deels for you."

"Absolutely not!" said Vic. "Don't *have* your wife do anything. If she wants to teach Lin and me so we could make our own, that would be fun."

"Yes. You can make winter deels for it will be very cold while you are here."

Because of the late start from Dalan bulag they had less than three hours before sundown, however it didn't matter. There were things they wanted to do but no time schedule to keep. About half an hour before sunset, Chu pulled off the road and headed for some boulders at the bottom of a small hill. They were nearly there when a desert hare popped from behind a bush and darted. Vic saw it and stood up and pulled her revolver. Chu didn't get a chance to stop. Vic fired one shot, and the hare jumped into the air, flipped and fell dead. Vic jumped out to retrieve the hare while Chu parked.

Lin pulled out some argol and started a fire.

Vic cleaned the hare and in a few minutes it was roasting on a stick. While it cooked they set up their pup tents and put on jackets.

"How long before it begins to get really cold?" asked Vic.

"It would not be strange if you notice it is more cold every few days," Chu told her.

Later as they ate, the howls of wolves were heard in two directions. "Sounds like finding a wolf won't be a problem," said Vic.

The next morning they rose early and were eager. They continued northwest, more or less, with mountains in the near distance on their left. Around noon, Chu said he would cook them a traditional Mongolian meal to write about and diverged from the path toward some low hills. In the foothills, they came upon a colony of tarbagans and were able to shoot two before they dived into burrows.

"I will show you boodog," Chu told them. "Tarbagans will soon begin to hibernate until Spring. You can make boodog with goat or other meat but I think tarbagan is best." They began a fire and dropped several stones into the flames. Chu showed them what wild onion looked like and Vic and Lin harvested wild onions for half an hour. Back at the campsite, they found Chu removed the heads and organs and most hair from the tarbagans. He took salt from one of the money bags, and rubbed it inside of the carcasses. Then he put heated stones inside the bodies and closed them tight with leather cords. The tarbagans were hung on branches over the fire for the outside to roast while the stones cooked the inside. The onions were put in water in their canteen cups and set on the fire. Half way through cooking, Chu opened the tarbagans to release steam, then resealed them. He warned that if steam wasn't released the boodog could explode.

About two hours after they began they enjoyed a meal of tarbagan boodog, very tender marmot meat with boiled onions. Vic and Lin loved it. The rest of the day was more of the same travel wise, as Vic made notes about boodog and asked Chu an unending stream of food related questions.

VIC: DOUBLE TROUBLE

Chapter 6

Heaps of Corpses

Three hours out the next morning, soon after they passed a vast expanse of els on their right, Chu saw riders in the distance and alerted Vic and Lin.

When the riders neared, they could see there was no need for alarm. It was a man, his wife and two children, a boy and a girl each around 10. They led two pack horses.

Chu spoke with them for a while, and Vic asked for and received permission to take a photo of the family. After she snapped two shots of the family, she thanked them with a brick each of salt and tsai. Before the people rode on, Chu handed them a note and said something which plainly made the adults happy.

When they were gone, Vic questioned, "What did you give them? They sure thought that paper was swell."

"A note to Bayarmaa and Bat. I asked them to help these people, just house their animals for awhile and let them work for anything they need."

"Aren't they nomadic? Don't they carry what they need," asked Lin.

"Usually, but they left Gazar quickly and abandoned some things. Red Beards were there two weeks past, and a week ago a group of Russians came who may have been men of the Mad Baron. Both groups took whatever they wanted and killed several people. He and his family lost many things. Then three days ago Mongolian soldiers came looking for Red Beards or the Russian bandits. There are several hundred camped outside the city and will likely stay awhile. The man was fearful for his wife and daughter, so they are going to Dalan bulag."

"That's terrible," said Lin. "You mean group after group of thugs or whoever they call themselves can terrorize an entire town?"

"Yes. Unfortunately, that is the way of life for now," answered Chu.

"Not an uncommon situation in history. How large is Gazar?" Vic asked.

"Ten times or more than Dalan bulag."

"Do we pass through it?"

"No, luckily. We would need to turn northward in a bit," Chu told her.

"Can we go there?" Vic asked. "Is it far?"

"Go to Gazar?" Chu looked unbelieving.

"Shouldn't it be safe if the men there are Mongolian soldiers?"

"Maybe. Mongolia does not have an official army. The Chinese disbanded it last year.

Groups have formed in anticipation of becoming a sovereign country again, but they are only as civil as the man who leads them."

Vic wanted to visit anyway, so a kilometer up the road they turned northeast, and an hour before dark they ran into more people abandoning Gazar. This time three families traveled together and left for the same reason as the others. They told Chu he should stop because they couldn't reach Gazar before dark.

The soldiers were eager to find anyone associated with the Mad Baron or the Red Beards. The government decreed that every other ger must keep a fire burning throughout the night, and in every fifth ger, someone must remain on watch all night. To attempt to enter Gazar after dark would probably get them killed. They camped early.

Mid-morning the next day they drove slowly into Gazar. Mongol soldiers were everywhere in groups of five or more. They all carried rifles with bayonets fixed, and none of them looked friendly.

The people the night before told Chu an official office was set up in the center of town. "We will go there. It is best if we ask permission. We'll find who is in charge and I'll explain that you are a writer and want to take photos of Mongolian cities. If he says OK, we will take photos, if it isn't OK, we will quietly and quickly leave the way we came."

Shortly, they came to a long rectangular

block building, not unlike the trading post at Dalan bulag. At one end was an office.

Several soldiers stood outside the office door, and Chu went up to speak with them Shortly, one of them went inside. After a few minutes, he came out and spoke to Chu who waved for Vic and Lin to come up, and the three of them followed the soldier inside.

An officer sat behind a desk and eyed them sternly as they entered. He didn't speak but looked intensely at Chu, who looked just as intensely at the officer. The officer stood and came around to face Chu eye to eye as they talked. It was evident that both men were asking questions, and the officer kept looking at Vic. Then the two men shook hands. The officer pointed to Vic and spoke to Chu and laughed. He held his arms open wide like he might be telling about the big fish that got away.

Chu looked at Vic and Lin and said, "This is Captain Unegen. His brother and my father were very good friends, and I met the captain once many years ago, and he recognized me. What is more important, he recognizes Vic Challenger." "What?" It still amazed Vic, but there was only one way. The picture and story of her and the jaguar in Mexico were syndicated worldwide. The captain read the story in a Russian paper.

"He is greatly surprised. He thought you would be bigger with massive muscles and maybe have a hairy face. He says you look too

360

pretty to kill such a beast with only a knife."

For an instant, Vic was dumbfounded and showed it, then she smiled and said, "Thank him for the compliment and tell him I love his country."

Of course, Vic got to take photos. The captain personally escorted them throughout the town and Vic retold the story of Mexico through Chu, as she took photos of groups of soldiers and gers and camels. Late in the afternoon, the captain took them to a field of what looked like large steamer trunks, each padlocked and with an oval slot on the side that was maybe 12 x 6 inches. Vic didn't count but there looked to be at least two dozen, and moans came from within several. With an ostentatious smile, the captain gestured and nodded toward the boxes and spoke.

Chu said, "He wants you to see how he punishes criminals. Most will be in their box until they die."

Vic was horrified but managed a small smile and a slight nod as though she approved. She looked at Lin and saw she must be horrified, too, so she put a hand on Lin's shoulder and looked her in the eye and with a smile said, "We shouldn't show disapproval. We are his guests, and they have a lot more guns. We can puke later," Vic finished as she gave the captain a smile and nod.

"Oh!" said Lin and she smiled and nodded as though she just understood something.

Chu translated that the captain invited Vic to take photos of their system. He thought it was more efficient as it didn't require as much space as a western jail and they did not feed those who committed the worst crimes, which saved money because they would die before long to make room for other criminals. To further assure adequate punishment, prison boxes were designed too short and too low for the prisoner to either fully lie down or sit erect.

Vic snapped some photos and just before the third one, an old, gray-haired woman pushed her face and a forearm through the hole of her prison box, looked forlornly at Vic, and in the most lamentable voice Vic would ever hear, wailed in Mongolian and repeatedly curled her fingers in a gesture of need. Vic bit the inside of her cheek and took the photo, while in her mind she screamed, *what in the name of heaven could an old woman do, to deserve being starved to death in a box?* Vic and Lin were ready to leave.

The captain, however, suddenly became excited. Through, Chu he told them an execution was scheduled for tomorrow, but they could go ahead so Vic could witness it.

"Oh my God!" whispered Lin with a forced smile. "Are we going to watch them kill someone? What if it's that old woman? What if it's a child?"

Vic said, "Relax. We must continue to fake approval because there is nothing we can do," said Vic. "And it could be worse. He isn't going to execute someone just to make a show for us. Captain Unegen said the executions were scheduled. We don't know the story behind any of the prisoners. Even the old woman may have murdered someone."

Chu agreed with Vic, but first told the captain they didn't want to change their rules or impose on the captain. The captain assured them, though, that it was no problem and afterward they could have dinner with him.

"Appetizing," said Lin.

Vic put an arm around Lin's shoulders and said, "It's just life, Lin. The very ugly side of life," and they both nodded at the captain and smiled.

Within minutes, a group of seven soldiers appeared and two prisoners were crudely yanked from their boxes and shoved out beyond the array of diminutive, solitary dungeons where they were forced to their knees with their backs to the town.

Vic asked about the crimes of the two condemned men. One killed a Mongol soldier, and the other gave information to Red Beards. The captain wanted to make an example. Vic said, "Well, one is a murderer and the other committed treason. We would execute them in America, too, and certainly, they knew their actions could get them killed."

There was no ceremony to the event. Once the men were on their knees, one soldier said

363

something to the others, three soldiers aimed at the back of the head of each prisoner and then the one soldier spoke one word, *rener.* All six rifles went off. Three rounds from a high powered rifle didn't leave much and the two now almost headless corpses collapsed into the dirt. Then a soldier took each leg of the two and dragged them away. Vic snapped photos during the ordeal. Lin watched the execution with a strange fascination but quickly looked away when a length of brain matter commenced to bounce along behind a corpse.

The captain smiled and said something to Chu who relayed to Vic, " He wants your opinion."

"Oh," said Vic, "It was so fast and efficient." As Chu translated, she nodded and smiled and so did Lin and the captain seemed quite pleased.

The sun was behind mountains and darkness was quickly descending. The captain now wanted to take them along to the outskirts of town they hadn't seen yet. Two soldiers went with them and conspicuously kept their rifles at the ready. As they walked along in the general direction of the office, along the outside row of gers, in the deepening darkness they could just make out knee-high, irregular heaps of some unknown.

Suddenly, muffled but vicious snarls and crunching sounds erupted nearby, and the captain ordered his soldiers to shine lights toward the unsavory noise. The heaps were not stones or logs, as one might expect, but piles of corpses. There were old bones, half decomposed carcasses and newer dead. The crunches and rips were wild dogs feeding on the carrion. They were not healthy dogs, but vicious brutes with conspicuous, weeping sores and missing clumps of hair. Not one was without fresh or dried blood and a sickly-yellow drool on its muzzle.

The captain was proud of how the dogs were useful. The wind, most of the time, was from the other direction so people need not smell the dead and the dogs served a valuable service as they cleaned up well and even acted as sentries for that side of the town. He cautioned not to go in that area without a weapon. Just two nights earlier, one of his men went to urinate too near the dead without his weapon. Dogs attacked him and tore him to pieces. It was just at that exciting bit of information that a new din of fierce growls and snarls commenced near them, and the soldiers shined their lights on the commotion. Several large dogs were ripping chunks of meat from the two men just executed.

"I'm hungry," said Vic, "Can we go eat now?"

Chu translated to the captain what Vic said, and he replied *of course.* Lin whispered, "I'm not hungry but anything is better than seeing more, and after a second she added, "Does he really think we might want to go for a walk among piles of rotting dead people, whether we

365

have a gun or not?"

Vic spoke to Lin quietly, "It's a horrible thing, but this brutality has been around for 100,000 years and may well be here 100,000 years from now. Remind yourself it could be worse. We could be on the pile."

"That doesn't make it right," said Lin.

"Not to us, but it is his country, his culture, and in his way, he is providing as much safety and civility to his people as he knows how. None of this is unusual for here and now. Even more important, you are a good person Lin. I know you will do good things in your life, good things for others, good deeds that would go undone if you were on that pile. That is why we smile and nod. That makes it as close to right as it will ever get."

Back at the block building, they went into the trading post tavern beside the office. The couple who owned the business cleared a table and waited on the captain and his guests while the two soldiers who were with them through the revolting tour stood solemnly against the wall behind the captain.

They enjoyed the simple meal in spite of what they witnessed on the excursion around town. They got all the boiled mutton and whole onions they wanted and drank tsai with milk and salt. During the meal, Vic entertained the captain with stories of big game hunting in Africa and the earthquake. Then through Chu's translation, she took notes about the captain's exploits and asked his permission to write about him, which seemed to please the captain greatly.

Afterward, the captain offered the back of the restaurant for them to sleep. They thanked him and gladly accepted. The temperature outside hovered around 30 degrees Fahrenheit, and it was windy.

Vic was about to go out for her sleeping roll when Chu stopped her and smiled at Lin and said, "Lin, you need to go get gear for all of us and seem pleasant about it."

"OK, I'm pleasant," Lin replied with an exaggerated smile. "Tell me why."

"The captain asked why you are with us, thinking you might be a spy for Red Beards. I told him you are from America also and that you are Vic's servant. It seemed the most believable story for his ears," said Chu shrugging.

Lin continued to smile, nodded and when she spoke, Vic fought to keep from laughing. Since their days in high school, Lin practiced and became better and better at what she called her 'southern belle' accent. Vic loved it; it always made her laugh. Unfortunately, Lin seldom used it unless she was upset.

Lin said, "Well now, I'll just take my little old self out there in the cold, the horrible cold, and fetch bed rolls for Master Chu and Lady Victoria as fast as this poor little servant girl can move. Thank you so much for the singular honor of waiting on the two of you. Did I mention the horrible cold?" she smiled and curtsied and started for the door. The captain said something and Lin heard Chu translate for Vic. "The captain says you have a very pleasant and obedient servant as befits a strong warrior." Vic struggled to hold in the laugh and thanked the captain through Chu, and as she closed the door behind her, Lin made a sound quite similar to the growl of a wild, corpse-eating dog.

Despite the cordiality of the captain, the three slept lightly, each with a hand on the revolver beneath their shirt, but there was nothing to worry over. In the morning, after more boiled mutton for breakfast, they thanked the captain for his gracious hospitality, and as Vic took a photo of the captain beside his horse, Chu disappeared inside for a moment. Just before they left, the captain spoke to Vic through Chu, "If you go west and high into the mountains you may find one of our leopards to fight or perhaps a bear, but if not, there are wolves everywhere. That would be a magnificent battle for you!"

Vic's answer was a big smile with much head nodding, "I would love to fight one of your wolves, maybe two at one time! Or even three!" Chu translated the intended exaggeration, and it greatly excited the captain who replied he couldn't wait to see the photos in the newspaper.

Then they said goodbye and went out to the auto. When they climbed in, Vic and Lin found a new bag in the floor and asked Chu. He told them to ignore it. It was fabric for their deels. Mindful that the captain might force the shopkeepers to give it without pay, Chu paid for it while the captain was not around, and the owner of the shop dropped it in the auto.

They drove slowly out of town and then sped as much as they safely could, to put distance between them and Gazar.

"Chu," said Vic after they passed out of town, "Have you heard the expression *hell on earth*? I think that is where we spent the night."

"And how!"said Lin. "I see you have another small bag, Chu. What is it?"

"It's sweet aaruul." Chu dug in the bag as he drove and pulled one out. It looked a little like a white cookie, smooth, the size of a silver dollar. Chu explained it was dried curdled milk. It can be made of milk from pretty much any handy lactating animal and can be cut square or round in any size. It could also be run through a meat grinder to make worm aaruul. "We make our own but most times with salt and this has sugar. If made from mare's milk it is sweet by nature, but we usually make it from sheep milk. The girls will like this."

"Original Mongolian candy," said Lin and Vic pulled out her journal to make notes.

After they traveled a few miles, Lin spoke again, this time in her southern belle accent.

"When we stop later, y'all eggs be sure and take it easy, find a place to put up your feet while I make everything ducky, like a good little servant. Maybe enjoy yourselves a nice little

369

nap while I prepare your royal tsai and coffee. I wouldn't want either of you to break even a tiny little sweat. Maybe I can fetch a whole pack of wolves for Lady Victoria to fight!"

"I'm sorry about that horrible cold last night," said Vic. You are hereby appointed to partner."

Lin looked back at Vic and grinned, "It's really this guy's fault. I'll need to come up with an adequate penance." Chu was smart enough to stay quiet.

By noon they turned back northwest, their route before they sidetracked to Gazar, and they covered about fifty miles before they stopped for the night.

Two days later in the early afternoon, they ascended slowly, steadily up a long gentle slope into mountains. There was no road, merely some areas with less vegetation than others. They didn't climb to the top of the mountains. Chu turned to go along the contour of the mountain between stands of trees and suddenly topped a little rise and shouted, "There is my home!"

A hundred meters ahead was a ger like any other, but in a setting which made Vic and Lin both catch their breath. On three sides of this ger stood a beautiful patchwork of green pine, blue-green spruce and the gray-brown orange of larch losing their leaves and behind it, rising above the trees was a backdrop of distant, snow covered mountaintops. Chu honked the horn and yelled out in Mongolian. A woman came out, and when she saw them she ran to meet the car, and a little girl ran on either side of her.

Chapter 7

Wolves and Weapons

Chu stopped before the ger and jumped out and hugged his wife and lifted her off the ground while the two little girls wrapped their arms around his legs and squealed over and over, "Aav, Aav!" The four spoke Mongolian for several minutes; then Chu introduced his family to Vic and Lin.

His wife and daughters were quadrilingual, like Chu. They spoke Mongolian, Chinese, and a little English and Russian. Of course, the girls spoke all four languages at a seven-year-old level, which Vic liked since she knew zero Chinese, Mongolian or Russian.

The given name of Chu's wife was Narantsetseg, which means *sunflower,* but she was called Narakaa. The twin girls were Mönkhtsetseg, *eternal flower* and Mönkh-Erdene, *eternal jewel.* Luckily, like Narakaa they had shortened names or nicknames, Segree and Monkkaa. All three were excited to have guests and the little girls immediately latched onto both visitors. They saw few Chinese other than their dad and never met a Westerner before Vic. Within a few minutes, they named their new friends. They called Lin *yanztai egch*, nice big sister and Vic was *yanztai bacgan*, nice girl.

They enjoyed a fabulous vacation at the ger for a few days. Vic and Lin learned much of Mongolian fashion and cooking from Narakaa. Vic used several rolls of film to take photos of the mountains and the family. They both often played with the twins, but Lin especially enjoyed the little girls, and they seemed to enjoy time with *yanztai egch*, since she spoke two of their languages.

A sizeable chunk of time was devoted to shagai or sheep-ankle-bones games. The twins taught them several shagai games, like cat's game, open catch, tossing three shagai, and four animals. Monkkaa or Segree always won. Vic was accustomed to losing, but Lin couldn't believe at first that seven-year-olds were beating her in games. Lin did best in cat's game, a form of jacks or knucklebones.

Of course one big project was their deels. Narakaa guided them to cut and sew the fabric from Gazar. They used sheep skin to line the deels and two fabric knots served as buttons. The sleeves were fashioned longer than their arms to create overhang to keep hands warm when not using them. Slits were cut in the deel for mobility, especially on horseback, and Narakaa gave them silk sashes. Vic and Lin wondered why both front flaps of the deel folded completely across their body. They found when they added the sash, that it formed a very handy pouch between the folds.

Narakaa also helped them fashion the hides of sheep rear ends, turned inside out, into warm hats with ear flaps.

They went horseback riding with the entire family several times and on the first occasion, they were astonished when Chu put each girl up on her horse and gave her the reins. They were excellent riders and Chu explained that all Mongolian children are taught to ride as soon as they can walk, if not sooner. At first Lin and Vic both were afraid the girls would fall on some of the slopes but on the second outing, the girls said let's race, so they did. The girls won and asked Chu why the nice girls couldn't ride better and Chu told the twins it was because they were not Mongolian. They thought that was funny and laughed until tears were in their eyes. They laughed so loud and long that Lin and Vic caught it and laughed until tears were in their eyes, too. Vic and Lin did not worry about the twins after that.

That night Vic borrowed a mirror from Narakaa and took the twins out to look at the moon. They positioned the mirror to catch the full moon reflection and used their magnifiers to view the lunar mountains and craters. Then Vic pointed out the asterism we call the Big Dipper and told about it and the legend of Calisto and Arcas. Then the twins, through Lin, told Vic and Lin about the Seven Gods, the very same set of stars. It was a night in a class of its own.

One day Vic and Lin played hide and seek with the twins in the forest beside the ger and Lin said, "Aren't they adorable. I can't get over how cute and smart they are!"

Vic said to Lin, "I would love to have a daughter someday, and laugh with her and watch her grow up."

"A little Vic would be nice, huh," said Lin. "Dress her up with pretty dresses and a little cloche! I'd like to have a little Lin someday, too." Then Lin looked toward the woods where the twins were hiding and called out, "Here we come! Wǒmen shàngqián yǐ nǐmen!"

On the eighth day, they enjoyed an outing of sorts. The night before, a wolf killed a sheep and that was not a thing taken lightly. Wolves were like mortal and historic enemies of the Mongols. Sheep provided meat and milk and wool. Even more importantly, for a wolf to come so close was a danger to the girls. Chu kept dogs like all Mongols but owned only two which were both killed a month earlier when they went into a herd of maral and were kicked to death. He didn't get a chance to replace them yet.

The wolf didn't chew on the entire sheep, so a hind leg and the head were kept to eat later. Chu took the rest to lure the wolf.

Narakaa followed a pair of wolves a couple of times but lost them, yet she had a good idea where they might be. They went down in a valley about two miles from their ger. Several openings were prominent on the far side of the valley on a steep hillside. Chu left the others behind cover about 200 yards from the slope and rode over to drop the bag with the carcass below the openings, then rode in a circle back to join the others. He said there were tracks where he dropped the bait and they settled where they could observe unseen.

Chu said Vic or Lin could shoot the wolf if it came out but they both declined because Narakaa said she wanted to kill this wolf. They could go on a hunt another day.

The twins amazed Vic and Lin. Neither ever saw five year olds so quiet. They didn't make a sound as they intently and patiently peered through the bushes for the wolf. An uneventful hour of watching ended when Monkkaa waved a hand and got their attention, "Psst! " Then she and Segree both whispered, " Chinua!" Of course, Vic and Lin were impressed about one second later when they saw the muzzle of a wolf inch out from a dark hole on the slope.

Earlier, Narakaa drove a long branch with a fork in the end into the ground with the fork at eye level. She now placed the barrel of her rifle in the fork and took aim. Then she relaxed and raised the barrel a bit. "There is another," she said to Lin in Chinese and immediately another wolf came out and the two animals sniffed the air for a sign of danger.

Narakaa spoke to Lin in Chinese and nodded right. Then she re-aimed on the post and Lin aimed without a post. For a few seconds it seemed no one breathed, then

Narakaa whispered "Rener." Simultaneously the two rifles fired and both wolves lurched just slightly and fell over. The twins immediately jumped up and down and clapped their hands and jabbered rapid fire in their mix of Mongolian, Chinese, Russian and English.

They all led their horses over to the wolves and Lin and Narakaa each pulled a knife to skin the wolf she shot. The wolves were on a ledge about six meters up and Chu climbed up and threw the bodies down. Both pelts were a beautiful bushy mix of dark gray to silver on the back and sides, with pure white bellies, and would be use to make handsome, practical winter pants for the girls. The twins ran to watch Lin and almost immediately tapped her on the arm and shook their heads. They spoke in Chinese, clearly to condemn Lin's technique.

Vic looked up at the hillside which went almost perpendicular to the ground from just above the lair. There was practically no vegetation on the hill and Vic said "These barren hills are beautiful. I think I'll have a look around."

Lin fought to not laugh as the twins continued to scold her. Vic looked over and said "I just can't bear to witness the humiliation!" Then she laid her carbine down, pulled up the sleeves of her deel, tightened the straps on her pack and scaled the steep hill without hesitation. Her five companions stopped what they were doing and watched Vic pull herself up the cliff as nimbly as a rock squirrel. Vic came to the ledge a good 25 meters above them and went out of sight and the others went back to skinning the wolves.

Three hours later when the wolves were skinned and their meat cut for food, Vic had not yet returned, so Lin moved to where she could see the ledge. Vic sat admiring the valley and Lin called to her twice before Vic noticed. Then she waved and scrambled down the cliff.

When Vic reached the bottom she smiled and told them "I got some great photos and wrote some terrific descriptions, if I do say so myself. I also took on a bit of cargo up top," and with a twinkle in her eye, she opened her pack and pulled out the bounty. "Look what I found!"

"That's jade!" said Lin.

"I'm going to make a knife!"

"A stone knife like you used to battle the jaguar?" Chu asked. Vic told him yes and Chu translated for his wife and she seemed very excited. "Narakaa wants to know if you will make her a knife," Chu told Vic.

Vic looked at Narakaa and nodded. Then, with just her empty haversack, she started back up the cliff face to collect more jade. As she topped the edge to the ledge, Lin yelled up to her, "Get enough for me, too! And for Chu." When Vic came down, she said she brought enough for the girls, also, plus a large slab to make an ax. Then she went to what was left of the skinned wolf carcasses and cut the ligaments from their legs. Then they returned home where the wolf hides were stretched on frames atop the ger.

The next morning after breakfast Lin and

Narakaa took down the wolf hides and crumpled them to keep them soft, then turned and re-stretched them and replaced them on the ger roof. Then they began work on their knives. First they collected tools - a hammer stone, points from maral antlers for a pointed tool, sheep skulls full of sand and fine gravel for sharpening and a pad of camel leather to lay across their lap for a work surface.

Each began with a block of jade larger than the knives which would be the finished product. Then under Vic's direction they plunged into the slow, careful process and with angled, almost delicate strikes, began to shape their new weapons from the raw, green stones.

After sunset on the fourth day, they wrapped the flat end of their stone knives with camel leather and all were happy with their jade knife, especially Segree and Monkkaa.

The following day, everyone else went to other activities and Vic pulled out the largest stone she collected and began to work on an ax head. It would not be as large as she liked, but it would be deadly and it would be beautiful. Vic planned to shape and sharpen only one side. She needed to find a suitable haft, and shape and harden it to take the stone, and then shape the back of the stone head for a good fit. She would then slowly scrape and grind furrows into the stone for her cordage. After sundown on the sixth day of her labor, Vic used the wolf sinew and pine resin to attach the head to the haft.

Vic told the others she regretted she was so absorbed for so long, but no one minded. For

Vic, no matter what other weapons were available, she felt unarmed without a war ax. Now Vic was armed.

After the evening meal on the day Vic finished her ax, what seemed to have become an obligatory part of her life happened again. Vic was asked to tell the jaguar story. Narakaa thought her twins would love to hear Vic tell the story, and when the girls clapped it was inescapable.

To begin, Chu described a jaguar to the twins and told them how big it was. Vic thought, from the way Chu spread his arms, that he might be exaggerating the size of the cat. When he held his hands apart to illustrate the size of the fangs, she smiled. Chu seemed to be describing a saber-cat.

When Vic finished the story of the jaguar, the twins bounced and laughed and asked their mother questions, then clapped at the answers. It made Vic feel so good to see their excitement that she thought that if she came all this way just for this night, the trip would be worth it. Then the night got even better.

While the twins bounced and laughed, Lin leaned toward Vic and whispered, "When are you going to tell me the rest of the story? Don't forget."

At the same time, Narakaa spoke to Chu and then he translated, "Narakaa thanks you. Because of stories like yours, she knows her daughters will grow to be great women."

Vic froze at those words. In Mexico, Pablo spoke those exact words about his nieces just before he died. For a second, Vic stared silently at Narakaa. "Tell Narakaa that she is a wonderful mother and that I hope someday I may be a mother as fine as her. I am honored to share the story with her and her daughters and I know they will be great women, but it will be because she is a strong kheezh."

Narakaa smiled back at Vic and nodded at the translation. For a moment everyone was silent. Vic looked at Lin then at Chu then at the twins and Narakaa then back at Lin. "Would all of you care to hear the rest of the story? The parts no one knows except those who were there. The secret story. It will take a while and it is late but if you want to hear it I will tell it."

Chu translated for Narakaa as Vic spoke and no sooner did Vic finish when Narakaa nodded and the twins did their clap, laugh and bounce again. Then the twins positioned themselves cross-legged in front of Vic with a beautiful look of childish wonder on their faces.

"Tell us Vic," said Lin.

So Vic told more of the story. The jaguar didn't just wander into camp but was attracted by Pablo's body. She told of the gunfight where Pablo was killed. "That's where I met O and JJ," she told Lin.

Vic described being taken by what the camp cook, Maria, called a thunderbird, and how she later killed the beast in the underground river.

When Vic stopped, Narakaa spoke and Chu told her "Narakaa thinks there is more. You were in that jungle for a greater purpose."

"Narakaa is wise," Vic said. Then she looked at Lin and half whispered, "Here's the scary part, where you might think I'm a fruitcake." Lin shook her head and said, "No way."

Then Vic told the secret story of Africa, the years of vivid dreams, the earthquake, and how she fainted and in the space of three minutes she re-experienced her last weeks as Nat-ul. She told of Nu, and how he killed Gr for her. Finally, she told how she visited the cave re-opened by the earthquake, where Nu died as he protected the head of Gr for Nat-ul. Then she said aloud what she had never spoken aloud before. Until that moment the thought lived privately in her mind. "I loved Nu above all else and I still do. We were buried apart and yet the love lives, and I will search for Nu until I find him, or until death stops me again."

When Vic finished, Narakaa and Lin thanked her for sharing her secret story and the twins hugged her. Nor did a single one of them harbor any measure of doubt of the story and accepted it as readily as if Vic told them she walked in a Nebraska cornfield. Nor did Vic feel any discomfort at sharing her secret with those present as she feared beforehand.

In the morning as they awoke, Lin grabbed Vic's arm and shook her, "Hey. I don't think you're a fruit cake. I'm glad I know why you want to visit these wild and wooly places. I want to keep traveling with you, too. Maybe I will be in the right place at the right time like you and will remember something wonderful."

"Thanks Lin. You have an open invitation!"

They were at the ger twelve more days. They took several day rides and were amazed at the array of wildlife. They saw a rare mazalai or Gobi's brown bear, lynx, saïga antelope, zeer, wild donkey, wild camel, and argali sheep. On one ride they spotted a small herd of takhi or Przewalski horses. Vic snapped the first photos about 800 meters distant, and stopped to take another photo every 200 meters. The takhi finally trotted off when they were about 100 meters away.

On one day trip Vic shot a lynx and on another Lin shot a fox. They used those skins for the outside of their sheep-butt-hats which made them warmer, and attractive enough to wear anywhere.

Vic wrote a lot in her journal, she and Lin taught the twins more English and learned some Mongolian from them, and both learned more about every-day life in Mongolia. Daily they reveled in playing shagai games with Monkkaa and Segree, although they continued to lose.

One morning Lin said exactly what Vic was thinking, "Could heaven be any better? A loving, happy family and scenery so fresh and beautiful it excites and amazes you all over again every morning. Mongolia is magnificent!"

Chapter 8

Monsters and Bad Guys

Chu was ready to take them to see the primitive rock paintings. They also hoped to see maral and Vic still wanted a wolf. They took horses this trip and waved goodbye to the twins and Narakaa just as the sun peeked over the left shoulder of the alpine ger home.

It was noticeably colder as Chu predicted. Days were generally no warmer than the mid-thirties and nights were near zero Fahrenheit. Heavy trousers and flannel shirts under the deels kept them warm while they were active and Chu gave each a sheep skin to add to her bedroll for ground cover.

They took it slow down the mountain. When they reached the steppes, they headed toward another mountain range. Chu timed it well, and before dark, they came to what Chu called a river, but Vic and Lin called it a creek. It was about fifty meters across but no deeper than a foot at that point. Just a few meters on the other side of the river were dunes, the els. Just feet from the water was a site where some trees and boulders broke the icy wind which gusted down from the northeast. That is where they set up camp.

Before the sun was up, they had coffee and dried mutton and broke camp. They crossed the river as the sun came over the mountains and gave them long shadows. Within minutes on the els, the campsite was lost behind a dune. All they could see in every direction was sand - no plants nor even rocks. Just sand. Of course, Vic stopped to snap photos.

Chu told them, "I've been across the els often and can usually travel a straight line by watching the sun move. It is important to keep a straight line. These els are not that wide. Perhaps only eight kilometers here. But the length is great. They stretch 100 kilometers north toward the mountains. If you lost direction and went the length, you could run out of food and water and die. The shortest distance across these els is to the northeast or southwest, give or take."

They were twenty-five minutes or so into the ride, probably half way across the els when Chu halted his horse and pointed to a half dozen small trees to their right, a miniature, scraggly oasis in the midst of thousands of square kilometers of uninterrupted sand. "Let me show you something useful," Chu said and headed toward the trees.

"We've seen these before," said Lin.

"A few times," said Vic. "We camped beside some the first night out of Kalgan."

"It is an important plant on the steppes and in the els. It can save your life, and now you shall learn about it."

The site included a couple of patches of semi hard surface where the sand was packed and was like a crust. The three dismounted and Chu stood beside one of the shrubs. "This is a zag tree. It is called saxaul tree by foreigners." Chu broke off a branch that appeared to be dry and peeled a strip of bark. Then he tipped his head back, squeezed the bark and water dripped into his mouth.

"Almost like the lianas in a jungle," said Vic.

"When the bark or a limb is dry it is good for a fire." Chu bent down and cleared sand from a root, cut it and pulled it from the ground. What looked like small potatoes grew along the root. "These are not part of the tree. This is cistanche." Lin seemed excited, and the two spoke Chinese for a minute, then Lin turned to Vic.

"Cistanche is an herb used in Chinese medicine. I use it a lot, but I've never seen it like this. We get it in jars imported to us. Chu, could I grow it if I took some home?"

"I don't know, but my guess is they would grow. They are very hardy," said Chu. Then he quickly added, "What if you need a zag tree, too? But maybe a zag root will grow you a tree."

"Worth trying," said Lin. This is great stuff, Vic," Lin stowed some cistanche and saxaul root in her pack. Vic snapped photos of the tree and Lin as she cut a root, then replaced her camera into her pack.

In spite of the temperature, the sun warmed them up in their deels and it was bright. Lin said, "Makes a nice shade tree, too." She dropped hard in the shadow of a zag tree and immediately stared up at Vic with a look of bewilderment.

"This doesn't feel right," Lin said as she pressed on the sand.

Under Lin, the ground seemed to move and suddenly just beside her, the sand exploded upward and the most bizarre and horrid creature any of the three could imagine reared up a meter high beside Lin!

Vic had no idea what it was, but it opened a mouth armed with multiple rows of pointy teeth and was large enough to easily gulp Lin's head. The mouth reminded her of a lamprey and she didn't wait to see what it would do. Making perhaps the fastest draw of her life, to date, Vic yanked the revolver from her deel sash and planted three rounds into the cavernous mouth.

Meanwhile, Lin rolled to the side and jumped up. Her revolver was in her hand by the time she was on her feet! "Holy jumping Jehoshaphat! What is that thing?"

"I don't believe it! Watch for more," Chu said as he warily looked all around them. "That must be a death worm. I thought it was just legend," Chu told them. "All my life I've heard stories about these creatures. When people disappear in the desert, it is always said the death worms got them, but no one ever produced a body."

Vic and Lin kneeled down beside the thing which was only partially visible. More was still underground and they guessed it must be at least two meters long. The teeth were not large. The longest were in the first row and only about an inch long. They both poked the body and agreed it felt spongy but firm, a bit like a giant caterpillar.

The body was thick and muscular, dark red and segmented with smooth scales. "For all the world, this looks like a gut," said Vic.

"Olgoi-Khorkhoi," said Chu, "Mongolian for intestine worm. Russians and other foreigners gave it the name death worm."

Then Chu cautioned them. "Be careful, you two. The stories say that they can shoot a death ray but descriptions sound like an electrical charge. They are also said to spit poison that kills instantly and dissolves the victim."

"What a useful pet," said Lin. "It could dissolve your garbage, control the mice, probably till your garden and be a guard dog."

On either side of the grotesque mouth was a horizontally situated pincer. Vic slipped on gloves and pulled the pincer nearest her. "Look at this," she said. "Look how it twists!"

"A mandible!" cried Lin excitedly. "A pair of mandibles! And they can be manipulated to grab you any way you turn." Vic twisted the mandible ninety degrees both right and left.

"The inside edge is like a razor and the tip is sharp," Vic noted. "They can be used to stab and hold prey or slice it in two!"

"How many ways could this thing kill you?" asked Chu. "Electrocute you, dissolve you, slice you in half, impale you or chew you up!"

"One's all it takes," said Vic as she allowed the mandible to fall shut. "This is big enough to easily take your head off, Lin."

Lin replied, "I'd rather not think about that. Whew, what a stink! Reminds me of working with acids."

"Yes. Mixed with a rotten egg stench and a little like something dead," said Vic.

"A nauseating mix," said Chu, "and I think it is fast growing stronger."

Vic picked up a dry branch and poked at the carcass again. It was no longer spongy and firm. When Vic prodded, the branch penetrated the skin easily and a yellow green sludge ran out and the horrible stench doubled! Immediately the branch began to dissolve where the odious mess touched it. Vic dropped the stick and she and Lin stood and stepped back. "Maybe we should leave," Vic said.

"We probably should leave quickly," said Chu. "Look!"

Vic and Lin looked where Chu pointed. The sand undulated in several places, as several large unknowns wriggled toward them just beneath the surface.

They kept their eyes on the movement below the sand as they backed to the horses. The horses were already jittery and needed no prodding to begin a gallop. They glanced behind and eyed the sand around them as they went, but galloped for only a couple of minutes.

Then Chu slowed and turned them at a right angle. "We are probably OK, now," he said. "Let's continue to the canyon."

"Well, Chu, you may be the only person in Mongolia who can tell why no one has ever produced evidence of a death worm," said Vic.

Lin added, "Even if the worm doesn't eat everything that goo dissolves victims to nothing and if you kill one it dissolves itself before you can show anyone." Then to Vic she said, "You didn't get to take a photo. Show the world!"

Vic shook her head, "That's OK. It would be like a thunderbird."

"You think no one would believe, even a photo?" Lin asked.

"What would you think if someone you didn't know showed you a photograph of a creature unlike anything you have ever seen, described what you saw back there and told you all physical evidence conveniently dissolved?"

"I think in Mongolia people would believe," said Chu.

"Maybe they would," Vic said, "but I need to remain credible to readers in Nebraska first and foremost, so I can have a job that pays my way to places like this. I have seen enough strange things I could believe it, but most people have no experience with such oddities, but they have heard of P.T. Barnum. They wouldn't believe a poison spitting, electric worm as big as a man with a mouth like a lamprey and looks like a pig gut and dissolves itself if you kill it. I just saw it and I'd have a hard time believing what I just said."

In another half hour they were across those els which represented only a fraction of the vast region known as the Gobi. They were on harder ground, a Mongolian prairie, with many zag trees and other small plants.

Half a kilometer ahead the mouth of a canyon was visible at the foot of barren hills and Chu thought it was the canyon they came to see. Chu told them it was only about 120 meters deep and very rocky, so they left their horses at the twenty-meter-wide mouth. Even from the entry to the canyon, what they came to see was visible. They walked almost to the canyon's far end where primitive animals and stick-like people were painted on the canyon wall about five meters above ground.   "How or why did they make drawings that high up?" asked Chu.

Lin asked, "You read up on this, Vic. What's the answer?"

"They probably didn't. These were likely made at least a hundred thousand years ago or it could have been a million years ago. Over that span of time, there has been enough wind and rain to wear away the valley floor until it is five meters lower than when the drawings were made."

"So the cave dwellers just stood and drew these where it was easy to reach," said Lin.

Vic replied, "Yes. The back wall may have been right here at one time and has been eroded back five meters. This was probably a ravine and these drawings were at the end. It was higher and there may have been a cave here. Over time, nature, wind and rain, eroded the ravine and dug this canyon."

As she spoke Vic took off her pack and brought out her camera. She opened it up and snapped photos of the paintings and one of Lin and Chu below them. Then Lin snapped a photo of Vic looking up at the primitive art.

Unknown to the three, they were not alone. As they approached and entered the canyon, they were intent on the goal and still talked about the death worms, so they did not notice the men who moved in the shadow of the mountain three-quarters of a kilometer distant. The men noticed three people on the open sands, however, and halted, dismounted and watched.

Vic just secured her camera in the pack when she felt a chill up her spine and her neck hair stood. Before she could look around or question it, a Chinese voice called out from behind them. Lin and Chu were startled, and all three looked toward the canyon mouth. Instantly, Vic began looking for a solution and Lin and Chu pretty much stopped breathing for a moment. Spread the width of the canyon were Chinese men in various forms of dress, thirty across and four deep, all armed. "Red Beards," whispered Chu.

Lin whispered, "How did we let ourselves get into this? What do we do?"

The man who appeared in charge yelled again.

"He wants to know if you are Russian, Vic," said Chu.

Vic smiled and called out "We are Americans from the United States." Eyes only, she continued to survey the area.

The commander impatiently yelled again.

"He wants us to drop our guns and go to him," Chu translated for Vic.

"Would that be a good idea?" asked Lin.

"Feels like a very bad idea," said Vic, "but so does a shootout. What do you think Chu?"

"If we don't drop our guns they will probably shoot us in about one minute. If we drop them they will probably torture us and then shoot us."

As they pondered their dilemma and Vic sought a plan, the trio continued to nod and smile as a stall, but suddenly the Chinese commander shouted and the first row of men raised their rifles and took aim!

There was no more time to think about it. Vic continued to nod and smile and whispered, "When I say jump, dive behind a rock, but don't start to shoot until you hear them coming. Jump!"

There were plenty of large boulders. Lin and Chu held their carbines in their hands and dived behind different man-high stones. Vic's carbine leaned against another - she grabbed her weapon and dropped behind that boulder.

Thirty rifles from the front row of Red Beards fired as they dove for cover! Then fired again and again. For a moment there was silence.

They listened for the sound of men coming

for them but there was no sound. Then the commander yelled out again.

"Holy crap!" said Lin.

"What did he say?" asked Vic.

Chu answered, "He says if we come out he will kill us quick without pain. If he is forced to come get us he will cause us great suffering."

Vic said, "Don't try to stand up, you'll just die. Shoot at the boulders in the walls of the canyon, a side each. The bullets will ricochet. Fire about every two seconds and alternate shots. That may keep them from rushing us immediately and will help conserve ammunition. I'm going to shoot at the top."

"The top?" Chu and Lin both wondered aloud.

"Start shooting," said Vic and rolled to position herself with a view of the top of the canyon at the point where she last saw the soldiers.

The Red Beards were still in the general location but were now crouched and tried to ricochet their shots the way Chu and Lin were, but it wasn't working. The three were too near the end wall of the canyon so the angle put the enemy bullets into the canyon wall behind them.

Vic's target was a boulder with a good four-meter diameter which jutted out at least ten meters, perched precariously seventy-five meters above the soldiers. Where that immense boulder met the cliff face was dirt. A one meter stone jutted out from the dirt wall below it as though it might be the one thing holding the enormous boulder in place. Vic hoped the top gargantuan rock was cantilevered over the small one and not part of an even larger formation stretching back into the canyon wall. She felt there was a pretty good chance since the entire canyon floor seemed to be a debris field of loose dirt and stone washed from higher up the mountain over the millennia.

Vic emptied her carbine into a spot at the base of the smaller stone, then reloaded and emptied it again. Then she reloaded again. Lin and Chu continued to alternate their shots and fired every few seconds. The Red Beards fired little more, an indication of the value of ammunition.

"OK," Vic said, "Here's my plan for what it is. If I can cause a landslide, it should cause enough distraction for me to get up this wall. I can work my way to the canyon mouth. These guys had to come on horses. If I can get to the horses and stampede them into the canyon, there will be a lot of confusion and dust. I will bring our horses behind the stampede and we can ride off into the sunset. I know it sounds a little lame, but you two can't climb the wall and if they charge we couldn't shoot and reload fast enough. Any better ideas?"

Chu just said no, Lin said, "I don't like it but I can't think of anything else."

A half dozen times they heard the cry of someone hit by a shot from Chu or Lin, but they didn't hear the two men who belly-crawled to them until they suddenly sprang over the boulders!

Vic jerked to one side as a bullet from one Red Beard tore up dirt where her head lay a second before. Vic's bullet hit the man center chest.

Lin and Chu both fell sideways and the other Red Beard blasted the hard ground between them as they both put a bullet in his gut. Immediately they rolled back in place and resumed their measured firing.

Vic was again shooting at the rock and her shots were having an effect. Large clumps of dirt fell from below the smaller rock and first the smaller and then the huge boulder tilted. The Red Beards began to yell excitedly and Chu called over to Vic, "They see what you are doing! They will either run away or charge us."

Vic yelled back, "I'll put my money on a charge. You'll need to take a chance. If they sound like they're coming this way, get prone and shoot from around the boulder at ground level. You'll be less of a target. Lin, you're good with either hand so every couple of shots switch sides, to keep them guessing where to shoot."

It all happened at once.

The Red Beards charged so Lin and Chu dropped and began direct fire and neither wasted a bullet.

Vic continued firing as she spoke and now the bottom smaller boulder broke loose and took an enormous amount of dirt with it as it rolled down.

The large boulder tilted downward more at the

same time which caused the Red Beards to pause and look up with apprehension. For one second nothing moved, then a massive volume of dirt was displaced below the targeted boulder and it broke free and half slid and half rolled toward the canyon floor. It brought with it rocks and dirt and boulders which were one and two meters across. Adequate debris to fill a dozen box cars careened across the canyon.

Vic rose and moved over to fire at the Red Beards, but there was no need. Maybe half the Red Beards were under the collapse and most of the remaining men ran the other direction. Lin and Chu finished the only six on their side of the landslide.

Vic didn't wait for the dust to settle, but called, "Let's go!" Then she jerked up her pack and slung it on as she ran toward the collapse with Lin and Chu beside her. "That was more of a landslide than I expected. Let's see if we can all slip by in the dust and confusion," Vic told them as they ran.

The cliff side collapsed and rolled across the little canyon floor to the opposite side and created a wall that split the canyon in two. The new wall was an arc of stones and debris highest at the wall that buckled. Against the far wall, the debris was only about two meters high so escape was not a problem. The three were at the barrier of fallen debris when they came to a sudden stop.

Zt. Zt. Zt. "What's that?" Lin questioned.

Suddenly it sounded as though every surviving Red Beard began to fire at once.

Zt. Then the screams began. A second later they heard an explosion. "They have grenades," said Chu. "But they are not throwing them at us and who are they shooting at?"

As they took a step backwards the three heard stones falling to their left. The air was clear enough they saw a bulge push out of the canyon wall and slide-roll along the column of debris.

The ball was writhing and began to disjoin into dozens of death worms! Most were a good three meters long with a diameter as great as a man. The screams and explosions seemed to attract them for every worm moved away to the other side of the debris.

The three continued backwards, eyes always to the front and the worms.

"I think you opened a nest," said Chu.

"Or in this case, it looks like that can of worms I'm always hearing about," said Lin.

Zt. Zt. The sound repeated every few seconds. Another grenade exploded and the tortured screams continued. "I hate to do nothing. They may have been fighting us but at least they are human," said Vic. As she finished speaking, two of the Red Beards came running across the top of the collapse. The faces of the two men were twisted in anguished terror as though they fled demons from hell!

The ground sprayed open to one side of the two and a worm reared up. *Zt!* From a small hole above the mouth came a yellow-white flash of light. It flared to the nearest man, who fell dead, and the three no longer wondered about the sound. The other Red Beard halted and fired. The head of the thing splattered but the man stopped at a price. Behind him, another worm burst from the dirt, closed the deadly mandibles around the man's middle, and sliced him in two. The extreme horror on his face before, was nothing compared to the look on his face as he attempted futilely to hold his intestines from spilling out as his torso and lower body fell in opposite directions. There was a single scream as the worm fell on the man to feed.

Vic's eyes narrowed and she growled. "Whether we can help them or not, we'll be trapped if we don't move. The chance to get out of here will not improve." Vic ran to the right edge of the collapse and pulled herself up, with Lin and Chu just behind.

As she passed near the feasting worm, Vic blew the creature's brains out. Worms burst up from the ground twice before they dropped to the other side of the debris wall, but the reflexes of the three were so adrenaline-super-charged that each worm died from three bullets at almost the instant it emerged.

When they dropped to the other side they stopped, mesmerized for just a moment by the sight. Only six Red Beards remained of the original hundred plus, and they were in a circle, back to back. Each yelled in desperation and fired, or clubbed worms with an empty rifle. All around were dead worms stacked one on the other, dozens of them, yet still more slithered down the hill and others popped up from the earth.

"There is no way we can help them, Vic," said Chu. In the time Chu spoke, another Red Beard fell to the electric charge of a worm, as a comrade lost a leg to the mandibles of a worm which came from the ground.

"I know," said Vic matter-of-factly. She sprinted and led Lin and Chu toward the mouth of the canyon along the wall on the far side from the collapse. Although it would not save the men, Vic still fired as they passed. She dropped three worms and Lin and Chu followed Vic's example and each brought down a pair of monster worms.

When the three came out of the canyon they found four horses of the Red Beards partly eaten and that told the story. Worms came up outside the canyon, too, and those horses were killed before they could bolt. The rest dashed into the desert or along the mountain. Chu's horses were well trained, however, and wouldn't go far. In short order he spied them a few dozen meters into the sands and yelled out to them. Obediently the horses came at a gallop, but there were only two horses, Chu's and Lin's.

As the two horses approached, a worm burst out of the ground between the three and the horses. Lin shot it dead but the horses stopped, neighed and shuffled and wouldn't come closer. Lin and Chu ran toward the horses, but Vic scaled boulders beside the canyon mouth and climbed to a height of six meters, well out of range of an electric charge.

Lin and Chu mounted before Lin noticed

Vic wasn't with them, and yelled back at her, "Vic! What are you doing? Come on! We can both ride this horse."

"No!" yelled Vic as another worm burst from the ground. Chu shot it dead before it could emit a charge, but both horses reared and were difficult to hold in place. "Go before a worm injures a horse or one of you. I'm OK up here. There are horses loose all along the mountainside. When things quiet down, I'll catch up with one and then catch up to you. I'll meet you later across the river where we camped before. It's too dangerous to do anything else right now. You two need to get out of the area! I'm OK Lin, go!" As though to emphasize the danger, another worm burst from the ground and pelted Lin and Chu with dirt before Lin put two rounds in it. The horses reared as two worms came squirming out of the canyon and something moved under the dirt near them.

"Ok," Lin yelled unconvincingly. "Hurry and find a horse, Vic! I won't budge from camp until you get there!" Then Lin and Chu turned their mounts and galloped away.

Chapter 9

Exploding Mountain

Vic watched them disappear quickly into the sun's glare on the white sand. Then she dropped her pack on top of the boulder in the clear, *just in case,* and propped her carbine against it.

Then she took extra cartridges for her revolver from the pack and stuffed them in her deel pouch. Armed with her revolver, stone knife, and war ax, Vic then scurried up the cliff where she could walk back and look down into the canyon.

Vic went with a purpose. They easily expended more than half the ammunition they brought. This was their first day away from Chu's home and they ran into Red Beards and death worms. They might now go weeks without firing a shot except to bag a maral or wolf, but Vic didn't want to bet their lives on it.

There were no more screams, no more humans standing. The worms feasted and from

403

even 30 meters above Vic could hear flesh sucked from bones and bones crushed in mandibles.

Vic found a place where a tremendous slab was pushed up in ages past to form a diagonal trail to the floor of the canyon, at least it made a trail for Vic. Another modern might find it difficult to lend the name trail to the narrow ledge. It was mostly smooth rock sloped at a thirty-five-degree angle and but a foot wide. Below were large boulders and jagged rocks that would surely kill anyone who fell from even a couple of meters. A shorter drop might leave one helpless until the worms came to feed.

With her back against the wall, Vic side-stepped down the ledge and stopped at the same level as the opened nest across the canyon. She had a good view of the three-meter-high tunnel situated about five meters above the canyon floor. Vic watched, safe from a charge at that height and if she didn't move, they probably would not notice her while they fed.

The scene below Vic was nightmarish, with dismembered, partially eaten corpses everywhere. Detached hands seemed to grasp futilely for some support to pull them from the hell of this day. There were many more dead worms than Red Beards, and all were quickly dissolving into the transparent, putrescent sludge.

Vic watched the charnel feast for a minute and noticed that the worms, as they got their fill of flesh, slithered slowly up the side of the collapse and entered the opened tunnel.

The first thing Vic wanted to do was venture down to the canyon floor and collect ammunition. The Red Beards used a hodge-podge of weapons. She didn't expect any of the unusual .351 carbines but sighted several .45's. If they got in another jam, especially if it was close quarters, more ammo for the revolvers would be welcomed. It wouldn't hurt to have a few grenades, either.

Vic looked for the nearest pack and spied one whose straps were held tight by the severed forearm and hand of a Red Beard, just half a dozen steps from the wall and almost directly below her. She didn't need to consider it. The moment she saw the pack she ran down the few meters to the floor, revolver in hand, and dashed for the pack, scooped it up, slung it over her shoulder, and retreated to the wall and up the ledge again. When she stopped, she saw that her foray seemed to go unnoticed.

Vic pried the fingers from the strap and dropped the hand to the canyon floor then looked inside the pack. It held one grenade, perhaps two dozen loose cartridges that looked like .38's and other things of no value to them. Vic dumped all but the grenade. She then took a quick survey below for grenades or cartridges loose on the ground. She spotted two grenades and three cartridge belts. Those would be first. Then she would need to take the time to look inside packs.

After six forays to the canyon floor, Vic improved their supplies by at least 200 rounds of .45 ammo and four grenades. By then, perhaps half the worms were returned to the tunnel and those that remained continued to gorge, so Vic jumped to the floor of the canyon and loped through the carnage for the seventh time. With the swiftness of a deer fleeing the wolf, she dashed from pack to pack.

As she rummaged the fourth pack, a worm noticed her. Vic pulled her ax and swung it to slice half way through the worm's body below the head. Then she bent down to clean the stone in the sand. While she wiped the caustic blood from the ax another worm came toward her, so she blasted it. Another worm immediately reared up in front of her. She shot it dead, too, but now several others were headed her way, so Vic retreated toward the ledge in a zig zag. Enroute, she twice jumped widening streams of the acidic sludge and shot a worm that burst up from beneath a pile of corpses. However, as she traversed that gauntlet, she was able to scoop up six more packs before she retreated up the ledge laden with at least sixty pounds of unknown plunder.

One by one Vic opened the packs and found a bonanza. Two climbing ropes, at least two hundred more .45 cartridges, and a dozen grenades! Vic looked back into the canyon which was fast transforming into a shallow pond of disgusting putrescence from which the fetid odor rose even to where she stood. With little conscious thought, Vic looked across at the tunnel entrance, a new purpose crystallized, and she thought, *We won't need all these grenades.*

At the level where she stood, Vic was able to circle the canyon with relative ease. She ascended a few meters twice and descended a few meters once, and shortly was on the opposite side of the canyon, directly above the entrance to the tunnel. On that side of the canyon, the level where Vic stood stretched upward into the mountains and was strewn with boulders and a few plants.

Vic pulled off the pack and took out the two ropes and a blanket. She kept four grenades for later and set aside twelve for her plan. She cut three strips of a Red Beard's blanket, each about two inches wide and eighteen inches long and then four strips as wide but a foot longer. Then she searched the slope and secured six stout branches, each about one-third meter long.

As she worked, Vic listened for sounds of worms under the ground. Since she didn't know if the worms could climb, she peered over the edge every minute or so to ensure none were creeping up the wall.

Vic put together three expedient bombs. For each, she used a strip of blanket to tie four grenades along a branch. Then she ran a smaller branch through the pins of the grenades. Next, she attached both ropes to a waist high boulder which would easily hold her weight. Vic expected to bounce from concussion and wanted to be anchored to something substantial which wouldn't work loose. She tied the makeshift bombs to the end of one rope and lowered it slowly until the bombs were just above the entrance of the tunnel. There was excess cordage so Vic tied a butterfly knot with a large loop to take up the slack. Then she measured out enough of the other rope to put her at the top edge of the tunnel beside the grenade bombs.

Forty-five minutes after they rode away from the canyon at full gallop, Lin and Chu arrived at the river and dismounted to let their horses rest and drink. Both were tired, and there was little talk. Finally, Lin stood up and looked across the dunes at the mountains in the distance. "Vic was up to something. She could have come with us. We could have ridden to find another horse. She has a plan, and it must be dangerous, and she wanted us safe. It's probably three hours until dark. Chu, go back to your family. Vic and I will find our way," and she mounted her horse.

"Wait! What are you talking about?"

"Vic is planning something, and she might need help. I've gotta go back, Chu. You don't. You have that great family to take care of."

"Don't get melodramatic, Lin," said Chu. "If you go, I go. You have become my friends, and even if you weren't, I am your guide. Professional pride dictates I go. Besides, I promised my friend Lao I would protect his little cousin."

"You really think I need protection?"

"Not really." Chu let go of Lin's reins and mounted his horse. "I'll just follow and take notes."

Lin looked at him and said, "Thanks, Chu. I've gotta talk to Lao about calling me his little cousin, but he does pick good friends. I guess this can be your penance for that servant girl thing." Then she spurred her horse forward.

The horses were tired, so it took longer to

return, about an hour. The mouth of the canyon was still 400 meters away when Lin said, "I swear I see Vic's pack up on the rock where she stood when we left her. I should never have gone. Do you see it?"

Chu answered yes he saw it, then pointed right. "There are some Red Beard horses in the shade of the hills." Then they heard an explosion.

"That was a grenade, I think," said Chu. "Except it sounded too big."

The two slowed as they came nearer the mouth of the canyon. A minute after the first explosion and while they were still a hundred meters away they heard a second explosion. Then came a series of rumbles and rolling explosions from deep underground.

The horses balked so they halted. "What's going on?" Lin wondered aloud. "It must be Vic. She must be in trouble."

The rumble grew louder, and Lin was about to spur her horse forward when there was yet another explosion, then an immediate louder rolling grumble from the direction of the canyon. Then came the big one. The final explosion threw them from their horses and knocked the horses to the ground. Before the air filled with sand and blinded them, Lin saw the right wall of the little canyon move to the left side and saw stones the size of houses fly from right to left. Then the sand forced her eyes shut. Lin and Chu both were knocked silly but didn't completely lose consciousness.

It was three minutes before Lin spoke. There

was still so much sand in the air that she couldn't hold her eyes open so she spit the sand out of her mouth and just asked, "Are you here Chu? Are you OK?"

"I'm OK. You?"

They heard the horses snort and rise. Chu spoke to them in Mongolian to calm them and keep them from wandering away. A few seconds later, Lin felt the muzzle of her ride against her head, and she pulled herself up to stand beside her horse. A steady wind blew, and it cleared the air within a few minutes.

Where the canyon mouth once opened was a wall of rubble that made it difficult to imagine there was an entry to a canyon right there just minutes before. Lin ran to the former entrance, but there was no longer an opening or canyon. Then she ran the direction where she saw Vic's pack. She found the pack and carbine quickly, a few meters from where they rested before. sand and gravel covered the pack, but Lin checked inside, and the camera and film seemed unharmed. Then Lin called out for Vic. She mounted her horse and rode 200 meters in either direction. Chu rode in opposition to Lin, and both called out, and every few minutes they would fire a shot into the air. After a few passes, they stopped at the thirty-meter-high rubble pile which was once the canyon mouth but now was simply a section of the mountainside.

"Maybe I can climb up over there..." Lin began.

"No Lin," said Chu. "If Vic was in the canyon she's gone. If she was not in the canyon, she'll expect to find us at the camp site like we said. Even with that explosion, there will be horses within two or three miles for a day or more. Or she may already be back. We could easily have passed just out of sight of each other. Let's go back and wait for her. If she doesn't show up in two days, we can return."

"Vic's OK," said Lin "I know she is. But I shouldn't have left her in the first place." Lin made a fist and slammed it against her thigh. "I shouldn't have left!" Before going, Lin took Vic's journal from her pack and tore out a page to write a note - *See you at the creek.* She secured it in the carry straps and put the journal back in the pack. Chu asked, "Don't you want to take her camera and notes just in case she...", but Lin cut him off, saying "Vic will want to make notes and take a photo when she returns for her gear." So Lin and Chu rode back across the dunes to make camp and wait.

Chapter 10

Many Faces of Death

After Vic lowered the makeshift bombs, she tied the end of the other rope around her waist and descended the cliff face, careful not to dislodge rocks which might alert the worms. Three meters before the end of the rope she spotted a large worm coming up the debris toward the tunnel and stopped dead still. While she waited, Vic noticed several yols, large vultures, high above. Probably the heavy scent of death attracted them, but they were not descending so likely they were also privy to the danger of the worms and the various forms of death they dealt.

It seemed forever, but finally, the worm was into the tunnel and Vic lowered herself to the end of the rope. There she dangled sideways with her shoulder at the top edge of the tunnel entrance.

Vic detached one bomb from the rope. She pulled the length of blanket tied to the stick that ran through the pins to arm all the grenades at once, held her arm out full length and hurled the bomb into the tunnel. As it flew from her left hand, Vic climbed to better avoid shrapnel and stone projectiles from the explosion. She just pulled up the third arm length when the grenades detonated. The explosion bounced her against the cliff face once, and Vic slid back to the end of the rope, untied the second bomb, pulled the pins and chucked it into the tunnel. She made it up three arm lengths again when the second bomb went off and bounced her against the cliff. There was another explosion from deeper followed by a grumble. Vic had no idea what it might be, so she just slid down to the end of the rope and lobbed the final bomb inside.

As Vic climbed, bomb number three detonated and was promptly followed by another explosion from deeper. Then a subterranean thunder began to roll closer, and the earth trembled. She didn't know what it was, but it could not be good, so she climbed faster. At the top, she didn't slow but jumped up, grabbed the bag, pulled the loop of the rope over the boulder and dragged the rope behind as she ran up-slope. She made it a hundred meters before another explosion forced her to stop and fight to keep her balance.

Then came the big one. Suddenly, Vic was in total silence and was senseless to physical sensation. The ground billowed the way a sheet on the clothesline ripples in a breeze. The earth lifted beneath her and tilted and just as suddenly it reversed and Vic had the sickening sensation of a sudden fall. Vic was engulfed by hot air and dust and her knees buckled from a sound so violent it made her bones vibrate! Like a flare of lightning the broiling memory of her final breath in a cave a thousand generations before seared Vic's brain! Then her world went black!

It took several minutes before Vic became conscious and opened her eyes. Dust still hung heavy in the air, but she could see well enough to move, and the explosions and grumbles were done. Vic stood and walked slowly around in a large circle. It was evident that the area of the hill where she stood was now several feet lower than it was just minutes ago. What had been a slightly convex upward slope was now the concave inside of a bowl.

Vic tried to find the way back around the canyon and quickly realized there was no canyon and no simple return path. A clutter of massive boulders and loose sand and gravel remained which would be difficult to traverse and may also still conceal live worms.

The possibility of worms seemed remote. Most if not all worms in the vicinity must have been killed in that horrendous explosion. Thus, Vic's second purpose was achieved. Vic seldom hosted any thirst akin to revenge, but a hundred men helplessly slaughtered brought it to life. The scene of destruction quenched that thirst.

Even if no worms survived, crossing the debris field would be arduous. The disarray of unsettled rocks and sand could hide deadly crevices. Loose rock might collapse from her weight. Travel would not be served by a fall into a crevice of unknown depth or by being clobbered in the head or even a foot by a heavy stone.

The safest, surest way to go was upward and look for a way around to where the mountains rose up from the desert. She turned to leave and heard a gunshot beyond where there was once a canyon. She paused. A minute later came another gunshot. Vic listened and yearned to investigate. Was it possible Lin and Chu didn't get away and were in trouble?

As she contemplated the gunshots, Vic realized she turned her head to the left toward the sound. She pressed the end of her index finger into her right ear and winced from the pain. Blood was on her finger tip. That ear drum was ruptured, but there was nothing much she could do. She cut a small square from her flannel shirt and folded it into an ear plug to keep the wound clean, dry and warm. If the ear didn't get infected it should be good as new in two to three months.

Six shots were fired. Ten minutes after the last, Vic coiled the rope and stuffed it in the pack, retrieved her cap which had been blown off, and headed up the slope to search for a path to the front of the mountains and back down to the steppe.

One hundred meters above where she fell, Vic found a goat trail which ran more horizontal than vertical. She moved along the trail as quickly as she could, for there was likely no more than an hour and a half until dark and the air was frigid. She wanted to retrieve her pack and bedroll for the bitter night.

Vic rushed quietly. There was a chance she might not get to the desert floor and retrieve her pack before dark. So she carried the revolver in her left hand and the ax in her right and kept alert for sound of any animal with skin enough to provide cover against the deadly cold.

Vic was not disappointed. Just minutes later she rounded a turn and came face to face with a large gray-black, lone male wolf. He barred his fangs, snarled and leaned back on his haunches to leap. In that instant, as the wolf prepared to attack, Vic swung the ax. It struck the wolf's head and knocked it to its fore knees. The wolf yelped, then growled and raised up. Vic back-swung without pause and the ax caught the animal on the other side of the head and finished it. Vic dropped the pack and pulled her stone knife. She rolled the wolf over on its back and began to skin it. She did not do a clean job and laughed about how the twins would scold her if they watched this. The skin was free in a few minutes, and Vic removed a hind leg and stuffed it into the pack. Next, she cut into the torso for the liver. It had a thin yellow cover which Vic knew was fat. She took enough slices to fill her hand and put them under her canteen in the metal cup. Then she continued.

Vic was on the opposite side of the mountains from the sunset, so already shadows were deepened, and the temperature was dropping fast

417

when she came to a cliff edge which overlooked the desert. She peered over the brink for a way down and saw the wall was sheer. She took the rope from the pack and dropped an end over the side, and it stopped about three meters short of the ground. It might be miles before she found a better place to get down. The dunes touched the mountain, and no sharp stones were apparent just below. Darkness was coming fast. Vic decided to go down, and she needed to move fast because once she got off the cliff, she wanted adequate light to aim.

She knew her weight would stretch the rope some, so the drop should be no more than two meters. Easy, if nothing went wrong. If she didn't land on her feet, it could kill her, or if there were sharp rocks just lightly covered with sand, she could break a leg and lie helpless to see if a predator or the cold would claim her first. If she couldn't retrieve her gear which she set at the canyon entrance, the odds were good that she would freeze to death.

However, Vic was not one to dwell on such baneful possibilities. Do what needs done and Vic needed to get down from this ledge, now. She tied the pack and skin to one end of the rope and anchored the other end around a boulder.

Vic lowered the gear then descended, and in seconds, she was at the rope-end with the pack. She slid over the gear, held to the rope at its lowest point, and pushed out from the rock wall. She swung back and gave herself one more push. At the farthest point from the cliff, she let go of the rope.

It worked, and Vic landed in sand. She hit hard from a meter higher than she expected, but there were no rocks, and she was up on her feet immediately, and whipped out her revolver. The weight of the grenades and ammo had already stopped the swing of the rope. She moved from directly beneath her gear where she could see the rope against the darkening blue-gray sky and she fired. Her third shot brought it down. Vic caught the pack and was already moving back toward the defunct canyon as she slung it on.

Minutes into the walk, Vic passed a stand of zag trees and collected an armload of dry branches. Vic didn't run or lope. She knew that under the layers of clothing she would sweat even in the frigid weather and if she became wet with sweat, it would make her colder. Although she walked to minimize sweat, nevertheless, she swiftly found the former canyon mouth and Lin's note with her gear. That was a relief. She quickly transferred the ammo and remaining grenades from the confiscated pack to her own.

As a precaution against worms, she hiked a couple of hundred meters away from that area and found a shallow dimple into the cliff wall. It would help block the wind which had picked up to more than twenty miles per hour.

With the zag branches, she built a small fire at the back of the dimple against the cliff and laid four fist sized stones in the blaze. For a quick meal, she cut the wolf meat into paper thin strips and cooked those and the thigh bone directly in the flames until charred. She knew wolf, like jaguar, is OK to eat but must be very well done to prevent infestation by worms or other disease.

Vic ate the blackened meat first, then cracked the thigh bone and scraped out the marrow with her knife. She just finished the quick meal when the snow began. Briefly, she warmed her hands over the dying flames and pulled on her gloves to set up her pup tent. Inside, she lay the sheep skin down for ground cover, wrapped herself in the MacIntosh blanket with the four hot stones and covered her head and upper body with the wolf skin. Vic guessed it to be near zero Fahrenheit, and the wind chill magnified that bitter temperature. She shivered a bit at first but quickly warmed and fell asleep.

About two in the morning, Vic was half awake, aware that the wind was now fierce. It howled through rocks and whipped up the edges of the little tent and slipped inside to flap the wolf skin and even the verge of the sheep skin beneath her. She just thought how glad she was to not be in the open when a powerful gust pulled the tent pegs out on the side hit by the wind and she was suddenly lying in the open, holding tight to the wolf skin. The tent, still staked by three pegs, flapped hard and loud and Vic knew it could be uprooted completely and gone any moment. It was no longer snowing, but a thin sheet of ice-snow carpeted the ground.

The wind was strong. Her pack now held the camera and film, plus the grenades and ammunition she collected, and still the icy wind moved it several meters. Before anything else, Vic found a stone that weighed a good fifty pounds and laid it on the tent to keep from losing it.

The temperature was undoubtedly sub-zero and the wind howled at forty miles per hour! Even if she didn't mind sitting in the open, if she tried, the blood would turn to ice in her veins!

She hastily took stock of what needed to be done in the situation and went to work. As she labored against the raging, frigid gale, she reminded herself that the situation could be worse and felt grateful that she was not out on the dunes fighting the full force of the tempest and that Narakaa helped them make deels.

Against the unrelenting wind, Vic used her ax to chop a crater of about one cubic foot at the opening to the tent. She broke the remaining zag limbs into a size to fit in the hole. She took the wolf fat from the canteen cup and rubbed it over the largest of the branches. The fat would help a fire catch and continue and location in the crater would help protect it. When a little blaze was secure, Vic dropped four fist sized stones in the fire as before.

The wind and slippery ground made it difficult to work. Her fingers were beginning to feel over-sized and stiff from the cold which made it a challenge to use her hands. Part of her thought a break would be good, but she shivered constantly and it grew worse by the minute so she knew she couldn't rest. She needed a shelter, fast!

Vic used another stone to hammer the loose stakes into the ground but did not make the tent taut. She left it just slack enough so she could further anchor the edge of the canvas with weighty rocks. Then she pushed her pack inside the tent.

At last, and none too soon, she was able to snap the tent entrance and roll into the MacIntosh material with hot rocks again. Immediately, she could feel her body begin to recover.

Before slumber took her, she understood why Chu said you could hear the banshees of hell in a wind storm. It was like the wailing of the old women if a hunt for Glu, the mammoth, went wrong and many men were trampled to death or mangled. Even though Vic knew it was the wind and there was no more Glu, her ears would not let her hear anything but wailing. After an hour the wind diminished, the wails faded and Vic drifted into a sound sleep and walked in thick humid warmth beside the Restless Sea, hand in hand with Nu.

Vic managed two hours of sleep and the sun was up when she awoke. She unwrapped from the MacIntosh and shook off the fine layer of cold wet sand that managed to get inside the tent.

Then she considered her next action. She had no water and was thirsty. There was no food but she wasn't too hungry after the wolf last night. It took 45 minutes on horseback at a gallop to get to the point where she planned to meet Lin and Chu. It isn't easy to walk in sand.

Vic figured it would take all day if she attempted to walk. The best plan seemed to be walk along the mountain and look for a horse.

Vic packed her tent, threw on her pack and began her hike. In the early afternoon, she found her horse grazing and making his way slowly back toward the former canyon. She retraced her path to the site of the closed canyon and turned across the els. It was a rough two days for both Vic and the horse, and they needed water, so she didn't push. She came to the edge of the els and stopped at the river to drink an hour before sunset.

Lin and Chu saw Vic at the river and ran out to meet her. They all had stories to tell and shared them as they sat around a small fire and ate maral steak. "You should have seen Lin," said Chu. "When we returned, four maral were drinking at the river. They saw us and bolted, but Lin rode after them and very quickly brought down the largest with a shot from the saddle!" Vic thought that was fantastic and bragged on Lin's shooting and thanked her for the meal.

Lin and Chu were both curious, "What was that big explosion?"

"I'm not positive. I'm no geologist, but I have an idea," Vic told them and took another bite of the maral.

Said Lin "It looked like the whole danged mountain exploded. I saw rocks bigger than my house flying!"

Vic finished chewing the maral. "OK. I read that the oil they get out of the ground to make gasoline for automobiles, not only will burn but sometimes has deposits of explosive gas around it. It's the gas in the modern stoves and like my house lamps. My guess is that Mongolia is situated over oil and explosive gas deposits. The first two grenade bombs opened a fissure to such a deposit, so gas began to leak upward and the third bomb caused the gas to explode.

"I think I was on a massive rock, perhaps 200 meters in diameter. Probably it weighed at least tens of thousands of tons. When the gas exploded, like the lid on a pan of stew boiling over, the rock lid lifted and the stuff inside went out the path of least resistance into the canyon, and the lid fell into the hollow it left. Two things are for sure, maps of that area need to be redrawn and there are a lot less death worms out there."

"That sounds exciting! Just think of what happened and you were on top of it and you're still alive," said Lin.

"That's the part I like," said Vic. "I'm still alive. If I was offered a choice, I would have been far, far away when it blew."

Vic divvied up the Red Beard ammo with Lin and Chu, wrote by firelight in her journal for a time, and then climbed into her pup tent. She rolled into the skins, grateful for the delicious meat, for warmth and a gentler wind.

Chapter 11

Lost Species

On waking, Chu began a fire, and they drank coffee and tsai as they recounted the past three days. Then Chu turned pensive and after a sigh said, "I have fought for my life beside the two of you. You have shared a personal secret, Vic. Lao spoke of Lin with nothing but praise. I feel you are both above reproach and honorable. I wish to share a secret that you must never share and then I would ask a favor."

"What is it?" Lin asked. "You look intense. Yes, we have fought side by side, and I say yes to the favor even before I know it."

Vic told Chu, "I, too, can say yes to your favor. You have shown yourself to be honorable, so I know a favor you ask will be honorable, as well."

"First let me share the secret. Show it to you. Then I will ask the favor. The favor will not seem so fantastic once you have seen the

secret." Chu told them he could show the
secret at the next sunrise if they rode hard all
that day. So they immediately doused the fire,
threw on their packs and were off. They
traveled at a rapid pace and only twice did they
pause a few minutes to eat aaruul and water
the horses.

"I believe we will make it," Chu told them
two hours before dark. They traveled along the
edge of the dunes and stopped in front of a
distinctive set of rocks which included a four-
meters-high blade of stone that rose from the
sand like a giant sword.

Chu pointed toward mountains beyond the
barren sand. "The els are narrowed again at
this point, and those mountains are only five or
six kilometers." Then he brought to their
attention a mountain in the distance that looked
like the pinnacle of a roof with eaves that
trailed off to either side. "As the sun sets, that
formation will cast a shadow spear-tip to point
our destination. We must reach the edge of the
els below the tip of the shadow spearhead
before dark," he told them. "Otherwise we will
need to wait another day."

They pushed hard, and the horses were
slick with sweat when they reached the far side
of the els. It was good they did, for they just
had time to mark the tip of the transient
spearhead before the sun and shadow
disappeared.

"In the morning, I will show you," said Chu.
They made a small fire and ate more maral
before they turned in.

The daytime temperature might now warm to ten degrees Fahrenheit in the sun, but nights and in the shade were well below zero. "I hope we don't get another wind storm tonight," said Vic as she set up the pup tent. "I thought I would fly away like Dorothy and Toto the other night!"

The night was calm and once they crawled into their tents and wrapped up no one ventured out again until morning.

It was still dark when Chu called to Vic and Lin. They crawled out of their pups and found Chu had water heated for tsai and coffee. In the east, the black sky was just lightening to dark blue with golden streaks to announce the impending sunrise. Vic and Lin sat by the fire with Chu, and he told them, "We can find it now."

"What is it Chu?" asked Lin. "You have my curiosity up! Is it treasure?" Lin joked, and Vic smiled.

Chu laughed and nodded, "Yes, there is a treasure, and I'm sure it is bigger than I can imagine!"

"You're kidding!" Lin said.

"He sounds serious," said Vic.

Lin asked, "What is it Chu? Is it diamonds, gold doubloons or what? Are you serious?"

"Well, I saw what I think was gold, and it is in a buried castle, and any castle holds treasure, doesn't it?"

Vic made another cup of coffee and Chu and Lin each got more tsai. Then Chu told the story.

Beneath the sand, very near where they sat, was an ancient castle, perhaps an entire city, covered by the sands for who knows how long. Chu first found it accidentally, many years ago in his teens. He mentioned it to a few people over the years but they thought he was joking, so now he kept it to himself.

Without the sun pointer, he could not have found the city again, for every year the els advanced nearer the cliffs and covered the city deeper. "Even knowing it is here, it may be difficult to find, but we need to do so before it is so far beneath the sands that it cannot be uncovered. It is good you came this season. The sun's movements make positioning of the pointer accurate for only a few weeks each year."

"That is why you wanted us to visit in September, isn't it?" Vic asked. "You hoped you could trust us."

"Yes. I have visited here several times so I could remember how to find it. I only ventured inside to the first lower room one time. I was alone with only a lantern for light. I needed someone to watch my back but never met anyone I trusted that much but Narakaa." Chu spoke the last words timidly.

"My impression of Narakaa is that she can handle herself," said Vic. "Yet, there is no shame in caring enough to let the treasure lie rather than expose her to unknown danger."

"Why did you need someone to watch your back?" Lin asked. "It's a buried city, so it isn't very likely someone is there to stop you."

"When I was in the room where I saw the gold, I heard something like padded footsteps, and I hurried out. Maybe no person is there, but after what we have seen, it may be worse."

"Maybe worms," said Vic. "Now we can watch each other's back, and even if there is no treasure, it will be exciting to explore a lost city! Do you know what city it is or anything about it?"

"No. I have asked many people who know the area if there was ever a city here in the desert. They all say no."

Chu knew the entrance to be directly out from the point of the shadow. "On my last visit two years ago the entrance was 230 paces from the edge of the sand. There was, at that time, a rift in the steppe, from an ancient earthquake no doubt, six meters long and two deep. It was parallel to and about three meters out from the edge of the els. The rift is no longer visible, so the els have advanced at least 3 meters, maybe more."

"I'm excited! Let's get going!" said Lin.

Just as the sun crested the mountain, Chu took slightly exaggerated steps in a straight line from the mark they made. Vic and Lin were at his heels for 250 paces. Then Chu turned and looked up at the mountain. "Not quite right," he said and went another ten paces. He looked toward the mountains again, then took two more paces backward.

"This is it!" he said and motioned for them to stand by him. He pointed to a glint as a mirror might make which flashed at the crest of the rooftop-shaped mountain. "You need to see that glint, and you can only see it for about the first half hour after sunrise. When you see it, you are over or very nearly over the entrance."

The work frustrated them. As they would pull sand out of a hole, more would slide down the side. The only utensils available were zag limbs retrieved from the steppe and their canteen cups, plus they made use of the tents. Two in the hole would use canteen cups to scoop sand and pile it on a tent, then gather the edges and hand it up. The one up top would drag the load several feet away and dump it. Their one bit of luck was the wind. There was almost none, and that helped.

They began work before seven in the morning, and it was mid-afternoon when they hit the first stone. Their enthusiasm re-blossomed and they quickly located a breach in the stone as Chu expected. It was perfectly round and about three- quarters of a meter in diameter. They extended the excavation to be about a third of a meter deeper than the lowest edge of the outlet, and a full meter from either side. It was late afternoon by then, so they decided to wait until morning to go inside.

What they referred to as a window gathered more sand during the night, but it was quickly scooped out, and in the light, they could see the opening was no simple hole or window. It was more like a chute that angled down. "How long is this thing?" Vic asked Chu. He answered it was two or three meters long and round all the way. Vic had no idea what to call it but didn't think it was a window.

Before he slid into the tube, Chu confused Vic more. "Oh, be careful. There may be some glass still in the tube. It was full of broken glass the first time I came in."

Then, armed with revolvers and equipped with empty packs and haversacks and their electric lights, and of course Vic with her ax and knife, they entered the tube, first Chu, then Vic, then Lin. At the end of the tube, Lin and Chu shined their lights around. Vic focused on the abundance of rubble on the floor beside the tube and picked some up and dusted it off. In a second she shined her light through it and said simply, "Oh."

"What?" asked Lin.

"This is not ordinary glass. This is fine quality optical glass," Vic answered and slipped a small shard into a pocket.

Then Vic shined her light at the wall and wiped dust away with her hand. It revealed a worn tapestry, and she could tell there were dust covered tapestries on all the walls. "I'd like to get a good look at this design," Vic told them. "I want to dust this off good and take a closer look before we leave, but right now let's go where you think there is a treasure."

The lone door-less exit from the room opened into a tunnel which faded into utter darkness in both directions. Chu led them right, and they descended for about a minute to a wooden door. Beyond that door, they went down a long set of steps inside another narrow, tunneled stairwell until they came to a new intersection. Chu again led them right, for about a minute before he paused at another opening and said, "I hope you don't fear heights."

They followed him through the doorway and found themselves on a stone platform a good thirty meters above the next floor. Steep stone steps, one-meter-wide and rail-less, angled down.

"I don't like heights," Lin told Chu. "Let's keep moving."

Chu warned them, "In many places the steps have crumbled and cracked." Chu pointed at a group of foot diameter stones at the head of the steps. "There are loose stones which fell from the ceiling, too. Take care where you step."

"I've noticed damage everywhere," noted Vic.

"Maybe an earthquake destroyed this place," Lin suggested.

At the bottom, they found themselves in a huge square room at least 50 meters on a side. Their lights scarcely illuminated the far walls.

"Over here," Chu said and went left from the steps. He shined his light ahead, and they saw where he was going. In one corner of the giant chamber, a dais rose a meter above the floor. As they neared it, their lights revealed a very conspicuous high-backed stone chair in the center. They rushed onto the dais and Vic ran her hand over strange symbols carved into the stone chair back.

"This is superb work!" Vic said, "This must be a throne, and we must be in a throne room! Do either of you recognize any of these symbols?"

Neither had a clue, and Lin said excitedly, "If this is a throne room, this really must be a castle, and there may be a real treasure!"

"Back here," Chu told them and led the way behind the throne through another doorway. It was a short corridor which led to a large circular room with an arc of six doors opposite them. "I only went in the first door on the right," said Chu. "That is where I saw the gold." So they went to the first door.

Vic and Lin both gasped when they entered and shined their lights around the room. The dazzling reflections were almost blinding! It was a narrow room, but at least twenty meters deep. Stone tables lined three walls, and gold ingots, plates, goblets, bowls, and jewelry covered all the tables. The sight stunned Vic and Lin, and they stood in silence and stared for a moment.

"It truly is a treasure," Lin whispered.

"And what a treasure," said Vic.

They paced the room to examine the trove, but their awe did not lessen, especially when they realized that more golden treasure sat beneath the tables. After a few minutes, Chu spoke. "Now for the favor."

Chu wanted their help to take some of the treasure out, as much as they could carry, and he wanted them to take it to the United States and invest it, and on a regular schedule send funds back to Mongolia. Chu wanted to build a school for the twins and their friends who lived in the area. "It will take years, perhaps decades before the government will build schools out here. I want my daughters to have an education. I want them to have a life somewhere besides on the steppes or in the mountains. This has been a good life but the future will be in cities and will be for those who are educated. They are naturally intelligent girls. With education, they can be whatever they decide. I want them to have choices. If they choose to live like their parents, I will not be sad, but if they must live like Narakaa and me without choice, then I think I will fail as their father. Will you help me?"

In unison, Vic and Lin answered, "Of course!"

In a few minutes, however, came the first snag. "Gold is heavy," Lin said. "I don't know if this will work. A pack filled only to a third will be a good hundred pounds on each of our backs. That will be a small fortune, but will it be enough to build and run a school for years? And wouldn't we rouse suspicion if we go back through the wall or board a ship bent over from the weight of our packs?"

"Lin is right," Vic said. The three sat on stone stools and looked at one another.

Chu sounded discouraged, "What can we do?"

They were silent for a few moments then Vic made a suggestion. They could take out several loads, over multiple days if necessary, and cache it at a location where they would be able to get to it easily in case the castle became inaccessible. She and Lin would take some now, and two or three times a year Chu could ship more, maybe with herbs to Lin's parents.

There were problems with the plan, but those issues would come later, and in the end, none had a better idea right then, so they began to pack gold items into their packs and haversacks.

Lin filled hers first and said, "I'm going to take a look in one of the other rooms."

Vic said, "Stay alert."

"I'll just be in the next room. Room two." She patted her revolver and said, "My friend is going with me."

Vic watched Lin go out and smiled. *Now I know how Barney felt in Africa when he thought my actions were risky.*

Scarcely a minute passed before Lin called out, "Vic! Chu! Come here!"

Vic and Chu ran to the next room, each with a light in one hand and revolver in the other hand.

Lin was on her knees in front of an urn, light in one hand, her other hand full of red stones. "I think these might be rubies," Lin told them. The stones were natural and uncut, but were breathtaking in their clarity and brilliance!

Chu reached into another urn and pulled out a handful of green stones. "Emeralds!" He then reached into another urn and brought out diamonds.

"Gold in one room, gems in this room.

What do you think are in the other rooms?" Lin asked.

"Let's not get crazy," said Vic. "First things first. This solves our problem, and remember Chu thought he heard something down here before. We may need to leave in a hurry so let's dump the gold, and fill our packs and bags with gems. Then we can look in the other rooms to satisfy our curiosity."

In less than fifteen minutes they were about done, and Lin finished first again and said, "I'm going to room three."

"Be careful," said Chu. "We have made a lot of noise. If something is down here, we have probably alerted it."

Lin left for room three. A couple of minutes later Vic was done and pulled on her pack and haversack. Chu just closed the straps on his pack when he saw Vic stiffen and look toward the door. He started to speak, but Vic held up a hand to stop him. The hair on her neck rose, and a chill ran down her back.

Chu stood and pulled his pack on. Vic kept her eyes on the door and stepped closer to Chu and whispered, "I'm sure I heard something. And my nose tells me there is something!"

Suddenly Lin cried out, "Vic! Chu! Watch out!"

Vic vaulted to the door and leapt through with Chu behind her, both with revolvers drawn again. They did not expect what they saw.

A hulking, man-like creature stood at the next door and gave the impression of immense power!   It appeared very solid with a height about that of Vic at five feet nine inches. It was well muscled, but especially the forearms. Compared to a standard man they were quite exaggerated, with almost twice the circumference of the upper arms. Those extraordinary forearms ended at hands fully as unusual - large, with defined musculature and each finger ended with a thick, slightly curved claw. Short sandy hair, fine like duck down, covered the entire body, including the face. The large eyes implied a creature that needed to see in the dark, like an owl or marmoset. The head hair was the color of the body hair and hung below his shoulders, all toward the back, which left the ears uncovered, perhaps to aid in hearing.

When their lights hit him, the man half turned and looked at Vic and Chu and narrowed his eyes.

"You OK, Lin?" Vic called.

"I'm OK. Got light and gun both on this thing."

"Can you talk? Are you a man?" Vic asked. "Speak in Chinese and Mongolian, Chu. See if it understands." Before Chu could begin the man turned toward them, growled and stepped forward. Immediately Vic stuffed the revolver in her pants and pulled out the ax. Instantly, the man stopped and glared at Vic. "Try not to use guns. They're too loud. We need to assume there are more of these fellas around, but maybe they don't know we're here, yet."

It looked intently at the ax and Vic. "An ax

has been a weapon for ages. Since long before it was an implement to cut trees, it was used to kill the enemy whether man or beast."

"That means it is intelligent if it recognizes a weapon," said Lin.

Chu said, "I'm pretty sure it's a man, just a little odd. He seems to be listening."

"There is no possible way for him to know English," said Lin, and she spoke in Chinese. The thing seemed to recognize she was trying to communicate but shook its head and grunted.

Vic spoke to him in the language of the apes and early man, but there was no recognition.

Chu spoke in Mongolian, and began simply, "We are friendly." The thing craned his neck toward them and emitted something like an *ah*. Then it spoke. The sound was not identical to the sound of Chu but was similar.

"He understands!" said Chu. "The words are not exactly the same. He uses words which were once common, but are seldom used now. His accent and tones are different, but close enough I think I understand."

Then Chu spoke again in Mongolian, and the thing answered him. For several minutes, Chu spoke with the hairy man and from time to time he translated. The hairy man displayed another odd feature. He craned his neck toward Vic and then Lin and each time his nose opened! What looked like an ordinary human nose split into five strips of flesh which rose until what was the inside now pointed outward and writhed! Each incident lasted only a couple of seconds, then he spoke.

Chu told them the man said they smell like women, but carry weapons, and Vic, in particular, handled the war ax like a warrior. Then he asked if Vic was a demon. Lin couldn't help herself and laughed out loud. "My friend the demon woman!"

Chu continued to speak with the man and relayed the story to Vic and Lin. His people live deeper, and they are many. They came from another world long ago, a world where a fire was always above them, and invisible forces moved the surface they walked on into the air so it was difficult to breath or see.

"Sounds like the surface with the sun and sandstorms," commented Vic.

Then long, long ago the gods decided to protect them. The world trembled and roared. The floor of the world opened and the city sank, and the sand covered their city to protect them from the demons who roamed that world.

Chu translated, "So they didn't consider the earthquake a disaster, but a gift from their gods. I gather that not often does anyone come up where we are. I believe it was once the palace, where the ruler lived, and now it's like a sacred place. He said he smelled us and came to check."

After more conversation, Chu said, " I think they have been here very long. I mentioned Temujin or Chinggis Khaan, and he didn't know about him. He never heard of Modu and the Xiongnu, either, who were here about 200 years BC.

Vic shook her head. "I think they have been down here much longer than that. It might take ages for their eyes and nails to change to how they are unless they are a separate species, a lost race of man. Even that begs the question though - how does he know Mongolian, even an archaic form? He didn't mention any names familiar to you?"

"No. He said his people were attacked often by wild people who lived in the rocks and demons in the sky threw fire at them. That's why they were glad the gods put them underground."

"How do they survive?" Vic asked.

Chu asked the man, and after a minute of talk and gestures, he had an answer - mushrooms and an underground river which abounded in fish.

After another lengthy conversation, Chu grew solemn and said, "I asked how it is they don't run out of space. He says their home is vast, but if their numbers grow too many, the old are cut up and used to feed fish."

"Oh, my!" Lin said quietly. "Then they don't have emotions like compassion or remorse, at least not the same as ours."

"Everything is for the tribe," said Vic. "They are very primitive. That behavior indicates they may not even have self-awareness."

Chu had more. "He is quite upset that we are here. This is a forbidden region, a buffer to the evil world above. He keeps asking if you are a demon, or a wild person from the rocks, Vic. I don't think he likes you."

Chu apologized for their intrusion, explaining they were unaware it was a forbidden place and they would leave right away. The hairy man was puzzled about how a demon could be ignorant of a forbidden place and when Chu translated, Lin laughed again, and Vic called, "You are too easily amused, Lin."

Then the man told Chu he would call more of his people to help. When Chu translated, Vic quickly said, "No! I think we need to get out of here! He seems to be done talking. Tell him we need to speak with our friend. Lin, keep your eyes on this fellow and come out with us."

Chu spoke with the man to keep his attention while Lin eased out.

"Tell him we will go now, and we don't need help," Vic told Chu.

The strange man became belligerent and raised his voice after Chu told him they would go. "He wants us to wait," Chu translated.

Suddenly Vic looked behind them and said soberly, "We need to go right now!" She backed toward the doorway to the throne room.

"What is it?" Lin asked as she and Chu moved with Vic.

"I have that feeling." Vic tilted her head back as she went out into the throne room. "I smell them. More are coming!"

The man followed them. They dismounted the dais and walked quickly toward the stairway up. Alternately they watched the man and the many dimly visible doors around the vast room. The nearer they came to the stairway the louder the man became. When they started up the stone steps, he roared and waved his arms wildly!

441

Chu said, "He is warning us not to go higher."

"Why? Is this a more forbidden, forbidden place?" Lin asked, but they didn't slow. They were twenty feet up when the subterranean man roared more like a lion than a man and charged after them. It was immediately clear that he could move faster than they could as he bounded up three or four steps at a time!

"You're right Lin. We are going to a place more forbidden. We're going higher, and he must fear we will breach the barrier that protects them," Vic said as she turned to face the man.

An aggressor, no matter the size, ferocity, or power, is in a weaker position when one foot is off the ground. Vic grasped her ax at the end and below the head as the creature leaped. With all her power she drove the side of the handle against the man's face. He had no feet on the ground, and Vic's strength and his weight sent him over the edge of the stairs, but his giant, clawed hand wrenched the ax from Vic's grasp, and it toppled to the floor with him!

At that same time, the howls of several more of the underground dwellers could be heard drawing near. Vic didn't hesitate. She dropped the twenty feet to the stone floor, grabbed the ax and clobbered the man in the back of the head with the handle. He fell forward, and Vic was on her way back up the steps as a half dozen more of the men rushed in through a doorway across the throne room!

Lin and Chu were waiting at the top of the stairs, and Lin had her pistol out.

"Avoid shooting them if you can, Lin. Run! I'm right behind and only one at a time can go up the tube!" Vic was halfway up the steps as Lin and Chu rushed into the first hallway and ran! By the time Vic reached the top the entire horde was halfway up, so she stopped long enough to lift a loose stone and hurled it down. The creature in the lead batted it aside, but another stone was just behind and hit the leading man in the chest, and he stepped back, tripped on another, and the entire group tumbled down the steps or plunged over the side!

Vic sprinted!

Back at the tube, Lin hesitated, but Chu agreed with Vic. "We can't all go up at once! Go! I'll wait until I hear Vic!" Lin hurried up the tube and pulled her pack and Chu's with her. Chu waited. In seconds he heard running beyond the door and called out. It was Vic, so he went up.

Lin and Chu were out when Vic reached the tube. She slipped her pack and haversack off and pushed them into the tube an arm's length and went in after them. She could hear the men outside the door!

Vic pushed herself up the tube once and thrust her pack before her. She felt someone pull the gear out, and started to push herself up again when a huge hand grabbed both her ankles and pulled! Vic cried out and tried to pull herself upward, but she was no match for the strength

443

of the man.

The subterranean man yanked once and suddenly, from the waist down, Vic was back inside the room! Beyond the man who held her, Vic saw several more. She didn't want to hurt them. They were not just wild beasts. Or were they?

The thing released her ankles and reached up for her and as it did the mouth opened wide. Vic didn't doubt. He was about to bite her, and it wouldn't be pleasant! In a blur, she pulled the stone knife, drove it through a hand and back out! The thing howled and stumbled back.

Vic quickly pulled her feet and pushed up the tube and then again! She pushed a third time as she reached above. Suddenly, hands grasped both her arms and she was wrenched out roughly!

"Let's get away from this hole," Vic said as she stood up and returned the knife to her belt. "If they are all his size, they are too thick to pursue us but they may have crossbows, guns or just throw things."

They crawled out of the trench and lay against their packs to catch their breath.

"Holy crap, Vic! That was close!" Lin said.

"It felt closer than close down there." Vic pulled her trouser legs up and unlaced her boots to look at her ankles. Bruises were already evident all around, on the outside of her ankles from the man's hands and inside where her ankle bones were pressed together with great force.

After a few minutes, Vic suggested, "Let's

cover this. I don't think we'll be going back in."

"I know I'm not," said Lin.

"Maybe next year," said Chu.

They covered the hole much faster than they dug it and there was still an hour of light when they finished. On the hard earth at the base of the mountain, they re-erected their pup tents in a triangle configuration. The wind was up a bit, but they were able to kindle a small fire in the center of the tents to heat water for tsai to drink with dried maral.

As they ate they admired the treasure, and it now stunned them how much they brought out. Every pack and haversack was stuffed to capacity with precious stones and pearls. They estimated that each carried a good twenty kilograms of treasure.

None had experience with gems, but they all imagined there was sufficient value to build a fine school in the far reaches of Mongolia and much, much more!

"What was in that next room, Lin?" Chu asked.

"Silver. Just like the room of gold, ingots, goblets, everything, except it was silver. I wonder what was in the other three rooms." Lin pondered.

"Could be anything," said Chu. "What was valuable two thousand years ago?"

"It could have been incense and perfumes," said Lin.

"Or salt and tsai," Vic said. "They were probably valuable then as now."

"Or medicinal herbs," said Lin and her eyes

got wide. "Unknown cures for diseases!"

"Or scrolls with lost knowledge of things we can't imagine!" Chu said.

"What do you think, Vic?" Lin asked.

"I think I don't want to think. We could drive ourselves nuts pondering what eluded us. Everything about this raises questions. There has been no sea here for millions of years according to my geology class, yet they had pearls. Did they make excursions to the sea or trade with others? What did he mean when he spoke of wild men and what about gods shooting fire at them? Their mutations are mysterious, also. Could their physiques and eyesight really change that much in a couple thousand years, or even ten thousand years? What does he consider many? Are their dozens of them, or thousands? I am frustrated enough that I didn't get more time in the room where we entered."

"Why?" Chu asked.

Lin said, "Yeah, what do you think was there?"

Vic answered, "I am pretty sure the dusty tapestries were star charts, and I would love to have brought one. I would swear the one I dusted off showed Draco."

Lin and Chu were both intrigued, and Vic continued, "I'd bet a case of Cracker Jack and all the coffee trees in my hothouse, that the room was a planetarium, and the tube was the remains of a large telescope unlike anything we suppose existed long ago. If I deemed to work as an astronomer, I dare say that I could base

446

a lifetime career on the contents of that room."

"Holy cow, Vic! Do you want to ..." Lin began.

"No!" Vic cut her off. "I don't want to go back. I'm a travel writer with an ulterior motive that has nothing to do with astronomy."

Vic noticed Chu staring into the night. "What is it Chu?"

"I remember something which happened when I was ten. It was on the third or fourth trip with my father. We were camped for the night and two monks came from the direction we were going. They talked with my father awhile, then continued. The next day we took a different route. I asked father why we changed our plan. He said the monks saw a demon, yǎn shǔ rén, a mole man, that day and it would be dangerous to continue. I asked what are yǎn shǔ rénmín, mole people, and my father didn't know but trusted the monks."

With a shiver, Lin said, "Holy jeez! That thing's nose. It did look like a mole!"

"Is there a Mongolian legend about mole people?" Vic asked.

"That didn't happen in Mongolia. It was in China." Talk did not continue long. It was below zero with a little wind, and they were all glad to crawl into their tents and get warm.

Sleep came quickly, and soon Vic found herself leaned against a fallen tree near the edge of the Restless Sea where she relished the warmth of the primeval equatorial sun. Then Nat-ul startled her, "Vic!"

Vic jumped up and faced Nat-ul who stood between her and the Restless Sea. "What is wrong with you? You were nearly killed! Why were you so careless?" Nat-ul's voice was that of a young girl, but the words were delivered as though with a bullhorn and her anger was unmistakable. Vic never before heard Nat-ul angry and felt herself blush. "Why do you make me ashamed, Nat-ul?"

"It is not my words but your actions that give you shame! You almost died!" Nat-ul yelled again and looked harsher than Vic ever saw her.

"You did well to retrieve your weapon. Life is more likely to depart when you are without a weapon. Later you hesitated. Your ankles hurt do they not?"

Vic nodded.

"One more heartbeat, one more yank by the giant and you would have been in the room. You saw his teeth! He could take off a leg with a bite! One more heartbeat and he would be feeding on your carcass! You were two heartbeats from death!"

Vic knew Nat-ul was right.

"You hesitated. You knew what to do, and you paused. In matters of life and death, mistakes will get you killed, and the gravest mistake, the cause of more death than any other, is hesitation."

As Nat-ul spoke, Vic could feel the hair rise on her neck, and her senses heighten. She started to think, *this isn't real*, but stopped herself, keenly aware that thought was itself hesitation. Vic trusted Nat-ul in all matters related to life and death. Nat-ul knew what it was like to face death, again and again, to wage savage battle, over and over, for another day of life. Now, without conscious reason, Vic's hand went to the war ax in her belt and grasped it beneath the head.

"You know what to do in danger, Vic. You cannot have doubts. You cannot talk about it with yourself. The span of a heartbeat can mean the difference between life and death for you and sometimes for someone else, too. It should not be necessary for me to teach you the things known by children in the tribe of Onu!"

An image flashed through Vic's mind how Nat-ul - she - as a child, rushed without hesitation to battle Ur!

"Do what instinct and your heart say needs done!"

Vic's grip tightened on the war ax, and she was on hyper alert. She didn't know why. Wasn't this a dream or something like a dream? Can you die in a dream?

One thing Vic surely knew, since her vision and her visit to the cave of Gr in Africa, she enjoyed a new sense that gave her a chill and made the hair rise on her neck to herald imminent danger and more than once it saved her life.

Suddenly three bodies moved as one. Nat-ul dropped and caught herself on her forearms, her face an inch above the sand!

A great gush of water fell over Nat-ul and hit Vic as a gigantic saurian rose from the Restless Sea! It hissed, and the jaws sounded like a guillotine dropping as they closed on the air where Nat-ul stood an instant before!

Vic pulled the ax from her belt.

All of that happened in the same second.

The next second, like a hideous water snake, the saurian's head recoiled to strike again!

Vic swung the ax, and it sliced a two-inch-deep gash in the front of the beast's long neck. At the far end of her swing's arc, Vic was about to power the ax back, but there was no need. The wounded creature screeched and pulled into the sea.

Nat-ul was up again, and they watched the beast retreat and saw the trail of blood in its wake and knew it was surer than a dinner call. In another second, the wounded saurian thrust its head above the surface with a horrendous shriek, and the sea below the long neck became a nightmare scene of frenzied feeding! Other saurians literally ripped the doomed beast to pieces. One second more and the lifeless neck and head were pulled under, and the sea was once again still.

"See how fast death can come, and how brutal it can be?" said Nat-ul. "You are strong and quick and know what to do, but if you hesitate when you must act, you will end as that creature ended."

"Thank you, Nat-ul," said Vic. "I will never again endanger myself or others," she paused and smiled, "talking with myself about what to do."

"I know," said Nat-ul. "You learn very

quickly." She took a few steps then stopped and looked back at Vic, "A time will be soon upon you when, if you hesitate, you will die and so will others. Do what needs done Vic, and when pain and exhaustion overwhelm you and when all your strength seems gone, call on the power of your heart."

Vic wondered at the implication of that cryptic guidance but knew it was useless to ask. She watched Nat-ul walk to the cliffside path and ascend the steep incline and enter one of the openings that she knew were the homes of the people of the tribe of Onu. She could hear laughter and people talking in the ancient language of the uprights. For a brief moment, Vic was gripped by a deep urge to again be with her people of that time, to be with Nu in that life, but the ache declined. She knew she could never ascend the cliffs either with Nat-ul or as Nat-ul, could never be with Nu in that place. That time was gone. She must find him in her new world as Vic Challenger. Then she thought, no, not as Vic. I must find Nu and be with him as Victoria Custer. I am now Victoria Custer, she spoke, and it felt good to hear her own voice affirm who she was.

Vic still didn't comprehend who or what Nat-ul was. Was she merely a dream, an imagined being, a separate part of Vic's own personality, an avatar of her subconscious mind interacting with her conscious mind, a truly independent life force who dwelled inside her, or something else? Vic did come to one conclusion, however: it didn't matter. It was incredible, whatever it was. She liked Nat-ul and Nat-ul was a voice of reason and life, her counsel

451

was always wise, and it did not matter if she had no inkling of Nat-ul's true nature.

Vic basked in the warmth of the sun for a few seconds, then felt she needed to go and she heard Lin's voice, "Vic! You plan to sleep all day? I can't believe you're not up!"

"Coming," Vic said and unrolled herself from the bedding, pulled on her deel over her shirt and trousers and crawled out into the cold, still-dark morning. Overnight, there was a light fall of more ice-snow, and as far as one could see, the world was under a three to four-inch white cover.

From there they headed back to Chu's ger and family. For Vic, there was good luck on the second day as they came around a bend onto a group of maral. She was able to pull her carbine and get a big one before they bolted. They spent the rest of the day at that spot and cut the meat of the maral, wrapped it in its skin and Vic carried it across her horse in front of her. There was no need to worry that it might spoil since the daytime temperature was now perpetually zero or below.

Chapter 12

The Destroyer

They were at the point where they turned upward onto the mountain toward Chu's ger, and Narakaa and the twins when they sighted a lone horseman racing hard toward them along the contour of the land.

"He is pushing that horse hard!" said Lin.

"No one would do that without an important reason," Vic noted.

Chu stared intently at the rapidly approaching rider and finally spoke, "It is Ganbold. He lives further around the mountain."

The man came to them so hard that the horse almost fell as it stopped. "Chu!" Ganbold spoke in Mongolian rapidly for a moment, then turned his horse and raced off toward the steppes.

Chu's face had no color. "The Mad Baron invaded Mongolia last month and is in Urga.

Burilgi, the Destroyer, one of his commanders, is here in the mountains. He is said to be as ruthless as the Baron or worse. He has burned gers and killed many. Ganbold is taking his family south and says I should do the same immediately. If the Destroyer comes, there will be many, many men. He is known for overkill. It is said that he likes to wash over his enemy like a flood from the mountains," Chu told them.

"I've been washed over before," said Vic. "If he comes to fight a mother and her babies, he can't bring enough men."

"Double that," said Lin."

The three pushed their horses to a fast walk up the mountain trail in silence. With no spoken coordination, each pulled their revolver to double-check it was fully loaded . "How far are we Chu?" Vic asked.

"Almost two kilometers."

All three moved their carbine from the saddle and slung it over their head and shoulder, and let it hang for quick employment.

Vic's haversack hung from the saddle, and atop the gems, it held grenades, two extra loaded magazines for the carbine and loose rounds for both her revolver and carbine. Vic transferred the magazines and loose cartridges to the sash pouch of her deel. Then she slung the haversack over her head to hang on the opposite side from the carbine. Lin and Chu followed suit.

They rode on but a minute more when from a distance, from straight ahead, from higher on the mountain, from the one direction they did not want to hear it, from the direction of Chu's home, came a sound that tore at their hearts and sent a chill up their spines! Gunfire!

"Narakaa!" yelled Chu.

"The babies!" Lin shouted.

As though a single rider the three immediately galloped at full speed and spurred and whipped their horses for all they had! Abreast they rode and each, in turn, jumped logs and boulders as they appeared. Not one of them ever slowed for any reason, and one or more steadily goaded the horses with "Choo, choo!".

Ahead, the shooting was continuous, and the horses seemed to gain even more speed.

Vic flung the maral skin to the ground and loosened the war ax in her belt.

A stand of young pines came up in front of Lin, and she drove her horse through them without slowing and jumped a small boulder just past them.

Then they heard new sounds - a shotgun. "Narakaa!" yelled Chu. "She lives! That is the trench gun O gave me." The trench gun sounded again and again.

Vic jumped her horse over a log.

"Narakaa is very good. but she is alone with our babies!" Fear was discernable in Chu's voice. As one, the three horses hurdled a dry rivulet.

A plan is helpful. Knowing the situation is advantageous. There are times though when you have neither, but something must be done, something that pulls at your heart and your humanity and whatever more majestic, unnamed things lie even deeper inside you. The three had no plan nor did they know what awaited above, yet they never slowed, they never hesitated nor doubted, and they came to the place of the ger with no intention of dying, but to do what needed done!

When they came over the final knoll, they were to the backs of two dozen men firing at the ger. Between the standing men and the ger, four dead Russians bore witness that Narakaa could indeed use the trench gun!

Another half dozen men crept along the tree line to their left to slip up to the ger from the side.

In the trees, 100 meters to the right, fully three dozen or more hardened fighters were still mounted, and watched the spectacle and waited for the men on the ground to do the job.

The three raised their carbines and fired as soon as the targets were visible. Three of the men fell dead, and the others turned. Before any could return fire, the three carbines sounded again, and three more men dropped where they stood.

They rode through the remaining men and used the carbines as clubs. Each blow sent one more of the enemy to his end, and the horses crushed others. The three turned their horses in tight circles in the crowd, again and again, The horses trampled the enemy, and the riders clubbed more! In intricate circles that became figure eights, they turned their horses to the right and then the left. The enemy fired wildly without effect. Within seconds, only four remained.

The mounted riders came toward them now, and as the horde spread for the charge, it was evident they numbered forty or so.

Lin clubbed at one of the men on one side of her, and another from the opposite side swung up and hit Lin in the side of the head with the butt of his rifle. It almost knocked Lin off her horse, and Vic was about to go help when Lin and her horse did an immediate and perfect rollback, and knocked down the man who hit Lin and trampled him.

The three rode toward the men at the edge of the woods. They let the carbines dangle and pulled their revolvers and fired, then fired again.

They heard the trench gun twice more. Narakaa took out the last two of the men on the ground behind them.

Those enemies at the tree line died quickly, and the three brought their horses to a dead stop and jumped off to take cover behind trees. Chu's well-trained horses each continued a few meters then turned and waited.

As the enemy on horseback charged, every shot by Vic or Lin or Chu killed another marauder, and when the enemy realized the marksmanship of the three, they dismounted and took cover.

Vic, Lin, and Chu dropped their packs and found each had multiple bullet holes. Death was repeatedly thwarted by the precious gems!

Vic yelled to Lin, "We can't all run out of

457

ammunition at the same time. Reload now, Lin. Both weapons. After Lin, you reload Chu. Then I will."

Soon they were all reloaded and firing deliberately, and with every shot, the number of the enemy was reduced by one. Then Chu noted, "The trench gun is silent."

Lin fired, and with distress in her voice, yelled, "She's just waiting to see what happens Chu. Narakaa is OK, the babies are OK!"

"I think they've gone." Chu fired.

"Gone?" Vic asked and fired.

"We have an escape tunnel for an emergency as this." Chu fired.

Lin fired.

"Where does it go?" asked Vic and she fired.

"Down the hill behind the ger. Then she will run down the mountain to a place where she can descend a cliff and hide."

"Let's get them, then," said Vic and without any discussion, they ran to the horses. All three fired, then mounted and at top speed drove boldly toward the center of the enemy line!

They let the carbines dangle and shot revolvers as they charged the two dozen remaining men. The handguns were emptied before they passed the soldiers, but they kept riding.

Vic pulled the ax out, and as she rode through, she swung to one side then the other and two more of the bandits' careers were ended. Lin and Chu again took their carbines from around their necks and used them as clubs.

As Lin swung at the last man she passed, he fired. It felt like someone kicked her in the shoulder and it burned, then it was forgotten, and Lin rode on. As they cleared the men, Chu felt a hot slap and burn against his right leg and looked down to see his trousers torn away mid-thigh, and a bloody, ragged trench through his flesh an inch deep and two inches wide. Then it was forgotten.

They had a head start now and in two minutes came over a hill and saw Narakaa and the twins running. Narakaa heard the horses and turned. The grit of determination was on her face and murder to protect her children was in her eyes. She came around with the trench gun at her shoulder ready to fire! When she saw who it was, she pushed the twins in opposite directions from her and spoke to them and then nodded to the riders.

The riders didn't slow. Vic scooped up Segree, Lin took Monkkaa, and Chu pulled Narakaa to the back of his horse. Vic thought, *these girls are fearless*, and almost like a whispered echo, she heard Nat-ul say, *they just know what needs done and don't question*.

They continued for a minute, and Vic said, "They will catch us like this." She brought her horse beside Lin's and without slowing lifted Segree over to sit with Monkkaa in front of Lin. "Keep going. I'll find you."

"Vic, you can't..." Lin began.

"Go, Lin, go! You have two babies to protect. I know what I'm doing. Keep going! I'll use grenades to slow those animals down

459

and buy you some time. Then I'll get away. It's what needs done, Lin! You need time! You know it."

Before they rode on, Chu told Vic, "There may be more. I did not see Burilgi."

Then Chu and his family and Lin continued hard up the mountain out of sight, and Vic stopped to look around.

Vic left the trail and rode upslope to her right and dismounted behind a clump of trees. She reloaded her carbine and revolver. Then she folded her haversack fly open and took out one of the grenades from the canyon of worms and looked around. Trees and underbrush were thick, so there was good cover to hide Vic but it wouldn't stop bullets, and it limited her use of grenades. Fortune favors the bold, however, and Vic found a spot with a straight view across the trail and on the other side of the trail was a scree slope. Vic estimated the distance and prepared to make the most important throw of her life. Then she waited.

The wait was short. The thunder of many hooves came from just out of sight. She could tell from the sound that Chu was right, there were more than she expected. When they came in sight, Vic estimated at least 100.

The numbers don't matter, Vic told herself. Chu and his family and Lin needed as much time as she could buy them. That is what needed done whether there were ten or a thousand.

Her original intent was to use the grenades to even the odds and draw what was left of the enemy to chase her, but she expected thirty, maybe forty men. There were now too many for that plan. Even if she killed a dozen and half those who remained came after her, there would be fifty or more after her friends, and those were not the odds she wanted for them.

Five men rode abreast at the lead of the troop, with the one in the center just a bit ahead of the others. Even if not for his position, Vic would have recognized the Destroyer.

Burilgi, the Destroyer, was a tall man, Vic estimated a little more than two meters. He was bony, like a skeleton with cable-like muscles covered by skin. His right cheek was a sunken scar, and he wore a black patch on that eye, both probably from a gunshot to the face earlier in his career. Even though the temperature was below freezing, the man's torso was bare save for his own thick curly gray-black hair, not unlike the wolf Vic killed, and it covered his chest, back, and arms.

On his wrists, he wore leather bands with two-inch spikes. The outer seams of his pants were also lined with spikes. Across his horse, he held what at a distance looked like an elephant gun, no doubt so he could blow men in half to engender even more fear of the Destroyer. Vic was most disgusted by his belt where scalps hung in such profusion they fell over one another. Vic had only two thoughts when she saw the Destroyer: he was bad, and she must kill him if she could.

When she thought the lead horsemen were about four seconds from reaching the scree

461

slope, Vic pulled the pin on a grenade, powered it across the breach, and scurried for a new location.

Vic learned how the Destroyer earned his reputation. Burilgi saw the grenade land in the loose rock and immediately jerked the horseman nearest him from his mount, and held him as a shield. The grenade exploded and blasted rock fragments into the side of the group and killed or wounded ten or more, but the Destroyer wasn't harmed. Stones were buried in the face and chest of the human shield and Burilgi casually tossed the corpse to the ground.

The blast also caused a small rock slide that filled the trail with loose rocks and slowed the horses. To her further advantage, the men did not see Vic, so they did not yet know her position nor that she was alone. They all held rifles at the ready and looked anxiously from one slope to the other. A few fired in the direction of the explosion, but the Destroyer stopped them and then shouted something in Russian and then Mongolian, apparently to whoever threw the grenade. Vic didn't mind she didn't understand what he said.

Vic peered through brush along a new clear line of sight. Every action must account for as many as possible, as quickly as possible, so she was thankful to see a tight cluster of men. Ten riders were bunched close, and Vic mused, *these men are untrained. Ten minutes with JJ in Mexico and I learned not to bunch like that.*

Vic pulled a grenade pin and stood and aimed for the grouped horsemen. It exploded in the center of the group and killed another half dozen men and wounded that many or more, but Vic was spotted. She pulled the pin on the third grenade and lobbed it in a high arc toward the trail. It exploded a meter above the heads of the riders. It killed two more and wounded others.

Now the soldiers all fired at Vic or in her general direction. Most were still mounted, but at least twenty dismounted and began to work their way up toward her. Vic's return fire was slow and deliberate, and every shot killed or wounded an enemy. Vic realized, though, that she didn't have enough ammunition to kill them all.

She pulled the last grenade from her pouch, instantly chose a location, pulled the pin and stood. She threw it, and a sharp heat raked across her right arm as she ducked again!

Vic would not wait there and be swarmed over by these animals who called themselves men. Nor would she retreat and scamper through the bushes like a frightened rabbit. She recalled the counsel of Nat-ul, do not hesitate. She must try to kill Burilgi, and she was already in motion as the final grenade exploded.

Instinctively, Vic loosened the ax in her sash and made the war cry of the tribe of Onu as she ran. The cry reverberated through the frozen forest and was so vicious that every man on the hillside stopped firing for a second to look toward the sound. After sounding the war

463

cry, Vic halted and quickly fired twice. Two men who stared upward took those shots between their eyes! Vic pulled her knife and set it between her teeth and went on the attack! She dodged from tree to tree, fired every few steps and made each shot count!

Suddenly, a man came from behind a tree, and Vic pushed the barrel of his rifle down as he fired. She felt a kick like a mule in her belly but ignored it and grabbed the knife from her teeth, drove it into the man's throat, and ran on!

Then her carbine was empty, and she used it once to club a man then dropped it and pulled her revolver with her left hand and the ax with her right. Just steps later, another man came through young pines and slashed at Vic with his fixed bayonet. Vic thought she felt the air of the blade close to her face as she turned sideways to avoid it. She rammed the barrel of her revolver against the man's forehead and pulled the trigger and continued to charge down the hill full throttle! Even though the temperature was near zero, perspiration soaked Vic's clothing, and every few steps she shook her head forcefully to expel the sweat from her eyes.

Seconds later, she felt a hot punch against her left shoulder and then someone slammed her in the back with a rifle butt! Vic jumped forward and spun around and shot the man through the heart. His last act was to pull the trigger again, and it felt to Vic like a hot claw raked her waist. She completed a full 360 degrees spin and kept going!

Don't stop, she told herself. Don't stop! Every inch of her body was in pain, stiff or burning or throbbing or cramping from the strain! She could scarcely catch her breath, but she remembered the fight with the jaguar and how she managed to hold on and she remembered what Nat-ul said. *When your body can do no more, use the strength of your heart.* The evil below needed to die, and Chu and his family and Lin needed time to live, and Vic wanted to find Nu. A potent, invincible blend of love and loathing filled her heart and Vic continued the assault!

Vic was just 10 meters upslope from the trail when she heard one machine gun and then another and then what sounded like a thousand rifles from the direction of the Destroyer's arrival. It must be the enemy firing on her, but until a bullet stopped her, she would focus on just one thing - Burilgi.

Through the trees she saw Burilgi, still mounted, the elephant gun held with one hand as though a toy. He faced back in the direction they came and yelled to his men. Vic continued to dodge from tree to tree and suddenly burst through the last stand of brush just four meters from Burilgi. The Destroyer saw Vic and smiled as he aimed the huge gun at her head!

It was one of those moments when total focus is finely directed upon one infinitesimal point to the exclusion of all else. For the time of a single heartbeat, Vic could see nothing but the index finger of the Destroyer, magnified and in slow motion, closing on the trigger of his prodigious rifle!

In the instant, the finest part of a second, before the Destroyer fired his rifle with one hand, Vic side-stepped, and in that split second, she recognized the rifle as a Wesley Richards .577. It was the same rifle she used to down the charging rhinoceros in Africa and Vic marveled that the man could fire it in one hand! The heat of Burilgi's missile warmed Vic's face as it passed and the massive slug toppled a tree with a six-inch diameter. While the boom of the massive rifle yet reverberated Vic jumped onto a small boulder, heaved her ax with every muscle in her body and leaped after it!

The way a cat paws at a ball of yarn, Burilgi used the rifle to bat the ax to the side, but there was no time to swing it back at Vic. She hit him full body and her weight and the thrust of her jump took them off the other side of his horse.

Even as they fell, Burilgi retained strength and presence of mind to bring a knee up to catch Vic and push her over his head. The Destroyer hit the ground with a grunt as his move twirled Vic over and she landed on her back with a grunt of her own.

They both immediately rolled, in opposite directions and came to their feet. Vic kept her eyes on the Destroyer, made two hops, then leaned sideways to retrieve her ax.

The Destroyer struck at her fast, swinging his empty rifle and growling. Vic's ax met the rifle in mid-swing, and the stone caught the trigger housing and wrenched the weapon from Burilgi's grasp! Then the man began to swipe at Vic with one hand then the other. It required but a few attempts for Vic to realize he wasn't trying to punch or backhand her, but merely rake her with the spikes on his wrists!

Vic dodged and backed and circled the man. She blocked his swipes with the side of her ax and when he suddenly kicked high at her face, she stepped back and leaned back at the waist in one move. His foot was just inches from her face and she got a clear view of the three-inch metal spike embedded in the toe of his boot. His foot went down but he kicked again and again Vic stepped and leaned back to avoid his boot and spike.

Then a concerned voice sounded in Vic's mind. *Defense is death* and Vic knew what needed done. When the next kick came, she didn't wait for the next but swung the ax hard and forced the Destroyer to jump back.

The man rebounded again with another kick and as it went down without contact Vic's ax swept across between them again. That pair of actions repeated again and as it was about to repeat once more, Vic stopped the arc of her blow short to back swing early. The back of the ax head clipped the Destroyer's knee and knocked him off balance. He didn't fall but hopped sideways and stumbled as Vic began another sweep.

Burilgi roared in rage and struck out with his arm. His anger caused the man to miss-time his blow, so his arm and Vic's ax met and the ax won. The man's right arm was taken off at

467

the elbow and his forearm somersaulted to the ground behind him!

The Destroyer bellowed like a wounded bull mammoth and swung his remaining hand at Vic again and again and all the while his blood pumped out from the amputation wound. Vic sidestepped and swung her ax and then dodged again. When Burilgi kicked at her again, once more she came back with the back side of her ax head and slammed his knee. The man stumbled back and before he could regain his balance, Vic swung the ax up. The side of the ax head caught the Destroyer beneath the chin and he fell back hard.

Vic raised the ax overhead but stopped. Burilgi looked fearful as he frantically tried to reach behind him and roared oaths in Russian!

Vic kept her weapon poised but didn't strike. Within seconds the blustery shouts became histrionic screams as the man thrashed wildly and still strained to reach behind him. Then the directed reaching became uncontrolled convulsions! The great Destroyer began to belch the sauerkraut of his last meal. His eyes were wild with the fear of death which he dealt so casually to countless others. Vomit spewed from his mouth and an equal amount was sucked into his lungs.

As she watched the man die, Vic noticed the tip of the severed forearm jutted from beneath the man's shoulder and realized Burilgi, the Destroyer, was skivered by his own wrist spikes.

Suddenly a pistol sounded to Vic's right rear and before she could turn a White Russian dropped to her left with a fresh bullet hole in his forehead. She looked back and gave a sigh of relief. Lin stood there with her revolver in hand.

"You OK, Vic?"

"I'm Ok, Lin." Vic breathed deep and looked toward the gunfire. "You were supposed to be away from here and safe."

"I left you at the worm place and felt like crap. Didn't want to feel that again, Vic," said Lin.

"Then let's finish this together, Lin."

"Rest Vic," Chu emerged from the tree line with Segree holding his left hand. He used his rifle as a cane in his right hand. Beside him walked Narakaa with Monkkaa holding her right hand, and the trench gun ready in her left hand.

"Let the others finish it. You've done enough," said Chu. "Oh, don't touch those spikes, they're tipped with poison."

Vic half smiled, "Yeah, I figured that."

"We have all done enough," said Lin. "Besides, from here I see four wounds. You earned a break." Vic looked at herself and found a nick on her right arm, and a hole in her left shoulder with an exit wound in back which soaked her deel and shirt with her blood; a wound across her right waist luckily ripped through only muscle and skin but did leak a lot of blood. Her ax stone had an inch deep impression in the center, surrounded by concentric circles where the first Russian who came from behind a tree fired at her point blank. The ax saved her.

469

Nor were Lin and Chu without wounds. Lin had a shoulder wound like Vic's, a bayonet slash on the opposite forearm and the right side of her face was swollen and bruised, her eye almost closed, from the rifle butt early in the battle.

Chu had a wound in his right thigh and the back of his left arm, and his deel was opened across his belly where a bayonet cut a skin deep gash across his full width and he couldn't remember when it happened.

"You said four wounds, I see only three," Vic said to Lin.

"Your cheek, Vic. You'll probably have a scar."

Vic didn't ask which side but touched her left cheek. She felt the blood and looked at it on her fingertips and smiled her recognition. The bayonet came closer than she knew. It wasn't just the wind of the passing blade she felt!

"Who are they fighting?" Vic asked.

Ganbold who warned them of the danger was not the first to flee the mountains. Others fled a week earlier. Some went to Dalan bulag. Bayarmaa heard of the danger and knew Captain Unegen was in Gazar so went to ask his help. He was glad to give it for friendship of Chu, but to crush the Destroyer's force was also the kind of single-handed exploit which could make a successful career, so the captain brought 200 of his most experienced Mongol soldiers and arrived just in time.

Captain Unegen witnessed Vic battle with

the rogue Russian commander. Literally in awe, he said "That jaguar never had a chance! You are a mighty warrior!"

At that, Vic laughed and couldn't stop a brief stream of tears. When the captain asked Chu what was wrong, Vic told him it was a great honor that a Mongol warrior and officer would say those things, then called Captain Unegen a hero and a treasure to Mongolia. The true reason for tears was joy, for no one had called her a mighty warrior for a thousand generations and earned recognition is a joy for anyone, even warriors and re-incarnated cave girls. Vic knew Nat-ul would look down on public show of emotion, but it was right for Victoria Custer. Her reply, of course, ensured that if Vic wanted it, she could have an escort of a thousand men for the rest of the trip, but she didn't.

Captain Unegen shook Chu's hand and told him his father would be very proud and if he wanted to join the army, he would be a captain.

The captain turned to join his men and then stopped, looked back and made the perfect finale to a brutal, bloody battle. "Tell Vic Challenger's servant girl she also is a brave warrior. Even Temujin himself would feel pride to battle with these two warriors!"

When the last Russian was dead, the captain told his physician to look after the wounds of Vic, Lin, and Chu, but before the doctoring began Narakaa got an idea and Vic thought it was good. Narakaa retrieved Vic's pack and camera and photographs were taken of everyone in various combinations. Many included the captain, and wounds were obvious in all. On his request, a full role of film was taken of Vic, and the others with the captain and the dead destroyer and given to Captain Unegen.

The captain's physician was not a physician but a hardened, professional soldier with a lot of experience dressing battle wounds. He carried needles and catgut to close wounds, and antiseptic and bandages, so he more than sufficed and they were grateful.

Vic sat on a boulder beside Lin, and as the man worked on their wounds, the Captain brought her knife. She thanked him and wiped the knife with antiseptic. Then she asked, "Lin, remember that blood brother thing? There's no law that says men only. Want to be blood sisters?"

"Sure thing, Vic!"

Everyone stared wide-eyed when each pulled her knife across a palm, then clasped their bloodied hands together and spoke, "Sisters!"

Then they heard another, "Sister?" Narakaa stood there holding her stone knife. Vic and Lin didn't look at one another, for each knew what the other would say. They both nodded and Narakaa pulled her stone knife across her palm then grasped the hand of Vic and then Lin and each time said, "Sister!"

The next day before Captain Unegen and his troops took their leave, Vic presented the captain with her stone knife and saluted him and the captain returned her salute. Beside Captain

Unegen rode his aide who carried a pole on which the head of the Destroyer was impaled. When he was gone, Lin said, "You were right Vic. It's his country and culture. He may seem brutal and vicious, but in his way he is a brave and honorable soldier; a patriot standing up for his country."

Chapter 13

Going Home

Vic and Lin stayed another five days at the ger to rest, but there was little of that. They spent much of their time with the twins. They played in the snowy woods and lost shagai games, and although the temperature was never above ten degrees Fahrenheit in those days, neither Vic nor Lin complained of the cold.

On the third day, they remembered to retrieve the other packs and gems. Vic also found her maral skin intact, and the meat for Narakaa and the twins was untouched, but Lin's camera took two bullets for her. Narakaa wanted to make them new deels because of the slashes and bullet holes, but they preferred to patch their original deels.

Chu planned to drive them back to Kalgan, but they defiantly refused. It would take him away from his family too long. They could easily retrace the path they came by, avoid people, and forego a side trip to Gazar, even though they knew the captain would treat them like royalty.

Vic and Lin returned the carbines to Chu along with the unused salt, tsai, and rubles. Of course, they gave their magnifiers to Monkhaa and Segree.

When they were leaving, Vic gave the ax to Narakaa and told her through Chu, "You are incredible. You faced a hundred men to protect your babies and not once have I heard you even speak of it nor complain of the ordeal. I hope you never need this but if you do, may it serve you well. I am proud to know you Narakaa, my sister."

The twins gave Vic and Lin each a bag of sheep ankle bones and told them to practice. As Vic pulled the auto away, they held their hands up and gave Vic their version of the war cry of the tribe of Onu, told them "Bayartai", then yelled between giggles, in Mongolian, Chinese, Russian and English how much they loved nice big sister and nice girl. After the ger was out of sight and they could no longer hear the twins, they rode in silence for over an hour.

"It will be nice to get home," Lin finally said in little more than a whisper, "but I'm going to miss those little girls. I'm pretty sure, for awhile I'll be waking up ready to run out and chase them through the woods, or squat in the snow for a serious round of cat's game."

Vic said, "Well, there is no reason why we can't visit again. We should inspect the school from time to time don't you think?"

That made Lin smile big, "You're right! We will be like administrators or big donors or something. Don't even need to go for a story. Just see the school and play hide and seek!" Lin took a deep breath. "I feel better. I felt so heavy. Maybe next summer when it's warm!"

Vic laughed. "Who knows? But you will still love them Lin, no matter when it is. Like your aunt and mother after years apart. For love, time doesn't matter."

Then Lin told Vic, "I think I understand when you talk about doing what needs done. When we charged up that hill and in the middle of the enemy, all trying to kill us, I never felt afraid, but I didn't feel brave either. I just knew Monkkaa and Segree were in danger and to save them I needed to kill as many men as I could as fast as I could. I never felt more focused in my life."

The trip to Dalan bulag was uneventful. They timed it so they rolled into Dalan bulag in the day. When they parked at the trading post, the same five men as before loitered outside and they thought there might be trouble, but were able to enter without incident. They delivered a letter to Bayarmaa written by her granddaughters, to thank her for sending Captain Unegen.

When they were ready to go, Bayarmaa walked with them. Just out the door, the man who seemed to be the leader of the loiterers stepped in front of them and spoke to Bayarmaa who told Lin in Chinese who translated for Vic. "He wishes to tell you, that he has never seen better shooters, and he heard how you defeated the Destroyer and thanks you."

Vic and Lin both smiled at the man and said thank you in English, then Vic asked, "How do you say thank you in Mongolian?" Then she and Lin both told the man " Bayarlalaa," and Vic asked Bayarmaa to tell him they were very proud to do something good for his beautiful country. He nodded and stepped out of the way. There was no smile on his lips, but Vic and Lin both later swore that behind his hard expression, they saw a smile in his eyes.

Three days after Dalan bulag, they came to the wall outside Kalgan. They sold the auto back to the man Chu bought it from for half what Chu paid, which is what Chu told them to expect. Then they packed the deels and revolvers.

Chin was at the wall and recognized them and said to say hi to Lao when they saw him. To make things look on the up and up to anyone who might be watching, they opened their packs and pulled out the wolf skins and the deels to show Chin. Underneath the wolf skins, in each pack was a bag sewn from two tarbagan skins and each held five kilograms of gems, but who would want to see a marmot hide? An hour later they were on the train to Peking and Vic wound and set her watch for the first time in 70 days.

For three days they ate, rested and shopped and each night they both took a turn, a long turn, in a very hot tub of bubbles. Vic took photos of Lin with her relatives, and later back in Nebraska, Lin's mother couldn't stop crying and laughing when she saw the photo of her big sister with her eldest daughter.

They didn't have booked passage, so when they took the train to Dairen, Lao went to help them get on a ship. He had friends on the docks he thought could help, but it turned out to be unnecessary.

They were at the harbor, on their way to see someone Lao knew when Lin punched Vic on the arm and said excitedly, "Hey look!"

The Red Dragon was there. They explained to Lao and approached the ship. The sailor at the gangplank recognized them so they said their goodbyes and thanks to Lao and went up to see Captain Chuluun.

Captain Chuluun was more than happy to take them as passengers again. Both yet wore bandages on their shoulders, and the scar, nicely healing on Vic's left cheek, was evident, as was the bruise on Lin's face. "It looks like you ladies might have run into some trouble," Captain Chuluun said.

"Nothing we couldn't handle," said Vic.

"Just did what needed done," Lin said.

Suddenly the captain's eyes widened, and he looked as though he was trying to puzzle something. Even though phones were new and not everyone owned one in China in the last month of 1920, and few people sent telegrams, somehow good news always gets around.

"Say! You two didn't have a run in with a fellow called Burilgi, did you?"

479

Vic was silent, but Lin replied, "We sure did."

The captain refused to take their fare. Their passage was on him. They tried again and again to pay, but he wouldn't have it.

Vic and Lin were putting on the Ritz every night at dinner and wore the prettiest silk dresses they were able to find in Peking, with their wolf pelts turned stoles. There were no boring dinners for that trip. They sat with a new group each night, and everyone wanted to hear about the bandages, how Vic got the scar and what bruised Lin so badly. Their favorite question was, 'Where did you buy those nice wolf pelts?" One or both would answer, "Buy? Oh, we didn't buy these, we..." They had a lot of fun with that.

The trip was a reverse of the trip over, so a week later they were ready for Hawaii. They planned only to stay overnight and continue with the Red Dragon, but Evelyn convinced them to stay. It was only a few days until Christmas, and they could not get back to Nebraska in time, so why not stay until after Christmas? Captain Chuluun gave them a name of another captain, a good friend, who could give them passage January 1st and make sure there were no problems getting everything safely ashore in San Francisco.

Vic and Lin were happy to have a vacation in Hawaii, where they wouldn't need weapons, or wake up cold, or worry about sandstorms. The day they arrived was perfectly warm and sunny.

Days were spent mostly at the beach. Nights were wild for Lin and Evelyn as they dragged Vic into games of mahjong with them, joined by Evelyn's Uncle Charlie, and his number two son and number one daughter.

Vic didn't mind the mahjong because there was also conversation of famous cases which Charlie solved. Charlie also provided plenty of witticisms, and Vic's favorite was, 'To lose is like driving very large nail in house. Make it stronger." Of course, Lin couldn't resist that opening and said, "Then Vic will last forever."

On Christmas eve they attended a service at Kawaiaha'o Church with the Chan family. The church planned to serve dinner for needy families the next day and give out gifts to children, and along with the entire Chan clan, they volunteered to help. Charlie helped Vic find a shop open late, and she used the last of her expense money to buy 200 little jade elephants and turtles on leather cords to give to kids on Christmas Day.

The remainder of their time in Hawaii was mostly fun in the sun with time also spent listening to more cases Charlie solved.

When they passed through San Francisco, Lin convinced a Chinese language paper to publish her stories of adventure travel, so she would be doing what Vic did only in Chinese.

Vic and Lin arrived back home in Beatrice on January 12, 1921. The parents of both, and Lin's brothers and sisters were there to meet them. Vic and Lin assured everyone they were fine, which of course no one believed when they saw the wounds.

Vic's mom told her that most men wouldn't want a wife with a scar on her face. Vic just laughed her good natured laugh and hugged her mom and said, "It's OK mom. It doesn't matter if most men wouldn't like it. Somewhere there is one who does." Vic was intrigued when her mother made a half smile and nodded knowingly.

Neither Vic nor Lin knew what she was doing so it took several weeks to go from marmot hides full of gems to cash and a business set up for the school in Mongolia. Once done, they began to wire money to Lao, who bought supplies, which Chu took by caravan from Kalgan.

Both nearly died and both had permanent scars. Their friendship grew even stronger. They made incredible new friends who regardless of distance would be a part of their lives always. Lin was filled with unbounded joy and pride that she was able to help Monkkaa and Segree. Vic was equally proud over the same aspects of the trip as Lin, but an emptiness yet filled her heart for there was never a sense of Nu.

Two days after returning to Beatrice, Vic and Lin had root beer floats at Mortimer's Drug and Lin thanked Vic. "That was some vacation! When do we go again?" Vic was already planning.

On the day after they arrived back in Beatrice, on January 13, 1921, Vic began to plan the next trip. She spent hours each day in the library, looking over maps of South America, Iceland, Great Britain, Australia and more, and hoped that some extra sense would prompt her about where to travel but no place seemed to beckon more than the others. Of course, she often wondered if Ann Darrow would convince Carl Denham to share the location of Skull Island.

Vic found no clues to Nu, but she had a strong sense of something unfinished or incomplete. She experienced the same sensation following the vision in Africa when she recalled her previous life. It was a vague inkling about something lacking or unconsummated yet the identity of the something was even vaguer than the sensation itself.

Wherever the future might lead, Vic knew fully there may be more danger, pain, and injury ahead, but nothing short of death would halt her quest.

True love never dies. To Victoria Custer it was a sacred commission, an inviolable commitment to search a lifetime if needed and face any challenge to find her eternal love, Nu, son of Onu, who slew Gr, devourer of men and mammoths for his one true love, Nat-ul, wondrous daughter of Tha, of the tribe of Onu, that once dwelt beyond the Barren Hills beside the Restless Sea.

Things which matter most must never be at the mercy of things which matter least. - most often attributed to Goethe

You don't need to be brave. You just need to do what needs done. - Vic's Motto

The Adventures Continue...

Join the further adventures of Vic Challenger.
Visit http://www.vicplanet.com

#1 *Vic: Time Doesn't Matter* 978-1-889823-38-6
#2 *Vic: Mongol* 978-1-889823-60-7
#3 *Vic: Never Give Up* 978-1-889823-61-4
#4 *Vic: Terror Incognita* 978-1-889823-63-8
#5 *Vic: Fast* 978-1-889823-62-1
#6 *Vic: Event* 978-1-889823-65-2
#7 Vic: Bloody *Reprisal* 978-1-889823-80-5
#8 Mystery & Magic 978-1-889823-85-0
ISBN's are for paperback editions.
More to Come!

Howlers Illustrated story 978-1-889823-37-9

Vic Challenger's Incredibly Delicious Recipes for
Bacon Lovers. ISBN 13: 978-1-889823-10-2

Several Vic Challenger journals are available.

Authors appreciate and need reviews. If you have a couple of minutes, please leave a review at your favorite site.

If you enjoy Vic Challenger adventures, share the fun and tell others about them!

Want to be first to know when another Vic novel is out? Join Vic at
http://www.vicplanet.com/joinvic

Get free posters at http://www.vicplanet.com

Curious?

1. Mongolian cities have had multiple names over time. When Mongolia was autonomous, cities were named in the Mongolian language. When under influence of China or Russia, cities had different names. Vic mentions Urga, the capital. Before 1911 it was known as Khüree. It is now called Ulaanbaatar. Notice the map at the beginning of this book - Peking is now Beijing. Vic entered Inner Mongolia (actually an area of China - Mongolia was referred to a Outer Mongolia) at Kalgan which may also be referred to as Dongkou. See the Thank You to Hawaii State Librarians in the front of this book for what it took to find the earlier name of Dalanzadgad.

2. The Mad Baron (Baron Roman Nikolai Maximilian von Ungern-Sternberg) was real. He controlled the Mongolian capital for a few months in 1921. He actually had the facial wound given the Destroyer in the book. https://en.wikipedia.org/wiki/Roman_von_Ungern-Sternberg

3. The game of Prosperity eventually became known as Monopoly.

4. Maral = wapiti = elk.

5. Cryptids - The most basic definition is a plant or animal whose existence is questionable. The Mongolian death worm has a history of sighting that goes back over a thousand years. http://theunexplainedmysteries.com/Mongolian-death-worm.html **Short video:** http://www.animalplanet.com/tv-shows/other/videos/freak-encounters-mongolian-death-worm/

In addition to bad guys Vic meets at least one cryptid on every trip.

6. Yes, Sears Roebuck once sold kit homes. They began in 1908 and generally discontinued in 1940. Some "company towns" used Sears homes after 1940. The early ones like Vic's did not have running water, electricity or other conveniences although later models did include those things.
https://en.wikipedia.org/wiki/Sears_Catalog_Home

Full references with links are available at http://www.vicplanet.com

So, What's Next?

The adventures continue for Vic Challenger. Want to keep traveling with Vic?

There are a lot of rough rides, deadly dangers, frightful monsters ahead.

In book three, Vic visits a mysterious cave in the Grand Canyon, then goes on to battle cannibals and sea monsters in Scotland.

Book four takes Vic to the Amazon rainforest, where she encounters a crazy-old shaman, and her cave-girl ingenuity comes in very handy!

Vic: Fast, the fifth book in the series, sees Vic crossing the Australian outback in pursuit of villains. Along the way, she encounters odd and vicious cryptids, but a common lizard and nature might be even more hazardous.

The sixth book, Vic: Event, takes Vic to Siberia. It's a tit for tat trip. Her friend 'O' does her a favor and asks for one in return. It was supposed to be easy, but Vic runs into something that may be from far, far away!

In book seven, Vic: Bloody Reprisal, Vic's friend Lin Li, is injured by hoodlums sent by a man they both thought was dead. Vic goes after him and his gang, hot for revenge. Along the way, she runs into a thing that people say is a demon from hell. Vic learns a lot - about the downside of revenge, and appearances can be deceiving.

Vic: Mystery & Magic, is book eight, and is a Christmas tale. Can a ghost, greedy men, hairy beasts, a blizzard, and a race against time add up to a Merry Christmas?

In book nine, Vic: A Savage Place, Vic travels to Madagascar. Attempts are made on her life before she arrives! Vic finds a forgotten canyon with savage natives and beasts but finds the so-called civilized men who follow her may be more savage than the natives.

Vic Challenger novels are filled with adventures you cannot predict. They are not your standard tales, and grueling action seems never-ending.

AND,

Vic Challenger continues! There are more novels to come. They are all the coffee-shop-story-telling type of adventures. It's like this. You and I are friends and meet at our favorite coffee house. We both know Vic, and you know she just returned from a trip. Then I smile and reveal, *I saw her yesterday and heard all about it. Want to hear?*

And of course, there is that backdrop to every adventure - will Vic find Nu?

You can stay privy to everything about Vic at http://www.vicplanet.com

Thanks for reading!